Some Great Thing

Some Great Thing

COLIN MCADAM

RAINCOAST BOOKS

Vancouver

Raincoast Books acknowledges the ongoing financial support of the Government of Canada through The Canada Council for the Arts and the Book Publishing Industry Development Program (BPIDP); and the Government of British Columbia through the BC Arts Council.

Lyrics from "Cold Cold Heart" by Hank Williams reproduced with kind permission by Sony/ATV Music Publishing. "Tender" words and music by Albarn, James, Coxon and Rowntree. Copyright 1988. Reproduced by permission of EMI Music Publishing Ltd, London, WC2H 0QY. "Big River" written by Johnny Cash. Copyright 1958, 1986, House of Cash, Inc. (BMI)/Administered by BUG. All rights reserved. Used by permission. Words and music for "Ring of Fire" by Merle Kilgore and June Carter. Copyright 1962, 1963 Painted Desert Music Corporation, New York. Copyright renewed. International copyright secured. All rights reserved. Used by permission.

NATIONAL LIBRARY OF CANADA CATALOGUING IN PUBLICATION

McAdam, Colin
  Some great thing / Colin McAdam.
ISBN 1-55192-695-4
  I. Title.
PS8575.A26S63 2004   C813'.6   C2003-906951-6

Raincoast Books
9050 Shaughnessy Street
Vancouver, British Columbia
Canada, V6P 6E5
www.raincoast.com

Published in the U.K. by Jonathan Cape and in the U.S. by Harcourt Inc.

Interior printed in the U.S. by RR Donnelly.
Jacket printed in Canada by Friesens.

10 9 8 7 6 5 4 3 2 1

dedicated with love,
to Jaci, Sean, Howard

Some Great Thing

Part One

1

Kathleen on Wednesday

"JERRY MCGUINTY WAS my husband for fifteen years."

"Oh, yeah?"

"Twenty."

"But Jerry McGuinty's rich."

"I'm rich. From a phone call, I'll be."

"But you weren't really married to Jerry McGuinty."

"Watch where you're cuttin."

"How come you're not rich?"

"I am rich. Where's Lisa anyway? It takes a phone call, like I'm, like I'm one of them people, you know, calling. Cut my hair. Where's Lisa?!"

"I told ya. She's sick."

"What do ya mean, sick?"

"The clap."

"Ohhh. Lisa?"

"Yep."

"Who are you?"

"Joanie. I told you. See, it's here. Look in the mirror there. Joanie."

"Joanie."

"So your last name's McGuinty?"

"It is."

"How come it's Herlihy?"

"It's McGuinty."

"Says in the book, Herlihy. Mrs. Herlihy, ten o'clock, cut and set."

"Don't you set my hair. I won't pay if you set me."

"All right, Mrs. Herlihy."

"Herlihy, eh? Haven't heard that in a while."

"But ya gave that as your name."

"Herlihy's a pretty name, too."

"Herlihy is a pretty name."

"A Herlihy doesn't get the clap. Not a Kathleen Herlihy."

"No, ma'am, not a Joanie neither."

"McGuinty's a name."

"McGuinty's a name all right."

"My name for fifteen years or so. Smoke?"

"No thank you."

"Give ya some cheekbones."

"No thank you, ma'am. I got cheekbones."

"Where?"

"I got cheekbones as much as you was married to Jerry McGuinty."

"Where's Lisa fer shit's sakes? You tell me where Lisa is."

"I told you. Lisa's dead."

"What?"

"She died last week."

"Lisa?"

"Yep. Just after she married Jerry McGuinty."

"What?"

"Lisa's sick."

4

"You tell her to get better."

"You tell me what it was like being married to Jerry McGuinty."

"You cut my hair."

"I'm cuttin your hair."

"Arse. Jerry McGuinty was the biggest... You mind your own biggest."

"Business."

"What?"

"All I know is, I wouldn't be sittin in that chair if I was married to Jerry McGuinty. I wouldn't be gettin my hair cut by me, that's what I know, if I was married to Jerry friggin McGuinty."

"I could afford! I could pay for more than this. Who are you?"

"I'm Joanie."

"You're not Joanie. I was married to Joanie."

"Joanie McGuinty?"

"Jerry. Jerry McGuinty was my husband for twenty years."

AND I GOTTA buy cheese.

I gotta buy cheese.

"Cheese?"

"Aisle three."

"Three?"

"Three."

I can count. I can count. Comb your freakin hair, you ugly freakin freak, is all I want, is all I want is cheese. Three cheese.

"Where's aisle three?"

"What?"

"Aisle three fer shit's sakes." What do ya want with cheese? "What do ya want with cheese?"

"What?"

"I'm so fuckin thirsty."

"Do you need help?"

"I want some fuckin cheese."

"Aisle three, ma'am. That way, ma'am."

5

"What?"

"That way, ma'am."

He was sweet, that boy. That way, ma'am, that way. Cheese? Over there, over there by that way, ma'am, ya grubby little freak. "Which way?"

"Pardon?"

"Where'd he go?"

"Who, ma'am?"

"The grocery boy. He'll bring me a stick of cheese." That's it, that's right. Run away.

"DRINK?"

"Ya can't drink here, ma'am. This is a hairdresser's."

"I'll just have a drink."

"Ya can't, Mrs. Herlihy. This is a salon. Put that away now."

"I'll just put it down here."

"Put the flask back in your pocket, ma'am. I'm not kidding ma'am."

"I'll just put it down here."

"Ma'am."

"I saw your cheekbones."

"You see anyone else drinking?"

"There's no one in here."

"Right."

"There's no one in here, and you're trying to trick me."

"I'm not tricking you, Jerry."

"Jerry?"

"Joanie."

"It's Kathleen."

"Your name's Kathleen. Put the flask away, Kathleen."

"No one else is drinkin cause you're trickin everyone."

"Just put the flask away. There. In your pocket. You want me to finish your hair, don't ya?"

"Eh?"

"Mrs. Herlihy, ten o'clock, cut and set."

"I won't have a set today thanks."

"So you say."

"So says the Lord."

"Put the flask away now, Kathleen."

"Smoke?"

"No."

"I'll just have a smoke to help your cheekbones along."

"Thank you, ma'am."

"You confuse the shit out of me, Lisa."

"Do I? I'm Joanie. Would you like a drink, ma'am?"

"You're feckin right I would."

"Cause this is a saloon."

"Right."

"Put that away, ma'am. Put your head back there. Have a rest. Have a rest while I set your hair."

"Get your feckin hands off me, is all I'm sayin."

"And all I'm saying is you should do your shopping elsewhere."

"Security!"

"I am security, ma'am."

"Security!"

"Come on outside, ma'am. Finish your shopping outside."

"Get your hands off me, and I won't kill you."

"You won't kill me?"

"Get your hands off me."

"Please keep your voice down."

"I want some flippin cheese!"

"You'll get some outside."

"Why?!"

"What?"

"Where the fuck is aisle three?"

"Mrs. Herlihy? Mrs. Herlihy? Wake up, Mrs. Herlihy. Wake up now, Kathleen. Wake up, ya friggin drunk. Mrs. Herlihy?"

"Yes?"

"You fell asleep."

"I fell asleep."

"I've done your hair, Mrs. Herlihy."

"Where?"

"Just on top of your head, ma'am."

"That's very kind."

"Are you all right?"

Kathleen on Thursday

"IT'S HERLIHY."

"Good morning, Mrs. Herlihy. Could you hold for one moment?"

"What?"

"Hold please."

Hold hold hold hold old hold old old.

"Mrs. Herlihy?"

"Eh?"

"What can we do for you today? The usual?"

"Quick."

"GOOD MORNING, Mrs. Herlihy."

"Robert, is it? Come in come in."

"Just on the counter, ma'am?"

"Eh?"

"I'll just put it on the counter. I have bad news, Mrs. Herlihy."

"Give us a drink."

"It's about the drink, ma'am."

"What is it?" Itchy, itchy bastard.

"Our supplier had no Dewar's. It's Bell's today, I'm afraid."

"Right."

"I thought you hated Bell's."

"Not just now. Hurry."

"I was worried."

"No ya weren't."

"Pardon?"

"I suppose you want some."

"Thank you, Mrs. Herlihy. Just a quick one. I've got four more deliveries this morning."

"Dewar's or Bell's?"

"You don't have Dewar's today, ma'am. I'll have Bell's."

"You'll have Bell's. I'll have Bell's. I'll have more Bell's than you cause you're driving."

"That's only fair."

"Where'd ya put it?"

"Just on the counter, ma'am."

"I'll just... I can pour the feckin thing... Here we go."

"Thank you very much."

"Give that back for a second, Robert, is it."

"Sure."

"I'll just have a little sip of yours."

"I wish you wouldn't do that, ma'am."

"More tomorrow. I'll give yiz."

"Can't I just have a bit?"

Fucker. "Here. One finger. One and a half fingers."

"Thanks."

"Pass that back for a minute. I'll just drink half a finger. There. You're driving."

"Thanks."

"Sit, Robert, is it."

"Thank you very much. Thank you. I like this couch."

"Fortune."

"Yeah?"

"Flippin right. I remember."

"I'll bet. How are you today, anyways, Mrs. Herlihy?"

"I want you to leave, Robert."

"Sure. I'll just knock that back."

JUST KNOCK it back goodbye son. Off then, ya freakin sponge? I'll just slip over here and ring the Bell's and call ya back for more. No? Tomorrow then. Come on back tomorrow.

"GOODBYE."

GOOD MORNING and goodbye to you Robert, ugly face, freakin mole, strawberry pus on chin.

Smell of old teeth. So old in my mouth, and look at yourself. Look at above the couch, dirty freakin mirror, lookin at yourself. Get yourself up for another, and for anyone else? Blinds down behind the eyes. Older than you look. Nothing like you look. Get yourself another. Goddamn couch cost a fortune, might as well enjoy life.

Feet!

Get a man to lay a carpet just as soon as I finish this here, this drink here cost a fortune. Three fingers at noon, get me through the lunchtime quiet. Half a glass, fat fingers today thank God. There's a toast to all my friends, I wanna thank you all for comin. Get a man to lay me down, three fingers behind the truck.

Feet! God damn the knees. Cover your knees ya freakin hag and lie down there on the couch. There ya go. There ya go. Peace and freakin quiet. I'll just have a quick cigarette, if that's all right with you, Robert.

Robert?

"IT'S HERLIHY."

"Hello, Mrs. Herlihy. What can we do for you?"

"Don't put me on hold."

"No need, ma'am."

"No need?"

"No, ma'am."

"I didn't...I need my cigarettes. Robert didn't deliver my god-damn cigarettes."

2

Jerry

WHAT I SHOULD say is my name is Jerry and I built this house. Four-square, plaster walls, buttressed from toe to tip with an iron goddamn will, my friend, standing proud proud proud. I hammered it into the ground and I pushed it up to the sky, and with the grace of God and the sweat of men I will build a thousand more.

All these houses you see around you I built, and neither you nor the grown-up child of your grandchild's grandchild is going to see them crumble.

I build, my friend, and up yours if you think me common. I challenge you to build something, and I defy the fist of time to touch what I have done. I challenge you to build a matchstick outhouse in the time it takes me to tell an endless tale. See if you have the will; then wipe that smirk off your flabby pink chops and listen.

It is endless. And I am worn.

My name is Jerry and my son's name is Jerry, and that's because my imagination was always saved for my work. And Jerry, my son my son, is the life hope love and death of me.

Please tell me if you see him.

A plague of years ago I put a cigar between my teeth and reckoned myself the greatest man on earth. For there in her hands, careful of the ashes Jer, was the pinkest thing I ever made. Flesh and wrinkles and a boneless chicken in the palm of my hand, screaming in a purple dribbling rage, my boy. My chest, my boy, as swollen as the proud blue sea.

But where do I begin?

He had a grip as sharp as needle-nosed pliers. And he grew up smart.

3

Simon

So I SAID to her, I said, listen, I said, Kwyet, I said, Kwyet, I said (the eager chasseur), I want, I said, to run. My little humming Quiet, my little thread of Kwyet, a birdbreeze lower than a breath said Come, she said, or so I had imagined, Come she said, Here I am.

She said nothing, but I took her to mean much, as she ran more than walked, cowered more than curved up the stairs through the door by the window.

I want to run, I said, but None, I said, of this Come here. My goose was bumped all over from the breeze of disquieting breath; to run was my need, not my wish. I was prepared to get song-of-songsy, all hinds and harts and panting, to sing with her as we ran. But when I was *there,* when I was right there with her, there was nothing but quiet: an open window and an invitation. Come, she says, here I am.

What a long way to the ground.

HE IS A FASCINATING man, awful, handsome, disgraceful, a subject of great interest for many and the subtlest beast of The Glebe. You have to search to find him but we know exactly where he is: Number Fifteen, Cowslip Crescent, Not Far From Here At All If You Know The Roads.

Twenty years ago he had twenty years stretched out before him, as they say, although he constantly searched for them and has found them only now that he looks back.

His name is Simon.

KWYET HAD a bottom like a pillow, where I rested my head to consider what I looked like from above. I sent my soul up there to have a look. Kwyet on the bottom, me on hers, my graceful raffish soul tilting his head in Botticellian pose above my grateful rakish body (recently sated on Kwyet's adaptable bottom). I smiled and my soul winked back at me. I looked good, I should say.

4

Jerry

HE SHOWED AN interest in building, my Jerry. He had strength and the right touch. You know, nimble. I am talking about Lego and Meccano, mostly, in the early days. Toys of course. I wasn't fooled. Don't think for one dirty minute that I was a fool. I know the difference between toys and real life. But there was potential there, in those little forearms of my little Jer. He could put up a Lego wall as fast as any Italian brickie.

Then when he was eight, I remember the day clearly, he built an impossible house. It was plaster. It had three walls and no drafts. I showed it to Edgar Davies, who showed little interest; but it was clear to me that I was raising a genius, my friend, a boy, my friend, with the promise of a prince.

5

Simon

LET ME BEGIN where she began, at the ends of her almond-sweet
toes. There began daily his lingual epigraphy, from toes to ankles
and upward: a world of liquid phrases sketched with the tip of his
tongue. Kwyet was every morning a dream of an unfound
America.

Toes, ankles, inward; my salt trail of reverence (delicious!)
formed a changing map.

When Kwyet ran, the elastic world yearned after her and he
could not resist the pull.

6

Jerry

I WAS THINKING nothing when the doorbell rang because I am and was a busy man. Paperboy? is maybe all I thought.

But when I opened the door.

This was, I don't know, maybe several years ago now.

When I opened the door there was Jer.

"Jer!" I said.

Or maybe "Jer?", because I will tell you now there was no way I could have recognized him if I hadn't been his father.

"Jer?!" I said.

And he said, with my voice but smaller, "Hi, Dad," he said, and came in.

Now there are two things I should tell you. The first is that he had stubble on his face, hair on his hands, and his mother's you'll-never-touch-me eyes. And the second I cannot tell you because you do not know Jerry or me or what it would be like to want to hug him.

"Hi, Dad," he said, and I knew it was my job to be cool.

"How are ya, Jer," I said, cool.

And he said, "How are ya."

And I said, "Beer?"

And he said, "Yeah."

And I went to the fridge and came back with a couple.

He was still standing there in front of the door, and we clinked them together, me and Jer, and no two beers in the history of man were sucked back faster, I tell you with no shame. We finished at the same time, and when I look back now I realize that's because he was my son.

"Another?" I said.

And he said, "Yeah." So I came back with two more.

"Come in. Sit down. Come in."

He had a knapsack on his shoulder full of his father's hope. I couldn't ask if he was going to stay.

He sat down over there, across from me, and I kind of wished I was his beer and don't call me a faggot.

"How are ya, Jer?" I said.

"OK," sip of beer, "OK... You?"

"OK," I said, and was going to say "You?" again. "Beer?" I said, and he said, "Yeah," and I got another case from the basement and put it in the fridge.

"So, you've been OK, eh, Jer?"

"Yeah. OK enough."

"You look thin."

"Yeah."

"Healthy?"

"Yeah."

"You hungry?" Too early, too early.

"No."

"Me neither."

"*You* look thin," he said, after a while.

"I've been on a diet," I said, because I'd been on a diet.

"Yeah?"

"Yep. Twenty pounds."

"Yeah?"

"Yep."

And it just came out again—"You hungry?"—and I watched him grow his thorns.

We sat there silent for a long loud time, I tell you with no pleasure.

But when the room warmed up and the floor came back, I looked at my son full in the face and I said this: "I know the guy who makes this beer."

And he said, "Yeah?"

"Yeah," I said, and I told him a story you can borrow if you want to send your kids to sleep. I'll tell you how it goes once I've finished this. There I was talking about yeast, a grandmother's recipe, a guy named Buck who made one or two himself, and there was Jer, a familiar stranger, older, smaller, a growing man, and as he politely nodded himself to sleep I might have walked over and put my hand on his head.

7

Simon

SHE NEVER HAD a lover as curious and adept, I told her to tell me. We were sitting on my windowsill (naked: downstairs), and we were both immensely pleased with me. She was at a loss for words.

8

The Story of Jerry McGuinty

THIRTEEN NEIGHBORHOODS, FIVE thousand roofs, thirty thousand outside walls, and a rock-hard pair of hands. That is what I have built. I have laid iron, I have laid iron mesh, I have breathed more iron filings than the men who built the railroads. And I have plastered.

My father was a plasterer. His father was a plasterer. His father's father was a plasterer (and plastering was the death of his father). I, my friend, am a plasterer. Lean forward here and I will show you my card. I am a member of the Plasterers' and Cement Masons' International Association of the United States & Canada, local one-one-five. There are fifty thousand members, and I am the best. My father was the best. His father was the best. His father's father was the best. And this is all due to two things: will, and a secret. Only Portland cement goes into my mix, and when it comes to mortar I use barely a pinch of lime. That is my secret.

Will. Until you know what it is like to join ten million bricks, don't say a word about will.

I have covered five thousand acres with my own creations. That's right. I have choked, raped, and tortured the earth, my friend, and in the end it is mightier than it was. Teach me about nature and I will show you a pair of hands.

We're in Ottawa, the capital of Canada, no less. Now look here at this map. The Oaks: mine. The Hunt: mine. Pine Grove: mine. Much Of It: mine. I will show you more later. I will drive you around them. Edgar Davies helped with one or two of them.

I have no sensation in my left little finger. I have missed more nails than you have opportunities, and I haven't missed a nail in thirty-one years. Frostbite has whitened both of my earlobes and sunburn has turned my forearms to suede. Before steel soles I stepped on five nails and after hard hats I missed death twice.

I have loved a woman.

I own my own company.

I have heard and told ten thousand filthy jokes.

My first day on a site without my father was the day my life began. A January day as cold as a nail. My apprenticeship was over and I was given a job with people who hated me because that's what builders do when they meet new people.

"McGuinty! Ya thick-headed cunt plaster shit on the cock-ass floor-cunt!"

I remember the foreman.

"McGuinty!"

He ate a cat once.

"McGuinty, ya lick-whore cunt drip wall fuck level or I'll eat your ass!"

I couldn't move my fingers and the plaster was slower than time. At lunch I sat with a man, Johnny Cooper, who had just finished five years for GBH. I didn't know that, and he looked lonely.

"You sit any closer and I'll punch your gut through your ass," he said.

I plastered half a wall and I helped one of the brickies, a guy named Mario.

"Jerry," I said.

"Mario," he said.

"What should I do?" I said.

"Eat my cunt," he said.

The foreman took me aside at the end of the day and stood me next to the half wall I'd plastered (still wet), and he pushed me slowly into it face-first without saying a word. I stepped back and saw an impression of a scared white Jerry McGuinty.

I LEARNED how to talk.

"I can't cunt find fuckin nails ass, shit, you seen them, hoor?"

"What?"

WE BUILT EVERYTHING in those days. We built hangars for the military and houses for their people. The houses were made of paper, nothing but chipboard and plasterboard, staples and glue.

Let me tell you what it's like building with plasterboard.

I'll tell you later.

It was the time to be in the construction business, I tell you for your interest, and a lot of guys I knew worked hard enough to start their own company later. We built the hangars and houses, convenience stores, gas stations, model homes that lasted for a month. Everyone had a finger in everything, and everyone's finger was gold.

But that first January. Girders stuck to my flesh like frying pans and my toolbox looked at me like a threat. Every hammer, wrench, and trowel I owned found different ways to hurt me. One day I wouldn't feel my fingers, the next they'd be there like a scream. Put your hands in a freezer for a day, if you have the time, and then thread a screw through a nut. Don't tell me how it feels.

"Ouch!"

"McGuinty!"

And the men I worked with. Italian, Irish, Canadian, the usual muddy mix. I was on that first site a week when Johnny Cooper came up out of the blue and clocked me in the jaw. That hurt. Tony Espolito shook my hand so hard when I first met him he pulled my pinkie out of its socket. He killed himself with a hammer once. There were ten of us on that site and there were nine hairy animals too many, I say with no restraint. I thought I knew what a man was.

EVERYONE'S FINGER was gold and the earth was hungry for houses. When I was in the middle of it I didn't realize what I was in the middle of. It took me a few years, a few sleepless smelly years, to realize it was the greatest boom this land has ever seen. One of them, anyway. We couldn't help but make a fortune.

I AM Jerry McGuinty.

YOU HAVE to have strength and you have to be right. Accurate. No one survives as a builder if he has to do work over. The best builders I've worked with have been like professional athletes. Little ones, big ones, thin ones, thick ones, perfectly made for whatever they did. Chippies have the steadiest hands, and the quickest. Tony Antonioni could put up an A-frame in an hour and a half, if he remembered his tools. He also knew angles. He could cut a plank at exactly 32 degrees with nothing but a hand-saw, if he remembered the wood.

I became an expert brick layer, but it was plaster—plastering anything—that wrapped my pride in a creamy layer of gold. To plaster the simplest wall takes grace, patience, and a solid sense of how the world stands up. Some say it stands up straight. Some say it curves like hips. I say it stands as I tell it to. My walls will change your life.

Walk over to the nearest wall in your house and knock on it. If it makes a hollow sound it is plasterboard and you should be out earning money. If it is hard hard hard and creamy it is plaster, my friend, and I want you to take down your ugly pictures, stand back from it, put your glasses on or take them off and give that wall a good strong look. Does it make the room bigger? Smaller? Do you feel a little sick? A strong wall is plastered solid at the edges, but the middle is where it lives. A bit of pressure on my trowel can make you love your kids, a bit less and God help you breathe.

Smirk at your peril.

FOR THE FIRST YEAR I was still living with my parents, but the next January, always freaking January, my father kicked me out of the nest and my mother shoved me for emphasis. I rented a room in Mrs. Brookner's basement, and I learned to like her as much as I liked banging my head on a beam.

Every morning I was up at four thirty and Mrs. Brookner made me eggs and ash.

By six I was at the site, no matter where it was, with my eye on a wall and my insides clawing their way to my mouth. Those early days were the hungriest in the history of my stomach. Trucks came by at eight o'clock, on the dot, and I still smell them coming: Jack's Little Griddle, Ye Olde Lunch Wagon. Meals on greasy wheels, my friend, and never were they sweeter. A cup of hot gristle at ten o'clock on a January morning (in those days it was fresh) was our hot milk and honey. At twelve o'clock the grease rolled around again, and once again at four.

IN THE FIRST two years we built a hundred paper houses—a hundred holes and a thousand dirty troubles. They were young people's houses, and to everyone but their builders they were dreams. I could put my hand against the inside of a wall—my own wall, the wall I was forced to build—and feel the wind blow through it.

By the time we were putting up the last house the rest had already been filled, and we got a close hard look at our victims. They were older than me, those dreamers who moved in, and I was too young to feel sorry for them. The difference between dreams and plasterboard, I tell you out of wisdom, is their shape.

Doors slammed loose and linoleum cracked, wires fizzled dead, hot and cold, hot and cold, all pipes burst, bottom edges curled in a hot shit-grime. For a while I answered complaints. My foreman sent me over.

"Good morning, ma'am, I've come to rebuild your house."

All the visits were the same.

"Good morning, sir, I hear you're having a problem with your upstairs window."

"You're goddamn right I am. There isn't one."

"There isn't one?"

"There's no goddamn window. Just the frame."

"Well, I'm here to fix that. Let me go to the truck and see if I can dig up a pane or two."

And he'd follow me to the truck.

"No goddamn window for six weeks. And my goddamn wife's trying to get pregnant."

"Well, I'm here to fix that." And I'd look in my truck and find a windowpane to make his wife pregnant.

I WAS NEVER home before ten o'clock and home was never home. Mrs. Brookner was always awake in the kitchen cutting up a head or a tongue which I'd find the next day in my sandwich. Even if I wasn't tired there was nothing to stay up for.

But I was tired. I earned a sleep which I cannot describe because nothing ever happened but sleep. Four thirty came again and for thousands of my years it has never stopped coming. I was too tired to be weary and too scared to be tired. But slowly, slowly, I was learning how to live. I made friends.

"Hey, Cooper."

"What do you want?"

"What?"

"You just said my fuckin name."

"Sorry."

And I got stronger. Strength is in the forearm, my friend, and I defy you to come near mine.

To SAVE MYSELF time in the future I put extra compound over some of the plasterboard in those first houses. The wind stopped blowing through them and the stupid young couples kept warm. That was the first of my plans.

I took no breaks and I had no time. But there was freedom between my ears, and I don't mean what you think I mean. Building is ten percent concentration and ninety percent habit. You have to think about what you're going to do, but you don't while you're doing it. It doesn't matter how busy your body is, your mind is always free. Free if you have good forearms. Once I know where to put it, my trowel moves steady as the waves— habit moves it, and my thoughts are free. And that's when you plan.

Johnny Cooper, Mario Calzone, and Tony Espolito, they don't plan. When they're staring at a wall or choking on sawdust, they're thinking this: Woman, Blood, Bone. They're thinking things you'll never know.

But Jerry McGuinty plans.

The future was there one day, drying around my fingers.

IN 1968 I met her and everything white turned red.

WHEN YOU build one hundred shameful houses, day after plaster-board day, you start to think that the world needs nothing better. You start building yourself into them. I caught myself one day, in the middle of Mrs. Brookner's breakfast, thinking I would throw up one of those houses for myself. It would get me out of here, I thought. I counted up what the materials would cost and I thought about where I would build, and I even thought about asking the foreman for advice.

They change you, all those Januaries. Those first few years had more than a few of them. I was only in my twenties and I was already growing this here belly. My eyes were always red. I suppose I drank a lot of beer, but up yours if you're going to judge me.

You change, you stay the same, or you do something in between. I didn't know what to do. I thought about changing crews—sometimes I'd get a taste of others during little jobs—but the men were all exactly the same. I've seen more Johnny Coopers than you've seen disappointment.

I thought about staying put, but then there was Johnny Cooper.

I thought about doing something in between but I didn't know what that meant.

Building myself an ugly little house seemed the perfect thing to do. I had money (in those days the unions had Strength). I could buy the materials, build the house in my sleep, and by the age of twenty-two have more square feet than my father had at forty.

So there I was, regretting breakfast, staring at a wall, waiting for the courage to come to ask my foreman for advice, when I looked at my hands and it came to me.

Plaster. I felt stupid as a sack of grade-two cement. I'll build a better house, I said. Plaster walls for smarter people.

9

The Story of Simon Struthers

CONTAINED IN SPACE, yearning to get out, that is how I think of Simon when I look back over his life. That body of his that has spread sympathetically with every yearning, his body was the trap he always ignored. It was the space around him he blamed. There were very few rooms which he ever wanted to stay in; but if there happened to be company for his body, he stayed beyond his welcome.

The day he turned eleven, he held a dinner party for eight friends, all of them girls. Long before he ever properly yearned for girls he was taught to respect and befriend them, to get along with everyone. "Nothing wrong with girls," his father said. Simon made a point of sitting next to them on the school bus. If there was an empty seat next to one, no matter who she was, no matter how the boys at the back laughed, no matter how the girl squirmed, he sat there. And it was in this spirit of getting along with everyone that his parents encouraged him to invite as many people as he liked to this dinner party, just like a grown-up, where conversation would bring everyone closer. "Just watch," his mother said, holding ice to his eye one evening after school, "the dinner table is the antithesis of the playground." He invited twenty-six girls and one other boy to the dinner in honor of his birthday, and eight of the girls, in honor of their parents' desire to hear what it was like inside the Struthers' house, did not return their regrets.

And they sat there.

The dining room felt fuller than when his father invited the PM and caucus. But not a word was spoken. Simon longed for his room. The girls were all seated, all silent, and his mother poured iced tea with such deft unobtrusiveness that even the ice in the jug was silent when it moved.

Silence through the salad, the roof closing in, silence when the beef steamed its charms on every girl's face.

It was Jenny Pearce who spoke, finally, first looking at Simon's mother but then addressing Simon directly with such sweet warmth.

"I love green beans. My brothers hate them. But I love them."

The table erupted into friendly controversy, most of the girls unable to believe that Jenny liked green beans. There was talk of food, generally, of food at school, of school generally, of Jenny's brothers, which invoked a few blushes.

Suddenly Simon found himself yearning so achingly to remain in the bounds of that room. Eight jolly friends. And pretty. He had to admit they were growing very pretty.

He giggled, laughed outright whenever a girl laughed, and giggled no matter what was said. He spoke, said interesting, outrageous things, laughing all the time. His giggles prevented him from blowing out the candles on his cake. He wanted to walk around the table and hug each girl, realizing for the first time how exciting it would be to know a few of their secrets.

When it all seemed to be going wonderfully, Simon, reluctant to leave the room but eager to bring more of himself into it, left the table and went to fetch something upstairs. Anything. A piece of *him* that he could show the girls. He found his newest book:

Great Houses of England, a guide to building models of a hundred noble estates. He flicked through the pages in his room, finding his favorites, and he even decided to show the girls the model he had started of Walpole's Strawberry Hill.

When he came bounding downstairs he found his friends all gathered in the foyer, thanking his mother and waiting for their rides. Jenny Pearce thanked Simon directly, but she had a curious smile when she saw his model house.

For the next few months, Simon was known as Lord Struthers Who Spits When He Giggles.

It was the first time he realized what a traitor a room could be.

In 1974 Simon moved into Number Fifteen, Cowslip Crescent, The Glebe, and used inherited money to do so. A mortgage was not for him, for through some political simony his father had accrued a fortune, the exact amount of which he has never looked at for fear that it would shrink. (He had an MP father and a Type A mother and his childhood was long, golden, and pestilent.)

The Glebe contains houses containing people discreetly proud of being contained in a house in The Glebe—people who say hello when you say hello to them and are otherwise quite remarkable if you get to know them. Many of his neighbors moved in at the same time, and they moved as one ought to move: they smiled, looked openly around, let each other know that here was a new one of them.

If only you could have stood there, in the middle of that crescent, watching them all about to grow, their milky blood so far from clotting into cream. They may not have had personalities but most of them had promise. One by one, sometimes by twos, they wove a garland of introductions across their lawns, "Hello" they all smiled, their cars exchanged pleasantries. But Simon was always the break in the chain.

The day he arrived, he began a routine of ignoring his neighbors. Not looking up when bringing garbage to the curb. Nodding not waving. Nodding not speaking. Not looking down when happy little children tugged on his unhappy trousers. (He had learned the power of mystery and silence.)

The point is that as they all whirled around in May Day glee, promising drinks and dinner and risqué revelations, Simon stood apart.

If you were thirty-eight in 1974, as he was, you will remember that year as one when you left behind some of the steak sandwiches and erections of your youth.

IT WAS A SENSE of change, more than change itself, which made that time memorable for Simon. It was more than the move to The Glebe. It was a move in the public service, a promotion, a new appointment. But it was more than that again. He knew that each day would bring more, and more. He knew that he would meet someone who could see behind his eyes.

HE HAD BEEN promoted for the third time in eight years, and now, thanks to the Struthers name, he was appointed Director of Design and Land Use at the National Capital Division. His new colleagues were intelligent, competent people whose job was to create thoughtful policies that would shape the capital city. It was interesting work, a promising time.

In those days Ottawa was nonetheless a bleak little place. It teemed with people with searching intellects—lawyers, foreign servants, civil servants—people who could capture the world in a memo, people who could have made it a wonderful city. But when they left the office they found very little to do. The Arts Center was built, but performances were amateurish. There was nowhere to eat, nowhere to drink, nothing to add to the store of experience (gained elsewhere) which allowed them to capture that world in a memo.

Simon loved it. He loved the potential, the blank canvas of it, the empty spaces across the city that suggested nothing but possibility. The population grew. Bureaucracy was growing. When Simon's father and his friends first launched the public service, there were only 130,000 people living in the city. By the time Simon's own career was underway there were that many people in the public service alone. Tens of thousands of capable minds— but the city still seemed to be empty.

Something was going to burst.

To tell his story one could begin anywhere. I could start with him as a teenager, when some habits first formed. I could start earlier, childhood, when his view of the world as a vessel of possible fictions first began to settle into the fabric of his body. But this later time stands out.

HE WAS A MEMBER of the Shakespeare Club, the Dance Club, the Dining Club. In the summers he joined the Five Lakes Fishing Club, which his father had helped to establish. He knew almost everyone. He associated with old Cambridge friends like Evelyn and Paul Overington (Evelyn and that cocktail dress!), Belinda and Henry Martin (Belinda in her bathing suit, "Please, Simon, no!"). He was close to some for a while.

Everyone knew Simon. They knew the Struthers name. Some thought they knew him intimately, but they could never tell you how.

THERE WAS one good restaurant, out of town, across the river, Madame Berger's, where desperate people with taste would gather to sample, as Leonard Schutz put it, "the finer fruits of the earth and human ingenuity." Leonard was one of Simon's new colleagues at the Division.

One night Simon was invited by Leonard to join a gathering at this restaurant, and it was the night he first heard Kwyet's name.

AT MADAME BERGER'S, Thursday at seven, table flat and pale like a doctor's wooden stick, say aah it's nice to see us all together, viz:

1 Leonard Schutz, puffing
1 Eleanor Thomas, scowling
1 Randolph James III, too many
1 Matty Schutz, shining (!)
1 Renée, the above not matching
1 Simon Struthers, pining
——

6 jolly burghers come to dine.

The civil service generally, and the Division particularly, was made up of people caught in a constant battle between insecurity and self-aggrandizement. Most of them knew they were important but they usually found no material evidence of this so they puffed themselves up. And they were dubious of each other. Some weathered their difficulties better than others, and around the table that night was a good selection of those who coped and those who did not. In addition to Simon and Leonard, there was Eleanor Thomas, Renée le Mesurier, Randolph James III, and there was Leonard's wife, Matty (who was not a civil servant).

Simon was suspicious of Matty at first because he could not comprehend why such a fresh turgid flower bloomed by Leonard's rotten oak.

Drinks were served and Leonard explained a sort of ritual that they always followed on these evenings. With each course a different person would be chosen to speak—to tell stories—on a topic agreed upon by all. Leonard suggested they all speak about food because that was his chief enthusiasm. So with each course came a different story about food.

Leonard was chosen to speak during the main course, and his story was appropriately substantial.

And then Matty spoke—Matty for dessert—a sweet ending and a prelude to everything sweet.

"I'm not very good at telling stories," she said. "Sorry.

"I don't know whether Leonard talks about her much with

you, but we have a daughter named Kwyet. She's fifteen. Whenever I think of anything, I think of her. I'm not just being a mother. Kwyet is…My point is, if I have to talk about food…

"When Kwyet was eight, a little boy in her class bought her a cheap metal ring from the post office because he loved her. She didn't love him but was too gentle to tell him, so for some reason she swallowed the ring in front of him and poisoned herself with the lead in it.

"I guess that's a story about food, but it's too short, isn't it?

"She's fine, of course.

"We had a funny little event a few years ago with Kwyet. I don't know whether it's funny, actually, but I will tell it quickly.

"Kwyet always has trouble deciding on anything. She has this puzzled, vague little face whenever she has to make a choice. So these two separate friends invited her to their places for dinner. One said, 'Come over on Saturday and my dad will order pizza,' and the other said, 'Come over on Saturday and Mom will make chocolate pudding.'

"It was a hard choice, so she told both of them she would come and all day Saturday I watched her face get all pale—her eyebrows going in opposite directions while she was trying to read a book, one toward pizza, the other toward chocolate pudding. Choosing between the friends was hard too. The friends hated each other, but loved Kwyet, and she liked them both equally. By Saturday afternoon, under pressure from me, she had to decide which one she would go to. It got later and later, and I thought she was being rude to both sets of parents.

"She went outside and I watched her running up and down the street, maybe trying to see which direction felt better. Sometimes she seems a bit simple. Finally she came in and called them both, and instead of choosing one she chose neither. She stayed in and had to eat something Leonard made. What was it?"

"Duck. Two roast ducks. I always make two, because they are small. One for three…"

35

"So poor little Kwyet asked me later if she could have these girls over the following Saturday for pizza and chocolate pudding. She invited them both, and as soon as she did that she remembered they hated each other. All week she had the same problem all over again. And that same little face. She couldn't bring herself to disinvite one or the other, and nothing I suggested was any help. Saturday came and she was silent all day. I tried to make chocolate pudding discreetly so she wouldn't feel like it was inevitable. And again it got later and later, until it was just too late.

"Both of these girls arrived at the door at exactly the same time, both were sort of pale and polite when I opened the door. The funny thing…the astonishing thing was that Kwyet didn't say anything all night. That indecisive look was gone and there was another weirder look she gets sometimes which I can't describe. She looked friendly and smiled at her friends and everything, but she didn't really say a word.

"I ordered pizza and sat with them for a while. I think it was the pizza maybe. Once they started eating the pizza these two girls started joking with each other and laughing, and Kwyet had nothing to do with them. She just sat back and smiled. She didn't even eat much. By the time I brought out the pudding, they were such good friends that I didn't want to be near them. You know how giggly they get.

"Kwyet had one spoonful of pudding. I can see it, one spoon of pudding missing from the bowl."

SHE WAS JUST a name then, you see. More than that, the name of silence—he didn't know how it was spelled in those days.

Take hold of a word and rattle its cage of bones, then you will understand Kwyet.

AND REALLY, she *was* just a name, just a little girl—of no more interest to Simon than as the subject of Matty's story. It was Matty who charmed, Matty who stretched his trousered mind to breaking point. Her mouth, when it teased out that phrase, "one spoon of pudding missing from the bowl," a smiling, kissing, mischievous mouth, "one spoon of pudding."

It is not much of a story, not much of an evening in itself, giving not much of an idea of the story of a man who is not much of a man at all. But it was the evening he met Matty. It was the evening he began his affair with Renée. There were consequences. Matty told her story, the dinner ended, Simon drove Renée home and kissed her in his car.

Perhaps I should be more straightforward.

From his personnel file, which he later doctored along with those of his colleagues, you can learn the story of Struthers, Simon:

Date of Birth: 3 April 1936
Place of Birth: Ottawa, Ontario
Mother's Maiden Name: Morgan
Father's Occupation: Member of Parliament for Kingston and the Islands; Minister of Finance; Minister of Foreign Affairs; deceased
Education: MA (Cantab.)
Interests: None discernible
Comments on Overall Character and Performance: Mr. Struthers has been an invaluable employee, and it is our opinion that at any moment he will burst into glory like a fountain at Versailles.

Part Two

1

THE LIGHT OF a welding torch is like nothing on this earth. You've noticed that. You've been on a site once or twice, getting your shoes a little dirty. You've looked at the frame of your dreams, the house you've put your money into, and you've seen hard hats and thick heads, bricks and wood, and black and gray men stooped in corners wearing gloves and welding things. You've seen their flames.

In 1968 I saw a flame.

Maybe you saw me. Maybe you were visiting the house two houses from the corner of Honeywood and Glyde, holding your wife's hand or your husband's hand, and you saw two men blowing fire on your dream, and all you really saw was two small people working on your own private miracle like you were God and we were your angels. Maybe you came right into that house that still had no *in* to come into and the foreman (the guy in the tie) pointed through the walls that weren't there at two men with masks and said, "They're welding your pipes." Maybe you were a little shy or scared.

In 1968 I was huddled in a corner on a weatherless day with Johnny Cooper, who was showing me the one thing on earth that kept him calm. He was welding sections of an out-take pipe together like they had nothing to do with sewage, like they needed to be some seamless piece of cloth for a bride. And I watched his flame, and he watched his flame, and maybe you watched his flame, but that was not, my friend, the flame that made the difference. You can't look at it, of course, that welder's flame. We both had our visors down while you took a quick look at it and realized you shouldn't look at all, and for maybe a split second we all wondered who could be angry enough to give men such a bright fire, but that is not, I tell you, the flame I have in mind.

In 1968, on that very day, a woman with no pity came up and tapped me and Johnny Cooper on the back, both at the same time.

Some flames you can look at for a long red time. This woman tapped us on the back and it was the only time I ever saw Johnny relax his fists when he was touched. Johnny looked at her, and I looked at her, and Johnny turned off his torch and we both watched the flame suck back in shame and I can still hear the silence. Up came our visors and there she was, smiling like everything perfect was inside her skin.

I don't know what we looked like—and if you were there looking at your new house feel free to tell me—but I have an idea that a picture of the three of us, Johnny, me, and her, would show this: two dirty welders in a silent land of promise. You'll have to look at the picture to find out what I mean and where she went, but I will tell you something about promise: it keeps everything warm and it burns when you touch it.

Hold on and listen to the Man in Black for a minute:

> *I fell into a burnin' ring of fire.*
> *I went down, down, down,*
> *And the flames went higher.*
> *And it burns, burns, burns,*
> *The ring of fire.*
> *The ring of fire.*

I felt it on my cheeks, my friend, and you know what I'm talking about. Her name was Kathleen Herlihy and the first thing she said was this:

"My name is Kathleen Herlihy."

Now, I DON'T KNOW or care about your life but there is one thing I'd like to say about mine. It changes every second, and each second changes the next, but there have been one or two seconds that were more important than others. Kathleen Herlihy watched Johnny Cooper and Jerry McGuinty raise their ugly selves from a crouch to a stand and it was the first few seconds after they stood up that changed all their lives for ever. For she looked only at Jerry McGuinty.

"My name is Kathleen Herlihy."

She looked at Cooper later, and she didn't look at me for all that long, but it was long enough to shift all our future seconds in a different direction, and I can tell you with as much truth as there is in the great deep balls of the black god Johnny Cash that without that look I would never have held young Jerry in my hands or lost him.

> *Love is a burning thing,*
> *And it makes a fiery ring.*
> *Bound by wild desire,*
> *I fell into a ring of fire.*

I didn't know what to say to her when she told us her name, but Johnny Cooper did.

"So?"

"So I was just drivin by and I saw yiz weldin." In those days her voice touched your ears like a petal. "I was in my truck, so that's why I came over." And she was shy. Not shy looking at your feet sort of shy, but shy like she respected you and knew that if she showed her true self right away she would blind you.

She pointed to a little yellow truck with some letters on the side that we couldn't read.

"It's a new truck I got," she said, "and it's my business."

"Your business. And why's that our business?" Johnny said.

"It's your business," she said, "when your stomach says it is," she said, and she impressed me as smart because I had no idea what she meant.

"What the fuck do you mean?" Johnny said, tired of flirting.

"I'm a caterer," she said.

"A caterer?" Johnny said.

"A caterer. Meals on wheels," she said. "But better." And she smiled, my friend, a smile that moved through a hundred different seasons and turned them all to spring. It made us all quiet.

"Better," she said, "because of pork."

And again I thought she was a genius.

"Pork?"

"Lard," she said, and said no more.

She handed us each a card, and we took off our gloves and I read it for Johnny. "'Herlihy's Meals on Wheels.'"

"That's me," she said. "Kathleen Herlihy."

And language came to me finally, smooth and warm as plaster. "My name is Jerry McGuinty."

"Hi, Jerry," she said, and she actually held out her hand.

I took her hand and let me say that I will never tell you what that felt like.

"It's nice to meet you." And she looked at Johnny and offered her hand, but he said, "We've got work to do."

"And I," she said, "am sorry to bother you. I just wanted to come over to let you know that I'll be driving round these sites for the next little while, and I hope that yooz'll try me out instead of some of them other wagons. And that's all I want to say. I hope yiz have a good day."

And she turned around like a ribbon in the wind and left me saying "Wow."

Johnny put his gloves and visor back on and told me he'd like to fuck her in the face.

THAT WHOLE SECTION around Honeywood and Glyde was built by the Rossi brothers, and the Rossi brothers were the kings of split-level foolishness. Those two brothers never got along, and I figure that whole trend, one floor two feet higher than the other, was a result of them never seeing eye to eye.

The house where we were welding was the last of an era. Giovanni Rossi died, his brother was an idiot, the suburbs were growing, you wanted a new style of house, and Jerry McGuinty had money in the bank. "Two thousand, four hundred and fifty-three dollars," my bank book said to me, and in 1968 that was nice to hear. While Johnny Cooper and I were working on that house I was putting the last stages of a plan together in my mind, and it does seem, when I look back now and think of meeting Kathleen, that my whole life was determined in a day.

After Johnny finished welding that pipe we sat with our backs against the house and I asked him if he'd like to do some work for me. He told me to shut my fuckin hole for a minute and give him some peace so I was quiet for a minute and then I just *went*. I told Johnny that I'd saved some money and that things had to change and that these houses we were building were going to blow away in ten years and that the ones still standing would make people sick. Who wants to live in a split-goddamn-level I asked him, knowing he would agree because he'd asked me the same a couple of days before. That's what I want to know he said and I said that's right and I've got an idea I said to change things I told Johnny Cooper with the voice of purest truth that what people want is a house standing proudly on its own two feet you can listen to me or not I said but I'm going to build some solid fuckin houses. I remember the passion was in me. I'm going to cover a neighborhood in plaster I said and I'm going to make it into a solid white fist you watch me I said and you watch the wind and rain go running think less and fuck more that's my motto Johnny said and so I had to repeat the whole goddamn thing to him because he had stopped listening which I did and I said watch the fuckin wind and rain go running. God I remember it now and my shoulders strong. And I said to him standing now and less scared than I had ever been around him Johnny I said I am going to make a fortune I'm going to buy some land Johnny out there by the airport and I'm going to build some smart fuckin houses and I *am* going to be proud my friend and if you don't want to come with me that's fine but if you promise not to hit me I'll tell you you're a fool I need a good crew Johnny and I know I can't do better than with you because the truth was I couldn't afford anyone better and besides he was a genius with his torch. And Johnny, I said.

I can't remember. I was still living in Mrs. Brookner's basement with ugliness everywhere, but I had been walking around with my idea like a flower in my heart. That talk with Johnny was the first time I let anybody know about it, and I think I knew even then that if I hadn't just met the beautiful Kathleen my idea might have died inside me. I was so excited. I had been thinking of her. She had turned and left and walked to her cute little truck, I went Wow, we went back to welding, I watched Johnny's back, and in my mind was a new Godmade face. For an hour I thought of her, and it was no surprise that there I was with all that beauty in my mind talking to Johnny Cooper about hope.

I wasn't thinking. Telling Johnny Cooper about dreams and hope was like telling Johnny Cooper he looked pretty, and I started realizing that before I finished gushing my idea. I remember Johnny stood up and looked at me and I thought I should brace myself.

But the fact is, or I like to think of it as a fact, that Kathleen Herlihy had loosened more than Jerry McGuinty's tongue. Cooper's fingers were limp when he stood up and I knew he wasn't going to hit me. I feel now that he had been thinking of the same pretty face when he went back to his flame, and for a few important seconds he didn't think of swinging. That's my theory, and you can smirk at me for as long as it makes you feel smart.

Johnny stood up and he said, "When do I start?"

And I do remember. I remember smiling behind my mouth, and I remember a face behind my eyes.

KATHLEEN HERLIHY was what colors tried to be. I have some pictures here, but they don't do her justice. This one here of her on our steps—that was our second house—comes close, but that's ten years after we met.

She wasn't just beautiful because I had no experience. I knew women. I know what you've been thinking. "Here goes Jerry the wet-eared virgin falling in love with his sister who's his mother and he'll be frightened of vaginas." The fact is, when I was fifteen years old I lost my virginity and it took me only several seconds to learn a thing or two about women. And I had girlfriends after that.

I WORKED LATE after that day and I wandered over to other building sites, hoping I might find her truck. I went home and I swallowed something awful that Mrs. Brookner left by my door, and I lay in my bed and my sleep never came. I went to work the next day before the moon even thought of disappearing and I had my eye on every road and my ear on every truck. Johnny Cooper turned up at seven as usual, and got to work without talking and I was glad of it.

I was starving. Other trucks came by with their horns more irritating than ever. Johnny bought from the first that came along and poured as much grease on his hangover as he could afford. I was glad again, because it meant he wouldn't want to buy from Herlihy's Meals on Wheels.

At 8:31 she came driving by—I noted the time for the future. She was later than all the other trucks, which I would have thought was a mistake if she hadn't been so pretty. Her horn was like this: JigaJigaJiga, like a laughing little animal. I probably smiled. JigaJigaJiga. I was sick by then. No hunger at all.

"Good morning."

"Good morning."

"Jerry, isn't it?"

Fantastic.

"Kathleen, right?"

"Cold one today," she said.

"It is cold," I said.

"What can I get for yiz?"

"What've ya got?" I said, cool, sick.

"What do ya feel like?" she said, tricky.

She pointed to a blackboard by the window that was decorated with chalk drawings—hammers and saws—that she thought the builders would like. Cute and realistic. I can't remember all the choices because all I wanted was honey from her eyes. I chose what I would never be able to eat.

"I'll have an egg sandwich."

"Egg sandwich. That's my favorite, too," she said.

She disappeared for a minute and came back with a sandwich the size of a farm.

"Wow," I said, meaning it. "How much?"

"Fifty cents," she said.

"Fifty cents! For all that?"

"Yep."

"Sheesh," I said, or something absolutely fuckin stupid.

"You tell your friends," she said.

And I said nothing.

It wasn't fear and it wasn't shyness, really, it was just the thought that this woman handing me a sandwich is what the world will always yearn for as it grows. I should just look at her for a few seconds, if that's all right with her.

"Anything else for yiz?"

"I'll have a Coke," I said, and she said, "Sure."

I got my few seconds and her truck drove away, with the promise of tomorrow and the mornings after that. Johnny Cooper looked uglier than ever when I came floating back. I watched Kathleen's truck through the wall-less house. I watched it drive around the block and Gone. I think I had some thoughts, but I cannot remember them, and then my hunger woke up like a frightened dog.

Let me tell you about that sandwich.

I TOLD JOHNNY that it was going to be a couple of months before I could get any work going for him. I had no idea how long it would take really. We had lots of work to do on the Rossi site and everywhere else—enough to let me wait for a long time. But I didn't want to wait, and if I did want Johnny working for me I had to get things going quickly because he would soon forget the whole idea and then I'd have to explain it again. My problem was that I didn't know how to approach the banks and all that.

IT ONLY TOOK one more meeting with Kathleen to confirm that she was a genius.

8:31 came around the next day but Kathleen came at 8:47.

JigaJigaJiga.

We talked like a pair of idiots.

"How are ya today, Jerry?"

"Good, thanks. You?"

"Good. Ya hungry today, Jerry?"

"Starving. You?" What?

She smiled that question away and I loved her.

"Did you enjoy the egg sandwich yesterday?"

We talked about sandwiches for a long time. I tried complimenting her on that egg sandwich and I had no idea what I was saying. She was confident, that Kathleen Herlihy, I thought to myself, and I was a whiskerless boy.

She showed me the menu on the blackboard again and told me she was going to change it every day, because you can put anything in a sandwich as long as it's clean. It was a joke but it was true. She looked in my eyes like Beauty and said there was "no greater good than giving the body a sweet new flavor to live for," I think. She said the only thing better than making a new sandwich every day would be wrapping the earth in two pieces of bread, so you could eat the world and die.

We talked for seventeen minutes, and they were the roundest minutes I could remember. Her confidence tied me up, and I'll tell you she was funny. I won't repeat her jokes, but they were funny because it took me just that extra second to realize she was joking. And she started talking in a way you don't find on a site.

"I like," she said, "drivin around here and seeing how hard all you guys work. It makes me feel safe."

That was something she said.

And also, "You can see, like, the work that goes into living."

It was the truth. It is the truth. A building site shows you the work that goes into living. And a finished building is a life—the end of a life when you can do nothing with what you've built but die in it. And she was beautiful when she was saying it, and what a warm sun after my lonely cold mornings.

I tried to talk like her and I talked like I hadn't spoken for days. My words were too heavy to come completely out of my mouth. So she did most of the talking and tied me up some more. She was leaning out of the hole in her truck and I was looking up to her, and I never felt anything like that. I was minutes into knowing her and I wanted to hold her and press her against the ache.

THE ONE THING I said to her that day that I really made a point of saying was, "I've got an idea."

"About what?"

"About the future."

And I told her about my idea to build. I didn't tell her all about it, because I couldn't, but I hinted.

"I need a bit more capital," is what I said, being proud at the time of that word "capital." I learned that she was a genius because the word didn't impress her at all. In fact, she had advice to give.

"I know all about that," she said. "I know all about raising money," and her truck was there all around her as proof. I could have been suspicious, because I myself already had enough money to buy that truck of hers and her business was never going to be as big as mine. But she didn't let me.

"I know you've got bigger dreams than this, Jerry, but I can tell you what to do about banks."

She told me to come and see her again tomorrow morning and she'd tell me what to do.

To start a construction business in those days a man needed a few important tools: a crew of eight; thirty thousand dollars; skin like brick. I couldn't have told you that so easily then, but I had some idea. I thought I knew how much money I would need and how many men, but I didn't learn about the skin thing until I realized I needed a lot more money and I couldn't trust the men. That took a while. The one thing I knew I needed before anything else was the money. It was going to be a long time before I bought any heavy machinery, but renting a backhoe alone cost a pocketful of blood. The people who rented them out in those days were the other construction companies, and they didn't make it easy for little boys who wanted to compete. A lot of the money I needed was to buy the trust of the guys who owned machines.

What I didn't count on was that the banks would know that too. It was something Kathleen warned me about.

"Don't go in there thinking all you gotta do is look clean and pretty and show them you can save. Those men are lookin for savvy. That fella who'll interview you will know everything that can go wrong in a construction company, and you shouldn't be fooled by his suit. Confidence is what ya gotta have, Jer."

I record this also as the first time she called me Jer. She gave me confidence and she told me what to do, and you can think what you want, but there is nothing unmanly about getting advice from a woman that beautiful. And she was exactly right.

She told me about getting a plan in writing and told me to be honest and proud.

Weeks later I got an interview at a bank. I walked in there with my chin set so and I butted chests with a bull of a banker who smiled like a boxer. And sure enough when I shook his hand I felt concrete, wood, and nails.

"I was in the construction business for twelve years, Mr. McGuinty, and I rarely encountered men as young and stupid as you. I don't know what it is that makes you think you can own your own company but whatever it is, it's not represented in this proposal."

And he went at me with the sharpest spears of honesty that were ever flung at me, and if I had been more reasonable I would have crawled out of that office and contracted my life to the Rossis to live in health and safety. But Kathleen had given me weeks of advice, and I told him that that piece of paper was bullshit for the bank and if he wanted the truth I'd tell him. I told him exactly how much I needed to bribe the machine renters, the councillors and him if he wished. I told him how I could fudge my insurance, and a hundred other things that won't make me look like an honorable man, but up yours.

I walked out of his office completely broke and rich, with more money than I ever thought I'd have and no way of paying it back.

FROM THE THIRD morning, my visits to the truck were about financial advice, preparing me for that interview. Kathleen drove by at a different time every morning, and I would put down my tools when I heard her and do my best to look serious and avoid the eyes of Cooper. Men like Johnny Cooper didn't tease you about women, they went to the women and made you look like a fool.

Her coming at a different time was the difficult part. Even these days, if a catering truck comes later than usual you'll find some angry-bellied workers. She made the best sandwiches that ever drove by men, and they were hard to wait for.

But it wasn't that. When you're cold and the sun's not coming when it should, it's harder to control the shivers. I would leave Mrs. Brookner's thinking of nothing but Kathleen, and whenever she was late she made me lonelier than before I had met her.

Advice. She could have told me that the best way to make money was to give it to the Pope and I would have believed her. But she gave me good advice.

The sun. Never did I think you could press it to your chest and enjoy getting burned.

She came later and more confident each day. I was sick and shy.

But I started learning how to handle her.

"How are ya today, Jer?"

"Good."

You just be quiet, you see. And you don't ask her a thing.

Or, "It's cold as a hoor," you say, or something like that, because it looks like she likes a bit of the roughness. And she laughs like a boy on a ride.

And you say something like, "Don't suppose you want to trade jobs?" and she says, "If only you had some skills," and then you laugh, quiet, and she starts talking like a bird you can't touch.

She told me all about herself in those first few mornings and to this day I don't know her. Her parents were Irish and she grew up in Dublin till she was eighteen. Sisters, brothers, she was the oldest, she looked after them.

The part of her story I liked was she came here on her own. She followed a man and I hated that part. Broke her heart, she said, and I only half hated her. She started struggling and struggling and she was still doing that now but it was looking like she might see the end.

I had a lot of money saved, I thought, and I wanted her to know that, so I told her sometimes the end is closer than you know and she nodded like I was wise.

I liked to watch her hands make my sandwich.

She said that looking after her sisters and brothers was like being a mother and she said she needed a break from that for a while because she was only young. "That's another reason kinda why I came here," she said. "But," she said, "I might want kids sometime." You could still hear the pretty Irish in her voice, but you could tell she was trying to cover it.

I hadn't thought about kids so I had nothing to say, and she liked me when I said nothing. She told me about Ireland, but my father was Irish so I didn't listen. She told me about the house she grew up in, eight kids and the parents with three beds between them, or something of the sort. "Sheesh," I said, or something to show that it meant something to me.

"You don't know what that's like, Jer, sleepin in a bed with so many kids," and I said, "No," to show her she was right. "I don't have any brothers or sisters," I said, in a deep voice, and she said, "Is that right, Jer?"

She told me a lot that day while she was putting the world in my sandwich. All I wanted to ask her was "Where did you come from, where did you come from?" even though she was telling me all about it.

ONE DAY WE had lunch together in her truck and one day, a couple of days later, she didn't turn up at all.

The day we had lunch in her truck was the day after I got my loan approved at the bank and my future appeared like a map. I was excited about the money.

"I'd like to buy you lunch, Kathleen."

And she said, "I'd like to make it."

She came around again at noon and we sat in the back of her truck on a couple of milk crates. I told her the good news, I said, "I got it."

As soon as I went into that truck everything felt different. I felt like I was in her bedroom and her parents were out. Everything both of us did was slower and closer and every word had skin. The blade falling smooth through an egg said, "Jer, you're a good strong man." Everything she did said something about me and everything I did said something about her, and that is the truth about a boy in a girl's bedroom.

"This calls for a celebration," she said. She went up front and reached under her seat and pulled out a bottle of Dewar's that she kept there, she said, "for bonfire nights." It was an Irish expression I never understood. "You must have impressed that banker, Jerry." And heavy came my cup.

The whiskey rubbed my nerves with velvet, and I ate half my sandwich without knowing it. She laughed a bit before she bit into her sandwich, and I don't remember why, but there she is, in my mind, laughing before she ate her sandwich. She moved her crate a bit closer to mine and it was natural.

And there is one moment in every man's life when Fear and Worry smile at each other and push him toward a woman. Something makes them decide you should forget about them, and there you are falling toward this woman with no real thought of being scared or pushed back— just a feeling of blood, chest, fast.

I gave Kathleen a kiss two lips. A kiss on the skin of her smile, then hand round the back of her head and Deep. And yes there is warm and yes you've landed soft and fast pushes further to a warm can't believe. I kissed Kathleen and my palm was behind her ear and her head was touching my hand like grace and this is a man and a woman, finally. In that hand there, that thumb there. Soft.

Go away while I remember.

I DIDN'T LOOK into her eyes because when a man does that he's an actor. It was so silent and I was so Jerry again and she the more Kathleen. There was my hand and her breath saying good.

Then Worry and Fear shut the truck up tight. There was a look around her mouth like love and What've you done.

She had the sense to smile and make a joke, and I was grateful because all I could have said was Wow and This is Serious.

"That's not how you'll keep the banker happy," was what she said.

We both leaned back and were each a kid on a crate, except really she was all grown up now. She picked up the bottle of Dewar's again and filled up both our cups and she stood up and said, "'Nother sandwich?"

I got so nervous then, I tell you with no pride, and I didn't know what to do. She walked around, getting bread and tomatoes and I was too scared to look at her. Maybe I looked at her legs in her jeans and was proud. But I was scared and I wanted her to say more and she was just slicing bread. I didn't know whether to say "Come back here" or "I'll go."

I forgot that we were parked there by a site and it was lunch-time for more than just the two of us. I heard other builders coming toward the truck and in a couple of seconds Kathleen was sliding open the serving window and was taking orders for food. It all suddenly felt exactly like it was: Jerry in the back of a food truck.

As soon as I got outside, my leaving felt like a mistake. I felt like I should be back in there in her.

SHE CAME BY the next morning with her "How are yiz" like a whisper. She made me a special breakfast, she said, and there it was all wrapped up, sausage still hot and a toothpick. I wasn't ready for that. I hated the thought of someone thinking all night about what it was like being kissed by Jerry McGuinty, and I still don't like the thought. I've kissed plenty of women, and I don't want to know how it felt for them. I was expecting her not even to show up that morning, or to show up with a look like No. But there was my special breakfast. We didn't need to say much because one right look is like the sun on fog. I was a confident man standing there by her truck with a sausage in my mouth, and I didn't say a word but "Nice."

I ASKED HER OUT to dinner. The day after the day after I kissed her I asked her. It wasn't my first time taking a girl to dinner. I did it once before, but that was no good because I wasn't clean.

Kathleen got a smile on her face and said, "OK."

I didn't have a car in those days so we decided she would pick me up in her truck and we'd go a couple of blocks over to Giovanni's, you know, Italian.

I got clean for that date, boy. I went back to my place early and Washed.

At eight o'clock she rolled around like luck and I met her on the curb. She wanted to come in and meet Mrs. Brookner and see where I lived but I told her no. "Let's eat," I said, like a man who knows his mind. We got up into her truck and it was the first time I had been driven by a woman and every time she turned a corner was like a long flirty smile. She drove that truck smooth.

"Giovanni's," she said.

"Giovanni's."

"I know what I'm gonna have," she said.

We didn't say much when we were walking into the restaurant. She just made a sort of squirrel-eating-nuts noise which in those days I found cute. "Smells good in here," I said. A waiter came and took us to a table, and I let Kathleen go first even though I was hungry. When we sat down we both had that phony look that people get when they sit down in restaurants. I saw myself in a mirror behind Kathleen's head, and it was then that I felt nervous. I looked like a fuckin idiot. Young. Kathleen took longer to get rid of her phony look, but it was only like the difference between a beautiful thing and a painting of it.

"So what are you gonna have?" I asked her, as soon as we were settled.

"I don't know yet, Jer."

"But I thought you said you knew."

"Sure I knew, but I don't any more."

"I see. I see."

We were flirting.

"I know what I want to drink," she said, "if ya don't mind, Jer," and that was a highball of Dewar's.

"Make it two, make it two," I told the waiter.

We sat there and smiled and there was her neck right across from me. I remember her dress and her hair but I won't tell you about them because why would that interest you.

"Jer," she said. "I've been so happy for you, since you got that loan. Happy, happy, happy."

The drinks came.

"When a man does something on his own," she said. "When someone does something on her own, he comes back a different person. I came back different. You came back different. Cheers. I loved that…I hope ya don't mind me saying this…but I loved that look on your face when ya came to the truck the other day because it reminded me of mine. I looked just like that when I came here from home. When I got off the boat…"

We both drank those whiskeys quick like Here Comes a Holiday and ordered a couple more. I ordered spaghetti and Kathleen ordered spaghetti because that's what Giovanni's was known for. And we got a jug of red wine.

"It's terrifying, Jer, thinkin that there's nothing between you and starvation, you and some great cold nothing, except your own courage. You've gotta…I've gotta…stand up, go out and do something, because if ya don't there's nothing but that cold, do ya hear me, Jer?"

She just went right ahead and got all thoughtful and it was just what I needed, just what we needed, to make a kiss in the back of a truck more than that. Just what I needed to make me hungry and easy.

"I knew about every step when I got here, like every time somebody said something to me I remembered it. Tom, the fella I followed, disappeared completely. I walked around, like, not knowing where to walk around. And ya decide, don't you?"

"That's right."

"You decide. Am I gonna be lost or not?"

"That's right. You plan."

"Exactly, Jer. You plan what yer gonna do next. What's your next move, as they say. That's what ya decide. And I decided."

"The truck."

"Exactly, Jerry. That's a lovely Irish name. Did you know that my father had a brother named Gerald? Gerald became a priest. That was his decision. Some of them find God, don't they, but that wasn't my decision. In Ireland, Jerry, ya make God your decision for keepin out the cold, or ya leave. It wasn't just Tom, ya see, Jerry. It was me. I knew, Jerry, that he didn't want me to come, but I came no matter. I was frightened like a little kid, I was, everything louder and bigger. None of it's louder or bigger but I felt so, Jerry, I felt so, and all the funny accents and the drivin, flip me, if I couldn't get used to the drivin when I got that truck. It was one of them little things ya have to get used to, like the little things on top of all the big things, on top of that worry have I made the right decision leavin home and that fecker Tom leavin me and it's colder here in the winter than the devil could have planned and my family's at home forgettin me, and there I am drivin on the wrong flippin side on top of it all. You know, Jerry? Ha! This is good, eh?"

Long sip spaghetti wine.

"So ya come here and ya sit in some rat's arse of an apartment and ya think who are ya, is what you think, and who would I be, you see, if I weren't sittin here in this apartment. And ya get some courage, some comfort, they say, thinkin of the bad things you've avoided and the bad things ya could've become or done, or even the boring things that weren't all that bad that you avoided because they just bored you, and ya think, right, I'm not so bad off, but that's utter bollocks is that, Jer, when yer actually sittin there with shite around you, isn't it, because deep inside ya know who you are and that no matter what comfort yiz are getting from thinking of the people you aren't yer still the person you are, who is a cold and lonely one sittin there surrounded by shite which slowly yiz are realizing only yooz can clear away. That's what I realized anyways, Jer, and that's in my circumstances, Jerry, where the plannin really starts, and could ya just top that up for me there, that's delicious that. I thought about what me mam said before I left which I won't repeat because I don't want ya to think less of her. She's lovely. But she told me yiz are making a mistake followin that man and she was right, I will grant the woman that. But she said yooz'll be lost, and that is where she was exactly wrong. Wrong, Jerry, because that's what I'm saying and you know it, that when yiz are sittin out there completely alone yer found, found, found, not lost. Ya sit there and ya think, so this is me. Ya find yerself, and that's the difficult part. And that's what I'm sayin. Ya reach that point and ya think, right, what do I do with this me. And there's some, Jerry, like you, who find some great thing to do."

There was something so exciting about that point right there that made us chew on our glasses when we drank.

"And no flippin thinkin yiz have done it all wrong, because you cannot, Jerry, you cannot think of the past. You burn your bridges, Jerry, is what you do, or it's what I did. Do ya have many bridges, Jerry? And maybe that was good for yiz, but for me it was, I'm leavin, you know, and it wasn't just one person it was one bridge after another and I don't want to think about it and get all sad, but it was me mam and me dad and me brothers and sisters and Gran and Tom, in a way, and everyone in a long line of people ya can feel like yooz've disappointed if ya let it, but ya mustn't. Moving forward is what yuv gotta do in that truck there outside. Isn't it beautiful? I mean isn't it a flippin beauty, Jerry, cause it's mine and I'm thinkin of repainting it even brighter yellow to cheer you miserable lot up in the morning. Driving around in that, free like that, is a beautiful thing, like the sight of a new plate of spaghetti. Do ya want more?"

Yes!

"And I will never be what I was, Jerry, just a flippin maid cleanin up and wiping the arses of all my brothers and sisters and the Catholic flippin Church, Jerry. The Catholic feckin Church lookin over every cold day when ya wake up and ya jump out of bed and kids, kids, kids, and yiz are never alone at all. Yooz have got it here and I respect that and if yer a Catholic Jerry, I apologize, but over there it's something else, Jerry, and it's what makes ya feel like ya have to clean up them kids all the time and I don't want to start ranting. But there it is outside, Jerry, that van and I hope ya like it. I was driving around the other day thinkin that if it wasn't for the petrol, and it's feckin expensive, Jerry, but if it wasn't for the petrol, and the money I owe on it, I could drive for ever, you know, like drive around these lovely streets and they drive into my dreams and I drive into them and it's just a lovely gliding feeling all free, do ya know? Because I'm all new Jerry and ya don't need to know about all them things from the past, and there's something in your eyes Jerry that's very sort of wise and I love it. I hope ya don't mind. And you know, if it wasn't for the money for the petrol I could drive absolutely everywhere sellin sandwiches, because that's the lovely thing about a sandwich. You can laugh, Jerry, but people eat sandwiches everywhere. That's what I like about it. And I love meeting the new people. That's lovely wine isn't it, that wine. I only drink on bonfire nights such as this one. Do ya like singing? Men don't sing over here and I respect that but I love singing. Will ya hum a tune for me, Jerry? I'm only joking. I'll hum for ya sometime, shall I, Jerry? And I have to say. Jerry."

We leaned closer across that table.

"Jerry, I've been thinkin about nothing else but what we did in the van, Jerry, the other day in the van. And it was lovely. I hope ya don't mind me saying that, a strong man like you mustn't like that talk, but it was lovely, Jerry. Because ya just came up into the van, didn't ya? Jerry."

Look at her there.

"Ya came up into the van and that was a lovely kiss on my lips."

I'LL TELL YOU WHAT it looked like in those neighborhoods before they became neighborhoods but while they were on their way. It's men like me you have to thank for making them solid and tight.

Much of this earth, in those days, was meant to be built upon. I didn't see much land that was pure and beautiful. A lot of it was sacred because the sacred part of land is the use you make of it, and most of this land was saying "use me." There was so much developing or prospecting around that the world looked like it was going to roll up and leave, and if you didn't hold on to it, if you didn't put your boot down on the dirt and say, "That's mine," it would move under the boot of the next man who would change it. The earth knew it, and it made itself as unfinished and in-between as a twelve-year-old boy. Hills weren't hills and rocks would barely need blasting. It was land that was either aching to be touched or aching to get back, and my choice was to touch it. And I'm not talking about some sort of Eden. It wasn't a case of spoiling or leaving innocent or doing anything at all of bigger meaning than building a house for Mom and the kids and a building for suit-wearing Daddy. I already knew about the sweat of my brow. I know the Bible. I know about woman and change and searching and evil, and none of it has to do with building a neighborhood, because a neighborhood, like the unused earth before it, is just a vessel.

So have a look on the map here and I'll show you. From here, which is now Hunt Club, all the way over to here, now, see there, McCarthy Street, was nothing but moving aching land, all, as I say, half land, half nuisance, half pitiful and perfect. There were some small farms but the rest of the land wasn't even clean, a lot of it. There was a young boy drank from one of the puddles before we built there who lost his eyesight for a little while because of it. Sometimes land comes poisoned before you bring the machines.

Eventually that area was taken by eight different developers, including me. My point is that there was a lot of land and a lot of interest. This section here, from what is now John Street to Uplands, is what I wanted to put my boot on first. You hear about homeowners now—that's what they call you people and me—who want their privacy, who want their hills and trees and all sorts of other things between them and everyone else, and I say it's a big bag of shit. First thing they do is wonder who the neighbors are and it's all the same in the end, love and gossip creeping over the hills as easily as straight across the yard. And you ask any developer even now with machines that can do anything what he thinks of a proper hill where he wants to build, and he will say fuck. It's easier to make hills than build around them, especially in those days, and that's why I had my eye on that section there. It was flat, my friend, like the palm of a friendly hand.

There was wet mud and dry mud and wild grass and dandelions and some cement laid down from years before when people had empty messy plans. It was land that people knew they could build on but hadn't finished thinking it through. It started at a bit of a rise, more of a rise before I crushed it, over here from the northeast and slid down smooth across the south-southwest onto the back of the old suburbs.

Good soil, some of it. Iron in it. One old man I liked kept a little garden out there that he shouldn't have and grew tomatoes, nice red ones. Wetter at the bottom of the rise but that's where the old houses already were, so the earth I eventually moved was dry, light.

It was foresight, and I don't mind pretending it's a gift. Some of the other developers, Edgar Davies one of them, thought that land there was boring. They thought they had foresight. And they were right in a way because they thought the people would want the interesting "contour" they called it, farther over here, and ignored the difficulties of building on it because they knew they could charge more. That's eventually, to tell you the truth, what I did. But that's not how you start. You start making the good solid houses, farther out, as many as you can, clean and simple, a white smile away from the frown of the city. I knew that then and you can feel **free** to admire me. Walk up to those walls and knock.

But the land, the land, that was how the land was. I won't declare I miss it. It was an interesting time and there it is for the record. It was dirt and water and rocks.

We kissed again that night like wine glasses Hooray. And we also kissed in other ways that only two people kissing know, and there's her mouth and hands and fast, and you sometimes just push hard. And we were drunk, my friend. I had never been so. Stumbling and knocking hips soft, and cheers, and where's the truck. Up against the truck but not inside. I am in Love and it is obvious to me and some time I might tell her. Push. You come to that crossroads, and I don't care what you hear about those days now but when a man and a woman wanted a manwoman body they just went ahead and did. And ohhh I thought about her. You're at that crossroads pushing against jeans and she's making noises and ohhh I *am* a lucky man. But we did not go inside that truck and it was the sweetest lasting choice I ever made, my body humming like a tire on a road.

"Goodnight, Jerry."

"Goodnight, Kathleen."

And I didn't see her again for almost fifteen days.

Fifteen days, my friend. I had no idea where she went. The next morning I thought it was just a hangover because I myself had a sick dizzy head. I waited thinking maybe she'd come by for lunch or maybe for the afternoon round but I never heard her horn, and waiting for it, stretching for it, put a whistle in my ears.

The next day no better and the next the beginning of Fear. Crash, kidnap, rape, or just plain new-kissed hatred. Whatever the reason, gone.

2

The Evolution of the Tongue, from Patricia to Renée

THE FOURTEEN-YEAR-OLD boy, so say the sages of ages, tires of yearning for the mouth of his mother, and should therefore grow up near a fat neighbor's daughter. Patricia Murphy, with breasts like toffee, gave Simon lessons in tongues. The fourteen-year-old boy ideally spends his days pressed hard against something else. Patricia Murphy, with crotch of impervious cotton, was free between three and four. Spin the bottle, postman's knock: she was an artful little teacher.

The tongue began at the hyoid bone in the back of Patricia Murphy's mouth, was first discovered by a boy named Louis, and was later explored and charted by Simon Struthers, esq., son of a great man.

Salt is tasted on the front and back sides of the upper surface of the tongue; sour on the middle sides; bitter at the back. The tip, indeed, tastes sweet.

Beginning at the hyoid bone in the back of Patricia Murphy's mouth, the tongue stretched over several years and continues to ignite the world with pentecostal passion and confusion.

But it briefly gave way to the finger.

The brutal dry palm of Natasha McSweeny shook his fifteen-year-old plasm to a jerky beginning. (Against the wall of the gymnasium for help with her grammar and spelling.) He couldn't suffer the abuse for long. He struggled till it was *her* back against the wall and he learned the might of his finger, when to deepen his inquiries or to dwell on the same point.

Then the tonguefinger was born, a rhetorician's dream, moving its audience—Jodie, his third cousin Lucy, whoever would listen—to new heights of understanding. But as understanding grew, new knowledge was sought, the tonguefinger became obsolete. Jodie found a deeper truth with his best friend Sam, regardless of the fact that he possessed an even greater truth than Sam's (he knew his from the locker room).

And a glacial freeze crept over.

Subterfuge began, a sign of things to come. His howling parts, so proud, so competent before, went underground. Sixteen. Seventeen. The greatest lesson still not learned, and the body turned against itself.

Then Sue Hawke came smashing through the ice, older, larger, and a new world was born, finally, and very, very quickly. Always too quick for Sue. He was proud again, roamed the earth again in wiser form.

He learned hands all over again from Catholic Marcia (even feet on one occasion). From two whose names I have forgotten he learned that the neck can taste like butter and if one smacks the buttocks just so they will blush like a nectarine. Anthea, Sarah, Rebecca his almost fiancée. The body settled into what he thought was its final form, and the tongue still licked its purpose.

He was not an unattractive man.

There are many I have not named.

So why, when he picked her up in the car, would Renée not take his kiss?

Was he nothing but a colleague?

———

HE WAS A MARVELOUS mystery to many in those days of promotion and change. Simon Zelotes, sedulous, defiant, triumphant amid the jeers of nonbelievers. He did the jobs that others could not. His skin had the sheen of conviction. Simon Magus, perhaps not moral, undeniably charming, he gave them what they wanted. He exhaled the smoke of Delphi and many gathered around him.

He changed memos from stiff syntactic graveyards into cloistered gardens of the Word. He, Simon Struthers, arrived at C Wing seemingly out of nowhere, and changed the warp and woof of the place with the elegance of his texts. He made C Wing (floor twelve, Thomson Building) into a long sword of concision, driven into the side of our dull civil edifice to startle not to kill.

He had one or two affairs, sexual.

WALK WITH HIM down the pale new hallway of the Thomson Building, strangers all around. Light blue carpet, men in brown trousers with pens clipped to shirt pockets.

What sort of man will he be in this new job?

Simon wears a suit, dark blue, and a fresh white shirt. He is not yet sure whom to mock and whom he should defer to.

The Thomson Building, on a square modern plan, has yet to reveal a comfortable spot for him to be alone. The toilet on level twelve is cold.

His first few memos are clever.

WHEN SIMON and Renée first met it was a perfect introduction to the challenges of the job. For the month leading up to the dinner at Madame Berger's, they worked on a minor memo. The issue, as it would always be, was land. Should it be touched, or not.

She arrived at his office with a folder in hand, and a friendly tickle of her nails on his door.

"Hello, Mr. Struthers. I am Renée le Mesurier, from down the hall."

He held her hand and squeezed it.

"I've got a C9 here that needs a redraft and a general change of focus before it gets properly adjusted for the perusal of the whole Division. The focus is all wrong, to tell the truth, thanks to Leonard, who, you may as well know, never understands this sort of thing. Do you have the time to do this?"

"Nescafé or percolator?"

He made a preliminary catalog.

Legs: tapered, certain, cereous behind the knee?

Wrists: like ankles of a doe.

Eyes: Greek! But blue.

Line from Ear to Chin to Shoulder: Serpentine.

Tan-skinned Renée is a patch of truffled soil, and he is a canny pig.

"The question is, how do we fill the memo? At the moment we are in the gathering stage, and for several weeks," she says, "Leonard and I have been trying to put this together. What Leonard doesn't understand is restraint, Mr. Struthers. A C9 tells us how to act, but never that we should. It is about information."

"Frank."

"Yes."

"But controlled."

"Yes."

"A guide stepping forward."

"Yes."

"His hands behind his back."

"I think we understand each other."

"I think I can help you, Renée. Tell me about the topic."

"I wouldn't want to tell you everything, Mr. Struthers. Not in one sitting. There is a long history to this issue, which I could not make interesting. For thoroughness you should probably go to Leonard."

"Let's hang thoroughness for the moment."

"I agree. Let's just say the issue is conservation. Preservation. Do you have an opinion on preservation?"

"That depends on the thing preserved."

"Interesting. That's partly our problem. What is the thing preserved? Do you like questions, Mr. Struthers?"

"That depends on who asks them. Would you like to call me Simon?"

"This topic is full of questions, Simon. The first question, when Leonard tried to help, was exactly as you guessed. What is the thing preserved? The thing preserved is land. Land. But the next question is, is it?"

The desk stands between them like a fat governess. "I think I understand you, Renée. The question of preservation of land is never about land. It is about preserving what land might be. Land discovered is land used: either land pretending to be unused (children flying flapping kites), or land already developed. Preservation of discovered land is a moot pursuit. And preservation is anyway irrelevant when considering what might be, since past and future lead us in opposite directions. The issue is promise. Since we are fooled by promise in preservation's clothes, it is appropriate only to ask questions, as we think something is lost as soon as use or preservation is decided. But questions won't fill the C9, our Division won't be informed, and what of the Public Good?"

Foreigners are often impressed by a certain sort of language, especially when they are not foreigners but Canadians pretending to come from France for the sake of cachet.

"Exactly. I have to confess, Simon. I was beginning to lose hope. Sometimes a new person, a new perspective. You may be just what the issue needs. I am so pleased you understand. It is actually all very interesting, but one forgets with all the process."

"Shall we sit down?"

On his desk they constructed a Stoic's porch, a brightly colored repository of learning that was all about inaction; and throughout he could only wonder if her fingers tasted like cinnamon.

"I don't expect that we can finish this in one sitting."

"That would be hasty." But stay.

"Would you like to stop?"

"No. But…"

"I agree."

His office has the same blue carpet, handprints on walls, and smells of budget. Its memories can be counted in days and its paint is like spit on paper.

Those prints over there, low, fingers down, were the hands of Renée supporting her affable self: black hair and a handsome smile. Renée visited his office most days, the issue was demanding but the visits were short.

"Basically," she says, "we are faced with a choice. I don't really know how to put the choice in words, but as a question it is this: What sort of a future will we choose for this city? It is simple enough. I don't know why I keep coming back to the beginning like this, to the choice. It is a choice between parkland or concrete, but it is so much more, isn't it?"

"It is."

"And Land and Environment can't help us. Ten years ago this wouldn't be an issue, but now it is not clear which way, politically, this should go. I think the Minister is inclined to encourage development. He is a practical man. And I am inclined to agree with him. But politically?"

"Politically?"

"Politically there are questions. The Minister could be credited with supporting a Division that specifically protects the environment."

"Protects the body of the environment."

"Hmm?"

"From depredations."

"Yes."

"From people."

"Yes. Which…I don't know, Simon. I am inclined to think that is nonsense. I like people."

"I like bodies. It is a matter of whether one likes restraint or not. Here are you and I, at this desk, discussing the fate of a piece of the city…Hand me that memo…"

Silk!

"Where was I?"

"I don't know."

"Will you be going to dinner on Thursday?"

ALL THOSE MEN in brown trousers. Whom would he befriend? They all have faces like clocks, expressions changing predictably as time ticks to ten, twelve, two, four thirty, home! when their true selves appear. Would any of them invite Simon home?

He never liked men.

AT THE PROSPECT of possible naked scrutiny, he tends to withdraw, momentarily. His confidence, like his penis, retreats. That explains why he was rather quiet in the car with Renée. It is not because he found her unattractive or uninteresting. Certainly not. In fact, he watched her through her window over the previous night or two, once he had got her address.

MANY OF THEM were below him anyway, these brown-trousered types. No need to consider befriending them. Rising in the public service was achieved by saying nothing to the right people.

But surely some were interesting. Hobbies, stories, collections of dreams on display in their homes. Certainly Simon was interesting.

BUT HE WAS the type of man, you see, who inspired distrust. It wasn't his fault.

As a boy, he was sometimes asked by his mother to read aloud for his father's friends when they came to dinner. What a precocious little monkey we have. He read with perfect enunciation. His apple cheeks were meant to charm. But there was a tacit acknowledgment shared between him and those friends of his father's, an acknowledgment that he didn't understand many of the words he read and that his charms were purely superficial. No one trusts a boy who seems clever; and he knew he wasn't clever. We will call you a genius, we will notice your beauty, but we will never be convinced. He accepted their lack of conviction.

The tie he wore at school when he strode into his teens was always perfectly tied with a neat little dimple. "Simon is always so *neat*," the girls would always say. "You always dress so *well*." The other boys hated him for the notice of the girls. And beneath the girls' admiration was that hint of distrust.

How fruitful this became when he grew up. Women watched him when he entered a room. He was charming at cocktail parties. He always had witty things to say when he had an audience. (And nothing to say when there was only one other.) The other men in the room, seeing the women so blatantly attracted, would distrust him, call him a poseur. To the women, this suggestion of being untrustworthy, hollow at the center, made him *sexy*. In this adult world, the consequence of his suspicious charm was that instead of being beaten up after school, he was promoted. People distrusted him to the extent that they felt he must be, should be, powerful.

Women loved him; men, despite themselves, ensured his rise because he could attract so many women. His rise made the women all the more amorous and all the more suspicious, and so on.

If his latest appointment owed something to the lingering force of his father's legacy, it was also the product of widespread distrust. And so here he was in this pale blue office.

DINNER WAS ON Thursday, and Simon had agreed to drive Renée. So on Wednesday, at around midnight, he found himself standing on the fence outside her house peering through a window down her hallway upstairs. He had a good view, could see clearly, but the bedroom, the bathroom, the livelier rooms of a stranger's house, couldn't be seen from outside. He saw her cross the hallway once.

It was not something he had done before. I think it was completely out of character. At other moments in his life as he walked down nighttime streets he had stopped, as we all do, to look into brightened windows. ("What a dramatic painting!"; "I wouldn't have put plants there.") But the stops were brief, they never gave him what he hoped for, and he never, very rarely, thought of going closer to the windows and watching for almost an hour.

Renée had given him her address so he could pick her up for dinner, and without thinking, without pausing, he simply found himself standing on her fence late on a Wednesday night, hoping for a look at her. And disingenuous as it sounds, he was only searching for a sense of belonging. He was trying to fit in. Certainly, he would have been pleased by a glimpse or more of her naked, but he was there to learn other secrets—any secrets that would help him to feel more comfortable in the middle of all the change. People and places belonged to him once he knew their secrets.

He saw her only once that night. The hallway was dark, so he saw his own face transparently imprinted on the scene, a sort of smoky portrait that he ignored as he strained to look through it to the hall. Every now and then his face would become his focus, but he paid little attention, looked through it again because acknowledging it would remind him that he was standing on a stranger's fence, and that the flesh around his jaw was beginning to soften in a mournful way.

Lights appeared under doors, altering his view, altering his face. And then finally a door was opened, throwing light into the hall, and he saw Renée in her pyjamas. He was beginning to forget himself.

ON THURSDAY EVENING he showered thoroughly and looked forward to the dinner. Renée dominated his thoughts at that point because she was the only new peer he had worked with so far. Eleanor Thomas seemed a bit severe; Randolph seemed neglible; Leonard, frankly, wore a dogsmell tweed; and his wife, Matty, if she was able to put up with a husband like Leonard, was not going to be of interest. But Renée; there might be some fun with Renée. Over and over he thought of how he might greet her, what they might talk about in the car on the way to dinner, after the dinner. He thought he might as well kiss her when they met, get it over with, kiss her deeply if she liked, and then touch her thigh through dinner. And afterward…He showered until there was no hot water left.

He drove to Renée's, proffered his lips in greeting and as a taste of things to come, but she took his hand, ignored his lips, and said, "Thanks for picking me up."

She wasn't wearing the skirt he had imagined, the space between his car seats was greater than he had remembered, and his interest had been lowered anyway because of his long and vigorous shower.

Not being kissed when one's lips are pushed forward is humiliating, of course, so he quietly thought about that while he drove her to the restaurant. "Am I nothing but a colleague?" And at dinner, as soon as he met Matty, the confusion was compounded. My God, there was something vital about Matty, a confidence (that was it, confidence, he was already yearning for it then, you see), and a smile behind her words as though she knew what liars words can be but didn't mind a bit.

No, he did not touch Renée's thigh during dinner. No, he did not, over coffee, feel her stockinged foot between his legs.

But, yes, he slept with her that night. He drove her home, but halfway there, with Matty on his mind (that mouth) he asked Renée if she would like to go to his place for a drink. And in the car (why not?), before they went inside his house, he leaned over to present his lips again, and, with Matty on his mind, he kissed Renée and she met his tongue.

3

STAND THERE WITH me in front of the walls of waiting. A young Jerry waiting for fifteen days for hips and hope and hair curled like questions. Don't look at me, because I looked like a kid, but listen to what I was thinking.

I was thinking of finishing touches. Sanding the walls of the last Rossi house, getting it ready for the painters.

I guess we can call what happened next a sort of beginning, the important beginning, the beginning of something that I didn't notice then or didn't want to notice and maybe only noticed a few days ago when I started thinking about all this. But there it was, definitely, by her goddamn little truck years ago. I don't even know what to call it or how to describe it, and if I had to build it I wouldn't be able to make a mix thin enough.

The fifteen days passed and I was walking back to Mrs. Brookner's after work one night, and I saw Kathleen's truck parked on the wrong side of the road. I didn't know whether anyone was in it because the lights were off, but the serving window was down which she usually closed when she wasn't around. I walked up to it and maybe I shat in my underwear a bit and I knocked on the side of the truck but there was no answer. I said "Kathleen?" through the window but I couldn't hear anything, and then I said it again in a higher voice like a little sister.

"Kathleen?"

She came to the window looking tidy and beautiful and completely different like she was borrowing someone's blood.

"It's Jer."

"I'm not serving."

"I'm not hungry."

"Just so yiz know. I'm not serving. It's what, it's eight o'clock, and there's no reason for me to be serving anyone."

"Right."

"I'm just having, I'm just taking a nap in there, in the back."

"Sorry."

"So you woke me up."

"Sorry. I saw the truck."

"And you were hungry."

"No."

"Well, everything's turned off, the griddle and all that and I can't be arsed to make anything, and there's no need or reason."

"I just saw the truck, and I was seeing whether, you know, you were all right. Where you've been."

"Since when?"

"Since, you know, a couple of weeks."

"What do ya mean couple of weeks? Where have I been? I've been everywhere I always am. In this truck. Where have you been, if it's any of my business?"

I told her where I'd been.

"Well, I don't know about all that, there, Jer, because, we've not been far apart and it's not like I've got to tell any fella where I've been and all, like he's the priest who's gonna tell me mam. I'm bloody tired at the moment to be honest with yiz."

"Well, like I says…"

"Yeah, well, it's like I says too, I've been doing nothing to make someone come asking after me like he's Father Flippin McGuinty, especially when I've just been here and if I haven't seen him it's not my fault. I've been here, right here in this spot for a couple of days with the men from the DeFalco site coming over every day for lunches and sandwiches and that, you know, for a couple of days, and you can ask them."

Which wasn't true because I'd been all over looking for her and I was sure I would have noticed that truck right there. Even if I never really looked away from the Rossi walls.

"And I've been driving around to new areas because that's the point, Jerry, of having this van. Ya drive around and find the new business, and so I've been working. And I was right here. And we saw each other just a few days ago, anyway, not a couple of weeks, Jerry. We had dinner, remember?"

"That was fifteen days ago."

"What's wrong with yiz?"

"It was."

"We had that dinner with all the talk and that. And afterward. I remember all of it. That was just a few days ago. I don't like that, Jerry. I don't like a man telling me what time it is. I know where I am and how long I've been here and it's always someone telling you where ya should be or where ya should have been, and that's what you're doing Jerry, so I wouldn't mind, if you'll excuse me, if you'd flippin stop, is all. I was having a nap back there, a bit of a nap after a long day of selling the sandwiches to the DeFalco men who's a bunch of flirts, and getting whistled at all day and I was tired of playing the game and I've gone and run out of the feckin sausages, so I got tired. It was just a moment of peace right now where a woman can have a small nip and a nap and God help her for relaxing. And maybe you couldn't have known, but you might know in the future, and, you know, here I am after a perfectly honest day's work and I'm confused because I just woke up and I've no idea what yiz are talking about with fifteen days like I just went asleep for fifteen days in some other city and I'm supposed to be here more often serving sausages and that."

"I'm sorry. I was, I don't know, maybe I'm…but I was worried, because, you know, fifteen, or so, days, and why was the truck on the wrong side of the road, is what I was worried about."

"Well, it's bollocks to be worried. I don't know. The truck, the truck is on this side of the road because I was tired and not thinking. I suppose you've never walked into the wrong room you're building or forgotten something, or maybe not, but that's the reason for the truck. And it's all the wrong side of the road in this country. And I've been thinking a lot since we had dinner a couple of days ago, Jerry, about a lot of things and I need to get my head together just now so don't expect me to be all nice and that. I'm not telling you, I'm not going to tell you to feck off or anything, but it's a fine thing to do, disappearing like that and then just turning up at the window looking for a sandwich."

"I wasn't looking for a sandwich."

"Well, whatever yiz are doing, I'm not in the mood. You've confused me."

So I remember that at some point I turned my mind again to how the last fifteen days had passed, just for a minute while she looked over my face for all the things wrong with it. And I saw nothing but those young white walls at first. She was looking at me thinking that's a small head on him and a greasy nose and he's not as smart as I thought; and I pressed my mind hard against what I'd been doing, what I'd been thinking.

Sometimes truth has a taste like smoke or metal. I hate it. I close my eyes, think of something else. I think: Forget it. Eventually it goes.

Anyway the troubles with Kath, usually, see, it was all something like a draft you don't notice till you're freezing. That was the day the crack appeared, maybe.

But next thing you know I'm in her truck.

———

So is it the story of a woman warming to her man?

My warm Kathleen.

A woman wakes up angry, growls a bit, looks at her man's gentle face and warms into steam?

She invites him up into her truck to stand by the bed where they both see the dent of her happier self and all their confusion is gone?

It was something like that, and excuse me if part of me wants to say you're goddamn right it was. I can remember the dark of the tarmac on the way to her truck's door, the yellow of the door, the smell of the truck—all of it certain, and all of it coloring over the minutes before.

I can remember the tickling heat of the truck inside like static, and there was that smell of pork that comforts and makes you sick at the same time. I wasn't so nervous as I had been, even though there was now a bed back there squinting at me through blankets like a challenge. I didn't ask her about the bed because now was a time for a quiet steady Jerry.

And quiet and steady he was, my friend, firm on the dizzying world. I could tell you all about it. Our squirming, what I look like in the nude. You might enjoy that.

Instead I will tell you about a line like "S" and the taste of the milk of lost hope.

I have known a number of surveyors in my life, a lot of good solid men as precise as their tools. And I have stood with them on some beautiful land and wondered at how they can gauge so calmly all those delicate misleading lines around them. Marking and measuring and rarely being taken in. I remember standing by one of them once, looking at a fairly simple plot of land by a creek that I was going to build on, and he was working there quiet, measuring the curve of the shore when all of a sudden he stood up from his slouch, packed up, never finished his report and I never heard from him again. It was the only love of a line I had seen as strong as the one I had for Kathleen's as she stood there inviting a kiss.

Now there was none of that "I was so happy, I didn't know where I was." When you're happy you know exactly where you are and I was definitely naked in the truck of Kathleen Herlihy. I was aware as I have ever been. I was aware enough to notice this taste that I can tell you about now and happy enough to ignore it then.

I ignored it for a lifetime. It was on her mouth and on her neck and on every other inch I was lucky enough to visit. As much a smell as a taste. The right touch would have made it weep from her skin and declare itself honestly, but I never had the right touch. And I don't want to suggest that there was anything obviously wrong. I couldn't name the taste then.

Maybe it was something like vinegar.

So we were lying on the bed in the back, having fallen asleep and awakened, and I was proud because I had done well on top of her, when she told me she had moved out of her apartment. That's why the bed was there.

"I couldn't afford it any more," she said, "and I like it in here besides. I told yiz I was going to do that."

"When did you tell me that?"

"The other day. So I just did it yesterday, just packed up and told the landlady her apartment was awful because that's who I am, and I moved all of my things in here, and I think, Jer, that the bed fits nice."

"So it does," I said.

"And I sold a couple of records and some other things, which is sad but feck it. I have to say, Jerry, that I'm a bit confused at the moment, you know, not quite myself, but when it all settles I'll be glad I done what I did. Cause it's not just the money. I don't mind telling yuz I couldn't afford rent and that won't surprise you cause yer wise, but I would have done this anyways, moved into this van. Freedom, Jerry, is what we're lying on. An apartment that moves with your life. Cause Jerry, I don't know whether it makes any sense, and God I'm craving something, something sweet or maybe fried, but having an apartment that moves around with your life makes so much more sense than moving your life into some sort of space you wouldn't go to otherwise, right? That's what came to me in a sort of flash, even though I'm totally penniless and that's why I moved."

"But you're making money."

"Oh, sure, I'm making money but it all goes, you know, on petrol, on gas or whatnot? Most of it. All of it. And there's lots of sites around to make money from and I think word's round that my food warms the gut, but it's driving to the sites that's the problem, and between them. All that petrol, and keeping the thing running while I'm serving, and that. Keeping the…keeping the oil hot, and that. But now at least I can just park at the site I want to start from next morning, I don't have to get up so flippin early. I can drive to the Y sometimes to clean up, but I don't get dirty generally speaking cause I'm a lady. Not like you lot. And to tell ya the truth, when it all settles down a bit, I'm a bit bloody excited. And you're lovely. So I've got to do a bit of planning, you know, do things at night that'll be right in the morning. If I'm out say somewheres else I've got to remember to park near where I want to be the next morning. But that's not difficult and I'm not a flippin eejit. There's some cement or something on your finger that's hurting me, Jer, just on my stomach there if you don't mind. So it's a big change, moving, you see, but I'm personally in favor of that."

Even though the place was decorated with nothing but grease, there was something womanly about it, and I let Kathleen know that I found it all exciting. We started talking again about twenty minutes later, and I started thinking about the situation a little more deeply. Kathleen was up digging out some doughnuts which she wanted, having poured us both a whiskey, and I was sitting up thinking about my own room in the basement.

As happy as Kathleen seemed with the idea of living in her truck, I thought there was something not right about it, and the whole situation seemed urgent to me. Why was I in a basement and she in a truck? It was my duty, which I was too excited to mention, to put us both in our own house, and I was pleased to think of the loan I'd got and my plans for my first development.

"I'm feckin exhausted," she said.

AND I BOUGHT land. Three thousand, three hundred and fifty-five dollars is what I paid for thirty-two acres, and if you think that is cheap you are not as stupid as the man who sold it. He thought I was giving him a lifetime's weight of gold, and I haggled over that last fifty-five dollars to convince him that I was. When we turned away from each other after we shook hands I'm sure we both had the same smile, and I know for a fact that he died a happy man because he wrapped a beautiful new Mustang around a lamppost six weeks later.

No development of land in the history of concrete-laying man has ever been a pure success unless it was bought from someone desperate or confused. If you see land for sale or land you want, don't measure it or stare at it or plan how much you would pay. Go to the nearest bar or church, find out from the locals what sort of person owns the land, and if he's a bankrupt, drunk or idiot, buy it. Like I said, in those early days it was hard to go wrong, but the fact that that man was a happy old fool didn't hurt.

I knew from what I'd seen, from knowing how long the building alone could take, that there was no point in sitting around being careful. Once I bought that land, the worst thing I could have done was sit on it and dream. I had already got a good corrupt surveyor who was willing to trespass to have a look at the land before I bought it, and he figured I could divide it into at least eighty-five lots, throwing bits away for paths, the road, and taking into account a few of those surprises that land always carries in its coat.

Once I bought it, the surveyor went out there properly and pegged it, and while he was walking around with string and orange tape, I was always near him. I met Johnny Cooper out there and told him, asked him, to look at what he would build on, saying I would meet him there in a month if he wanted, when I expected municipal approval. I said I'd match his wages at first, and if he helped me get things going quick I'd give him time and a half.

I needed at least six other men, and sometimes more than that, so I turned my eyes over all the men I'd worked with during the past couple of years. Antonioni I would definitely want for the wood, Espolito and Calzone I hated but needed for strength. Men can be good with their hands, but they're not good builders unless they can stand for nineteen hours in the rain. I knew I wouldn't be able to afford the most experienced builders I had worked with, but the strong ones who were quick were what I hoped for. Tony Antonioni and Johnny Cooper would be worth some extra expense. I'll tell you the rest of their names when I need to.

I worked nights at other jobs, and spent the days visiting other sites to meet the men I wanted or the men I could afford. One of them, Edgar Davies, had started his own crew. Some of the others said yes, some laughed at me. It took me longer than I expected.

Summer was starting, we all had more light, so Work was what the smart men did. My surveyor had a lot of other jobs so he came late in the day doing bits at a time and I would meet him, follow him or just stand still and watch, before I started a late shift elsewhere. Sometimes I would meet the men I wanted there on the land, like I did with Johnny, because you can get some builders excited by showing them what they can change.

Tony Antonioni met me out there one evening and I told him more about what I had planned. Tony was the stupidest genius I knew and I continue to respect him.

I said to him, I said, "Tony, what would you like to make of this?" sweeping my hand all grand across that thirty-two-acre world, and he got a shiny look in his eyes like wise people get, and said after silence, "Me?"

I figure Tony was a bit like God: he didn't really know what he was doing or why, but the end result made it seem like he did. He walked around the land and listened to the designs I had in mind (simple), and I doubt he understood much of what I said, but he looked like he was understanding more than I could ever know. He said, "You like me to work here?" pointing to the ground, and I said, "Yes," and we talked about money, and there was a long silence.

It was a warm evening, and there was always something relaxing about Tony even when he wasn't doing what you wanted. Eventually he put his hand on my shoulder and said, "Yes Jerry OK Jerry," and his smile showed me a vision of perfect wooden frames. I shouted over at the surveyor, who was tying his orange tape here and there, that I had just hired the best chippy around, and the surveyor smiled back like he meant it, which was a happy moment among three strangers.

And that is when building is at its best: when out of nothing and nowhere, unknown bricks and men appear and promise they will one day join. There are parts of the work that I like, a million that I hate, and there is some satisfaction when it all looks finished; but that is the part I love, when it's not together but might be.

Kathleen met me on the land that night, just as Tony was leaving. She said she had some shopping to do for bread and whatnot, so she could only stay for a few minutes. I told her I had so far got Johnny and Tony and a couple of others to work for me, and she was proud. We might have got into her truck for a minute to see how proud she was, quietly because the surveyor was around and quickly because the shops were closing and sometimes I get too excited.

When Kathleen drove away I walked back to the middle of the land and stood, not far from the surveyor.

I knew what I looked like from above, dustcloud slapped out by my glove on my jeans. It's a blackening blue sky, isn't it, and there I am in the middle of the land, yellow truck driving off to the right, and no noise left but unraveling string and the sound of orange tape saying here, here, here.

So MANY SWEET nights I sat there. Cool dirt, smells of mint and other things that my mind has no name for. Owning land swells out my skin, makes me proud, bigger, real.

That rock is *flat*, that one tilts *so*.

It's mine like my boot, like my heart.

Stretch your arms out an acre and take some. It's yours like nothing ever can be.

SUMMER NIGHTS are blue in Canada, which might sound meaningless or obvious to you, depending on your nature. The sky never goes black, it just gets sadder and a bit more honest. It never gets too dark to count steps, so I did that sometimes after work, before dawn, around the thirty-two acres.

There was that one white birch stuck at an angle like someone else's claim. I loved owning that. And the rock so round at one end. I still do own that rock—I moved it to my house when I had one and have moved it with me since (out there in the yard).

I'll tell you, my friend, when you own your own land, don't dig in it like some fuckin long-hair to look for sad little memories. Dirt's the future, not the past. Change it, move it, smell it, use it. That birch is a tree, not a bone. I realized I would have to uproot it: lot eighteen where number twenty-six now stands, firm.

Other decisions were made, pacing.

I'll have to lose that lot to make the road curve smoother.

Those four lots will have to be cheaper than the rest.

A backhoe can't lift that boulder.

Pace steady, know your land.

Decide.

And when the man from council comes, tell him your decision. Present the future to him. Or let him help you shape it.

"So, Mr. McGuinty, developing some land, are we? Taking a bit of the soil away?"

"That's right, Mr. Councillor. Come and walk around with me."

"Don't mind if I do, don't mind if I do that at all, Jerry. It's a nice piece of land."

"That it is. That it is, my friend."

"Yes. And I have seen your surveyor's plans. Looking good, looking good, if you'll pardon the repetition."

"He's done a good job."

"Quick."

"That's right."

"He's done a lot of work around here lately."

"I bet. It's coming up. It is all coming up."

"That it is, Mr. McGuinty. So tell me more about it. I have read your proposal, which is all nice and tight, correct and co-pacetic, forgive me, but tell me more about it."

"Well, look around and tell me what you think. I'm not good with words, but I'd say I was meeting a need."

"I would agree with that."

"Maybe you have some questions."

"Maybe. Yes, maybe. Tell me, Mr. McGuinty, what is it you see before you, there, on that land?"

And we both know that what we see is tax, a nice long future of tax, so I say, "I see families, Mr. Councillor. Families with jobs and houses that won't fall down."

"Well, I like to hear that, Jerry. I will be honest with you: That I like to hear."

Tax on their driveways, tax in their streetlights, tax in the water not there.

"I do like to hear that," he says. "And tell me how you feel about land."

And I say I've learned to love it.

"Because we do have a policy on parks," he says, which was the first I'd heard.

And I say, "So I hear."

"That's right," he says. "We need to keep some green. We're not a very green council, but there's no harm in it. You might have to lose a lot or two. Either green or ten percent of the value of the land, is what we say."

"Ten percent, eh? Ten percent. And I suppose you've seen the deed."

"That's right. I'm the one who looks at the deed, at the plans as a whole. The buck stops here and basically starts not long before me."

"So you decide it all."

"We are a council, Mr. McGuinty, but if there is something you would like to say to me as a man, I can listen discreetly."

"Thank you, Mr. Councillor."

"Because there are a few things I myself have learned about land over the years, Jerry. There is nothing certain about it, nothing you can trust. Men, some men, me, you can trust. Land, no sir."

"I might agree with that."

"Men can adapt. I can adapt, Mr. McGuinty, and if there was something you wanted to propose to me before your surveyor comes and joins us, you must tell me. Let me show you that I can adapt."

"All right."

"You might, for example, want to suggest to me an alternative to the park, maybe an alternative to the ten percent."

"Indeed I might, Mr. Councillor. I might want to suggest that, for argument's sake, I overpaid on the land."

"You didn't."

"That's right. I did not. But let's say, for the sake of argument, that you, as the man who has seen what I paid, have had a good look at the land yourself, independent of me, and have had a sort of surprising conviction that what I paid was too much. Just like that: Bang, it hit you when you met me on the land—that McGuinty's paid too much."

"And how do I come upon such a conviction, Mr. McGuinty? Do I get it from wandering?"

"You get it from talking."

"I see. Negotiating. Is it a matter of figures, sir? Mathematics?"

"Well, I never understood mathematics until it became money. Let's talk money."

"Let's say…that I came upon the conviction that you over-paid on this land by, say, ten percent. Yes?"

"All right."

"And this conviction led me to believe that, in order to make you look better for the sake of history, for people looking back at you, I ought to change the record of how much you paid by, say, ten percent."

"Yes."

"That way the ten percent you would pay council would be a more just amount."

"That's right."

"And so, talking figures, how much do you think that sort of justice, that surprising conviction, might be worth to the man who offers it?"

"Well, mathematics, who knows? I'd say about three percent of the difference."

"I would say five."

"Done."

"Well, I think it will be a fine development, Mr. McGuinty. Very nice, indeed. And I am sure that council will agree. I have a family, Jerry, a wife and a daughter, and I believe in them. Families are a noble thing to plant in this municipality…"

And on the bastard goes. That's how it might happen to you, and I was smart enough to expect it.

Within the month I got the approval like I'd hoped, and that particular council didn't bother me for some time. As for that particular man, Schutz was his name, he soon left for Big Government, but it wasn't the last I saw of him.

———

AND, YES, IN the blue I looked for her truck, and I could never find it. The last time I had found her truck was that day it was on the wrong side of the road.

When I was on my new land I was gradually realizing that I was doing what I dreamed of, and I didn't know how to feel about that. Happy that it came; worried it would go; sometimes surprised that it was a flat patch of dirt and I was actually nowhere near my dream. But most of my surprise was provided by Kathleen.

One night, for example, she drove onto my land to tell me about going to the bakery.

"Feck all of them, is what I said. Because she was telling me, Jer, while she was handing me the bread, that the supermarkets were promising them jobs. Feck em, is what I advised her. They were telling her, we'll buy your shop, knock it down, change your business entirely, but we'll employ you, if you like, serving bread behind some flippin little counter that is no longer yours.

"I said, what the arse would you want to do that for, give up your own business like that, and she agreed but said she had no choice. Most people were buying from supermarkets she said, and they were offering a good price for her shop, more than she could hope to make from baking for years on flippin years."

"I heard they were looking for the right land."

"They're looking for blood, is what I told her, Jer, or words like that. I felt, I feel truly sad for her, and I was also hoping a little that she might give me some of the bread for free. Have you ever bought bread from her?"

"No."

"Don't, Jerry. But she gives me discounts because I buy so late in the day. And she did give me some free bread, which is a good price for advice."

"It's a good sign that a supermarket's moving right there, if that's all true."

"Why?"

"Because that's toward my development. A supermarket there means people will live even farther out."

"But what about her?"

"If she's getting a good price it's even better news. It's all becoming valuable."

"I doubt that I'll be getting free bread from a supermarket. Discounts even."

"You won't need to. You won't need free bread. I'm going to make a fortune. That's what…that's what that conversation should have told you."

"What? That has nothing to do with me, Jer, making a fortune. I've still got to earn a living, just like she does, except there's no big market on wheels that wants to take over my van. That's what that conversation told me, and you'll forgive me for thinking yiz are a bit insensitive to the struggles of that baker lady. She's been there for years, Jerry, and she likes owning it."

"I didn't mean…"

"Well, it's feckin awful, is all, the idea of that supermarket coming and just buying her like that. Being able to buy her like that just because they're giving her a good price. Nobody's ever able to do anything about that, though, about realizing that there's more to things than a good price. She knows that staying there baking—pour me some more of that, will yiz—that staying there baking on her own is a bloody lot better than working for them and all, but she just can't…you can't do anything. It's like a big check is worth more than a gold coin, and you can't question that even if you know it bloody well isn't, to look at it there in your hand. That coin's what you should hold on to. I feel awful for that woman, and yooz are insensitive."

"I just meant that, I was saying you won't, you shouldn't need free bread."

"Well, I like free bread. I got lots of it last night and it's around that flippin sandwich in your hand."

We didn't see much of each other when I was getting the land ready. We both had a lot of work, and by the time I finished my piece work at night it was too late to meet her before she served the sites at dawn.

"There's nothing flippin wrong," she said, "I just don't like the thought of that baker woman, and yooz have got me thinking about her now more than I want to."

"Well, let's talk about something else."

"You talk. I always talk."

"OK. The man from the municipality met me and the surveyor."

"Well that doesn't help that baker lady, does it?"

"That's not what I'm talking about. You said I should talk."

"I'm just making a point."

"He came last night. I think I have to do a bit of paperwork, but…"

"There's no time. There's no time for any of it, is there. I'm feckin tired."

"You've worked a long day."

"Bloody rights."

"So you should rest."

"Nothing else to do."

"That's right. Just relax."

"I might go round to see that nice baker lady. I said we should have a chat some more, and I want her to know I meant it."

"You should relax."

"And you should feck off, Jerry McGuinty!"

"What did I do?"

"Go on, fuck off! Get out of my van and work on your flippin land. Go on, get out!"

"But I don't need to."

"You'll need to now. Get out before I throw hot oil on yiz! You vex me."

"How?"

"Don't how me. That lady's got a lovely face, sort of a jaw on her, and now there's a sad sort of light in her eye just here, sort of wet, and it's flippin awful to see her not herself. I've bought bread from her for a year, and she never had that light before and we said hello to each other like two strong people, and it makes me angry as fuck! Now get out! They're buying her and it's put that light in her eyes, so fuck off, Jerry!"

"I've got nothing to do with that supermarket."

"My arse you don't, and I don't care if you don't anyway. What makes you think I care anyway, you standing there looking stupid because you don't understand. I don't know what I'm doing here and I don't know why yiz are in my van standing there like that. There's not time for anything, and there you are, standing there. Get out or I'll put this out on your face."

She had a cigarette.

ON THE FIRST DAY of work five men turned up with tools. Johnny, Tony, Tony, Jerry, and Mario Calzone. Four of them had the look of sleepy *so what* that everyone has who arrives at a new site that's just an old site in a different spot. They stood apart from me and spat and smoked and shared some morning farts.

Dirt, arms, dawn-red eyes, backhoe standing ready, rusty, day-old beards that never grow. Every site looks the same on the first day, no matter how you multiply it.

I was scared as a bird. All the joking and smells and silences of those early mornings are part of a crew getting used to each other, testing and poking and settling in. Then there is a final silence when the foreman gets men working, but the foreman this time is me.

No time for nerves because Tony Espolito decides to test me early.

"You're the boss, big Jerry, where the fuck do we start?"

He was wearing the same plaid shirt as me, which pissed me off.

"Where do you fuckin think, Espolito?" and I tossed him a set of keys.

When an engine fires up, men get to work, because noise takes away choices. That's something I had learned. One rumbling old backhoe with Espolito at the gears made the rest move straight to what they knew. Johnny to the dozer, Mario guiding Espolito, Antonioni looking thoughtful with a shovel, and Jerry waiting for two dump trucks that were meant to be there, now.

Being the boss is all about posture: hunch like a gorilla when you're angry, but otherwise stand straight because you're smarter than the rest of them.

But I couldn't stand there for long. Dirt had to be shifted. The first long phase is push, push, get your head down, dig and push, shift it and pile it and make some unnatural holes. Basic work and there's comfort in it. One of the dumps finally arrived, a day before the other, so we had somewhere to put the dirt.

I was ignoring most of what I'd learned and was giving the unions the finger. Proper outfits use the right people for everything, and by rights men like Cooper and the rest should not have been there so early in the project shifting dirt. If you're a brickie, you come in when the bricks need doing, and if you're a union type you stand by your wall, build it beyond your reach and you wait for the union to throw food over it until you feel like dying.

We loved and feared the unions like they were big boozy uncles, but it was only the fools who followed everything they taught. As long as I paid these guys a fraction more than their union wage, they would do the work I gave them.

But money, boy, money.

That old bulldozer idling in a thundercloud of diesel while Tony smokes a cigarette: that's my money. That hour when Mario limps around useless because he dropped a rock "Cunt!" on his foot: it's all my borrowed money.

THERE WERE LONG breaks of nothing at first because those dump drivers had not yet learned to respect me. Dirt piled everywhere. Espolito kept digging the big holes, and the other Tony kept running around shoveling this and that. And Johnny and Mario.

Johnny and Mario hated each other because they were exactly

the same height. Johnny was tougher but Mario could swear more powerfully than any man I've met, and the battle between words and fists was never so muddy as when those two were together. Mario was always shouting at Johnny while Johnny was driving the dozer: "fuck…fuck…fackunt"; and Johnny would always have to shut down the dozer to hear.

"You're sucking on that cigarette like a fag tasting cunt. Why don't you give me one and I'll show ya how it's done."

And down comes Johnny with fists like heads and he smiles and says, "How about I fuck your eye with my knuckles," and he blows smoke directly in Mario's right eye. So I've got to come over because I'm the boss, fully aware that these men could rape me, and I call a general Lunch! even though it's ten o'clock.

At lunch we all sit near but apart, and a round of stories begins. Stories on sites have always been the same collection of words—hard, woman, father, beer—used in combinations that continue to grow. They are perfectly timed to add up to forty-five minutes, and they are nicely designed—though nobody mentions it—to take our misery away. You can get a sad story sometimes that makes your heart feel tired from all the uphill crawling in the world, but you'll somehow still feel better about going back to work once you hear it. Or you get the stories that start nowhere, finish in the same place, and offer no real fun or interest along the way; but they still feel necessary and go very finely with a roast-beef sandwich and a Coke.

Tony Espolito often started things off. He had instinct, Tony, he sensed things. He sensed that Mario, a fellow Italian, was going to lose his face bone to Cooper, so he always jumped in with a story to change the mood. Espolito's head, however, was a hollow, mysterious place.

"Last Saturday I drank thirty-two Old Milwaukees and didn't feel a thing. I rode the wife for three hours and cracked my head on the kitchen counter. It was a fuckin blast, and I'm never gonna buy a TV because, fuck it."

"What do you mean?"

"I don't know."

"Radio!" Antonioni shouts, smiling, and there's silence for a while as he looks wise and reminiscent.

"What radio?" Mario asks.

"My father, he have radio."

"That's great," says Mario, "but we're talking about television right now, and I don't know why. I'll tell you one thing. When big Jerry over here pays me a few times, I'm buying a TV."

"I drank thirty-three Old Milwaukees on Sunday. I like the way it feels."

"I know a guy in Kingston Pen drank sixty shots of Listerine." Johnny's stories were always about prison, and were short.

"I remember," says Mario, "when I was eighteen, fuckin nineteen, we followed this fuckin friend of ours around, who said, "Boys, my friends, I'm gonna show yooz lady cunts what beer was meant to do to a man, and if yooz want to put some money down, I say I can drink one hundred Labatt's 50s before the clock strikes twelve." And this was fuckin three o'clock or something, and we all put our money down and followed this friend, fuckin Giuseppe, around the neighborhood, carrying cases—we all had beers with us, cases—and we walked and sat for hours, fuckin clink! twenty-one! clink! twenty-two! And we was all getting drunk ourselves watching Giuseppe, you know, clink! pssht, and he'd eat the bottle. Couple of the gals in the neighborhood, you know. And beer comes in cases of twenty-four because that's all a man needs, right?"

"Just about," Espolito says.

"So fuckin Giuseppe's up at forty-five beers, and it's dark outside and we're just watching him, because, he was a fuckin brag, Giuseppe, always loud and shit, but we was watching him because he was just doing everything, you know being every person a fuckin man can be, quiet, mad, laughing, crying like a little hoor, and running around being funny after the girls. And at forty-five he just goes all quiet and he gets that look and boom, passes out. I threw up something brown that night."

"My father," Antonioni shouts again, "have radio, because my mother, she no want my father on top of her, and my father, he...does not drink."

He clapped his hands once, and I've never seen such confusion among men.

JIGAJIGAJIGA!

"Hey, fellas. How are yiz? Tony? Ya look filthy. Doesn't your mother bathe you? Hey, Mario."

"Hey, gorgeous. Whatcha wearin under your jeans?"

"A cleaver. What can I get you Mario?"

"Get me one of them egg sandwiches, baby."

"Tony, you made up yer mind yet?"

"I have egg."

"Two egg sandwiches. What about the rest of yiz?"

"Same."

"Same."

"Four eggs. I'll give yiz a discount."

"Don't forget your man."

"I know what he wants."

"I bet you do, baby. Two melons and a mouthful of prosciutto."

"Yer a riot, Mario. Feck off and play in the dirt while I make these sandwiches. How's it going today, Jer?"

"It's going good. We're clearing it. I'm going to get Johnny to do the blasting by the end of the week."

"Ah, good. He'll like that, won't you, Johnny?"

"My sandwich ready?"

"How's it going with you?" I say.

"Good."

"Good."

"Fecking awful cause of all the filthy mouths, but I'm fillin them. I've got to get over to the other new site there, that Edgar Davies one."

"How's that lookin?"

"About the same, same as this."

97

"The dumps keep going to him first. I've got to do something about that."

"Here's the sandwiches. I've put an extra slice of tomato in there for ya, Jer."

"You're not going already, are you?"

"I've got to. I can't live off you guys alone."

"That's because my sandwich is always free. Here, I must owe you ten bucks. Here."

Kathleen started sneezing. She always sneezed after making a round of sandwiches. Lots of small ones, like she was counting the tasks she had finished in a cute little language that I didn't speak. The men always said "Bless you" in tones of love and religion.

"Well, I might take a break since yer paying, Jer. Don't mind if I do in that case. I'll just sit up here."

She never came out of her truck, and I wouldn't go in while the men were around. And there were rarely any stories when she stayed. I leaned against the counter, just there, by the serving window. And the men stood around, silent, cool, looking at different parts of the world. There was always a good ten minutes of nothing, just the sound of mouths and eggs and whatever washed it down. There's an invisible thread connecting that sort of group. I've noticed it around country people too. Faces look like they're lost in a private dream, but everyone's actually observing the same thing. A noon wind crawls across the group like steam, say, and right when it reaches the last of us, Mario will say, "Hot as ass," and we all silently nod.

We would all notice when Kathleen moved. If she shifted in her chair, Espolito would shift a bit, kick a rock or something, maybe Mario would cough. We were watching her even if we weren't.

Crusts were usually swallowed at around the same time and that was when someone might spit, tell a joke, make an order, or, in the case of Kathleen, sing some new thought that made you want to hold her up naked and smile.

"You've got parsley on your lip there, Jer, looks a bit like Ireland."

JigaJigaJiga!

"Gotta go, boys. Gotta go."

4

By the end of that night the tastes on his tongue were of onions, cognac, and the butter of Renée. O the things he and Renée got up to, as the world looked through his tiny window.

I should tell you about his job.

The job, you see, the job was created for the man: slippery, hard to know, potent.

Simon and his colleagues shaped a vast area of this city.

The National Capital Division had existed in one form or another since 1899—always with the mandate of planning Canada's capital. In the early days, the issues were infrastructure, determining how much land the Government would need for itself. The city had changed from a lumber town to the seat of government, and the challenge for the Division was to accommodate the multiplying bureaucrats, scientists, military moustaches and the thousands of burghers they spawned. It was a glorious race of demi-giants in need of an appropriate landscape.

The city was prosperous, and poor, in a way many of us have forgotten. Income ranged from nothing to solid. Words like "railway" and "milk" still had a significance that has partially been lost. There was one hill of obvious wealth in Rockliffe, at the foot of which was obvious poverty, and from there the solid citizenry spread, west, east, south along the canal.

The spread farther outward was as inevitable as that of a middle-aged belly, and the questions raised by both are the same: Can this be stopped? Should it be stopped? What does it say of our character?

The Division removed the old railway lines from downtown, they created parks across the river, restored old buildings, transformed industrial sites into museums. They rehabilitated, reinvigorated, reinvented. Some of it thanks to Simon.

Issues became increasingly theoretical. When Simon's job was created, the words "culture," "heritage," "values," and "future generations" were mumbled into coffee and were gradually growing louder. The Government knew what it needed for itself, more or less, and it now felt responsible for setting in the landscape an idea of what it was to be Canadian.

Matters of placement and determining uses were the concern of Simon. It was up to him to decide where the eyes, ears, nose, and wrinkles would be placed on the municipal face: their shape, beauty, depth, where they would go or whether they would appear at all.

And his primary tool was the memo, the oldest and noblest form of official advice, born with bureaucracy itself. It told Solon and Cleisthenes how to spill their democratic mess, Augustus whom to tax, where to build, how to grow a god. In Byzantium, in fulgent rooms, it sat on the lap of a meddling clerk. Ancient styli cut its waxen belly. That's how Simon saw it anyway. He was the inky part of fate.

Once a memo from Simon circulated through the Division, the Division would inevitably follow its advice. The idea behind the memo would metamorphose into an object on the landscape. The Division owned thousands of acres, had the right to expropriate anyone from any land that it wished to acquire; and it was autonomous. No Government department—Public Works, Land

and Environment—had direct power over the Division. It was a unique situation, the absence of red tape, the power over so many Government branches, and, in Simon's case, the power over so many colleagues.

His name, you see, carried *weight*. Struthers. His father had been one of the Mandarins, the group of great men who created the public service. They had all been to Oxford (Balliol men), they had all been clever, incisive, shabbily genteel. Public Works, External Affairs, the Department of Finance—these had all been the creations of Simon's father and his friends. And his father had gone farther, stepped bravely, openly, into the public arena as a member of Parliament and was the trusted friend to two prime ministers. A rare combination of vision and power. Ideas. Ideas had never been so golden.

And Simon inherited the gold. He polished it. The children of these Mandarins all had a destiny to refine the work of their parents. They sailed on their fathers' names, moved by their advice: Possess an orderly mind, my sons; use guff when you must, but never accept it; keep a strong head for drink—never mix; and before you die, apple of my eye, create something great for your country.

He was just as clever as his father.

A sentence, whether moral or grammatical, was his servant.

But it took Simon years to see, to understand fully, just how powerful he was, how much he could accomplish. So much time was spent settling into that pale new office, determining what sort of man he should be to all his new peers. True power, he suspected, was not just in a name, but in one's knowledge of one's colleagues.

Let's say one spends a lifetime acknowledging the fact that people rightly distrust oneself. This face, this glib demeanor, ready wit, ease of expression—"I don't like them any more than you do," one might say. "It's not me, I assure you. What you see is not the real Simon. I don't know who he is."

Simon could become an exaggeration of what people imagined him to be. Or he could prove that he had substance. He could prove that he was not the creation of others' perceptions— he was more than just a collection of predictable desires.

BY THE TIME he was twelve he had built most of the models in *Great Houses of England*: Hatfield, Theobalds, several others. Not very quickly, but well. He had an obsession with gluing his fingers together: that unique combination of numbness and permanent touch. But when he finished the models as best as he could, he felt huge.

If Simon's father was a great man in the House, how great was Simon, building great houses so much smaller than he was?

His father could build models from scratch. Cardboard, paper, matchsticks. "I will build a ship," he would say, and he would, indeed, build a ship. Simon needed a kit. "It's a simple matter of imagination," his father would say. "Imagine what you want, and build it." It was his guiding principle throughout his life. "The public servant must find out what the public wants. If he cannot find out what the public wants, he must accurately imagine. And once an image is before him, the servant of the public *must* create it." That was a pompous speech his father once made upon accepting some medal or other.

Simon built his kits with brilliant precision.

Eventually he realized that the city that contained his father's house that contained those houses Simon built was small enough to sit neatly on his desk in the Thomson Building. All he had to do was unglue himself.

5

I'VE GOT MYSELF a beer going, and when I swallow there's a pain high up in that canal that memories run along, you know, between the spine and the heart. Fear on one bank, yearning on the other.

I MADE A PACT with Edgar Davies, a while before he fucked Kathleen, that we would pool our resources. There was too much land for one of us, we both agreed, at least at that stage of things, and we could both be powerful if we worked together.

Edgar Davies was a little older than I was and from pretty much the same background. He did a year of college but I'm a foot taller than he is. I can't say whether his motivation to build was similar to mine, but I know that his goal was different. It is Edgar Davies you can thank for walls that show their studs like pimples, for houses that look too new when they're built, for the aging sugared porridge of choiceless making-do that all the world has drowned in. And I'm afraid that's why we got along. We wanted different things.

"Jerry," he said. "You make the strong houses, I'll make the shit. If people can't afford yours, they'll choose mine. We can split the market."

He dressed his houses up with language, "half-timber, Tudor living," "a taste of the dream of Italy," and sold them in divisions of two hundred. All of them exactly eleven hundred square feet, and identical inside except for the way they collapsed. He had a new alternative to wood every two years, materials like polypropylethylfiloplasticene, which an all-knowing God could never have imagined. It was a shame, because he's a good craftsman, Edgar. But at least he kept things cheap. They were houses for people like I would have been, one notch above poor, and he only charged one notch, maybe a notch and a quarter, above free. He made his money from volume.

Anyway, we made that pact very early on, on account of the dump trucks. They just weren't coming to me, so I rode around with Kathleen in her truck to talk to Edgar at his site one day. He was maybe a hole or two ahead of me, which I liked to see. (Close competition is what helps a city spread—without men showing off, a city will never unfasten its girdle.)

Edgar told me the dumps hadn't been coming to him either, until he started slipping the drivers an extra twenty bucks a week. Christmas fund, donation to the union, that sort of thing. We agreed that the thing to do was to tell the drivers that for the same amount again from me, for the Children's Hospital or the wife's family back home, they might do a couple of extra shifts some nights and make sure they concentrated on me for a while.

Soon the dumps came steady, blowing flowers of diesel at the sky, loading up and driving off to share with an unseen pit that "this dirt belonged to McGuinty."

And Johnny got ready for blasting.

"OHHH, JER, ya do me good like that there, Jer, like that there, Jer, like slow…there, Jer."

EVER CRACKED your head on your spine by jumping on your heels? Try it while I tell you about explosives.

Let's not make too much of this first job, right, no: I had only two boulders and one small gradient to destroy on that site. But like any other builder I hated the thought of blasting.

Professional blasting is the construction world's dentistry: pain, expense, and unexpected smells, all for the sake of someone else's idea of what looks good. I hate the fuckin dentist. The solution is to smile rarely and to handle your own explosives.

You drill the rock in a grid, holes about six inches apart across the area, and you drill down as far as you think an expert would. I did the drilling because grids didn't exist in the minds of my men. Once I was finished Johnny took over with hungry dribble in the corners of his mouth, running wire down the holes with blasting caps at the buried end.

No sirens in those days, just a hope that everyone's been told.

"Tony! Get behind the fuckin truck!"

ARE YOU STILL jumping on your heels? Keep it up and I'll tell you how to make a baby.

I made a baby. Right then. Right when we were laying those charges.

Funny coincidence. Laying charges. Babies. You think I'm making it up.

Threading, blasting caps, Boom! Ha!

Cheers.

See, Kathleen and I, I don't mind saying, had some good strong sex in those days. And most of the time, after she came like a fist, say, I would shout my pearls on her belly or whatnot. But sometimes not.

"*BEHIND THE TRUCK*, you fuckin *idiot!*"

And Johnny hooked it up all wrong, so back you go and try again. This wire here, that wire there.

Farther back! *Farther* back!

Then when it all works right there's thunder from the earth and the world seems upside down.

Stop jumping if you want.

My point is that when you're near those explosions you feel it Whack! at your feet first. It's unexpected every time. The smoke, flying dirt, noise—you expect those things. But the Whack! at your feet, the first smack of a long whip that Smacks! again at your neck.

I like it.

JERRY WAS NOT a mistake. Jerry was not my mistake. Jerry was not a beautiful mistake. Jerry was mine and was beautiful.

Seven pounds, small as a finger.

KATHLEEN DISAPPEARED for more than a month when the first set of frames went up. I was pretty sure I saw her truck just up ahead, rounding that corner over on Glyde or crawling up the McCarthy Hill. But I never saw her at breakfast, never saw her at lunch, or when I wanted her like a cure.

"Hey, Jerry. Seen your lady the other night driving like a fuckin wild horse. How come she's not fixing us lunch these days?"

"Where'd you see her?"

"I don't know. Thirty-six beer in me."

She didn't drive away forever. I think. She's just there—you can smell the exhaust—don't blink or she'll speed up.

I thought I saw her one night and I ran a bit, broke a toenail on the steel in my boot. I ran after everything yellow.

It is best to run after everything, especially if you know that it's probably not what you really want—just a big yellow bag blowing in the night, something ridiculous from who-knows-where, twirling around a corner to who-cares. No meaning, just a flat disappointment that leads to more running. Better than knowing you should stop.

"THE TROUBLE with you, Jerry McGuinty, is that you exaggerate. And yer blind. I was not gone for a month, I just spent a few days or a week tryin out some new things, sites and that. I like the warm welcome, the flippin hero's welcome I get—don't get me wrong, it's lovely—but bloody Mary, Jerry, a woman can go for a little while collecting herself and it doesn't have to be a year or whatever ya say it is."

"A month."

"A month. Don't talk to me about months. I can tell you with a great deal of truth, Jer, that you have no idea what a month means, what…one flippin month can give and take away."

"What?"

"Never mind. You think I was gone for a month, but it's the month that's gone from me. I'll tell you honestly, Jerry, I don't feel like getting naked with you just now. What I feel like is a flippin shout of a night, a bit of a bonfire or a bottle or two. That is honestly what I want."

"All right."

"But we don't need to leave the truck. I don't mean going out or anything, seeing that filthy crew of yours in the bar."

"What?"

"If ya reach just under that seat there you'll find a bottle of Dewar's, there, yeah? Is it there?"

"No."

"Well, there's one up…yeah…there we are. Now, do us the kindness, Jer, if ya don't mind, and we'll just get happy feckin drunk, if that's all right witchyez. A month. A month my arse, I couldn't leave yiz for a month. Now, just stay where you are, for I am a bit fragile at the moment. There now. Cheers. To time flying. To flippin time flying."

Kathleen didn't cry very often. Bonfire nights and special occasions. Usually when she cried it was a tactic during arguments. But not tonight, my friend. Tonight she wept from her stomach.

I stood up to comfort her and I rammed my shoulder into that shelf where she cuts tomatoes. Here's the scar. When I got near her she was crying in such a powerful private way that I never felt farther from her.

We got drunk that night, boy. I got drunk because it went

well with my confusion. I didn't have a clue why she got so drunk.

I was bleeding from my shoulder and we talked about houses, basements, chicken, whether or not she should keep her butter in the fridge, and how there was no feckin way you'd find her accountable for anything, of any sort, just this minute, because she's mad, drunk, mad, and it's all a feckin mess.

That truck felt small, so out we go for a drunk of fresh air, and the whiskey's alive in the throat, breathes thoughts out lost.

"Why are you so drunk, Kathleen?"

"We're both drunk, and I'm not."

"Neither am I."

"Where did you go, Kathleen?"

"I'm here in the truck."

"Are you?"

"No."

"You're so small."

"Don't talk in that high voice. Ya sound like a man who's a lady."

"I'm drunk, Kathleen."

"It's good for ya."

Back inside the truck with half a wrestle, half a fuck in the doorway, and a drunken smile from my beautiful, who'll fix me a roast-beef sandwich always fresh. I tell Kathleen everything, cause I'm a small man in my heart right now and she needs to know that now because that's what I am, frightened, kind of scared of her.

"I'll tell ya what it is to be a strong man, Jer, and that's stay the feck away from me tonight, but don't leave, for here's yer sandwich. Kiss my teeth there, Jerry, that's nice. I just don't have the energy...for more."

We talked shit, and I woke up trying to forget a lot of it because somehow it ended up with her punching me in the ear. Certainly, yes, I asked her to marry me, and she said I hadn't a feckin clue. She kept hinting at things that I truly had no clue about, mostly to do with little Jerry floating inside her like a poisoned needle.

I asked her to marry me maybe four or five times while she was telling stories of mystery and nothing, and I can't remember exactly what happened, but I woke up on the floor of a half-framed house with blood on my shoulder, a ringing in one ear, and Tony Antonioni saying,

"Jerry, Jerry, to wash out blood, my mother she use water with gas. Fizzy!"

And I am sorry to report that Kathleen was then gone for two months.

THE FIRST TIME I met Jerry, he was a bulging explanation in front of Kathleen. She had just washed a pot, and had decided to get naked—turned toward me and slung a dishcloth over her arm and there he was in the middle of her, shyly winking through her belly-button eye. She was pushing out her stomach instead of talking.

Sure, I felt shock, joy, worry, but most of all I was happy to see Kathleen returned and naked.

He was Jerry right away because I had forgotten that babies could be girls. He was maybe the size of an orange, I guess, and Kathleen echoed his mystery standing there all calm and quiet and totally unknowable. She stayed quiet and let me get naked and away I went, easing into the thought that Jerry wasn't an orange and could be a girl, knocking and shivering against the fear that I was in a stranger and a stranger was in her.

It was a cold, hot, necessary place where Kathleen, Jerry, and Jerry came together.

TONY DID A FINE JOB on the frames. Beautiful. And the bricks were coming up thanks to me and Espolito. Five houses done by the time Jerry was born.

Beat that.

6

SMALL PROJECTS SUPPOSEDLY kept him busy. Despite the fact that his job was newly created, he inherited a number of tasks from differently titled predecessors. Parkways were to be laid here and there. There was talk of creating museums. Nothing to awaken the best of Simon. The first time he made love to Renée on his desk inspired him to stay behind until midnight, transforming those parkways into minor Appian Ways. But nothing entertained him as much as the idea of how he probably seemed to Renée. (He barely spoke, maintained a witty spark in his eyes, dressed impeccably. She was enthralled.)

He was told of a book that everyone in the Division either mocked or adored, the creation of a man who had Mandarin status but died in obscurity. It was a simple list, ten pages long (then), bound in leather, of all the projects dreamed up by the Division that never became reality. Those who adored it also added to it, updated it every year, rebinding it if necessary. Everyone called it the Dreambook (those who mocked it called it the *Dreambook*, with the same vocal italics given to *girls* by boys in the playground). Simon adored it as soon as he heard about it, but he heard about it only after being in his job for over a year.

Looking into it might have stopped the incipient blur of his career. Once he heard about it, he was afraid to look into it, afraid to attract derision, afraid to open it like those who avoid reading scripture for fear that it will spoil the mystery. It was also hard to find, being passed from desk to desk to be augmented, consulted for a laugh. Eventually he opened it, looked deeply into it, and the best of Simon *was* awakened.

But in the meantime there were the parkways. There were estates of great men to be "designated" sites of national historical significance. Nothing to give Simon dimension or a sense of what he could do.

It was sad how quickly it all began to blur for him. All his promise steadily trampled under the march of Monday to Friday. It was a civil servant who first gave names to days, realizing that every week each different day would behave as it had before.

THE DREAMBOOK was in Eleanor's office once when Simon was waiting for her. He quickly glanced at a random page.

He saw that a community center was once proposed: not the degenerate sort that now proliferate, but an elegant one, fantastically expensive, where children could be left in comfortable, imaginatively padded rooms with an impossible array of activities and minders; where adults could associate as comfortably and nobly as Romans in their baths. It could have dominated a city block left empty by demolition.

Silly, Simon thought.

But not really.

He closed the book when Eleanor came in.

"IMAGINE WHAT the public needs. Imagine what the public needs," said the ghost of Simon's father, over, and over, and over.

7

AGE OF TWO, Jerry my Jerry McGuinty the Second was the proud soft spokesman for the idea of silence and skin. Round little shoulders, nipples dappled pink by a painter's little finger. All the right parts for a boy, yes sir.

Who's a strong little soldier, eh? Hop up here on my knee now.

He was always cute chewing a banana—like it needed more chewing than it did. It occupied his mouth for half a day, which was often why he was so quiet.

And he was no taller than that chair leg there, in that first house there, whose smell of paint still hid in some of the closets. (I built it as quick as Kathleen could swell.)

Age of two, Jerry could stumble around the first little neighborhood created by his father, and I have no doubt he was proud. Sod freshly laid all around by Mario and Johnny, badly done in some spots to trip up little Jerry. Up you get there, big guy.

Age of two, our Jerry had three neighbors. It was a good start. I don't recommend living in the same neighborhood as the people whose houses you've built, since you become the resident repair man responsible for every woe.

But I had a House. I lived in my own House. Yes. Knock on those walls, buddy, and hear your knuckles say *Here*. And my Jerry could give his curiosity a tall square shape.

What's that roof?

It's Daddy's.

Da-doe.

Eee!

Da-dee!

"Give him another banana, Jer."

I WAS THE awful sort of neighbor who wanted more neighbors. Come on, gather round, tell your friends it's a great place to live!

I had no clue what it was like to live there, of course. I knew it in the dark coming quiet through the door. I knew it for that sweet smell of babies and a few little snorts, but it was all a blink in the dark.

"Yer a great feckin help, Jer, a right feckin champion. In at midnight, out at dawn. Would ya like a break from parentin, arse...ya feckin asshole?"

I was home when Jerry woke in the night sometimes. You know, awake for a cry and it's all right because Daddy's here. I don't feel guilty about *that*. I gave Kathleen a break.

"Fecker."

He was quiet as a stone compared to other babies, so I hear. I didn't have to cuddle him often, as far as I know.

"Do you know, Jer, I've been with other men before. I don't tell yiz about that much, but they say we should talk about that sort of thing more, you know, a man and a woman. And they've been *men*, Jerry, real men. I'm not going to say anything more, and all, but let's just leave it at that, or let's just say that some of them, if they'd be coming home at one in the morning, wouldn't necessarily be complaining about all the work they were doing, or wouldn't be lapping up to me, licking like a feckin little dog. You know, take it easy, Jerry, and let me get some flippin sleep. I've been with the other Jerry all day."

It was a three-bedroom house, so I got to try out some of the other rooms. Not a bad size. Can't hear a thing through the walls: good walls, quiet boy. Sleep was like being pushed backward in the dark—mornings were for steadying myself.

FOUR HOUSES SOLD!
Five houses sold!
The sixth was bought by a doctor!

I'M SURE YOU'VE had a bad carpet somewhere in your life. Maybe in your first house? Maybe in the closet where your parents forgot you?

I made a deal with a carpet maker in that first development, to cover all the floors in a one-inch blue plush. A young friendly color to hug my homeowners' feet. When I showed some of the first buyers the houses I remember a lot of them did say,

"Nice carpet."

But I myself learned to hate it. I never got any complaints about it. The guy who sold it to me made a fortune from it, selling a shorter-pile version to all the Government buildings. But I couldn't stand it. All around the edges, you see, around the walls, the twists of fiber would come loose, wriggle loose, one by one by one, like cheerful maggots, like a million little itches, you see.

At first I didn't pay much attention because it was freshly laid. You expect strands of carpet in a new house like you expect hair in your collar after a haircut. Fine. But not six months later, not three years later.

"Kathleen?"

"What?"

"Have you noticed that the carpet is still losing its fibers? You know, around the edges?"

"What?"

"The carpet."

There was Jerry looking up at us with a strand of blue carpet on his lips.

"No."

I was sleeping in the spare room more often, and the carpet was especially bad in there. It shone at night like a ragged moon and I was always trying to tidy it. If it shone more cleanly I would be more comfortable. I don't know why.

"The more I pick at it the more it sheds. But in fact, Kathleen, when I don't pick at it, it still sheds."

"Fascinating, Jer."

Once when I kissed Jerry goodnight, *I* got some on *my* lips. I told him, "Jerry, you put carpet on my lips!"

"*Ips!*"

But it became serious. Kathleen made me sleep in the spare room for two weeks and I couldn't stop picking at the rug, hunting maggots. I found them more easily in the dark, and I made piles to gather in the morning.

I couldn't sleep in Jerry's room even though I wanted to sometimes. It was always beautifully warm in there, but Kathleen warned me not to wake him.

"He's been twirlin and screamin like a jumpin flippin banshee, Jer, and if you wake him I will slit yer throat."

I slept in the closet sometimes, which is embarrassing, but I hadn't meant to tell anyone. It was darker, and perfectly built. If you had four hours to sleep, bruised your body all day, and had to sleep near a squirming plush of blue, you would occasionally choose the closet. I could cover the carpet with a blanket in there.

Also, you see, I could hear it moving. I wasn't scared of it, don't be a fool, I was just angry with it for changing, for growing out of the house I built for it.

Replacing it was out of the question. Do you know how much a carpet cost? It was money, my debts, that got Kathleen so angry—that was why I was in the spare room.

"We wouldn't have needed such a big house, such an expensive house, if you'd have kept yer bleedin wick out of me in the first place."

So the understanding was that I was to keep it out of her for a while and to think as much as I could about money. I'll just give you a quick idea of what depended on me selling the rest of my houses:

Tony Antonioni
Tony's wife: Pia
Tony's children: Tony, Joe, and Tony
Tony Espolito
Tony's wife: Pia
Mario Calzone

Johnny Cooper
Johnny Cooper
Johnny Cooper

John (Jack) Mackay, owner of the backhoe
Colin (Co) Maloney, for staples, nails, and spackle

For Franklin Thomas Murphy, surveyor,
five percent of the first four houses.

For Roger Boast, bull-chest banker,
blind eyes turned and bottomless hanker
for interest, "Jerry, no thank you, Jerry,
twenty percent is treating you fairly,"
twenty thousand dollars.

DeFalco Cement
DeFasco Steel
Delancey Hardware
Dia-Real Diamond Bits™
supplying all your drilling needs
since nineteen-forty-six
—a fella there named Rick.

I owed my pride
I owed my hope
I owed my brags
I owed that Jer that said,
Keep Kathleen, she will not drive away.

My mind was prepared to recognize a certain amount of money, a certain level of debt that I might possibly repay, and as long as I could distract myself with work I could occasionally greet that sum without emotion—just a daily face, walking the other way, "mornin," and nothing more.

SO WE SAT THERE, the three of us, a picnic on a blue carpet, and Jerry's got her eyes, the latest model, and I've got a coffee or something, and proud am I, my friend, yes, velvet warming the back of my heart because I am part of a three-folk island looking human and safe, looking so much better than the sea we sat in.

No one is caring about the carpet. Jerry's got a strand just on his eyelid there, but we can get that for him later. Kathleen just kissed me of her own free will.

"I'm gonna build you something, Kath."

"That's nice, Jer."

I didn't know what I meant.

Jerry holds up a cup with Mickey Mouse on the outside and orange juice within; he's a little priest sitting down there on his rump, cup up high in both hands. Not that I had seen a lot of him, but it struck me at that moment that I had known this person Jerry for almost three years and had yet to have a conversation with him. I felt close to him and I knew he knew what I was thinking, but I had yet to hear an adequate account of what was occurring to him.

Kathleen had her hand low on my stomach and she kissed me again, so things were looking good for tonight. I'm playing it cool, watching Jerry while she's watching me. Jerry starts talking while he's holding up the cup.

"Mickey, Daddy, walks on top cause heeess."

"What's that, big guy?"

"Issy?"

"Sure he is." It was important to laugh when you didn't understand the guy. "Huh huh."

"Hee!"

He had a happy face when he spilled that juice, very happy, a proper smile, interesting, like he just became a person.

And Kathleen turns her head when she hears the wet sound of the juice pouring on the carpet, watches the stream from the cup.

I suppose what we have to imagine, you and I, as we look at Kathleen watching Jerry pour his juice out from up high, is that Kathleen was in a jungle. She was an explorer, like me, totally lost, a surprise around every corner, never knowing where to go next. There she is in this jungle, and she's had a rare moment of rest, when she turns her head and sees a terrifying waterfall, raging fuckin orange, and maybe she thinks for a second that she is a drop of that orange and she's falling with no air in her lungs and she wants to get back up, but she's falling.

Whatever we imagine, there she was punching the cup from Jerry's hands so it flew across the room, and the look on her face sees nothing but horrors—no people—and then...

"THE CAARPET!

"RUIN!

"THE NEW

"FUCKIN

"CAARPET!"

The back of her hand hits me in the mouth, the other hand hits my nose.

I had never seen anyone that angry, and by the time I could realize that humiliation of being hit in the face, she had screamed a new world into being. That was not the room I had built.

"How MANY fuckin messes will he pour?! The beautiful FUCKin carpet! You, never, fuckin, see!"

She ran over to the corner to Jerry's box of toys, picked one up, threw it down, picked another up, threw it down, over and over like she was demonstrating something, and her anger just grew.

Sometimes when a person's angry you can keep yourself removed, be a little superior, laugh at them a little. Not Kathleen. All you can do is worry about what she'll do next.

"That orange will never come out! It's like...fuckin paint! And the two of yuz are standing there looking so fuckin stupid. If you were a man?...If you were a man?...If you were a man?... you wouldn't let me get like this. I'm fuckin sssick."

She threw that word like a silver knife at me.

"FUCK."

The three of us were moving slowly into the hallway, shuffling to the drums in her head. When I tried to hold her arms down she hit mine out of the way. Lunge, slap, shuffle, dance, slap, reverse, "Ssshit!"

Then, the doorbell rang.

You should have seen her.

It was like one of those miracles you can work on babies with a silly rubber pacifier. She just stopped.

And she walked toward the door, opened it, and I heard this man's voice saying,

"Hello, I am Simon Struthers."

And that was when Jerry started crying.

Part Three

1

THEY WERE TWO minor bureaucrats approaching middle age, trying to forget themselves in tragicomic frottage. She even said his
name, "Simon!," when they rubbed and fumbled, as though he
were transporting her; when naming him would only remind
him of where he was—here, now, in this silly office (you should
have seen the blue of the cut-price carpet).

It was obvious from Renée's face that she did not have hope,
that she was pretending as much as he was. It was probably her
pretending that called to mind his own.

"Simon!"

They giggled when they finished.

THERE WAS A CRUCIAL difference between the parkways, the building restoration, the heritage designations—all these minor projects—and the one major project that dominated his career:
possibility. Possibility in the form of undeveloped land, you see, in
the form of a huge green space that had yet to be used for anything. Museums, parkways, old estates were built. It is an obvious
distinction, but it is worth spelling out since Simon, at the time,

could not himself pinpoint what it was that made this other project so exciting.

Simon, Renée, Leonard and the others determined what would happen to a broad swath of the city in the south, forming an arc, quite elegant, from west to east, approximately three miles wide throughout. The city had expanded to the inner border of this arc, with a few unregulated exceptions, and beyond its outer border were farms and other unspeakables.

Developments, clusters of construction, necessarily arose. People needed houses. Local councils (which many in the Division, including Leonard, had sat on early in their careers) were responsible for allowing these developments. But their numbers had increased to a level that excited the imagination of the Division, eager to use its powers, eager to seize the opportunity to give the capital a distinctive shape.

The idea of taking control of this green space had occurred to someone in the Division fifteen years earlier. At first the idea was relegated to the Dreambook, but after rounds of new appointments, changes to the constitution of the Division, the idea was crossed out of the Dreambook and given serious consideration.

Leonard and Renée had begun to prepare preliminary briefs when Simon arrived in the Division. Leonard had conceded that his voluble mind could not be accommodated on the pages of memos, so, as Chairman of the Division he took a consulting, supervisory role while Simon worked with Renée on getting things down on paper.

The noblest aspect of a bureaucrat's realm is the distance between him and his subject. Although Simon and Renée determined the uses of this land, it was months before they ever looked at it. (Renée, in fact, never did.)

Simon's greatest mistake was setting foot on that land.

Early on, now, at this point when the hair on his temples was still brown, they knew the land from the 1:25,000 topographical map, which, as far as any of them knew, told them all but the smell of the flowers. Leonard contributed some knowledge that he felt was important. Because of his expertise in agriculture and foodstuffs he was well positioned to commission surveys and fieldwork. There was a period when he even squeezed into the galoshes he hadn't worn since university and ventured into the field himself. His observations, shorthand "Field Notes" that Simon later translated into a memo, were invaluable:

March 29, land wet, probably melting snow

March 30, patches of snow here and there, puddles, "a plashy place" (Byron?)

March 31, have observed various native trees, though few, viz Birch, Maple, Oak perhaps (not a botanist)

April 5, but it is mostly grass, mud, etc.

Surveyors' reports filled in many of the gaps, as did those of land-use consultants and others, but they were largely technical.

Information, infrastructure, science, man-hours, abundant, irretrievable costs soon mounted to the point where a preliminary official decision had to be made. The land was formally declared to be under review.

ON THE EVE of that declaration, late at night in Simon's office, Renée was straightening her skirt after a fairly goatish session.

"Simon," she said.

"Yes," he said.

"I am not getting any younger."

"I know."

"Neither are you," she eventually added.

"That is true," he said. "Have you eaten?"

"When would I have eaten?"

They had been at Simon's desk for hours.

"I think we should make a decision," she said.

"Well, that's what I had thought before you…before we…"

"I think we should make a decision right now," she said.

"I myself am not hungry," said Simon.

"I wasn't talking about dinner. I was talking about this land."

"Can a decision be made on an empty stomach?"

"Yours is not empty."

"But yours is."

"That is irrelevant to me."

"But is it irrelevant to this decision?"

"To the decision about the land, yes. Simon, I find you a little evasive."

"About what?"

"Everything. I think we have a number of decisions to make, the least important of which is dinner, Simon. What about us?"

"What about the land?"

"Which would you like to focus on?"

"I would like to focus on you."

"Well, I am not in the mood for that again, and it only raises the same question. What about us? Quite aside from the demands of this project, Simon, I don't think we can go on like this forever. On your desk like this...and going to your place. I don't...I am not an adolescent."

"I don't know what we should be discussing in that case," Simon said. "I don't think that we would arrive at anything but more questions. I don't mind questions, but are questions what we need? That is why I asked about dinner. I myself am not hungry. There is an answer. I do not have answers about us."

"Well, I am not relying on you to have answers. I am not expecting you to tell me how I should behave with you, or to decide on my behalf. That seems a little arrogant of you."

There was silence for a while. Simon must have affected some pathetic look or other, some sort of pout, because Renée reached for his hand and held it.

"We needn't make a formal decision," he said, almost as a question.

"Not making a decision gets us nowhere."

"Well, I just don't think a decision like that needs to be made. After all, we are colleagues, we are working closely together, we... I am still attracted to you. Our involvement on this project will continue for a while. Dispassionately speaking, I think such a decision is unreasonable. And that is not to say that you are unreasonable. Just the decision. Granted, some distance might do us good."

"What are you talking about?"

"Let's make a decision on the land."

"Now?"

"Yes. I think we should. We are on the verge of it. It is all there." He tapped on the desk.

"We should act," he said. "You think...you have said, and I have agreed, quite consistently over several months, that something must be done. We wouldn't be here if there was not a decision to be made. How will we use this land? we ask.

"Well, that is getting ahead of things, being hasty, and perhaps should not be the issue at all. The issue, at this point, is, simply, that a decision needs to be made on this land. So, why don't we decide, officially, that this land needs to be decided upon?"

"What?" she said.

"Decide, mark on this map, that this land needs to be decided upon."

"And that is progress?"

"Yes. What have we done so far? We can't decide. But something has to be done, something will be done, developers will move, take it over, for good or bad. And since we can't distinguish between good and bad, yet, let's decide to be indecisive. It's so marvelous, I can't believe that it hadn't occurred to you earlier!"

"To me? Oh, no. To you. No, no, Simon, you are the clever one."

1:25,000.

They seem to be mapped minutely. Twenty searching fingers (1,000,000 inches when still) quickly reached their boundaries.

They needed a bigger map.

Simon and Renée's decision of indecision meant several exchanges of title. They could enforce their review more confidently if the government owned as much of the land as possible. If that meant spending an unprintable amount of revenue and removing a few farms, it was excused by the nobility of the exercise. The arc of land would be a rainbow, each band of color serving a different public need—this for industry, that for housing, this for the recreation of putty-limbed children.

Leonard, more than once, saw Simon coming out of Renée's office after the hour of five, and Renée coming out of Simon's. He seemed rather jealous of Simon.

"I see you two are working late."

"Your voice seems shaky, Leonard."

"There is nothing shaky about me, Struthers. Perhaps you have some time, Renée, to go through a few things with me?" asked Leonard.

And Renée, having been through much with Simon, would have to excuse herself.

"Well, things do not get done at this pace, Renée."

"I SEE YOU two are working late."

"Have you been crying, Leonard?"

"I have been concentrating, Struthers. Do you have a moment, Renée, to look something over with me?" asks Leonard.

And Renée, whose knees are shaky, would have to delay on account of her health.

"I hope it is nothing serious, Renée. Nothing you might pass on to Struthers."

"I SEE YOU are working late, Leonard."

"That's right, Renée."

"Well, Simon and I have come to a decision. Simon more than me."

"I hope it is the right one."

"We have decided that action should cease."

"What do you mean?"

"No development should take place."

"Have you written the C9?"

"Simon has."

"Is that what he has written? That development should cease?"

"Not that it should cease. That it should be in abeyance."

"Well, I disagree."

"But it's too late."

I SUPPOSE SIMON might never have explored love with Renée if he had known the scale of it. There were clues from the beginning that she was fingered, elbow-pressed, browning at the edges; but the real limitations of love cannot be measured by signs like those. Deciding from a wrinkled eye that love has so much time to run is the business of desperate emperors looking into livers to determine the length of their reign. A bit of plumpening, some unexpected joy, will renew that wrinkled eye. Sometimes tragedy, even a lingering illness, can firm the skin just so.

Love can be measured by a strict rule of inches, which Renée used thus:

1 "You wear the most elegant suits, Simon."
2 "It's what I love about working here, all the people from such interesting backgrounds. Your father was a great politician."
3 "You don't say much, Simon. I feel like I am always the one talking."
4 "Perhaps you should wait till I've finished brushing my teeth."
5 "I sometimes admire your mind, Simon, but…are you really saying anything?"
6 "There's something to be said for getting things done."

And so on. She may not have reached twenty-five thousand, but she might have. Before they could ever really know each other, before Simon could have any idea, really, who Renée was, he ended the affair abruptly, pfft, like a match dipped in water. She was beginning to voice questions about his character.

WE MOVE ON. We all move on. Simon moved on. He had never really stopped. Run, run, run, run, run. He chased his travel agent for a while. His accountant. And the unions in his mind...

One sweaty session over the sink brought the image of Eleanor Thomas to mind, and that led to a deplorable interlude. Simon timed his trips in the elevator to coincide with Eleanor's, and first with a series of looks, then with this series of words—"I love you, Eleanor"—he coerced her into a bony kiss.

Shock, bites, unspeakable confusion accompanied many of their subsequent meetings. Later she put his hand on her breast, no larger than a Brussels sprout.

It was the beginning of real complication in the workplace. Simon's affair with Eleanor was due simply to his curiosity about death—that is the only way to make sense of it. Certainly, he could learn from her. She was fascinating—as profoundly attractive as repellent people can be, as long as they are slim and clean. It was, as I said, just an interlude, some trips in the elevator, but the complications became obvious during a plenary meeting, when the C9 had been submitted. Leonard liked to call an Assistant Deputy Minister from Land and Environment to meetings whenever an important public decision was to be made.

Eleanor, Leonard, Simon, and Renée were present, along with a few others. Simon scarcely opened his mouth to say the following, "You will notice...," before Eleanor said, "I don't understand you," her voice shivering like an autumn leaf, and Leonard barked, "There are flaws in this report!" while Renée murmured that Simon had written most of it.

The voices all arose at once, and then Simon began again.

"You will notice that..."

"Profound flaws!"

"It is not how we agreed to put it."

"I don't understand what you want."

Leonard, as Chairman, put it to the ADM that the issue should be reviewed in six months and that some of the crucial studies outlined in the memo would be repeated. Leonard left the meeting with a triumphant smirk, as did Eleanor, it seemed, until she came closer and revealed to Simon a sideways dagger of a mouth. Totally inscrutable, frightening, sexy.

HE BECAME preoccupied. He stole more kisses in the elevator, stealing less and losing more. Simon's stranger soul was drifting toward her world.

They were seen sitting together in the cafeteria where Eleanor normally sat on her own, frowning at a book. She now had a surprising look of dominance. Her kisses in the office became more frank, overwhelming, an orator's tongue in deed not word. In word she was chastening and correct, which somehow pulled him closer.

"Do not *move* one millimeter closer, Mr. Struthers, *not* in front of my colleagues."

She gave him the key to the cabinet in her office where there was barely enough room to hang her winter coat. He squeezed in there and waited like Casanova at the foot of Madame X's stairs— but with no promise of a meal or satisfaction. *Love makes waiting precious to the lover who is sure that Love will keep his word.* He pressed his face into her coat and waited, inhaling the smell of teeth that distinguished her body and clothes.

When she arrived she would kiss him, say nothing, occasionally put his hand on her breast. And she would send him out, desperate.

BUT THAT TOO ended quickly, as abruptly as it started.

"I wish to have nothing to do with you," she said one evening in her office.

"Nothing?"

"Not one thing."

"Not even professionally?"

"Mr. Struthers, to me you are a cipher. A mystery once, and now a perfect zero."

She was so offensive as to be arousing.

"But you scarcely know me."

"I believe there is nothing to know."

"Nothing?"

"At first I thought you were interesting, but you are quite vain, a bit of a phony and rather vapid. You look well enough, as far as that goes. But I am looking for someone either considerably stronger or considerably weaker than I am. *If* I am looking for anyone at all. I do quite well on my own."

Simon did not do well on his own. All that restraint over the fantasy of Eleanor had to find relief in Eleanor proper.

"Can't we embrace, Eleanor?"

"What a dainty expression. You might have *embraced* me weeks ago. *Taken* me. Have you no strength?"

"None."

"Are you powerless?"

"Yes."

"Completely?"

"Yes."

"I want the key to my cabinet back."

"It is in my pocket."

"Can you not get it?"

"No."

"Are you powerless?"

"Completely."

"Which pocket?"

"This one."

"This one?"

"Deeper."

"Here?"

"Please."

"I have it."

"Please."

"I have it."

"Please."

"There."

"God."

It only took a few strokes.

THE LAND BECAME known as the Greenbelt, but I mustn't get ahead of things.

The decision to review the issues was followed months later by a few eager applications for development on separate parts of the Belt. The names of the several applicants were Campo Partners, Davies Construction, Atlantic Commercial Builders and McGuinty Construction, all of whose applications can be found in the archives of the National Capital Division [files (1973) C41, D10, AC11, Mc4].

Given the urgency of some of the applications and the inchoate policies on the ultimate purpose of the entire Belt, the National Capital Division was thrown into an exhausting phase of labor. The applications were mostly for domestic development, with one proposing a large shopping mall to serve the proposed local needs. The mall relied on the houses, the houses on the mall. If Simon had looked into the matter he might have found that all of the applicants had something to do with each other, but Simon had no interest in such things. He was preoccupied with navigating the strait between Eleanor and Renée.

Besides, developers are the grown-up versions of the towny boys who bloodied Simon's nose whenever he left the bounds of school to search for tangy lollies. Their fists created his sense of furtiveness and shame. It would be foolish to get too close to them. Leonard, however, knew the developers well. That was his little secret.

ELEANOR, SIMON, AND Renée did not work well together.

Renée wished to favor the applicants from the beginning, which suggested to Simon that she was allied with Leonard. Eleanor had such a pedantic approach to any problem that she couldn't help but be allied with Simon. But she opposed him despite herself.

Leonard wanted their disagreement to lead to further hatred, so that he could step in and do as he pleased. Simon wanted delay.

If only he could spend *more* time with them, and if only spending time meant becoming more mysterious to each other. If only conversations, polite laughs, tedious mundanities would diminish rather than increase over time. Simon didn't want to be himself, he wanted to get back. He did not want to be the chap with sperm-stained trousers who had stood in Eleanor's office. He did not want to be the growing bore not quite so interesting as Renée's career (there were hints that she felt this way only seconds before he abandoned her).

He was the Enigma who subjected Renée to ecstatic humiliations. He was the sublime Undefinable who conquered, for an eye-blink, the categorical precision of Eleanor. He wanted delay, to sit in the room with them and make them wonder.

"This McGuinty proposal," said Renée, finger on the *M*, "looks fine to me."

"It is full of errors," said Eleanor. "Here he says phase one will take 'eighteen months,' and here he says 'eightee moths.'"

"The 'n' didn't work," said Simon.

"Pardon?"

"The 'n' on his typewriter may not have worked."

"That is hardly professional," said Eleanor.

"It is hardly important," said Renée.

"It might give us pause," said Simon.

"Not for a moment," said Renée.

"It may be of interest," said Simon.

"It is of no interest," said Eleanor. "It is unacceptable. Anyway,

Mr. Struthers, you make no sense. He could not type 'eighteen months' in the first instance if the 'n' did not work."

"It was faulty."

"I don't think we need to say anything about typographical errors. I think this McGuinty proposal looks fine," said Renée, tap tap on *t*.

"'O e hudred and te houses of first class quality for the smarter family,' he proposes. I find it laughable," said Eleanor.

"What we are discussing here, Simon, Eleanor, is, as usual, whether we should be the guardians of this land. I, for one, am sick of this discussion. We *are* the guardians of this land. We own it. And we are the guardians of this land on behalf of the citizens of this capital city. Our mandate is to enhance their experience of the city. To experience the city they have to live in it. To live in it they have to have houses. Mr. McGuinty's proposal is fine." Finger (white-tipped) atop *u*.

"That is an admirable syllogism," said Simon. That finger had been in his mouth.

"The proposal is a shambles," said Eleanor. "Mr. McGuinty also has a poor grasp of arithmetic. He says, if we approve phase one before winter he can complete 'seven houses in the first three moths, and eight in the next three moths, a total of fiftee in the first half year.' Last I knew, the school system was still healthily functioning on the premise that eight plus seven was fifteen, not fifty."

"It is the 'n,'" said Simon.

"How do you know? He clearly can't spell. I have no doubt that he is a stranger to numbers."

"He is a builder, Eleanor."

"No, Renée, he is more than a builder, he is a developer."

"And his proposal is fine, Eleanor."

"It is a shambles, Renée."

"Look at the substance of it, Eleanor."

"Form is substance," interjected Simon.

Both women shot him a scornful glance.

"So you believe," said Eleanor.

"So you agree that form is unimportant?"

"No, Renée, I do not agree. It is unimportant in the case of certain people. Meaningless. The opposite of substance. But not all people."

"We are going nowhere," said Renée.

"Yes," said Simon.

"So you are on my side?" asked Renée.

"Of course," said Simon.

"Of course he is."

"I am on yours too, Eleanor."

"Can we please focus on the substance of this proposal? Phase one is only thirty houses. Why can we not approve the building of thirty houses?" asked Renée.

"Because if we approve phase one, we will be expected to approve the next five phases, and that will be a large development."

"That is very true," said Simon.

"I do not need your glad hand, Mr. Struthers."

"He does not, Eleanor, need your...what's the word?"

"Truculence, perhaps."

"Thank you, Simon."

"Thank *you,* Renée."

"Now, for God's sake, focus on the issue, Simon. I don't need your glad hand either."

"Yes, Renée."

"*Yes, Renée,*" Eleanor mimicked.

"Oh, to hell with you both," Renée said, gathering her file. "Let's meet in a month."

She left Eleanor and Simon in the room together.

"Well, Mr. Struthers, why don't you run after her?"

SIMON WAS AGING. You are wondering what else was happening while he settled into his new life, as he met and disappointed new people. He was aging.

Do you live in the same drowsy autumn?

There is no need to picture him doing anything when he was not at work. Picture him doing nothing, in a raiment of nothing, against a background of nothing, a pendulum swinging from each eye.

Or don't.

He yearned. He wished age *were* so static, or that its only effect was the gravity of skin. He yearned more every day, and no matter what he did, no matter what adventures he had riding on the picaresque heels of his own libido, no matter what minor things he accomplished, he still awoke at half past seven, was a public servant at nine, at eleven o'clock his tongue tasted like tea and then, now, still, whenever he goes to bed he is one cruel inch from the nipple of fruition, no matter what is in his mouth, who is underneath him.

He yearned.

His stomach melted like wax.

THAT RUSH of applications, the houses, the shopping mall, took more than eighteen months to approve. They all had other duties, other responsibilities. Despite Simon's love, they all hated each other. Simon did not understand why Leonard, especially, hated (with a fervor that grew by the day) the fact that approval took eighteen months. Simon became isolated at work. He never saw anyone socially, he bowed out of working with Eleanor and Renée, letting Leonard make his decisions for a while.

And life kept blurring. His work was tedious on a daily level—assessing applications, considering needs was more minute and messy in practice than his mind could bear. Never a hope of seeing an idea come to life, never a policy that wasn't sullied by others' opinions or needs.

One small initiative kept him occupied briefly—a survey he created of new residents in the south of the city, near the land that was under review. He wrote the questions, and, despite protocol, visited people door-to-door presenting his survey. "Hello, I am Simon Struthers," he would say, assessing them immediately. The questions on the survey gave him great pleasure: Are you married? For how long? Why? One in every twenty questions was bewildering and intrusive—often simply "Why?"—and its effect was honesty, people answering presumably out of confusion or fear. "Why?"

But learning secrets on paper wasn't the same. Ultimately he was never, truly, invited in.

HE FINALLY got his hands firmly on the Dreambook, and secreted it in his office. He looked slyly through it, at first.

There was a plan for a memorial to great public servants.

There was a plan for an art gallery made of glass.

He had yet to realize what it all might mean for him.

After Eleanor and Renée, after the travel agent and his accountant, no one, for months, perhaps a year. Years. Just the women in his head, scenarios and desires from the past reimagined with limited variation.

The scenarios with Matty, in his head for so long, kept growing. He knew her better than he ever actually came to know her. That mouth, her confidence, that face insisting itself on the face of everyone else who populated his fantasies. But how could he ever see Matty again when Leonard had ceased inviting him to dinners? When all his colleagues, her friends, were beginning to shun him?

People in marriages say they lose their identities; they become, for better or worse, an amalgam of two people. That may be the case. But what was this life alone? Would Simon amount to the sum of the people he met, whom he wouldn't meet often or long? He tried befriending some of his neighbors, some of the men, to test himself, to see if he could refrain from desiring their wives. He tried to prove that his house, in the middle of all theirs, was legitimate, was indeed a house, not just a vessel for a single, restless man. But the most he could ever bring himself to say was,

"You'll have to come over for a drink some time." He shouted it from his car a few times. The neighbor to his right was once remarking upon the weather, and before he finished his remark, Simon shouted that invitation.

"I can't believe how much snow we've had this year," the neighbor said. "Last year, around this time, it was definitely looking like…"

"You'll have to come over for a drink some time!"

And of course the man just stared. He did his best to seem grateful, cheerful, but he certainly never came knocking, and Simon never repeated his invitation because what was the point of having a man over who talked about snow? The man's wife might have made snow seem charming, but the man himself…Men are predictably earnest or jocular. He knew all their routines.

No one, nothing, would ever surprise him or grow to a pleasant conclusion. The houses around him, especially his own house, seemed more and more like manifestations of mediocrity, not just vessels, but constant reminders of the boundaries that prevented Simon from growing, from learning who he really was. The people within them might once have been fascinating, perhaps still were, but how could Simon ever truly reach them? How could they ever learn who he was?

All he could keep was an unchanged persona and a hope or a hunger for other people's lives.

THE DREAMBOOK once mentioned converting the canal into a skating rink in winter. That idea was crossed out and made real. The longest skating rink in the world!

But most of the ideas remained dreams.

Someone had once proposed a wind tunnel. A gigantic white tube, is how the proposal described it.

ONE WAY TO STOP the blur, to keep things still and give them color, was to learn as much about as many people as he could.

He looked through the personnel files of his colleagues.

He read everyone's, including his own, which he discreetly improved and corrected. He took the liberty of correcting Renée's here and there, not according to what he had learned from her, but according to what he had originally imagined she should be. He created new lives for himself and all of his colleagues.

Susan, his secretary, with contacts in personnel, was his aid. She was not only helpful, she was slim and lascivious, five feet six and three-quarter inches in heels stuck firm in the mind of Simon.

"Susan," he said, "let's have a look at our colleagues."

She was an excellent facilitator, knew where to find every-thing, was open to all suggestion, gossiped homicidally, wore clothes like fleeting thoughts. It was inevitable that Simon would love her. She was always dropping things and bending far forward to pick them up. He was often there to help her. Bosses and their secretaries don't really fall in love with each other. They don't really even sleep together. They unite to share knowledge. The beating heart of any successful organization is a coupling boss and secretary: her wisdom, her acuity, her knowledge of process, of people, her dreams of dominion, combined with his jerky move-ments—such union is the only guarantee of an organization's vi-tality. Simon's coupling with Susan did much to improve his knowledge.

For one, he soon learned that he needn't read their files to gain knowledge of his colleagues. Susan knew it all.

In Simon's kitchen at home, on a Sunday morning in June, Simon mumbled the following thought with his lips on Susan's thigh:

"Leonard's file gives no home address. I wonder why that is."

"Because he doesn't want anyone to know where he lives."

Simon thought for a moment. "Why do you think that is?" he asked.

"I *know* why it is. He's bought a new house. Use your lips. His secretary told me. Mmm. But he doesn't want mmm people to know. He has suspicious deals. With builders. Mmm. His secretary told me."

Simon's chin was wet like he was dreaming of hunger. A breeze was blowing through the house, from a window in the front, into the kitchen, over the counter, past his chin, out the kitchen window where the world was watching.

"He's always taking bribes. His secretary's been through his trousers. Mmm. Wads of cash. I think I'm going to come…no."

"I wonder if it is a very grand house. Why does he not want people to know where it is?"

"Keep going. I think he just, you know, yeah…just doesn't want to know, people to…I'm not…where…how he got his house…God…there's something suspicious."

"I see," said Simon. His face was getting wetter. "Do you know where he lives?"

"Yes. Would you mind if I sort of…turned around? There. Nice. No, I don't…I do know where he lives but…I don't know exactly…God, that's nice…"

Why did Simon want to know Leonard's address? Why not keep it all imaginary, everything, everyone, where Leonard lived, what he looked like in his living room? Why did he want to know?

"I know the address. Why do you want to know? Don't tell me…don't tell me yet…don't tell me…don't tell me…"

The breeze, persuasive, kept blowing through the house— through the foyer, through the dining room, into

"I'm coming."

Past Simon's chin.

He did not wait to be asked again. He hadn't even known the answer until it came out of his mouth. "I want to know," he said, "because I think I am interested in his wife, Matty."

THE BREEZE BLEW over the houses, carrying Simon's sentence with it. The sentence tickled its belly on roofs, luxuriated in the sun, spent several weeks blowing around. It took a while before it caused trouble.

Susan did not like to hear, naturally, that Simon was interested in someone else, not while she was there on his counter naked from the waist down. So she curtly told him where Leonard had bought his house and within a couple of weeks she had told enough people at work that Simon was interested in Matty that Leonard caught wind of it.

And, eventually, when he tired of his own surveys and introducing himself to strangers, Simon went to that area of new houses, and knocked on Matty's door.

2

THERE'S MY JERRY up high.

Look up there.

Giggling.

Having a jiggle.

I discovered when he was around the age of five that he liked to ride in the shovel of a tractor. He was on-site one morning and I guess I lost track of him for a while. Next thing I see is Tony Espolito driving toward me in a tractor about to pick up a load and there's my Jerry sitting sort of primly in the shovel with a laugh on his face, Tony unaware of it all. Jerry was up high, coming lower, lower, lower with his smile and a pair of bouncing happy fists. (He wasn't hurt.)

So I'm taking him for a ride now—that's what he's doing up there. He is still around five or so, maybe six. And that's a new V6 John Deere (maker of the finest tractors since I don't care when), which I bought cash in hand, on the barrel, bang.

If you keep looking up, seeing Jerry's dangling feet, the new yellow shovel, the blue sky he's eating, you don't have to notice that it's January, that you can't feel your fingers. And if you just hold on to that lever there, just hold this speed and keep it straight, I'm going to climb up the arm and join Jerry in the shovel.

Ohh, it's blue! It's bright and goddamn loud, isn't it, buddy?

I think he loved the noise, the rumble of it. I loved that smile on him. He just kept looking forward, rumbling into the blue, bouncing his fists on his knees and swinging his feet.

I'll tell you what the feeling is from my point of view. It doesn't feel like flying. It doesn't feel like you're sitting on a tractor looking like a goof. It doesn't feel comfortable. It doesn't feel fast. It doesn't feel like nothing. It's slow enough and the sky is empty enough that you feel like you're standing still. But the noise and the shake of the thing make you feel like you're moving in every direction, and you are actually going fast enough that if you fell you would feel it (especially if you were five) and you would probably be run over.

But everything's all right and Jerry doesn't need me there in the shovel with him, so I'll climb back down and drive, thanks. That's how I prefer it—Jerry up high, sun in the sky, and me driving after him.

That's, at least, how I preferred it then. I don't know why. It felt safer. Not for Jerry, for me. Driving straight down a half-built road, Jerry always in front of me.

THINGS WERE GOING well (my friend). I was into my second big development. I had a couple of crews now.

I owned things. New things. Some equipment is better to own secondhand, but some that was smarter to own new, I owned, and when I wasn't using it I leased it out. Admire me, if you wish.

I was still completely in debt, but I was in a phase where I felt rich despite my debt. I understood that there are huge mountains under the oceans, which are still mountains even though they're not above ground.

The first development was sold, every brick in it (boy), and that's a happy moment. I loved—I still love—being able to look at that development and turn my back on it. To turn around, or walk past it, like it's any other neighborhood that has been there for a while. That is true manhood, I tell you, it's a sign that you are becoming one of the wise ones, when you know you have created something big and you can walk right past it because it is just your modest contribution to the bigness of the world. It's just another neighborhood. It melted my insides and chafed a mile of skin, but it is just another neighborhood. I truly had the wisdom to think that.

I wanted to turn my back on it, too, because I was also sick of living there. Our house wouldn't keep clean, for one thing. Kathleen *could* not look after Jerry and keep the feckin house clean, and it occurred to me that I could actually build a house that looked after some of the cleaning itself. (I was ahead of my time.) And a new sort of house was exactly what I needed for another development.

KATHLEEN AND I HAD been through a rough patch, a bumpy ride, some trouble, whatever you pale, lazy people like to label the plights of strangers. We had some trouble, I'll be the first to admit it, but we worked through it.

It reached its worst when, on top of all my labor, I realized that to make it all worth anything I had to perfect my business sense, my office work. You can't just build in secret, draw back a curtain to reveal what you've built and watch while strangers start bidding for it. From beginning to end, it has to be planned, plotted, written down, proposed, asked for, noticed, advertized— all that. It's not the side of things I liked.

I had to set up a small office at home, get a calculator and typewriter, filing cabinets, all sorts of expensive stuff that welcomed me home after a long day at work, and I never saw Kathleen. It was too much for me sometimes and it appeared to be too much for Kathleen.

One thing I never quite understood was the fact that Kathleen would get angry when Jerry and I were together. He would come into my study sometimes, sneaking out of bed, and we'd have a little chat. (It was very rare, because I was usually home too late.) Within thirty seconds Kathleen would be in my study telling Jerry to get back to bed. It didn't matter where she had been, whether she had been fast asleep or in the farthest corner of the house; as soon as Jerry and I exchanged some words Kathleen was on to us.

I was only just getting used to Jerry as a human, so they were important chats. I have some shame in admitting that I had been a bit scared when Jerry first changed from a baby to a boy to a bigger proper boy. It's a little spooky to watch a thing become a person. So our chats were about testing each other, partly. He would look at me closely and I would feel a bit shy.

"What's up, big guy?"

"I painted."

"Oh yeah. What did you paint?"

"I dunno."

"Oh yeah."

But it wasn't like I wanted Kathleen to come screaming at him, or at us. We should have spent more time together.

It felt like Jerry and I were conspirators. Maybe it was something to do with where we met: a typewriter, filing cabinets, and a calculator were the tools of conspiracies.

No?

Anyway, after Jerry came and chatted maybe ten or so times (probably spread out over a year, so that each time he was a different boy), Kathleen really lost her temper. She pushed the typewriter off the desk, I really shouted at her for one of the first times, and Jerry stopped his visits.

I don't remember exactly how that fight started—it was something aside from Jerry talking to me. I think that might have been the time when she ran into the room and threw an empty roll of toilet paper at me, wondering how I could use so much if I was never at home. Anyway, it was soon "What is he doing in here at this time of night!" and then the usual buildup with Jerry somehow disappearing from the room and Kathleen hitting something. This time she knocked the typewriter off the desk.

That's what pissed me off. I hate the sound of things crashing, and I hate a broken machine that I don't know how to fix.

I grabbed Kathleen by the shoulders, shouted and shook her, and there was one precious moment (the kind that grabs a man by his joint and says, Do it Son, you can Do as you fuckin Please) when Kathleen was totally submissive and boneless. She looked like she really loved me for that moment. But then either I said, weakly, "What *is* it?," or my eyes said it, and off she went shouting again. My strength made her weak, her weakness made me weak, my weakness made her strong again.

But what *was* it? She didn't like the idea of me and Jerry having fun together; that was one bit of truth we chipped away from that fight. She didn't have much fun with him because he was five years old and apparently he was flippin hard work.

I won't describe the fight more because I realize, buddy, that you don't want to keep listening to other people's fights. But I will tell you one thing that led to a solution. Basically, piecing everything together over the next couple of days (I was plastering ceilings at the time and when things were upside down against a background of white, they were clear), I realized that really the problem must have been her past.

She had been free before, and she had been in love, and now she was in love again, you bet, but she wasn't very free. I hadn't really thought much about her past love, Tom, the guy she followed over from Ireland, but it was Johnny Cash who reminded me.

I was doing a ceiling and listening to the radio and on came the Man in Black with "Cold, Cold Heart" coming straight from under his joint. I said, "*That* is what it *is*."

Tom treated her badly, dumped her, she set up on her own, she met me, we had Jerry, she lost her freedom, so she started thinking about some happy past with Tom. I understood.

So the solution was to pick up the typewriter, forget about the shouting and the crying, and borrow from the Man in Black. I wrote Kathleen a Johnny Cash love letter to show I understood. The typewriter actually worked, most of it, so I made the letter neat. I've got it here:

> I tried so hard, my dear, to show
>   That you're my every dream
> Yet you're afraid each thi g I do
>   Is just some evil scheme.
>
> A memory from your lo esome past
>   Keeps us so far apart
> Why ca 't I free your doubtful mi d
>   A d melt your cold, cold heart?
>
> A other love before my time
>   Made your heart sad a d blue
> A d so my heart is payi g ow
>   For thi gs I did 't do.
>
> I a ger u ki d words were said
>   That made the teardrops start
> Why ca 't I free your doubtful mi d
>   A d melt your cold, cold heart?

It worked, my friend: she was like fire, but soft.

I MAY HAVE HATED the office work, the writing things down and all that, but, I tell you, I was good at it. Especially the plotting—I was good at the plotting.

Edgar was cornering the market on blowaway cheapness, I was making a name for myself for *quality*. I designed my own signs, advertising the *quality* of my first development. I had called it *Pine Grove Park*, because I jammed a few pine trees into the ground. It wasn't a park because it was covered with houses, but promoting developments is usually a matter of calling them what they aren't. (I enjoyed that part of the plotting—being free to create my own world.)

I met Edgar over on his sites, and I'd see his crews putting up walls. They'd use round-headed screws on their studs which would dimple through the plasterboard. The boards were always four-by-eight, they never staggered sizes, always ran the boards vertically so the seams were as predictable and obvious as long bad jokes. There would always be cracks over the doors. They wouldn't bother with wood strapping on ceiling joists, so if your husband wiggles his hairy toes upstairs you will hear it downstairs when you're trying to relax.

I might as well take the opportunity to mention that I profited from their half asses. With a designer buddy I knew I developed a steel corner with tape already attached: it made cornering easier for the less intelligent plasterer, and around here it is still known as the McGuinty Corner, which I named after my son, Jerry.

I myself linger on my walls like I wished I could on Kathleen. I use fine gypsum laths which I ice with the ree-al thing, boy: Plaster. I even used wood laths instead of gypsum on the first two houses of Pine Grove Park, but you don't want to be an idiot about tradition.

I built thirty houses for every hundred of Edgar's, and I will rest in heaven.

I knew what he wanted to do, he knew what I wanted to do, and when we promoted ourselves, when we made tenders and when we made proposals to councils, we had a quiet agreement to keep our different ambitions in mind.

I kept little jobs going all the time. I was one of the few plasterers with any real skill, so I got some odd jobs repairing proper old plaster, which is as rare as beauty. (In fact, at this very moment, this very Jerry—with the drooping chops—is spending some of his retirement repairing old plaster: Chateau Laurier, that sort of building. Yeah.)

But mostly it was my plans, my plotting, that kept my crew busy, so busy that, as I said, I put together another crew. I've decided not to tell you much about that crew. Too many names for your little head. They were guys I knew, that's all. And they multiplied. At the height of my career, at the very peak of Mount McGuinty, I had over a hundred men (including subcontractors) working for me.

I kept the original boys tight with me—Cooper and the rest of them—because we were working smooth. They almost respected me by the time we finished Pine Grove Park, and I was almost paying them on time. They never complained to the unions.

We got one big private commission to build a monster of a house that ten years later was made into apartments. And then my second big development came through, basically a repeat of Pine Grove Park but its name was an outright fib: *The Oaks*. (Although I did use oak for the cupboards.)

While The Oaks was underway, Edgar Davies and I hatched a plan for two huge sets of houses and a shopping mall, which about ten separate bodies (investors and builders) became involved in.

This is when things started to get complicated, when people and types of people appeared out of nowhere like monsters in a dream. Things had been more or less within my control until then. I at least knew who I owed. But suddenly here are these investors, slick as oiled sharks, who somehow always knew exactly what I would do—what ought to be done—a few feet ahead of me doing it. They wore clothes and spoke a language that I had never witnessed. I thought they were a rank above men that God and the scientists were too dumb to have labeled.

For example, one of these investors—one of these angel demons—is listening to me tell him about a little problem I foresee with distributing water to the planned phase four, given the lay of the land and whatnot; and he is nodding to me, wearing a suit as shiny and deep as a pupil, politely waiting for me to finish; and I do; and he produces some figures that are like a map in math of all I said in English; and he starts explaining all sorts of additional problems that my mind had not yet encountered, which he then offers beautiful solutions to; and all this time his mouth is like a ballet.

Cooper thought they were fags, but they were better than that: stronger. I knew that I should obey them, learn from them, follow their advice. It was their money, and they taught me that there really is such a thing as "smart money," which most of us will never understand.

It was my smart plan that got them involved in the first place, though. Edgar and I wondered how we could put two opposite developments near each other without one detracting from the other. A mall is what I proposed. Keep the developments separated by shops, cater to necessity and greed under one warm roof, the neighborhoods can stay distinct and both take advantage of the building that keeps them apart.

It was too big for me and Edgar to think of doing ourselves, but it didn't take long to attract these angel demons. They were interested in the mall particularly, and right they were. I always thought it was ridiculous how rarely Canadians kept their shops together, how you would have to suffer like a settler braving miles of winter wind if you wanted to buy food and clothes in one trip. The investors knew that shopping malls would keep our country together.

Hang on a second while I get a beer.

———

So, FUCK ME, it got complicated.

One reason Edgar and I wanted to build near each other was that out of the ever blue blue came a surprise that regularly pissed me off for the rest of my career. Mile after mile of the ripest land in the history of possible plucking was brought under the control of Federal God Fuck Government. Miles of it. The best of it. One day we were buying whatever plots we pleased, dealing with tax-happy councils; the next we had to contend with some mysterious Crown Corporation, who saw no benefit from what we builders did. For them it was all ideas, and a bother.

I have no clue how it happened. I approached local council to get approval to build The Oaks, council tells me that I couldn't build all of it, that they no longer have control of it: "Apply at head office," they said, meaning the Federal Boys.

Kathleen was with me that day, and Jerry. We were driving in Kathleen's truck, which I figured Jerry would love. (It would be like knowing the ice-cream man. I figured he could tell all his friends, but he was, what, maybe six, and might not have had any friends.)

Kathleen's there waiting in the truck with Jerry while I'm talking to council.

"It's the big boys, not us," they tell me. "Apply at head office. They've taken over. And mind your p's and q's, McGuinty, it's a different set of rules."

So I come out and tell Kathleen, who immediately comes up with the idea of joining up with Edgar.

"Why don't ya see how Edgar's handling it?"

So I did.

That was a nice day. The three of us drove around and stuff.

EDGAR TOLD ME he was having trouble with it, with getting his mind around how to approach Big Government. I cut down the scale of The Oaks so that none of it actually ended up on this Government land, and while The Oaks was going ahead I met Edgar occasionally and we figured it out.

The Oaks is a little gem, a little pearl of a neighborhood. It's easy to drive by, thanks to the Government, but if you catch a glimpse of it, stop. It's worth a look. You might like to marvel at its *quality*, especially when you remember that there were little more than two years between the first foundation and the dying breath of paint.

The second crew made a difference, with babysitting particularly. As part of the reconciliation that I had brought about with the help of the Man in Black, Kathleen determined that it was time for Herlihy's Meals on Wheels to roll again. Little Jerry had prevented her from working, and she told me in one of her honest moments that the truck helped her to feel free. So while I built The Oaks, Kathleen drove a yellow smile across the face of local construction. And Jerry…

Jerry was such a beautiful boy. I'm going to tell you about his smile sometime.

Kathleen would drop Jerry off at the site in the morning along with a bacon sandwich or what have you, and he would stay on-site all day. We had forgotten about school at that point, but we remembered eventually.

I tried to watch him as closely as I could, take him for rides in various machines, but it was hard because, as foreman and The Boss, I already had a lot of kids to look after. So various guys in each crew would watch him.

Adults don't talk to kids without trying to teach them something, so even though my crew were morons they taught him things. He learned about accents and fear, as he would at school.

Understandably, the men did not much like having to look after him. He was a jolly little distraction for them sometimes, but you don't want to worry about ten tiny toes when you're riding a jack, and you do like to find your tools where you left them ten seconds ago. Cooper was often telling me to get that cunt *child* out of his face—and, as these things always go, Jerry loved Cooper.

If I had a moment, say, between sanding a wall and, what, helping a brickie on the next house, I would show Jerry little things, important things.

"Don't throw oily rags anywhere, not just anywhere, Jerry. Throw them in that bucket there. K, big guy? Fire. We don't want fire."

I taught him my secret mix. "Just a *pinch* of lime, K?"

He learned a lot from watching. It was always the noisiest things that he liked. Steamrollers. You've never seen a kid get a more private pleasure than Jerry on one of those old rollers. I have recently had occasion to learn from him that the pleasure was like flying, and that flying, for him, is all about noise.

THOSE DAYS ON The Oaks were when I first noticed the clouds gathering in the head of Tony Espolito, usually when he was telling stories at lunch.

"Your wife's a fuckin drunk there, Jerry boy, Jerry boss. Your mommy's a fuckin drunk, Jerry Junior boy."

"Shut your hole, Tony."

"It's true, fuck."

"Listen to the boss, Tony, and shut your fuckin cunt."

"Up yours, Cooper. I'm just talkin, I'm just saying. I seen her is all I'm sayin. I was up there. Been up there around whatsits-name and I seen her is all I'm tryin to fuckin say. You know."

"Forty beers a day, or a two…twenty-four…a two-four of beers a day," said Antonioni, "and you see a lot of things, Tony."

"He's drinking on the job, Jer," Cooper told me.

We all drank on the job in those days. We all had beers in our hands when Tony was telling his stories because it was lunchtime and that's what you do. I never had more than two while I was on-site. A man like Cooper had four or five—any more and he knew he would do something criminal. But Espolito had a lot, always.

"In Italy: no!" Antonioni said. "A man does not drink the beer on the job."

"Fuck Italy," Cooper said.

"What's Italy?" asked Jerry.

"Prison," said Cooper. "That is where a man does not drink beer. Ya can't have all those bottles around in the yard, cause if there's some fucker around like Espolito here, you'd *cut* him."

"Look, I see things is all I'm saying, fuckin *clear* sometimes, like I'm on high, like I'm a fuckin prophet, boys, and you can, and you can, fuckin listen or not. But I seen whatshername, and I seen terrible things in the future."

He would switch. We were all becoming familiar with his switches. He would look like he would be crying a bit, and then suddenly he'd be furious.

"Fuckin *clear*. I'm fuckin telling you!"

And he smashes his empty on a rock near little Jerry.

Espolito was aware of those clouds, at least. He would look surprised and remorseful after he did something ugly. Whatever it was that made them gather (whether it's the booze that makes the clouds or the clouds that make the booze—I'm not the person to ask), he had some sense that something was going wrong, and eventually he did something about it.

Edgar Davies came by the site that day just as Mario was punching his countryman in the gut for smashing his bottle near Jerry. I was ashamed of the scene in front of a visitor. I took Edgar aside and invited him into one of the finished houses. I would show him that if my men couldn't get along, at least they could build.

"The fighting keeps them warm," I said, and I lit a propane burner to make things feel civilized.

"It's cold as a nipple, Jerry. I don't blame them for exercising. This is a *nice* room, Jerry. Shit. How much did this cost you?"

"My right arm, Edgar. My right priceless arm."

He was one of those handsome men, Edgar. Smile and all that. He still is, I suppose, but old men with all their hair look like women with too much makeup.

"I'm glad you came by, Edgar. I think I've got a solution."

I told him about the mall and we worked out our plan. Truly speaking: *I* told him the plan, *I* did the thinking. I was generous with Edgar in those days because I knew Kathleen liked him.

"He's a chum," she said.

We worked it all out. Edgar knew how to get the investors' attention, and I held one little magical piece that I told him about. I'll tell you about it in a second. Altogether we chatted for a couple of hours and I felt excited about the future.

I came outside when Edgar left and noticed Jerry looking pale and shivering so I brought him into the room I had heated. That did the trick.

"Ah, JER, I HAD a good day today, I'll tell yuz, a great free day, and I made us a bit of money."

"You didn't…"

"I know I didn't need to but feck it, I did. Maybe forty dollars or so. Edgar's got a lot of fellas working for him."

"So do I."

"I'm only saying. I made a lot from them. And I drove a lot, now, free as a bird for a couple of hours there, love. The van will need some work, though. I'll be putting the money toward the van, if ya don't mind. Jerry, in an unrelated point, would ya mind trimming some of that hair in your ears? You're lovely, though."

"You're lovely. You look happy."

"Ah, feck, am I. What was the monster doing today? Did ya have to clean his arse?"

"Why are you always asking about his ass?"

"Because I'm sick of it."

"He was good. He worked hard and the boys treated him well. Except for Cooper. Cooper made him do some sanding because there was no sanding to do in the house Cooper was in. I had to take a few splinters out of him."

"The truth is, Jer, I don't think forty dollars will entirely cover the work on the van."

"Let me have a look at it."

"You're too busy."

"I'll look at it tomorrow."

"You're too busy."

"I'll look at it first thing."

"I said you're too busy, now stop arguing. I just thought you might give me a little money, for the van and other things sort of freedom-related. I found myself without tomatoes this morning, which is not a good sort of a thing, and I quite like the idea of having a beer, like a little one, with the likes of you at lunch."

"That's a great idea. You've got to join us more at lunch. Stay with us."

"That's a lovely idea. But it's hard, now, isn't it, because lunch is when I'm selling the most. Forty dollars. It's not to be sneezed at."

"You don't need to sell all the time. Join us for lunch."

She started a round of sneezing then, which, given what she just said, seemed like the cutest little joke imaginable at the time. Up yours if you think it's corny. I gave her a hug that I can still feel, which makes me sad to still feel because her hugs, when she meant them, rolled up from her feet and pressed all the right places.

"I've got twenty bucks I think," I said.

"Lovely. That would be lovely."

She said it in my ear.

It was freezing in that house and we instinctively stayed within an inch of each other even if we weren't getting along. It was a feature of the winters in that house, me and her acting like Siamese twins.

I could be an honorable man on occasion, too. I was on that occasion. I had her an inch away from me, her gratitude in my ear, and I stayed an inch away. No pressing, no pleading, no "Hey...look what I've got!" Just an inch away like the air of her body is all a man needs.

I build cold houses. I should warn you.

————

MY LITTLE PIECE of magic was a fat fucking chump by the name of Leonard Schutz. I had known him from one of the local councils seven years earlier, and now he happened to be in Big Government, a Chairman of some sort, happy as ever to lick the bowls of others.

"Mr. McGuinty," he says, "I see you have built some fine houses," he says, "even I myself would buy one."

"Is that so? Is that the case?" I says, and "Yes," he says, "it is the case, my good Mr. McGuinty, and I wonder if you plan to build more." So I says, "Yes, as a matter of fact," I tell the man, "I do, in point of fact."

"I admire a man of fact," he says, "and what," he asks, "are the facts that you might *not* be of?"

"I am all ears, my kindly gentleman buddy, ears and hungry for facts."

"Well," he says, "one fact that you might not know is that you cannot build just anywhere, Mr. McGuinty, sir, not just anywhere at all."

"Well," I says, "I was possessed of that general fact, the sort of father of that fact, but I don't know all its children."

"Well, before I introduce you to them let me provide you with the fact that I am your friend, Mr. McGuinty, a good friend, with things to offer, as well as certain needs. Would you like a chocolate?"

"No," I tell the man, and he says,

"I know the sort of environment that exists at the moment in the planning of what you might call the future of this city." And he sucks on a fuckin chocolate. "In fact, I have a hand in it. You and I are friends, of course, and so we can be frank with each other. But before we be frank, would you mind telling me what sort of a price you might be asking for a three-bedroom house of the sort you might be able to build?"

I can't remember the exact figure, but these days you would laugh at how small it was, because money has been putting on some ridiculous airs in the last twenty years.

"That is a fair amount, my friend," he says.

"It is a solid amount, my friend. Fair in the sense of *fair,* is what I think you mean."

"Indeed, Mr. McGuinty, it is fair in every sense. As am I, I believe. And I believe that it would be a shame for you not to be able to capitalize on a number of houses at such a fair amount."

"I'm all ears," I says.

"In the current environment I would have to say that your chances are not so fair. This is not local council any more. It's one hundred percent different."

"A hundred percent," I says.

"That's right, Mr. McGuinty."

And so I say, "Let's say it's not a hundred percent. What percentage difference from the days of local…what percentage difference, generally speaking, would make my chances of building more fair?"

"On a hundred percent, I would say a difference less of eighty percent would make a likely difference."

"Twenty percent?"

"Eighty percent less. That's right, Mr. McGuinty."

"I'd say forty percent less sounded more believable."

"Well, I wouldn't want to say less than sixty-five percent."

"How about fifty?"

"Fifty-four."

"Fifty-three."

"Done."

So, who cares, a fat goof gets a house at forty-seven percent of the price I charge everyone else. So what? He promises to sprinkle chocolate on the tongues of Big Government. It's worth it.

It's magic.

A NAKED KATHLEEN in the blue light of our bed at night could blind me for a year. Only on occasion, let's say once a month, would I see her like that: pale, nude, open, her and the bed like some sweet bruise that I had to press on. She gave me a sense of sadness and fragile human bones that I got from no one else. I might have learned about fragility from my quiet little son, but in fact I wouldn't have. The past few years have taught me that Jerry is the strongest substance known to man. My business is in things that can't break; I don't know why it took me so long to appreciate Jerry and reject Kathleen.

You there listening to me, know this: she blinded me till there was hair on Jerry's chin. Don't expect to hear about a very Big McGuinty for the next little while, not until you hear the sound of a woman hitting a window.

I won't tell you more about that until its proper place, but the window comes to mind when I'm talking about fragility. Just know that when you hear that sound, I have smartened up—strengthened. Until then you might occasionally wish to have a laugh at my expense. Go ahead and watch me in that bruise of a bedroom and laugh until the tears come.

WHEN YOU'VE FINISHED, dry your tears and picture me in a furniture store, if you please, because that is what I remember next in the establishment of my life.

I had sold a chunk of The Oaks and was looking for furniture with my friend Kathleen, who knew what every salt drop of me tasted like, and we were at the height of happiness buying things with some shiny new wealth, hoping to make our house look different.

We weren't very good at furniture. I am the first to admit that I have no taste, but it occurs to me that having good taste is usually about living for other people. Kathleen had no taste, but I thought the things she did with cloth and curtains, what have you, were kind of glorious, even if they were usually kind of funny and flammable.

We decided to spend a lot of money on this occasion. We bought a couch that cost as much as the room cost to build, and we bought these four swivel chairs that were made in Finland, or one of those other countries I've never wanted to visit. Height of fashion, is what the salesman said. They looked pretty silly, like they would last as long as a haircut, but these four chairs were the craziest fun I ever sat down on, and they eventually played a big role in my life. They lasted for ages.

Kathleen, Jerry, and I sat on them in the store and loved them immediately because they Spun, buddy. One touch of your toe on the ground and you turn from noon till nine before you realize where you are. The three of us went for a spin together—they had the four chairs set around a circular table in the store—and we had a good giggle, turning slowly at first just from the force of sitting down. Then faster. Then faster. Kathleen's face flying by, smiling, Jerry reaching down to the ground with a foot, climbing back up when he'd pushed himself off, squeaking his laugh. Those chairs are like ice that you can't stand up on—you never get where you want to go, and the effort makes you laugh. They were gold velvet; I knew Jerry wouldn't like the material (I don't know why kids hate velvet and adults think it's a treasure), but he loved the spin.

I got up from mine and went over to Jerry, grabbed the high back of his chair and spun him hard. Yaayhaay! He spun like he was falling. And then Wham! I stopped his chair fast to make him dizzy, boy. The second time I whammed my hand down I declared that I would buy the lot—the four chairs and the table (and the couch). I left Jerry spinning in his head and Kathleen spinning for real, and I went and paid for some priceless fun.

When I came back to the two of them about ten minutes later I saw a red mark on Jerry's cheek, purple anger on Kathleen's face, and puke on the table and on the arm of Jerry's chair. It smelled like the raisin toast that Jerry liked for breakfast.

I should have realized that those chairs would cause me trouble. I should never have taken them home.

"I'M PROUD OF YA, Jer, proud of you building all them houses."

"Thanks, baby."

"It's a hard thing to do."

"Thanks, baby."

"Sure, I am proud, baby."

"Thanks."

"I've only driven my truck around, in my life. I'm proud of yiz. That's a nice thing, is it, to have someone to be proud of. I've never felt that before. Feels like a luxury. I like it. Like it's a feeling you, like, someone, could do without, but it's lovely anyway, right, like you've got your love and you've got them sexy feelings, and hate, and all them things that shake the world around, and having someone to feel proud of isn't anything that will do much shaking, like it's all just for my own benefit, which is lovely. It's a feeling on top of a feeling, like a sauce. Am I sounding like an arse?"

"I think you should sell your wisdom instead of your sandwiches, baby."

"Ah, tanks, Jerry."

She said thanks without the "h" sometimes.

"It's doing something, isn't it?" she asked.

"What's that?"

"Driving the truck around, and all. It's what ya might call doing something. I'm not wasting my time, is it?"

"Of course not."

"Sometimes I feel totally useless, though, love, which is why I ask. I'm feelin a bit useless, Jerry, a bit…I'm feelin confused and a bit like I want to cry, because, pardon me, Jerry, it feels a bit empty. Christ, it feels empty sometimes, Jerry, doesn't it, love?"

"Just hold my hand there, Kath."

"Yeah. I'm only saying, Jerry. You know, we don't talk that much, and I'm only saying that I wonder whether it's me or the world that isn't worthwhile—I'm only trying to work that out. But not really, love, I'm just a bit down, is all, and also quite happy. That's a nice hand, and I'm proud of yiz. I might just go for a drive."

"It's midnight."

"Just a quick drive. Have a think. Stop thinking."

"I'll come with you."

"Someone's got to stay here."

"Why?"

"Jerry."

"Right."

"Stay here, Jer. I won't be long."

IT TOOK ALMOST TWO years for Government to approve that development. And every phase after that was a struggle. The investors had their thumbs on me and on Edgar, I had my thumb on that Schutz character, and he had his thumb wherever he thought it would cause a reaction, but with all that it still took two years. I even paid Schutz openly, outright, above and beyond the discount I gave him on his house. There probably was a better way, a smarter political way to get things done, but I think that would have meant cocktail parties and dinners, which no free man should ever contemplate attending.

Besides. Free. Who mentioned freedom? There were Planners' Meetings, Stakeholders' Meetings, Developers' Meetings, Union Meetings, Community Meetings, Jesus Meetings, Not Another Meetings, my friend, Meeting Meetings, surrounding me like a religion. I have no doubt that I cut my personality on a lot of the dull heads I met with, but I also lost my freedom. And somehow the more organized things got the more chaotic they felt—goals slipping further from our reach the more we met to discuss them.

I should admit that I liked meeting with the angel demons, even though they reminded me of how much money was at stake. They always gave me tips, but they didn't deliver them as tips; they just had so many facts inside their suits that everything they did was a lesson or a glimpse of the future. They shared some secrets to succeeding which I am afraid I won't tell you.

Edgar came over sometimes. I made a point of being home, Kathleen made the house look nice, put some colorful food on plates, bit of perfume on her wrists, and we'd have a little Party Meeting. Edgar and I would share stories about our crews, each of us pretending that his was the most hopeless, each hoping the other was telling the truth. The three of us were funny together, and we drank just until Sorrow and Drowsiness approached the front door. Edgar had good timing—always left at the right time.

I had good timing, too, mind you. Even though that approval took two years I had it all well planned. There was time for us to move, to try a new style of McGuinty. I intended to move into one of the *big* new houses I was going to build in the *big* new development. My stroke of genius was in the *style* of the house and in the *timing* (*big*, *style*, *timing* were what you call my marketing concepts for the development—*timing* because *now* is the *time*).

I had changed my ideas a bit, often actually, while we waited for approval. The houses would be this style, then they would be that style. I would discuss that sort of thing with Edgar because it was important that we did different things.

I finally settled on a style one night after Edgar had left our place. It is true that they were fun Party Meetings we had, but Edgar took a lot of the fun away with him, and all we were left with when he left was a mess, that awful blue carpet, an unexpected fear in the face of Kathleen. Houses swell and breathe like bellies, don't they, always shifting and fluid inside, goddamn it.

You've got your record collection organized, let's say, in an alphabet of moods, but you play those records, you have your favorites, and soon enough they all collect on the shelf around the stereo, on the speakers, under Jerry's feet, and the room is no longer familiar, your moods are scattered. It's not just a matter of mess, it's a matter of what's going on in your belly: you have to control it because it affects everything else.

So the new style—I mentioned this earlier and you didn't quite believe me—the new style would clean itself.

A simple matter of smart ventilation and no sharp corners can take care of a lot of that dust, ladies. Nothing obvious—I didn't make big goofy curvy corners, they were just curved enough that you only noticed standing close to them. Try doing *that* with plasterboard. And the ventilation was discreet, in floor and ceiling. Furthermore: marble floors. Grey marble floors in the kitchen and in the foyer. If you can notice dirt on those, you're a nut.

Further yet: no open plan. I never cared how hip it seemed to see your buddies shaking drinks in the kitchen while you smoked in bed; it's messy. Big rooms with high ceilings, that's what I built, with walls like mountain borders.

The angel demons liked the ideas—one of them bought one.

Big.

Style.

Timing.

Clean.

Smart.

AND IT'S A CITY. It basically amounts to a city, that land we developed. No skyscrapers, sure, no churches just yet, but a school was part of it, yes, and all those shops, and all those houses, and more underground necessaries than you would ever dream necessary. And the churches did come, those geometrical ones with blond bricks and the devil's artwork. The first school became a high school and two junior schools appeared. It still grows, without me, and one day it will be an important link in the world's iron armor.

Call it a suburb, if you want, but it was still part of the city itself, the spreading roots of the buildings downtown, and I figure you can say a man built a city who laid roads, built houses, and had a hand in the magic that brought up the rest. I'd say he was man enough for you and I'd say that the ten years of my life at the heart of that expansion were the hardest, ugliest, most confusing string of laborious days a chump should ever face.

———

DRIVE WITH ME for a while and I'll show you the area. It will be useful to see it from a hill nearby. Hop in the car here. It takes about half an hour. I'll tell you about Tony Espolito on the way, and then you can have a look at where I spent the days of confusion.

Buckle up. I'll just get a bit of speed up here, a nice cruising speed. Nice smooth ride. A little faster, eh? What do you say? No one around. A little faster? Faster? No one behind, eh?

Wham!

Ha!

Sorry.

I should have warned you. Take it easy. That's the point, you see? No warning.

Where was I? I was just, it was just

Wham!

Sorry.

You've got an idea what the Espolito experience was like.

Things were getting started, you see, getting properly under way, like we were cruising just a second ago. Work had begun. There were armies of workers, everyone in his proper place. A few roads were down, and even in those early stages there were close to a hundred guys around. It was totally different from having just my own crews. Powerful. Professional. I even wore a tie when my hands weren't busy.

Jerry was at school, Kathleen seemed happy enough driving around, everything was saying "Smooth...nice." But about six months into the thing, Wham!

"Boobleloodleoodleoodle oss man Jerry, oss man Jerry!"

Espolito turns up on-site drunker than he was Italian, and he's up on some scaffolding throwing stuff down at me and at some guys who didn't belong to me.

"I've seen it all, Jerry Werry, seen it, fag it. You're gonna die, you're gonna ssssuck on the end of it. What are they looking at? Who the fuck are they?"

He had been complaining more and more loudly over the

past couple of months about the other workers, all the guys he didn't know who weren't working for me. He seemed scared of them, but then he'd pick fights with them.

He was throwing bricks down at us.

"Had some whiskey, Jerry Berry, had some. I'm gonna piss it down on ya. Here you go, ossy. Big bossy. Ooh, it hurts when I pee, bossy wossy."

And he's throwing stuff while he's trying to spray us, more bricks and things. He nailed a guy with a bag of dry mortar, which would have freakin Hurt. So this guy goes wild.

"Get down here, get down here!" he's shouting, and Espolito's like, "Get down here! Get up here! Get over here!" Barking like a blind old dog, and laughing, "Wooooooooooooh."

And a few of the guys down there with me go over to the scaffolding and start shaking it, which was a dangerous thing to do. They all had their hands...here, hold the wheel...their hands like this, white-knuckled fists squeezing the uprights and shaking the whole thing...thanks...and Tony's up there all serious suddenly and even more confused. These guys wanted to kill him. We had all wanted to kill him for months. But I didn't really want a man dying on me. And he was a great brickie.

So I shout, "Whoa, whoa! Fuckin whoa!" I was wearing a tie that day.

They stop, and then Espolito starts laughing at me again. But he slips, and the moron's too drunk to think about hanging on with his hands.

If his wife hadn't buckled him into his overalls that drunken morning he would have fallen straight to the ground. I don't know whether that really would have killed him, but anyway there he is hanging from a bolt by the shoulder strap of his overalls and totally lost.

So I climb up the scaffolding carefully to try to help him. When I'm up there he's just dangling and mumbling and there's puke down the front of him.

I haul him up and try to keep him upright. I used to think he was just an annoying drunk, but at that point I thought he was a retard, you know, a man with a sad medical explanation behind his stupidity.

"I'm a prophet, fuck it, fag it, Jerry. I seen it. I'm telling ya, I seen it."

The puking probably did him good, because he was a bit less hysterical.

"Oh, I seen it, though, Jerry. Seriously. I seen it all, and it's not what they want to hear. Not what Jerry wants to hear down there. My head is hurting with it. Tell Jerry..."

"I'm here."

"Tell..."

He was quiet for a while and he squirmed out of my arms and sat across from me. He was looking around and rubbing his face like something was irritating him. A hammer and a couple of other things were lying on the boards up there, and I pushed them toward him like toys—like I would do with Jerry. "Here, Tony," I said. He picked up the hammer and hit one of the bars with it, like a reflex. He sobered for a minute. A well-swung hammer is a builder's mother's milk.

"I seen it, Jerry." Coughs a bit of puke. "It hurts, Jerry. My head hurts so fuckin much. I taste it. Like this bar. Seriously, Jerry, I seen it in her eyes."

He whacked on the bar with the hammer again once or twice.

"You're gonna lose it, Jerry. I'm a prophet. You're gonna lose it all."

He was calm, and he was swinging the hammer idly, but he seemed to know what he was saying. When he said "it all," he hit the bar twice, bing bing, and put the hammer down.

"Everything," he said. "It hurts so much," he said. "In here." He poked at his head. "You're gonna lose it all," he said, picking up the hammer again, "and it hurts in fuckin here," and he hits his head with the hammer.

It was a light swing, just a thoughtless wave of the hammer, and I just stared at him waiting for whatever was next. I stared at him, he stared at me, and it took me a minute—I don't know, long enough for me to look around a bit, to let him know that I was waiting for him to do something—until the hammer dropped and I saw some blood and hair on it.

I should have got you to drive…maybe…it's best just to keep going, yeah? I can't…

He was staring at me like he was…to make a point: *Your head is weak, Jerry, our heads are eggs, Jerry.* I guess he was sitting far enough forward that his gut was keeping him upright. If you were there, you wouldn't have thought he was dead either. You would have looked in his eyes and taken his point: *Your head is weak, buddy.*

I thought it was the only wisdom I could get from him—his action, you know, showing the truth. But I remember saying to the guys on the ground, "He was a prophet." I know they laughed—about five of them laughed. But he was a prophet.

THIS IS IT. Get out here. I'll show you. Come over here, there: you see from those pylons over there? And the water tower *way* over there? From there basically to the foot of this hill—not quite to the foot, about half a mile from where we are, but then all around there. From there…to there.

Yeah.

WHEN I THINK of him staring at me like that I feel like I have the flu.

"I feel like I have the flu," I told Edgar and Kathleen one night.

"Have a drink," Edgar said. "My grandparents called it 'beaver fever,'" he said, "but I have no idea where they got the name from. You know, when you feel funny but all you need is a drink: beaver fever."

"Bang on," Kathleen said.

"It's got nothing to do with beavers," I said.

"I know," says Edgar.

"He knows," says Kathleen. "That was his point."

"That was part of my point," says Edgar.

"I know your point. I don't need a drink. What I need...grab me a beer there, Kath. I need to stop thinking about Espolito dying."

"Forget about it, Jer."

"Yeah, forget about it, Jer. Listen to him. Yiz have to forget about it."

"I feel like I have the flu."

"Yiz'll have to forget about it or you'll make yerself sick."

"She's right, Jerry."

"I am sick."

"It wasn't your fault, Jerry. If you're worrying about the union, forget about it. The investors gave them insurance before the whole thing started. Don't worry about that. And it wasn't your fault."

"I don't care about the union. And I don't care that it was my fault. I gave him the hammer, so it was my fault, but I don't care about that. It's the...it's just the look of him. It's hard to explain."

"Well, it's hard to like the look of him. I never liked the look of him," Kathleen says. "I can't imagine what he looked like with a hole in his head."

"There wasn't a hole."

"Whatever."

"It doesn't matter, Jerry. It barely set us back. There could have been an investigation and all that shit."

"Ah, look, have one of them sausage rolls I made—look, sliced all nice."

"Yeah, have a nice sausage roll. You know, think about something else. Like what it must be like to have such a good cook for a wife."

"We're not actually married," she says.

"Really?"

"Not actually," I says. "You can't imagine what that was like, though. Seriously. The hammer hitting him didn't make a noise."

"Fer fuck's sake, Jerry, have a sausage roll."

"It would have made a noise for him, I guess. He wouldn't have had time to hear it."

"Instant, was it?"

"That's what they say. It's what it looked like, I suppose, because he just turned off, but really what it felt like was the opposite—like he is still *on*, staring at me somewhere, that same stare. He said he was a prophet."

"He was an eejit."

"But how would you feel if a guy said he was a prophet, and then made himself look like he permanently had his eye on you? Something like...like he was teaching you something forever but he's not around to explain it."

"Eh?"

"He's staring at some piece of knowledge that you can never understand."

"Eh?"

"Fuck it, Jerry. You know, it's a lesson to us all about insurance. Yours is going up a bit, and I'm sorry for you, but there we are. That was probably what he was trying to teach you: 'Good thing you have insurance' or 'This is gonna cost you,' or something like that. So you two aren't married?"

"Did you put Jerry to bed?" I ask.

"If I didn't, who did?" she says.

"Anyway, Edgar," I says, "I'm surprised your men aren't all dead after all those houses you've made them build. Exhaustion, eh, my friend?"

"Ah, you know as well as I do that they're tents, not houses. The only thing that'll kill you from building my houses is the shame of it."

"I think they're nice houses," she says.

"That's nice of you, Kathleen. Jerry's the one who builds nice houses."

"I need a new brickie."

"Have one of mine."

"He was good," I says. "I feel sick."

"You look pale, Jerry."

"He always looks pale because he's never flippin home. He works too hard."

"We all work too hard. *You* work too hard, Kathleen. Eh, Jerry?"

"Yeah."

"Breakfast, lunch, dinner, she's around, cooking, serving, what-not. It's fantastic. Did you hear, Jerry, the other day, Bill Cookson, you know, Cookie, the fatty, he says, 'Shit, Kathleen, that's the sweetest fuckin chicken I ate.' Did you hear that? Fat guy like Cookie? That's the highest praise you could get, Kathleen."

"I might lie down," I says. "Why don't you stay, Edgar?"

I HAD A vasectomy once.

We weren't having sex, Kathleen and I. I'm sorry to have to tell you that. We had sex a couple of times a month for a while, and then nothing.

"It's Jerry," she would say. "The other one. I can't have another."

Having to kiss her, but not too deep. Looking at her face, but not too deep. Our conversation had no depth.

"Corn?"

"No thanks."

"Ketchup?"

"Please."

And you try waking up to Kathleen, her back toward you and her hips just so. And you think she's finally liking it and wishing you a warm good morning, when she wakes up and slaps you away.

It was intended as a surprise, a sort of wedding vow in early middle age. I don't know. I wanted another Jerry; the more Jerries the better, I thought sometimes—or ideally another Kathleen. But also, certainly, I didn't want another kid. I didn't know the Jerry I had. And Kathleen was like that, too—back and forth—although she was more extreme. Mostly she didn't much like kids, but some nights after a laughing time with Edgar she would go up and look at Jerry with me and say with a little shake in her voice, "We should have had more. We should have had six." Unfortunately that was after the fact.

Clamps, is what they used. They didn't snip anything. They slapped a clamp on me—a new thing at the time. I respected that. Faith in their trade. The clamp could be removed and I could feel pity on past generations who only knew the knife.

I took a little time off work. Told Kathleen I had to go to Toronto for a union meeting so it would all be a surprise for her. Don't worry: I accepted an anaesthetic as general as the dark and woke up with a painful memory of something I couldn't remember. It was nothing at the time really, just a slightly uneasy feeling that someone visited my body while I was away and left without cleaning up. I never took advantage of the clamp business, the option to have it removed.

I came home and kissed Kathleen, deep, and I said, "Don't worry..."

"What do you mean?"

"Don't worry..."

"What do you mean?"

"Don't worry."

I was on top of her on the couch and I realized I couldn't do anything. I was half a cripple, really, afraid of the pain, couldn't make anything stir even though my head was full of wildness.

"Jerry pissed in his bed while you were gone," she said. "He's seven years old," she said. "He doesn't like me. He's always doing these things and you're not around, at your bloody union meetings, so I've got to give him...I've got to teach him."

"I wasn't at a union meeting."

"Where were you?"

"Hospital."

"Hospital?"

"So we could make love."

"Eh?"

"They tied me up, fixed me, slapped a clamp on me."

"Who did?"

"I wanted it. We're…we're not close."

"You're flipping lying on top of me. Do you mean you got snipped?"

"Clamped. They can take it off."

"Who can?"

"I wanted it."

"Jesus, Jerry. You could have…ya might have warned me. Now you can't…we can't…"

"We can."

"But we can't have…what about Jerry? He'll want a friend, a brother or something."

"Will he?"

"Of course he will. We were going to have more Jerries."

"What?"

"I want a house full of kids."

"When?"

"Now."

"You never said *that*! You never said you wanted a house full of kids."

"Well, I feckin well do, Jerry. I might."

"But we can…"

"Yeah, we can fuck. Big deal, Jerry. What's the point in fucking if we can't have kids?"

"What?!"

"What do you mean they clamped you?"

"They clamped me. They didn't cut anything."

"So they can take the clamp off?"

"Yeah."

"Fuck, Jerry. Go get yer flippin clamp taken off."

"I'm a bit sore."

"What am I asking for here, Jerry? Just a bit of independence."

"Having more kids doesn't make you independent."

"You clamping yerself for me does not make me independent. Yiz have clamped me, is what you've clamped."

"That's clever, Kathleen."

"Don't you fuckin mock me!"

"Well, whose stitches are these, if you're the one who's clamped?"

"Oh, don't…I do not want to see that right now. That is the last thing I want to look at right now, Jerry. Put that away and have some decency. They've gone and shaved you like a queer."

"What?"

"So what do we do now? We just happily go on fucking?"

"What do you mean 'go on'?"

"Quit being smart with me, Jerry. You're not looking too smart with that ting you just showed me, so stop being flippin smart. Jesus, Jerry, I'm in shock!"

"Mummy?"

"What do *you* want now? I'm talking to your father."

"Hey, Jerry. How's it goin?"

"Good."

"Talk to your father some other time. I'm talking to him now. I told him about your accident in bed, and he is not impressed, Jerry, so you'd better go away…Jesus, Jerry, I'm in shock."

I myself hadn't expected to be in shock, the operation having been smooth and the feeling of anticipation sweet. It's funny to think of shock now, after so many years of having that clamp in me. Nothing shocking, just plain silly. I feel like one of those Christmas puddings with a poisonous old coin inside.

"WATCH ME, Jerry, make sure I don't hit my head with this hammer."

"That's funny, Cooper."

"It is funny. He was a fuhuhcking idiot."

"I saw his wife the other day. She was too drunk to see me."

"I don't want to hear your sad little stories, boss man. Fuck off."

"EDGAR'S COMING to dinner."

"When?"

"Tonight."

"I've got to work tonight."

"Well, I invited him and bought all the food."

"OK. Maybe I'll be home in time for dessert."

"Edgar doesn't eat dessert."

"Then there will be more for me."

"I didn't buy dessert."

"Well, I'm sure you'll make him a nice dinner."

"Flippin right. It's what I do."

IF YOU WERE UP on that hill where I drove you the other day, you know, the one we looked…yeah. If you were up there at night years ago and looked down at the land you would have seen as much activity as if it was midday. So many men doing shifts. It was hard to get peace anywhere. I drove up on top of the hill sometimes to get away, see how it was going from above. All I could see was headlights. The workers left their motors running and their headlights on, shining in every direction like swords. I thought it was a stupid waste of money but that's neither here nor there.

I was up on that hill looking down one night trying to get a bit of peace when I got my first sensation that something was wrong. Something in my life was wrong, and something right there was wrong. I thought for a minute that someone was behind me and the more I thought that, the more I was convinced that it was Espolito. I never looked behind, I just became more convinced. I didn't hear anything move, or feel anything—but I knew that Espolito was behind me, about to breathe some drunken ghost's riddle on the back of my neck. I waited for him, waited for him. "What do you have to say?" I started whispering. "What do you have to say?"

That's a fuckin riot. I was whispering to myself.

I never looked behind me. I must have wanted to live a little ghost story. "What do you have to say?"

I wish I had turned around. That's my problem right there: I never looked. I let this feeling take over me. There's something wrong, there's definitely something wrong.

I didn't know whether to go home or not—whether there was something wrong at home, or in me, or just behind me. I walked backward to my car. Seriously, I walked backward to my car, got in, and drove home as fast as I could, and along the way I became certain that there was something wrong at home. She's gone again, she's gone again, she's gone again.

I burst through the front door, ran up the stairs shouting, "Kathleen! Kathleen!," threw open the bedroom door, and sure enough, no Kathleen. I checked the study, Jerry's room, the spare room, and I couldn't find her. She was gone again.

So I go to the kitchen, grab a beer and start feeling sorry for myself. I go into the living room, flop on the couch and "Aaaah! Feckin hell!" I sat right on Kathleen's stomach.

WHAT I DID KNOW for certain was that there was a conspiracy against me. I had thought it was funny, weird, that Kathleen seemed to think that Jerry and I were conspiring against her, but now I started to feel the same way about her, and that the conspiracy was bigger, that it started with little Jerry and went all the way up to the Federal Government. Basically, everyone had agreed to walk away from me when I approached.

Let's say I would need to talk to Edgar. I would go to his site office, go up to the door, and just as I would go in, I would turn and see him walking away toward his truck, always just out of

earshot—"Edgar! Edgar, buddy, over here!"—always just ten meters away. He wasn't out of earshot, that's what I realized. "Edgar!"

And Kathleen: same thing. She was out of the house earlier
than me often enough. Sometimes I would forget to tell her
something over breakfast, if we were eating together, and she
would always run away from me while I was running after her to
tell her. As soon as I would call her she would start running to
her truck. And she would slam the door of her truck in perfect
time with me shouting "Kath!" It was important sometimes too,
like once she forgot her barrel of butter and I ran out onto the
driveway carrying it, and again her door shouted "Kath!" She
would have to drive by later to pick up the butter, but the conspiracy seemed to dictate that driving back would be better than
turning around to listen to me.

And Jerry: same. I was home on a Sunday once and I wanted
to see what he was up to. I looked into his room and called him,
but he was down at the other end of the hall walking away into
the study, where I had been. So I called him, "Jer!," and walked
back to the study. Sure enough, no Jerry, he was walking down
the hall again, heading downstairs. "Jer!" No answer. No recognition. And there was another time—I don't know whether I'm
making this up or not because I actually have no recollection of
teaching him how to ride a bike—he was riding his bike down
the street and I was running after him to let him know about dinner. "Jer! Jer! Mummy says be home at five: Jer! Jer!" And he rode
farther and farther away from me.

That may have been a dream, that one.

It was happening all the time. Everyone was doing it. Even
that Schutz goof. I called him about fifty times one month to find
something out and he never returned the calls. I threw such a
stupid amount of money at that guy.

But this minor conspiracy had me bothered. I said, "Jesus,
Edgar, I have been trying to find you for a week."

"Where have you been looking, buddy?"

"Here! Every time I come to this office, you're walking to your truck."

"Well, it's all heating up isn't it, buddy?"

"Well, that's right. That's what I've been trying to let you know."

"Well, I know. Shit. I'm as busy as you are. It's going. It's moving."

"Yeah, but the Government."

"What?"

"The Government."

"Yeah."

"That's what I've been trying to tell you."

"What's that, buddy?"

"I haven't heard from my contact there for a coon's age."

"Right."

"Well, what's that all about?"

"I don't know, buddy. He's your contact."

"Exactly. I don't know what's going on."

"Well, it's all going on. I've got thirty frames up. Phase one is on its way."

"Right. Same here. My phase one is definitely on its way. What's going on? I've called the guy fifty times, and then you're… I was having trouble catching up with you."

"OK. I'm seeing you tonight, aren't I?"

"Where?"

"Your place."

"Again?"

"Yeah. I guess I've been coming over a lot."

"No, I didn't mean that. But you were over there…I didn't mean…you were there last week, weren't you?"

"I didn't know you weren't going to be there."

"No, I'm glad you went. We'll talk business, won't we? We should catch up."

"Yeah. Everything all right?"

"Yeah. Yeah. A bit overworked."

"Tell me about it," he said.

"It's all going on," I said.

"That it is," he said.

I WAS UP on the hill trying to get a bit of peace again, and once again that Espolito Ghost of Something Wrong crept up on the neck. Fuck off, is what I whispered this time, but the feeling was undeniable and I still didn't want to turn around. So I raced home and this time the feeling was right. It was midnight and the house was empty. No Kathleen. No Jerry. Espolito on my neck.

I grabbed a beer and fell asleep on the couch and when I woke up at dawn there were footsteps upstairs. I didn't care how much I felt sorry about Espolito dying: if he was still alive I was going to give him a fatal poke in the jaw because he was scaring the hair off me. The footsteps were in our bedroom. I knew it couldn't be Kathleen because I would have heard her come in with Jerry, plus her and Jerry's coats weren't in the hall.

I grabbed one of my boots by the door so I could kick the ghost's face with my hand, and I went upstairs slowly. I did make sure I was awake and thinking clearly. Trust me.

I couldn't hear a sound from the bedroom once I was up there so I checked the other rooms first. Jerry's bed had not been touched. Typewriter and calculator were still in the study. No more noise.

I went into the bedroom and there, lying on the bed, was a skinny black weirdo in a cape.

I flicked on the light and screamed with my boot in the air as a fist, but Kathleen barely stirred. She was out cold, passed out in her coat.

I was able to wake her up eventually, a couple of hours later, but she wasn't very friendly. I was wondering where Jerry was.

"He's over there, ya feckin eejit."

"Where?"

"Edgar's."

"What's he doing at Edgar's?"

"Let me sleep."

I drove over to Edgar's wondering what was going on. Edgar answered the door and Jerry was behind him playing with a toy airplane.

"Hey, Jerry, there you are," says Edgar.

"What do you mean?"

"Well, there you are. We've been waiting for you all night."

"Where?"

"Here."

"I was at home. Kathleen and Jerry had disappeared, just gone. All night."

"Come in."

"They were gone all night, and then Kathleen turns up at home and scares the shit out of me. Hey, Jerry."

"Hey, Dad."

"How's it goin?"

"Good."

"He's got his airplane there."

"So what's going on?"

"Well, I thought you were supposed to come over last night. Over here. And we called your place all night until around midnight or so. And Jerry here, he was all tired so it seemed best that he just crashed. See, I...Kathleen and I had drunk a bit, we were pretty looped, so we couldn't really get her home. I didn't know she left, actually."

"She's at home."

"Right."

"So, you've been looking after Jerry?"

"He doesn't need much, do ya, buddy?"

"I had breakfast," says Jerry.

"I dropped a couple of Pop Tarts in the toaster. I don't have much else."

"Well, thanks, Edgar."

"No, it was…I laid on quite a spread last night. I'm sorry you missed it."

"I didn't know, I honestly had no idea we were invited over."

"I had steak, Dad."

"Did you, buddy?"

"He had a steak as big as a cat."

"Did you, buddy? Good boy. Lucky boy. I'm starving."

"You want a Pop Tart, Jer?"

"Yeah, all right. Please. Sorry, Edgar."

"No, man. Have a Pop Tart."

WHEN I DROVE HOME from Edgar's with Jerry I asked him if he would like to build a house, you know, not a real one but a small one out of plaster on the floor at home. He was a hundred percent agreeable.

We instinctively tiptoed into the house from the garage. There didn't seem to be any noise from upstairs so I opened the door for Jerry and followed him down to the basement.

I had fixed the basement up as a sort of distraction until I could build us the self-cleaning house, so it was really quite nice down there—couple of workbenches, a television, no carpet.

"Now, of course, Jerry, the basic principle behind plastering is that you can't have a wall without a frame, and a frame is nothing unless it becomes a wall. Right?

"What we're going to do here is ignore that basic principle."

We heard a noise above, a creaking, and we were both quiet for a second.

"We're going to ignore that basic principle because I think we should go ahead and get our hands dirty, and it's a pain in the ass to build a small frame, right?"

"Right."

"Furthermore, Jerry, and I mean this seriously, plastering as you and I know it is a dying trade. Nowadays people—and, sure,

I'll have to admit, I do it occasionally myself—people use plasterboard; and the only art of the trowel that remains is in smoothing the mud over edges and studs, and occasionally smoothing over errors in the boards. And by mud, I mean compound, don't I, buddy?"

"That's right."

"So we're just going to make some plaster, dip our hands in it and make an impossible house. What do you think?"

"Can I make my own?"

"Is Daddy getting bald and fat?"

"You bet."

"You bet you can, big guy. I'll make one and you make one."

"I'm no good at Art or Spelling."

"That's OK, buddy."

"And Damien Lowther says I'm stupid."

"Well, how about Daddy rips his tongue out if he meets him?"

"You bet."

"You bet your genius head, big guy, now let's make a couple of dwellings. You've got to... when making plaster..."

There was more shifting upstairs.

"When making plaster, we have to pay the mixture some respect. We don't have to worship it or, necessarily, pretend it's a woman, or any of that shit, but we have to give it due respect. The one thing both you and the plaster know is that if it doesn't feel right, it's not going to hold. Now, you know my secret, don't you?"

"Pinch of lime."

"You're a star, Jerry. Pinch of lime. Don't tell anyone."

"Is Mummy awake?"

"I don't know."

"Maybe she's in bed still?"

"Maybe, buddy. So we'll just use this bucket here and so... right?"

"Yep."

"And so?"

"Yep."

"And Portland cement. Yes?"

"OK."

"There is no alternative, Jerry."

We set to building, Jerry and I, and we spread a quiet gray mess over the floor. We didn't say a word to each other, and gradually, upstairs, Kathleen grew into a storm of cupboard doors and footsteps. We didn't talk to each other in the basement for more than two hours.

Kids can be weird. Bunch of freaks, really. That's one thought I dwelled on for a while. Jerry was moving his lips, making little sounds that must have been the people who were living in his house. If I did that while I was building I'd look like a nut.

His house was ingenious. It gave me a lump in my throat. I can't describe it. You will never know. He wrote a "J" on each side and he made a little ball of plaster that he said was a cherry (for Jerry) and he put it on the roof. He was a bright, quiet little freak, and those whitening hours with the suspense overhead were some of the sweetest I ever spent with him.

"Your house is pretty ordinary," he told me, which made me laugh, which was a mistake.

The door to the basement opened and Kathleen shouted "Jerry!" from the top of the stairs.

We each waited for the other to answer.

She shouted "Jerry!" again.

We both said, "Yeah?"

IT WAS MY MISTAKE, apparently. Kathleen had told me about dinner at Edgar's ages before. I don't know how I forgot. Never mind. Nothing a slap round my ear wouldn't fix.

Everyone started walking away from me again. I was finishing the walls of phase one.

I don't think I have ever lived in myself. I had a glimpse of that realization when I was looking at one of those walls. If a wall is something hard, something real, maybe even an end, or an unmistakable truth; and this is me, here, this body, here; then I think where I, my mind, always actually lived was somewhere between me and the walls. I think I've always run around between truths, between myself and the end. It is not a big space between me and the walls, but there is room to imagine anything.

3

GALATEA, SAUCY GIRL, pelts me with an apple, then runs off to the willows...

"HELLO, SIMON!"

"So you remember me?"

"From dinner."

"It was a long time ago."

"Not long enough to forget you. Come in, come in. Are you here for Leonard? I've just come back from running. Excuse the shorts. Are you here for Leonard?"

"Not at all, no. Is he here?"

"I think he is out eating somewhere."

"I was looking for you, actually."

"For me?"

"I heard that you had bought a new house, so I thought I might intrude, warm your house, bring you bread and salt."

"Where's the bread and salt?"

"I could get some."

"That's fine. We have some. Lots. Leonard's tastes are richer. Can I offer you a drink?"

"What are you having?"

"A shower is what I was going to have."

"Shall I come back another time?"

"No, no. It occurred to me as a witty thing to say."

"It was."

"I would have champagne if you joined me."

"I will."

"So, you aren't here for Leonard at all?"

"No."

"It's a good thing he is out then. I hope you don't mind my appearance. I don't actually run very much. There isn't anywhere to run to, really, and I find it boring anyway. Nothing like a good walk. But I went running anyway, you see. Do you walk?"

"Only when there is no good in sitting."

"Maybe you would like to walk with me sometime. Would you mind opening the champagne? I blinded my grandfather once with a cork. I don't...I don't feel confident."

"I suppose not."

"It was just the one eye."

"I see."

"I'm kidding. Don't give me a full glass."

"Here you are. Cheers."

"Cheers."

"I hope you don't think I am intruding. Or that I am odd. Please don't think that I am odd. I have been meaning to look you up ever since we met at dinner, to call on you. Awfully long time ago now."

"It doesn't feel that long."

"I could have had you and Leonard over, but I'm not good at having people over. I am much more charming at other people's houses."

"Cheers again."

"Cheers. I remember your story, from dinner."

"Which one was that?"

"About food. About your daughter and her friends."

"The Friends and the Pizza story."

"Yes. 'A spoonful of chocolate pudding.' It was the best of the night."

"Not much of a night then. I tell it all the time. Leonard gets me into a bind with his role-playing at dinner. I always end up telling the same story, no matter what theme he sets. He can be pretentious, my husband. Do you like him?"

"It's a story about indecision, really."

"Yes, it is. The heroine is upstairs, in fact."

"Who?"

"Kwyet."

"Quiet?"

"Yes. She is still Indecision itself. She's a student. First year at McGill. But she keeps coming home because she can't decide whether to keep studying or not."

"So she lives in Montreal?"

"She can't decide. I mean, yes, theoretically she is in residence there, but she comes home every weekend. Would you like to meet her?"

"Yes."

"Don't be offended if she doesn't come down. I suspect the champagne will lure her. But don't be offended if not... KWYET!"

"yes, mum."

"WILL YOU COME DOWN FOR A MINUTE—she's actually quite social—WILL YOU COME DOWN? WE HAVE A VISITOR."

"just a minute."

"There, that was easy. Cheers."

"Cheers."

"Leonard tells me you are having a difficult time at work."

"I..."

"Oh, here she is. Kwyet, darling, this is Simon Struthers, a colleague of your father's."

"Hello."

"Hello. It's an extraordinary name, 'Quiet.'"

"Mum's a Kinks fan."

"Pardon?"

"*Kwyet Kinks.* It's a nickname, technically."

"We renamed her. Have some champagne."

"Nice."

"Bit of a reward for being social. What were you doing upstairs?"

"Reading."

"What were you reading?…Darling…What were you reading?…There now, you see, Simon, that look? The silence?"

"I'm thinking, Mother. I'm just thinking about what I was reading. It's Latin, but I can't really read a word of it. Ovid."

"Why are you reading Ovid?"

"…"

"Darling, Simon asked you a question."

"Sorry. For a course. I just don't know why I'm taking the course. I don't know any Latin."

"Plenty of translations."

"Well, that's what I'm thinking about. It's sad to look at words and not understand them, and then to look at these translations which say they are the same, but…"

"I know what you mean."

"Do you?"

"Do you, Simon?"

"Yes. What you need is someone to translate for you. I could translate for you. Orally. Read it out. That's what you need. If you hear a translation it doesn't seem like such an impostor."

"Right."

"Really?"

"Yes."

"Right."

"Cheers."

"Cheers."

"Cheers."

"Where's Dad?"

"Eating."

"I'm hungry."

"Simon, are you hungry?"

"Not really. Yes."

"You sound like Kwyet."

"She just said she was hungry."

"I am hungry, Mother."

"Kids. Eh, Simon?"

"She is hardly a kid."

"She is nineteen."

"Why do I feel excluded from this conversation?"

"Because you don't participate. Are you really hungry, Simon?"

"I could be, yes. This champagne is making me hungry."

"It's making me silly."

"Me too."

"Me too."

"We don't have food here, though."

"Dad eats it."

"And we have barely moved in. I suppose you've noticed, Simon. It's an empty, hungry house."

"I like that."

"I agree with Kwyet. I like that too."

"How's that champagne going, Simon?"

"There's some left."

"Would you mind pouring some more for us? Finish it off. That's it."

"I feel like something fat."

"Food?"

"*Yes, Mother.* Cheese. French fries."

"Think of your father, darling."

"That's true."

"It's the champagne. It makes me hungry."

"So how do you know how to translate Ovid?"

"I read Classics. I...I was never very good at it, at the scholar-ship. Never clever enough! Ha!"

"What's so funny?"

"I don't know. Sorry. I was never much of a scholar, but I could, seriously, translate for you. I loved the...I loved the myths. The stories."

"Maybe we should go for a walk. Walk off the silliness."

"But we're hungry, Mother."

"We could eat something on our walk. I've seen a chip wagon by the park. Is that disgraceful, Simon? Are you as snobbish as Leonard about food?"

"I don't know how to answer that. I like french fries."

"Well, so does Kwyet. Don't you, darling? Darling?"

"I love french fries."

"Let's walk to the park, then. Shall we, Simon?"

"Please. What park?"

"There's a nice park near here. Sort of a park. Kwyet and I walk there."

"Lovely."

"And we will go to the van?"

"Yes, Kwyet, for french fries."

"What an extraordinary name."

"Thank you."

"Thank you, Simon. Would you mind if I went out without showering?"

"Of course not."

"Let's go then. It isn't far. Shall we start the big talk on the way?"

"All right."

"How long have you worked with my father?"

"Excellent, Kwyet."

"Thank you, Mother."

"Umm...several years now. Gosh."

"And in what capacity do you work with him?"

"Excellent, Mother."

"Thanks, darling."

"In a limited capacity."

"Excellent, *Simon*."

"Thanks, Matty."

"He is limited. I don't know why I feel so inclined to be cruel about my husband today. It must be the hunger."

"I only meant that I don't always have much to do with him. We have worked on matters together, occasionally. This land around here, for example."

"..."

"..."

"..."

"Why so quiet, Mother?"

"I can't think of anything to say, Kwyet."

"That's the fault of big talk. It's my fault. My work is boring."

"It's not that at all. Let's pick up the pace a little. I hate all this construction."

"But you said you liked your house."

"Kwyet said that. I like the house well enough. It was Leonard's idea. Come on, everyone. Pick up the pace."

"I could beat you both in a race."

"Of course you could, Kwyet."

"But I am a man."

"That's true, Simon."

"An older man."

"Really, Kwyet. Don't offend your father's friend. You are younger than Leonard, aren't you?"

"Probably."

"There now, Kwyet. Don't offend him. I can see the chip wagon ahead. That's where the park is."

"I'm not sure my silliness is being walked off."

"You seem sober, Simon. Very…what's the word? Upright."

"I feel silly. It wasn't much champagne. Maybe it isn't the champagne at all."

"Come on."

"I'm going to run."

"Don't run, darling."

"I'll buy the fries."

"Bye."

"She's only boasting, Simon. It's not that far."

"I am tempted to run."

"After her?"

"Toward the van."

"If we get there at the same time she won't buy the fries for us. Look, she's there already. You don't have children to support, do you, Simon?"

"No."

"And Leonard tells me you are unmarried."

"Yes, I...What did you mean earlier when you said I was having trouble at work?"

"Did I say that? I probably meant Leonard. I gather you all have a big project. So you have no one to support?"

"No."

"Leonard's always talking about money, supporting her at McGill."

"Well, you have a big new house..."

"Here she comes. That was quick. Aren't you lovely, Kwyet?"

"It was your money."

"Yes. I was just shocking Simon with that. Good God, I am hungry. These fries aren't very fresh."

"I think they're good."

"They are good."

"They're good, but they're not fresh."

"How do you spell Quiet?"

"K-W-Y-E-T."

"How extraordinary."

"Let's go to the park."

"You've never been to this park, Simon?"

"I don't really know the area. I mean, I know it intimately from maps and so on. Surveys. But I have never been here."

"How *extraordinary*."

"Are you mocking me, Kwyet?"

"Sorry."

"It never occurred to me to consider this just a park."

"How extraordinary."

"It is extraordinary. I…one gets so *involved*."

"When will you translate for me, Simon?"

"Really?"

"Yes."

"Whenever you like."

"What did Ovid call french fries?"

"I don't think Ovid went to Belgium."

"Wrong answer."

KWYET, SAUCY GIRL, pelts me with pommes frites, then runs off to the willows.

TO CALL ON MATTY and then to meet Kwyet. Gentlemen speculators: hold in your eyes the diamond of your dreams, blink, and behold what diamonds dream of.

"HELLO, MATTY, it's Simon Struthers calling. I hope I am not disturbing you."

"Not at all, Simon. How are you?"

"I am well. I am at work, but I am well because I had a marvelous idea. Do you have a moment?"

"Hold on, I'll ask the turnips I was peeling. Go ahead, Simon, but hurry."

"I don't know whether it registered with you how important it was for me, professionally, to spend time with you and Kwyet in the park the other day."

"Professionally?"

"Absolutely. It was a pleasure personally, of course."

"That was obvious. I have never known friends of Leonard's to hum unless they were leaving a concert."

"Well, professionally it was crucial. I don't think you have a sense of how absorbed in that land I had been. And then to see it. My idea was to go out to that park today, now. It is work, after all. And I was wondering if you would join me."

"It would be a pleasure."

"You have no plans?"

"No. I should take up bridge, but I am willing to wait another day. Kwyet is back in Montreal."

"Oh. Shall I come over soon?"

"Do."

"I want to come out here often. Not just to this park, but all around here."

"It is a nice park."

"There's something about it. It isn't all that nice objectively, but there is something wonderful."

"I expect that is my company. I like coming here with Kwyet. Maybe it's Kwyet who makes it wonderful."

"Maybe. But it feels lovely now."

"Maybe it is me. I believe it may be me, Simon."

"Yes. The Government owns this land. It isn't actually a park. It's just land waiting for something."

"Kwyet's seen this land from above."

"So have I."

"From a plane?"

"Survey."

"That's not the same, is it?"

"Same as what?"

"As from a plane. Kwyet has a friend at McGill with a pilot's license. The airport's near here."

"Yes."

"So she saw it from above. I'm not sure whether he is a boyfriend or not. Normally she tells me."

"I would like to help her with that translation."

"She would like that. I was jealous of her for flying. I bet he is

195

handsome, too. Pilots normally are. You really want to help her with her studies?"

"I would be happy to translate for her."

"Is that something her father should do?"

"No."

"She would love that."

We have made you of marble, Priapus, for the time...

"Leonard tells me you have been quite close to some of your colleagues."

"Does he?"

"Yes. Why?"

"Why what?"

"Why have you had affairs with your colleagues?"

"You're awfully frank, aren't you, Matty?"

"Sorry. I think Leonard likes Renée. He feels he is getting old, Leonard. I think it makes him a bit desperate—to have affairs and that sort of thing. Prove he is still attractive. It's all a bit funny. No offense, but I find affairs a bit funny."

"Why should I take offense?"

"Because you have them."

"Just because I am a bachelor, it does not mean I have 'affairs.' You imply that I am an adulterer. I am not always an adulterer."

"What I mean is, I find the whole thing funny. Sex, physical attraction, lust. Shall we sit down on the grass?"

"If we come here often I will buy a picnic blanket."

"Yes, lovely, let's have a picnic."

"You were talking about lust."

"Yes. It's funny. I married Leonard because I lacked imagination, in a way. He seemed to like me. My father wanted to give me away because he liked the idea of offering a dowry. It made him feel noble. Do you mind my being frank? I thought for many years that I was only with him through convenience, lack of imagination, as I said. I thought that there might be better husbands available if I ever chose to put some effort into seeking them and so on. But through experience I've learned that it wasn't a lack of imagination at all. My apathy was, is, satisfaction. That phrase is rehearsed, but it's true. I'm not convinced that there is anyone 'better' than Leonard, because having someone is all the same to me. I like sex every now and then, but it seems amusing to me to want to seek it all the time. And I've found it difficult with Kwyet. I think she might be a bit more interested than I am in that sort of thing, and I don't really know how to give her guidance."

"I don't think you should."

"Perhaps not."

"Perhaps she doesn't need it."

"Maybe. She has that pilot boy in Montreal. He sounds good—maybe I was wrong about myself, maybe I would like a pilot. She has other boys too. Has she told you about any of them?"

"I haven't really spent much... You know everything she has said to me."

"She is very charming, Kwyet. Maybe, though, she *is* like me—I have never known about any definite boyfriends really. She could have many, or none. Do you know the kind?"

"When will she be visiting you again?"

"In a couple of weeks. You must come over then. Why don't you read with her then, or whatever you wanted to do? I can listen. Shall we meet here?"

"In the park, two weeks from now. The three of us."

... BUT IF *births make full the flock, then you will be of gold.*

FOUR DOLLARS ninety-five for a picnic blanket was a perfectly affordable way to silence the earth's cold reminders.

———

"SILENCE, PLEASE, everyone, now. Here. Silence. I will read my translation for you, Kwyet. A bit of Ovid that I like. Do you both like the picnic blanket? Yes? Silence. Ready?

THE TALE IS TOLD by Venus, bully Venus, love-weary Love, not weary of love but *by*, *with*, and *from* it. They say that by this stage in her career she was a little worse for wear. There were ghosts behind her eyes, and her breath, though still sweeter than the freshest flower in Tempe, tasted sour on her tongue in the morning. (Whiskey, whispered some.)

It was pectoral Adonis, hunt-boy Adonis they all blamed. The hunt, he loved; Love, he didn't. Venus could only chase him as he ran after animals and it was tiring her.

One day she managed to pin Adonis to the ground, her Lovesick head on his lovenone chest, beneath the shade of some tree or other—they don't say which or how—and she told him this story, apropos of everything.

"You may," she said, "have heard of a girl who ran more quickly than any man alive. Atalanta was her name. I used to go to school with her. And whether she was more beautiful than fast or faster than she was beautiful, even I couldn't say.

"Like all young girls in those days she went to Delphi to ask the Oracle about a husband. And the Oracle said, 'Husband,' it said, 'now there's a thing not to mess with; run from that thing: husband.' And as usual the Oracle felt mischievous so it added, 'But you will not run, and running you will lose yourself.'

"Atalanta was scared by the Oracle. She lived in fear for a good few years, hiding alone in her bedroom and in the shady woods out back on warmer days. But despite her attempts to hide, suitors came knocking or they would bump into her in the woods sometimes. She had to have some defense if they tried to woo her, which, of course, they did.

"'Run,' she would say, 'and see if you can catch me. Beat me in a race and you can have me in marriage.'

"And just to adjust their leery smiles she would add, 'But if you lose, you must consent to die.'

"Atalanta had no mercy.

"She was so beautiful that even on those terms, in the face of death, a rush of suitors leapt forward to race her.

"Now, this is where Hippomenes comes in.

"Hippomenes had taken a seat to watch this race. He bought a glass of wine and a few sprigs of mint and he said to the vendor: 'Who would risk such danger for the sake of winning a wife?'

"And the vendor said, 'Check her out.'

"If you were a woman, Adonis, Atalanta would be as beautiful as you are. She was almost as beautiful as I am. And when Hippomenes realized this, when he had seen her undressing for the race, he held out his hands and cried to the runners, 'I'm sorry! Forgive me! I hadn't seen the prize!'

"And while he was thinking of words to praise her, and while those words ran ahead of him, he fell helplessly in love.

"Atalanta shot by like an arrow. The race had begun. Her skin flushed pink as she ran and she looked like a statue of Me that has borrowed the blood of the sun. 'Why am I not running?' thought Hippomenes.

"He watched as Atalanta crossed the finish line victorious.

"All the young men who ran with her had to pay the price. But the groans and the blood, broken hope and teeth, would not deter Hippomenes. He sipped his cool Riesling, wiped his lips with mint and shouted to her, 'Atalanta! Isn't it an easy title, beating the slowest youth in town? Come on and give me a shot! If fortune gives me victory, there will be no shame for you to be beaten by so worthy a chap. My great grandfather is Neptune— owns all the oceans. If you beat me, you will have a properly memorable fame!'

"Her eyes softened like the evening when she watched him utter his challenge. She wavered between winning and being won.

"'You're not bad looking!' she shouted in return. 'Who is it that wants you removed from the living? Maybe I am not worth it. Maybe you are not the right age for me. Maybe other women would not refuse you, and you could marry them more safely. Marriage with me is cursed. For my sake, for your sake, I wish you hadn't looked at me.'

"A crowd had gathered around and they were getting eager for another race. Atalanta's father was among them. 'A race is due,' he mumbled.

"Hippomenes turned to prayer at this point. 'O Venus,' he said, 'help me with this race that I think I'll dare to run, and smile upon the love that I might coax out of her.'

"And a gentle breeze blew his prayer to Me, and I saw some room for fun. There wasn't much time.

"Not far from there was a park, quite magical. They've changed all the names now so I can't find it any more, but back then there was a tree that grew in this park, whose leaves and branches were covered in gold. I had an idea that would help Hippomenes. I jogged over to the park and plucked three golden apples from the tree and returned to Hippomenes, showing myself to him so I could teach him how to use the apples.

"He was weak in the knees because I was Love bearing fruit, whispering in his ear.

"Trumpets sounded for the race to begin.

"Atalanta and Hippomenes shot from the blocks like a thought. 'Run, Hippomenes, run!' half the crowd shouted. 'Kill, Atalanta, run!' the other half shouted.

"It seemed sometimes like the girl was deliberately waiting, holding back to look at Hippomenes' face. Or perhaps Hippomenes imagined this. Sometimes I do that to people.

"It soon became clear that Hippomenes was slower than Atalanta, and he regretted having that wine. When it looked like he was losing he tossed one of the golden apples so it bounced off the track to Atalanta's right. The fruit caught her attention and when she realized it was gold she had to have it. Away she ran and Hippomenes burst ahead.

"With the jeweled fruit in her hand Atalanta felt a surge of conflicting cupidities that did nothing but push her forward: gold! freedom! race! And soon she caught up with Hippomenes.

"Again she moved ahead of him, so again he tossed an apple and she was distracted from her course. More carats!

"But again after picking up the apple she caught up with Hippomenes and got ahead of him. There was one last chance for him to win.

"All this time the more she ran ahead of him the weaker he got with love. But I gave him strength of purpose, and he threw the last apple farther than the rest.

"This time Atalanta hesitated for a moment longer, but I forced her to run after the fruit and once she picked it up I made the three apples heavier than they had been. She was overburdened by the treasure and at last Hippomenes crossed the finish line before her.

"In front of a half-disappointed crowd he led away his prize, golden apples in her arms.

"So, Adonis," Venus said. "Didn't I deserve a bit of a present? Some thanks from Hippomenes, maybe a bottle of something? I didn't receive one puff of incense from him. He completely forgot what I had done for him.

"I got angry. I decided to punish them both.

"On their way home Atalanta and Hippomenes were walking through the woods and they were tired from all their running. They noticed a holy temple, sacred to some god or other—they've changed all the names—and they went in for a moment to rest.

"It was there that I struck Hippomenes with my strongest spell of lust. Completely without control, he grabbed Atalanta and he defiled both her and the temple.

"And then as they entwined and augmented their offenses,

we gods ganged up and changed their skin to fur, arms to legs, moans to growls, and before long they were lions. Helpless, separate and enraged.

"Really, it is a story about how I had a hand in creating lions," Venus said. "But I am telling you as a sort of warning, Adonis. Do not underestimate the anger of the beasts you meet on your hunt."

Adonis paid no heed, of course. As soon as he heard the word "hunt" he sprang up, letting Venus's head fall rudely to the ground.

She sat up and called her limo. In the backseat she got some gin from the fridge and mixed a little something for her head.

It was in the back of her limo, watching TV, that she later heard the news. Adonis had been killed in the woods.

"WHY DON'T YOU come to Montreal sometime? Come and visit me."

"Really?"

"Sure."

"When?"

"Whenever. Come on a weekend."

"But you are usually in Ottawa on weekends."

"I'll make an exception."

"Why do you come to Ottawa, anyway?"

"I miss my mother."

"Of course. Stupid of me. It's a boring place compared to Montreal. That's why I asked."

"Why do *you* live here then?"

"I don't know. It's appealing. Blank."

"Exactly."

"Really?"

"It's like a place where I do nothing and feel comfortable. Plus my mother's here."

"Yes. That is it for me. Minus your mother. More or less. Although I'm very happy I met your mother. And you. Do you know, Kwyet, before I met you and your mother I felt awfully wise around everyone I knew? I felt like I knew everyone. I don't feel like I know you. I hope I am not embarrassing you. I feel at a loss."

"For what?"

"I don't know. I feel hopeless…overwhelmed."

"Why?"

"I don't know. Can I buy you a present of some sort?"

"Why?"

"I don't know."

"KWYET SAID she bumped into you."

"Yes."

"You are around here a lot now, aren't you?"

"Yes, for work, you know. Do you feel like I'm around you too much?"

"No. I wonder why you are always here during the days."

"For work."

"Nothing to do with Leonard's not being here?"

"What? No. Leonard knows…my colleagues know that I am here. I have recommended that they come out and look at the area. It's a dramatic initiative of mine."

"Why don't you come over tonight?"

"Tonight?"

"While Leonard's here. I can make supper for you both. Kwyet is still in town but she will be out baby-sitting."

"I see. Yes, thanks, that would be lovely."

"You do like Leonard, don't you?"

"Of course. We have worked together for a long time now."

"I know that."

"Yes."

HE HAD TO BUY flowers for Matty. Lilies seemed right.

Wine for Leonard. What wine does one bring a pompous bladder of a man whom one despises for no reason? How can he be father to the daughter of Imagination?

Contradiction bottled. Something impossible, something to sum up: fire, fruit, silk, rot, dust, blades, bother and temptation. A young Pommard, perhaps.

What was he doing?

"Hello! I thought you were baby-sitting."

"I am. I'm leaving. Mum will be down soon."

"You look angry."

"Excuse me."

"Sorry. See you?"

"Simon. Hello."

"Hello, Matty. Was there something wrong with Kwyet?"

"I don't think so. Lilies! How lovely."

"Where's Leonard?"

"He isn't here."

"Oh. I will give him this wine when he comes."

"Put it down here. You and I will drink it. Leonard won't be here at all tonight."

"What?"

"I'll put these in water. No, Leonard went out to dinner with Renée and Randolph and that lot. It's Thursday, remember?"

"Of course."

"Did you notice that you weren't invited?"

"I have stopped noticing."

"Well, I thought it was cruel of Leonard not to invite you. You do know that he deliberately stopped inviting you?"

"I...no...I thought it was my choice."

"Anyway, I wanted to test you, to see if you liked Leonard enough to come over. And you have. It makes me very angry with him."

"Yes, well, that's not quite it."

"Anyway. He was wonderfully perplexed when I told him you were coming over. Most upset. I must apologize for him, Simon."

"That's all right."

"But we will have a nice dinner."

"I'm sure we will. Perhaps I should go, though."

"Why? Oh, no, I have offended you. This wasn't all a test. Don't be silly. I wanted you to come over. I wanted to spend time, you know...I didn't like the idea of one of those dinners again without you among us. So, really, it was just a way of ensuring you were among...me."

"Yes, but your test...it didn't really test...shall we have some wine? It didn't test whether I liked Leonard. It only tested whether I could put up with Leonard to be with you."

"...I see."

"Now I have offended you."

"No. I...cheers...gosh, this wine..."

"Yes."

"I'm not very hungry."

"No."

"I feel a little woozy. I thought...I don't think I want this to happen."

"What?"

"This. Hold on...Please, sit down for a moment, Simon. I don't...Kwyet's just left, you see."

"Yes."

"I don't know who you are."

"Yes you do."

"Simon?"

"Why don't we go upstairs and have a shower?"

You who pick flowers and earth-born strawberries,
Take off: a cold snake lurks in the grass.

He saw it, his wet little paunch in the mirror, toweling off, an athlete with no pride in his victory.

The end of his pastoral? Not quite. Let him yet pretend for as long as he can stand it. Pretend everything is what it isn't.

But it was such a peaceful time. Such a lovely, silly, almost imaginary park, too. Fine in its center, but don't go near the edges, beyond the trees: on one side construction, on the other nothing, such a miserable nothing, then an airport, beyond which, nothing. And soon to be a scene of struggles, then more struggles, then the site of something, well, wonderful. He put it there.

Matty. Matty's daughter. You couldn't blame him for loving them. His Kwyet.

He was so at ease, unaware of himself, unaware of artifice. None of his usual low-church priapism; just respectful sacred attraction, a delicious vibrating stasis between the three of them, sweet to be a part of.

Then he joins Matty in that sweaty shower of Leonard's. Leonard's own shower! Familiar moans—please, please, please, please, please just stop.

Matty may not have enjoyed that. Perhaps not. Did she? Perhaps not.

"Did you?"

"What?"

"Nothing."

HE NOTED THE WAY Kwyet stormed out of the house that night when he arrived at the door. Jealous of her mother and her visitor. He was worried about offending her, giving her the wrong idea about his interest in Matty. He had to signal to her somehow that she was his real goal.

HE HAD TROUBLE catching Matty at home for several weeks. He seemed to be convincing himself that he was just popping by, randomly, and wasn't it a sad coincidence that she was never there? In fact he appeared at her driveway regularly, constantly, like a foolish little cuckoo bursting wide-eyed from a clock. He almost ran into Leonard a few times, and after a while he gave up.

He assumed there was some extraordinary reason for her absence. Perhaps she had retreated to a nunnery, afraid of the passion he had awakened in her.

What was the truth? Was she not interested in him? Already?

He returned to spinning texts, to narrow hallways, lunch breaks, Wednesday afternoons.

It was he who retreated to the nunnery and it was becoming very clear that he was no longer enjoying it. He deliberately wiped his dirty shoes on his blue carpet. He caught himself whispering once, "Is there nothing real to do?" and was a bit embarrassed to catch himself. He had to do something, something grand.

Reading those myths reminded him of the glorious things the imagination produces. When he had read Ovid at university he had lost himself for hours, thinking of nothing but outlandish events and the sweet tortures of love. He imagined that when he left university his life might be as rich as all that; once the prudish restraint of childhood was shaken off, once the expectations of his family could be forgotten, the real world—his world—would be populated by giants, wit, and desperately romantic encounters. Sounds naive, but he wasn't. He was always wise enough to know that if things can be imagined, they can be created.

But how many years ago did that conviction first arise? What had he created?

It is the curse of being involved in policy. If you are involved in making policy you will know that no matter how active or industrious you may be there is always a sense of having done nothing in the end. You know perfectly well that it was your policy which led to a concrete result. But somehow in the face of the concrete result your policy looks like nothing. You feel a niggling uneasiness. Was your policy really responsible for that? Your policy alone? You start to forget how you had come up with that policy. You realize that no one else credits your policy for the creation of *that*, and as your own memory fades of how and why you came up with the policy it becomes even more insubstantial next to the result itself.

It is more than a fear of not being noticed, it is a fear of thinking you are one person, but then not remembering that person when you look back at him, or not believing he can have amounted to you.

THE DREAMBOOK mentioned a Museum of Childhood.

It mentioned an Odeon, a three-thousand-seat theater where only poetry would be read.

There was a plan for a hundred market gardens, which would leave the city self-sufficient in vegetable terms for three weeks a year. Laughs in pencil, "ha ha ha."

Sometimes when he opened the book he thought it laughed at him personally, but he realized that if he left it open long enough the pencilled scoffing of his colleagues would disappear. At the inky heart of the book were some serious, sad lost dreams.

Something could be built that would create rather than take away choice. Human possibilities could be examined rather than stifled.

Anything on the landscape takes away choice; he knew that. Houses, neighborhoods were the worst offenders—the same shapes framing everyone's potential. Put walls around a child and the child can't be free; take away paradise and Paradise will have to be imagined. But what if a building could be created where choice would be endless, where all substance, known and unknown, could be examined in miniature? A building where imagination could take form and where the consequences of taking hold of what is imagined would be minute.

There was such a structure in the Dreambook. I mentioned it.

Whenever he tried to visit Matty he would pass by that park on the edge of the Greenbelt, perhaps enjoying a rosy flush thinking of the flirtations he had enjoyed there, perhaps feeling regret over following flirtation too far. But whatever particular thoughts he had of the park, it was always in his mind when he was doing other things, when he wrote memos, when he looked through the Dreambook, when he spitefully wiped his feet on his carpet. It was no surprise that he thought of the park soon after he whispered, "Is there nothing real to do?"

MATTY HAD SEEMED pleasant enough, polite, when she and Simon said goodbye, but her absence had grown chilling. He didn't know whether he would have any better luck finding her at home this time.

"Hello, Simon."

"You're home! Finally. I was going to check for fresh graves around the city."

"We're having dinner at the moment."

"I'm sorry."

"Hello, Struthers."

"Hello, Schutz. Sorry to interrupt your dinner."

"Not at all. Come in. I'm afraid we've finished eating."

"I can't stay long."

"Oh well. Come in. Did you want to talk about work?"

"Um. Yes."

"Could it wait till tomorrow?"

"Absolutely."

"Do you really want to come in then?"

"Perhaps not."

"No, do come in, Simon. Heavens, Leonard. Come in and have a drink, Simon."

"Thanks."

Never mind what happened next. The door closed behind him.

Matty had been in Montreal, she said, visiting Kwyet, getting out of Ottawa, that sort of thing.

———

"It probably isn't a good idea if you come to our house when Leonard might be there, especially if you don't really seem to have any reason for visiting."

"I do have a reason."

"A reason that Leonard would like to hear."

"I was just curious about what you were doing. I was beginning to worry."

"That I was dead?"

"That you wished I were."

"I was in Montreal."

"Yes."

"And I didn't wish you were dead. I've just never…I've never had an affair before. It is an affair, isn't it?"

"I don't know."

"That's not very romantic. Aren't you supposed to say, 'It's Love,' or something like that? Anyway, Kwyet says it's a passing fancy."

"You told Kwyet?"

"Only that you had sex with me in her father's shower. None of the other details."

"I see."

"I'm kidding."

"I know."

"So why do you look pale?"

"Love."

"I don't feel like joking. I don't want to have an affair with you, Simon."

"Really?"

"Yes. I didn't…"

"You didn't like it?"

"Well, it's more than that, isn't it? I told you that sex is a bit pointless with me. Anyway, you don't have to feel like you're betraying someone. I know you don't like Leonard but he's the only man I've been with for more than twenty years. He can be pompous and I have to coddle his insecurities constantly, but when all you see is someone's vulnerabilities you hardly want to hurt them more. I know him. I know him like my own skin. I mean, I do want to hurt him sometimes, but not like this. Now you look hurt."

"No."

"I am attracted to you, Simon, but I just can't have an affair."

"Right."

"That seems to mean nothing to you."

"No."

"No?"

"Well, yes. What do you mean?"

"Perhaps I should visit your house sometime."

"Really?"

"I don't know."

"WHAT DO YOU want to know, Simon?"

"About what?"

"About me."

"Everything."

"Really?"

"No."

"That's honest."

"I have a theory."

"What?"

"That I am only interested in sexual things."

"Sounds like you may be right."

"Well, I am interested in you entirely. I mean private things more than sexual things."

"I must be dull, then. I do nothing in private. Leonard and I do nothing in private. That's not entirely true. We do things but I don't want to tell you about them."

"Why not?"

"Because I myself don't find them interesting. And now that I am reminded of them I feel a bit sick."

"Is he that unattractive?"

"No, Simon, I feel sick because I am betraying him. Would you mind putting your clothes on? I can't get used to you naked."

"I'm sorry."

"I don't mean to ask boring questions, Simon, but what are we doing together?"

"Let's not talk about that," he said.

"What should we talk about?"

"I don't know."

"Should I ask you what you do in private?"

"No."

"Why not?"

"Because it's private," he said.

"I see."

"I seem to do nothing but think of myself in private."

"That's no good. What do you hope for?"

"By thinking of myself?"

"No, I mean generally," she said. "That's something we can talk about. What do you hope will happen to you? What do you hope to do? Those are things I think about, in private."

"What do *you* hope for?"

"You first."

"I don't know. That's why I'm always thinking of myself. I'm always wondering what I want, I never know, but I am always aware of wanting."

"Like an alcoholic."

"Is it? I would have thought alcoholics knew exactly what they wanted. I don't know at all. I think I know, but then I try having it and I realize I am wrong."

"That's how one learns, presumably."

"I suppose. Alcoholics don't learn. What do you hope for?"

"I don't know."

"Really?"

"Not a clue. I hope for daily things…that Kwyet will call, that I won't lose my health, that sort of thing. That I can have peace and quiet but not be lonely."

"It sounds like your hopes are precise."

"No. I don't know what I want any more than you."

He wants to bite without tasting, taste without eating, eat without digesting, digest without losing, lose without regretting, regret without shame, feel shame without anger, grow angry without biting, bite without tasting.

"Matty?"

"Yes?"

"Can I take my clothes off again?"

The air in the park is like cream. The grass is fat and the leaves blow like flutes.

"Why don't you two skip?"

"Because mothers and daughters don't skip in the grass unless they're alone or in a man's fantasy."

"Really?"

"No."

"But I have seen Mum and Dad skip together."

"You should go ahead and skip, Simon. Kwyet and I will chat."

When the lion spies a herd of knobble-kneed delicacies cudding on the veld, he must, on occasion, feel confused. The delight, certainly, of running at them en masse must be great. But then two peel away. The finest two? One hopes. And when one of these peels away from the other, is there an epic battle of minute duration between instinct, hunger, mania, and indecision?

Yes, oh, yes, he was that lion. He may have been skipping in dew-lapped loafers. He may indeed have been skipping away from his prey. But he was that lion, oh yes.

"You said my daughter's name when we made love."

"Kwyet?"

"Yes. 'Oh, Kwyet.'"

"I was just saying 'quiet.' I thought we were loud."

"I wasn't loud."

"No, I was."

"You were telling yourself to be quiet?"

"Yes."

"'Oh, quiet'?"

"Yes."

"I wouldn't be surprised if you loved Kwyet. I don't know where she came from. Proud mothers always say that, but I think all mothers would agree that Kwyet can't have come from Leonard or from me."

"She has your intelligence and beauty."

"Your lies are predictable sometimes, Simon. What did she get from Leonard then?"

"Yes…Perhaps, not speaking in medical terms, her beauty is a metempsychosis of Leonard's voluptuous ideals."

"That was unpredictable. You've paid it some thought."

"No."

"Seriously, Simon, why were you telling yourself to be quiet when there was no one there but me? It's not as though our parents were downstairs."

"I don't know. It must have slipped out. It's your fault for not taking it seriously. If you took sex seriously I wouldn't feel self-conscious. Then I wouldn't tell myself to be quiet."

"I find it hard to believe that you wouldn't be self-conscious. You are the most self-conscious man I've met."

"Am I?"

"Don't look stunned. It's not a bad thing."

"I can't help it."

"Simon?"

"Yes?"

"It is getting late. Your colleagues will be wondering."

DID HE THINK of Kwyet?

Kwyet had been on his mind since the world first said no and his mind insisted, yes. No more jellies, Simon; no more playing, Simon; no more sleeping, Simon; no kissing, Simon (I'm your teacher); no cookies in bed, Simon; no more money, Simon; no kissing, Simon (she's your cousin); no making fun of fat boys, Simon; no crying, Simon; no leaving school grounds, Simon; no tongue, Simon; no, Simon, not there; no, Simon, not now; no ogling, Simon; no fondling, Simon; no, Simon, leather pants on boys are ridiculous; no, Simon, it goes like this; no, Simon, think of your father's reputation; no sex in dorms, Simon; no sex in girls' dorms, Simon; no sex with dons, Simon; no sex with Dawn, Simon (she's my wife); no sex for two months and *never* with me (I'm your doctor); no biting, no talking, no slander, no parking, no time, and no wine on a weekday.

"Simon?"

"Kwyet?"

"Don't forget about my invitation to Montreal."

"I haven't. I thought you might have retracted it."

"Why?"

"Last time I saw you—when you went baby-sitting—you seemed upset."

"..."

"Kwyet? Were you upset?"

"Come to Montreal in a few months. In a year."

"Why?"

"Don't you want to come?"

"Of course I do. Why in a year?"

"I don't know."

UNTIL HE KNEW everything he would never be at rest.

The wise cleric, sour of tongue, says, "Until you are at rest, you will not know everything." And you, pragmatic children of Locke, "Rest or not, you cannot know everything."

He didn't wish to know God. He didn't wish to know wisdom. He had no inclination to know the magic, faith, or chemistry that turns coal into motion, gas into water, a spinning jenny into glory of a nation. He wished to know nothing of the ground he walked on or the fabric of his bones.

But he did wish to know what private man and woman do when their doors are closed at night. The universe isn't hidden in an atom, it sits in the mind of a man at work who thinks a dirty thought; it's in the mind of your neighbor in her living room, flicking through her coffee-table book of dreams. What noble, envious, grasping, divine aspirations are playing behind her eyes? If he could collect each scintilla of emotion and perception. If he could record the precise notation of her coloratura climax as she writhes in the arms of adultery. If he could know you all, alone, the extremes of your despair, the remedies you barely dare to contemplate, your thoughts before they are tainted by language, your language, untainted by thought, which you babble in your bathroom. If he could learn every happynasty secret of each solitary mind, then he would know everything. Then he would know more than the men who search for wind on Jupiter, more than the men who know financial markets as farmers know their fields. Then he would be at rest.

And it follows, logically, that he would be interested in finding out where Kwyet baby-sat and observing her through a window.

There she is now, in the room through there, in this filthy house.

Where did Mummy and Daddy go? What does Daddy think of his baby-sitter, this dark-haired answer to every conceivable yearning?

There's our Kwyet. Who's the lucky little boy? I suppose he is handsome enough, but not enough for her. None of the requisite age and experience. Unhand her.

Oh, look, an airplane! Where did she get that from? She consorts with a pilot. Does he give her model airplanes?

Good heavens, the boy likes the airplane more than he likes Kwyet. Look at *her*, son, *her*.

Neeeeeyoooww, vvvvvvvv—no, no, give the plane back to Kwyet, there we are, they can't fly backward—vvvvvvvv. Look at her hand, little boy, look at the grace and force of it: an argument with five elegant conclusions. Ask her if you can touch her hand. But you do, don't you? You can. There you are now, touching whatever you like. Ask her if he can come in and join you. Please?

Oh, look, there he goes. Yes. He is off to the bathroom. That's right. Leave her alone for a minute. What do you look like alone, Kwyet? The smile slowly dwindles. How long? Still a trace of a smile. He is long gone, Kwyet. Why are you still smiling? He can't be that charming. Perhaps you can hear him in the bathroom. Is he singing? Maybe you hear an adorable tinkle. No, you are above that. Why are you still smiling?

Now here he is, back. With a banana? Why do they keep bananas in the bathroom? He must have gone to the kitchen, not the bathroom. Get Kwyet to peel that for you—yes, clever boy. She does that very well. Perhaps you would like her to have a bite? No?

What are they talking about? What is he saying that's so engaging? There is room on that couch for Simon. Perhaps he should ring the doorbell. What would his excuse be? "I heard you were flying planes. Can I join you?" They would both like that, a fellow enthusiast.

Is that a book now? How many props do they need? A picture book? Surely he is too old for that. Maybe it will make him sleepy.

Oh, she is coming over. Wait. Careful. She is coming over. Can she see him? No...don't...no...no!

There must be more windows somewhere. Who designed such a fortress of a house?

HE EVEN WATCHED Leonard on occasion—followed him in his car when he left the office. He had his reasons. Not an interesting man, Leonard, mind you, but the information gained became useful. Simon's secretary had suggested that Leonard had arrangements with builders. Simon followed him, saw him affording indulgences that even those in ministerial ranks seldom enjoyed (meals at Madame Berger's twice a week; a new car for Matty). Matty herself may have known that Leonard was doing something suspect. She often pretended that keeping Kwyet at McGill was difficult, as though Leonard had coached her to plead financial hardship when they were obviously well-off. A bit of disingenuousness from Matty made her all the more attractive.

Of course, Simon was careful not to find himself cornered into conversation with Leonard, but it happened sometimes.

"Struthers."

"Schutz."

"I've noticed that you have been visiting my house a lot."

"I have been in that area lately."

"In the precise area of my house."

"As part of a general exploration, yes."

"I have smelled your cologne in my house."

(Simon wears a beautiful cologne, repellent to all men.)

"Certainly, I have visited your house, yes."

"All of our colleagues know that you have visited my house."

"And now you will have to invite them over as well?"

"That is not my point. I am perfectly happy to have my colleagues over."

"I wouldn't blame you. A house like that. Very new. *Very* grand. The cupboards are oak, aren't they?"

"That's not my point."

"But I'm sure it's nicer than my house. Not inside, but structurally."

"I'm sure it is, Struthers. But that is not my point."

"Before you come to your point...will you come to your point?"

"Yes."

"Before you do, I should say a few things about my visits to your house. An official report, in effect. I have been remiss in informing our colleagues of my activities. Shall we sit down?"

"No."

"First of all, of course, I have visited your house socially. I called on you one evening, you will remember."

"That was not social. You came for professional reasons."

"It became social."

"Yes, but you came for professional reasons and I am not sure you really came for them. I find it hard to believe that you came just to see me."

"Touché, Leonard. And subsequent visits, aside from being sweetened by the presence of your wife..."

"Watch your tongue..."

"Were professional. I have been gaining a sense of the area, following your lead really. Those initial field reports you conducted were invaluable, inestimable. I thought a similar sort of investigation of the area as it has developed..."

"Get to the point, Struthers."

"As it has slowly developed, would be useful. Glossing over my observations of several crucial areas of undeveloped land, I will concentrate on your house—our mutual 'point,' I think. You see, your house, on the edge of this developing territory, is indicative, I think, of the sort of development, dwelling, we might expect. Am I boring you?"

"..."

"The sort of dwelling we might expect in the future. Affluence. Wealth. What do you think, eh, Leonard?"

"What?"

"Wealth. I can scarcely believe the sort of wealth your house represents. I could scarcely afford a house like yours. I'm sure you are one of those solid, not-quite-noble people who despise inheritances, so you may not take this point. But without my inheritance I could scarcely afford a house as sound and grand as yours."

"It was not that expensive."

"You are too modest, Leonard. I have long recognized that fault in you. It represents remarkable affluence..."

"A mortgage can get one anything."

"It is remarkable, and, maintaining my professional observations, I think we should take you, and your family, as indicative of the sort of person generally who will be interested in that area."

"That sort of development is not indicative of everything going up in the south of the city."

"In the Greenbelt."

"I think it should be less green."

"So do I, Leonard. Less of your remarkable *green*, eh, Leonard? Have a laugh with me. What was your point?"

"What was your point, Struthers? Are you threatening me somehow?"

"I was only giving you an idea of what I might report to our colleagues. What was your point?"

"Never mind."

"I have a meeting."

"So do I."

And so good day to you, you oozing bag of faux foie gras, may God forgive your excesses. Is it really possible that you are the planet around which those moons who are his eyes revolve? He won't pretend to understand what isn't superficial, Leonard, and he cannot understand your charms. What drew those women to you? I realize that Kwyet had no choice, but what an impossible issue of pestiferous loins.

And what if he really upsets you? What if, one day, he is relaxing on the toilet in C Wing and you are shuddering in the cubicle next to him, shaking with grief over something (what, your wife's betrayal of you?), will you realize he is next to you? Will it all be so revolting, empty, and cruel?

You are on to him. I know that. He is in love with your wife and your daughter. Maybe he feels the same as you did when you first fell in love with Matty. I doubt it. Oh, your Kwyet, Leonard! He had no idea who she was.

SIMON'S SECRETARY had let it be known that Simon was interested in Matty.

His colleagues shunned him all the more. He made decisions entirely on his own, when in the past he would have had some sort of discussion. His silence at work had once been a voluntary ploy. His mystery was being exposed.

He began to feel that his juniors in brown trousers were scornful of him. Did even they know that Matty was only the beginning, the mother of desire?

EVEN BACHELORS—the ones he knows who never talk about sex, the ones who do great things—even they are more precious than the philosopher's stone. That land they occupy by the shores of celibacy in the tropic of self-love, what do you know of that, my wise men of science? Perhaps some of you occupy it yourselves, or look through one of their windows. Publish what you see. He wants to know. I watch them often. Not as much fun as others, but fascinating. I am one myself, but I am not the sort I mean. The clean ones, the kind ones. They read books at night, some of them. Imagine reading a book on your own, at this youngish age, no pleasant distractions to look forward to, no fooling, no wife to grope or child to scold, no dalliance with pornography. Are they celibate, truly celibate and content with solitude? Tell me. I can't see them in their bedrooms.

And what is in the mind of a nine-year-old boy, who toys with an airplane in the lap of impossible Kwyet?

What about a nine-year-old girl? I'm sure there are wonderfully bizarre, kaleidoscopic fantasies that can barely be embodied by teddy bears and favorite dolls. I am not talking about sex, my stout captains of industry, nor, necessarily, about your own dull daughters. I just want to know their heights of madness and apolunes of reason. Where have we arrived if we can thrust impregnable buildings into space but have no idea why a girl would hit another? Where do we arrive if, as we drive along macadamized roads to new places, we roll up our windows when we feel the breeze of psyche?

Where have I arrived?

At the verge of this park with two Cokes, one for Simon and one for Matty (who will be along shortly).

Here she comes.

"I NEVER THOUGHT that an affair would be acknowledged, more or less calmly, by a husband and a daughter—you know, not quite accepted, definitely not approved of, but at least recognized, and without fights and tears and all that. By both of them. In totally different ways, mind you. Leonard hasn't said anything, really, but he told me he approached you at work. He said he 'confronted' you about why you were spending so much time at our house. So I asked him why he would do that, and he didn't say anything. I think he has decided not to say anything in case I feel embarrassed."

"Your straw fell out of your Coke."

"And Kwyet…she knows all about you. I think she might be ashamed of me."

"Surely not."

"She hasn't been upset. She just says barbed things. I feel ugly, Simon. I think she *is* upset. I'm alienating my family. For what? I always thought there would be more obvious drama. Leonard shouting, Kwyet crying. All the drama is in my head and it's very small. Ugly. It's my family watching me. I am the silly drama. Do you want to hear any of this?"

"Of course. I'm just fascinated by what your straw looks like on the grass."

"I wouldn't feel so small if we all had a fight—a huge confrontation."

"I wouldn't enjoy that."

"I'm not talking about you. My family."

"Right. Wouldn't it be preferable to carry on deceiving?"

"Why?"

"Well, you say you feel small now. Doesn't the truth make everything smaller?"

"No."

"It takes away possibilities. It would take us away—this moment in the park."

"What is this moment in the park, Simon? I'm telling you about how miserable I feel."

"Exactly. Anyway, it's more than that. It can all be more. I think you would find your drama larger if you didn't actually fight. It can be so much larger in your head. Every look of Leonard's could mean so much more."

"You're speaking quite dispassionately, aren't you?"

"I just don't want you to say what you met me to say."

"What...Let me put it this way. Being with you..."

"That straw, for example. That can be much more than a bit of litter in the middle of the park. Let's say we are giants, Matty. What could that straw be?"

"It would be smaller if we were giants."

"It would be bigger. Bigger to normal people. Let's say we are giants."

"I don't *want* to say we are giants, Simon. I think I would prefer to tell you what's bothering me. You are a total stranger to me. You may as well be a giant."

"Really?"

When you people finally build your buildings, or feel the wind on Jupiter, do you feel a bit disappointed?

I suspect that when Atalanta and Hippomenes were changed into lions they were pleased to be able to run again.

"It's over, Simon."

"Let's say it isn't."

"It is. I want it to be."

"Let's say it isn't. Let's say we are giants, Matty. And that straw is gigantic. It's a wind tunnel. It's a glorious great wind tunnel and we are giants."

"I'm betraying my husband."

"I have nothing, Matty."

Part Four

1

Now i'm dancing. We're all dancing. Kathleen's there, Jerry's having a dance, Edgar's there, in the corner. You will notice that the four of us can't dance for shit and that Edgar's hair is looking ridiculously big.

Jerry's nine or so (ten?)—old enough to know what music is and that dancing is supposed to match it somehow. I'm dancing like there's something I've got to nod yes to all the time. The music's fine, good enough to make me want to nod, I guess, and, sure, we're having a good time. But it isn't Johnny Cash.

And look at Edgar's fuckin garden of a hairdo. Hilarious. Kathleen's doing her arms-raised-above-her-head dance, like she's cheering for herself. Looking down at her hips and cheering for them. And she's turned toward Edgar, maybe cheering for his hair as well.

No, it's a celebration, definitely. It is a fun little party. The last in that house, you see—that's why I'm encouraging everyone to spill drinks on the carpet. We just finished eating our last meal there, which Edgar, of all people, cooked. I didn't tease him too much about that, but, come on; a man frying a steak is one thing, but a man trying to make little *things*, little eaty *things*, that I don't like the names of—that's a man who needs to take life more seriously. It was a good enough dinner, not as good as one of Kathleen's, but Kathleen was carrying on, you know, "Edgar, sure, that's truly feckin delish," and all that. Good old Jerry didn't eat much of his dinner, and he threw it up later because, whether he tries to or not, he will always make me proud.

So, yes, I'm a little tipsy like the rest of them. Sober little Jerry has no excuse for dancing badly. But he's not so bad.

"You're not dancing so badly!"

"What?!"

No, he's not so bad. But look at Kathleen. She's stumbling.

"What?!"

Such a pretty stumble.

We raised a glass to leaving. That house was old, not that old, but anything old has to be examined, evaluated, and usually left behind. Why choose old when I can make it new? Cheers.

Look at Edgar now, though—skinny shoulders and that gigantic animal on his head.

"You're a riot, Edgar!"

"What?!"

Cheers.

It was nice of him to cook. It's nice to have friends to celebrate with, but, you know, I wouldn't have insisted. Kathleen said let's have Edgar over and have a last blowout, we'll dance and it'll be grand, we'll blow the arse off the house or some nonsense. I said we should have a bit more respect, maybe just the family having a nice dinner, maybe the Man in Black humming deep-felt solemnity in the background, you know, baby, humming praise into these walls I built, because we may have had a couple of struggles here but it was our first house, and we made life where there was nothing, you know, I was feeling kind of biblical. Well, I'm sick to my guts of cooking for yez, is what she said, and little Jerry, with a funny wise look on his face that I'd never noticed, interrupted her and said, "I want a party."

Anyway, it's nice. This song's kind of fun. I don't know what it is but yes…yes…yes…is what I've got to say. And Edgar and I did, after all, have a fair amount to celebrate. The suburb is underway, my friend, two phases McGuinty, three phases Davies, completed, and, I'll be darned, if that isn't a shopping mall emerging between them, of which Messrs McGuinty and Davies have a sweet little percentage. There is also, of course, the fact that I am moving into a huge white beauty of a self-cleaning wonder with marble floors, a piece of the sky under every ceiling, and walls of creamy steel.

Oops, I just spilled an entire bottle of beer on the carpet. Look at that, Kathleen, you try it. No? She's celebrating Edgar's hair.

We did have all that to celebrate, Edgar and I, but we had done enough I thought. We were out together all the time. Constantly. Little Jerry wanted a party because we were always leaving him at home while we celebrated with Edgar. Maybe he just wanted what Mummy wanted.

Oops. Mummy stumbled again.

I'm going to bed.

NOW, IN THE NEW house the floors were in fact marble, and we had sliding doors. Sliding doors are very clever. You probably don't have them in your house. What other doors can be truly half open like sliding doors? There's no point in having normal doors half open, but when a sliding door is half open you get a better circulation of air and they let other rooms wink at you.

WE MOVED IN ourselves. I never use professional movers because they are without a doubt the stupidest men in the world.

It took me about a week to get everything from the old house into the new, and Kathleen was responsible for arranging it all. Cleaning it, fluffing it up. She was terrible at it.

Going from one to the other like that, from the old blue house to the new, huge white one, made me feel like we were jumping from evening to noon, like a bruise was healing.

But guess who helped us with the move. You could never imagine how heavy one end of a couch is when you have to look at Edgar's hairdo holding up the other. I told him, I said, "You might as well help Kathleen. Stay and help her move things around."

Little Jerry always asked if he could come and help me, but I told him he would be more use to his mother.

"Stay here and make fun of Uncle Edgar's hair," I said. But Jerry didn't find that funny. He really started developing his serious face around then. I had expected him to be all excited about being in a new house, but he always wanted to ride in my truck. "Seriously, Jerry," I said, "you're more help to Mummy. She'll need your strong arms to help shift things around." I myself have always appreciated being called strong.

So, after a while we were in, and I said to Kathleen, "Now that we're getting settled we probably don't need Edgar's help so much."

"No?"

"No. He's always wandering around here. He's a nice guy, but let's ask him to wander somewhere else for a while."

"You ask him."

"I will."

I didn't see him socially for a while. On-site I saw him often.

"Jer."

"Edgar."

But not in my house.

I was busy. You would expect nothing less of me by now. I was spinning, running, buzzing, trying not to touch anything for too long because the world was white hot. Everything was going, boy, humming, you needed to watch it all, everything. Just those few hours each night that I spent moving cost my business thousands. The phone was always ringing, at home, in the office— once, in my sleep, I picked up Kathleen's hand and answered it, "McGuinty here."

Buzzing, ringing, the telephones became white hot, and I stopped answering them. There was no time to sit still on the phone.

Phases three and four in the works, five on the verge of approval, I needed more men, more administrative help, I needed agents now to help me sell the houses.

"McGuinty here."

"McGuinty here."

"McGuinty here."

Endless goddamn meetings. I got so lost and tangled in that shopping-mall project, making sure my investment and bit of labor were working the right way. Those angel demons in the suits had me hypnotized, had everyone moving wherever they wanted, because they were so smart.

Whenever I was at the site office, an angel demon would step through the door and say, "Mr. McGuinty, I've just got to confuse you with mathematical language for a minute and then take you outside to introduce you to an unforeseen complication," and when I followed him outside the complication would be so white hot that I couldn't look at it for a month or two.

One day I discovered that a surveyor had pegged a road directly through the middle of eight intended houses, and my men had already started paving. "It's only a few hundred thousand," I say to the surveyor, while I see out of the corner of my eye one of the angel demons actually stuck in some fresh cement—both shoes stuck—and who runs over and clocks him in the eye? Mario Calzone. So while I'm arranging to sue the surveyor, one of my men is facing an assault charge.

It was like that constantly, not always so dramatic, but Hot.

Same for Edgar. I caught up with him at meetings sometimes and chatted with him afterward, but he always had to run away. He was too busy to look me in the eye.

I was too busy to watch my men, my men were too busy to listen to instructions. I made Cooper and Antonioni my deputies, foremen of small crews. Tony started wearing a tie, "for respet," he would always say, forgetting the "c" like he forgot that his tie got in the way of his carpentry.

Everything got more political. Unions started behaving like sulky girlfriends. If I didn't give them little gifts or promise a Big Gift in the future, they would send men out with clipboards who had little talks with my men, just near enough to me so I heard certain words: "action," "lose your rights," "can't afford," "danger." I had to do things on any union whim.

And, eventually, I had sex with a Real Estate Agent.

LET ME PUT it this way: over the last year in our first house I had spent exactly 31 minutes inside Kathleen. Never mind how many separate occasions it took to reach that total, and as for how I knew the total precisely: we had a new digital clock with big numbers.

Let me put it another way. I wish numbers like 31 could tell a complete story because I would leave you with a number and you would understand me perfectly. 1 = loneliness, 2 = want, 3 = revenge, 4 = the effect on my goof mind of a woman's apple ass, 5 = the total irrelevance of 1, 2, 3, and 4, 6 = every thought I don't have time to number. $1 + 2 + 3 + 4 + 5 + 6$ = half a minute between the legs of a woman with a blazer and a golden scarf, who was probably funny and nice.

Up yours if you want to judge me.

"DAD?" SAYS MY young ten-year-old to me. Maybe he was eleven or twelve.

"Yeah, buddy."

"I want to fly airplanes."

"OK, buddy. Where do you want to fly them?"

"Do I need to understand numbers to fly?"

"Maybe. Probably."

"I don't understand numbers."

"Fuck it, buddy. You don't need numbers. Fly your dad somewhere warm."

I THOUGHT THAT Kathleen would be a bit more hospitable, you know, in the new house. I bought us a new bed and said things like, "We've got to break that in," "Time to get our money's worth," things that were neither funny nor effective.

She was hospitable in other ways, though, to strangers. After about a year she said, "Do you know, Jer, we've been here about a year?"

"Really?" I said.

"That's right," she said. "And it's time for us to have a party."

"Really?"

"That's right. A real party. What's the point in having such a big flippin house if we don't have a party?"

"We could have another kid."

"I know that I could, but whether you could is another ting, Jerry, and besides which a party is less work. Let's have a party."

It didn't seem like a bad idea to me, actually. I could invite a few of the union guys, maybe even some angel demons. But what kind of party?

"A classy party," she said. "Like the house. A big flippin blowout, but classy. It'll do yiz good, won't it? Invite some of them bigwigs of yours. But yooz'll have to mind your p's and q's. Wear a tie. And I'll make some classy things, whore doves and what not, little tings like what Edgar made for us."

"Everyone will laugh at us."

"What?"

"They'll laugh if we make those little things."

"Ah, Jerry, that's class, you see. You don't recognize it. Just trust me now."

So we had a party, a huge party—about a hundred people or so. We could fit most of them in the foyer, which made me proud, but gradually everyone spread through the house like a spilled drink.

I greeted most of them at the door.

"How are ya?"

"How are ya?"

"How are ya?"

I knew most of them, but I didn't know the wives of some, and there were a few people Edgar had invited (Kathleen said he could). Buzz Harmon was there—union guy (Plasterers). Hank Buley, Rip Hancock, Wayne McKenzie. Solid union men you had to have on your side. They admired my work for most of the night, which they were obliged to do on account of politeness and the quality of the work.

Kathleen served food.

"Whore doves?"

"What's that?"

"That one's, like, chicken, but wrapped up special, those are stuffed mushrooms, and those are the devil's eggs."

"Shit. I'll try them."

They actually liked the food, and they liked Kathleen of course, so that little pocket of union acquaintances was successfully taken care of. I wandered to people. People wandered to me. It was a party.

One of the angel demons came, a Mr. Singleton, who I always liked. He spent his time talking to little Jerry, who was stationed behind the bar.

("People ask for a beer," I had told him before the party, "you just grab the opener and pop off the cap, pour it in a glass if someone wants a glass. Some of the ladies will want wine. Ask them if they want red or white, then pour it in those glasses there…"

"I know, Dad."

"OK. And if people want rye or scotch, you just pour a bit in the bottom of those glasses…ice over there…"

"I know, Dad.")

It was a great little job for him, you bet, and that Mr. Singleton was complimenting me on my son while we stood in the family room.

"Your son Jerry, Mr. McGuinty, made me an excellent scotch and soda. Just the right amount of each. And he says he would like to be a pilot. I am most impressed, Mr. McGuinty."

That Schutz guy was there as my Government contact. All bases covered. I had been getting his daughter to babysit Jerry sometimes, which is why he said, "Kwyet says hello to that young man of yours, Mr. McGuinty." And I said, "Right," because I didn't want to say much to him.

I told him my young man was serving drinks so he should go and make use of him. It wasn't kind to Jerry, but I couldn't stand that Schutz guy. I can't explain why. His daughter was nice. Beautiful. But I didn't feel much of a need to talk to him, and I also wanted to show that I was mad at him as my Government contact (they had threatened rejection of every phase).

Who else was there?

Antonioni was there with his wife. I had invited Cooper but he told me he would rather fuck his own ass. Tony and his wife stood near the union guys to let them know he had done some work on the house. One of them started hitting on Tony's wife, so he grabbed her and left early. It was a party.

Where was Edgar? I caught glimpses of him, but I couldn't find him when I looked. You need to have friends at parties so you can talk to people who don't mind you not listening to them. But I couldn't find him.

Oh, there he is!

No, he's gone.

I couldn't talk to Kathleen because she was busy passing around food and wearing this terrifying face of happiness. When she finished with the food I tried to catch her, but I couldn't move quickly because of the crowd.

I was in the family room and I saw Edgar go through the sliding door toward the foyer, and Kathleen go through the other sliding door toward the kitchen. Either way I went, then, I would catch up with a friend.

"Excuse me."

"Sure, Jerry."

"Excuse me."

"You bet, Jerry."

"Excuse me, Schutz."

"Oh, sorry."

"Excuse me."

"Jerry! Have a drink with us!"

"I'll come back. Excuse me."

I chose the kitchen door, expecting that Kathleen would be in there more or less alone. When I slid it open the kitchen was full and Kathleen wasn't there.

"Excuse me."

"Sorry, Jerry."

If I pressed through to the dining room I would catch her, but she moved too quickly. Once I was there I saw her go through to the living room.

"Excuse me."

"Hey, Jerry!"

"How are ya? Excuse me."

And at least when I was in the living room I would have a good chance of bumping into Edgar there.

"Excuse me."

But when I got to the living room, I couldn't see Kathleen. I looked through to the foyer and saw Edgar going back through the door into the family room, in a circle. I made it into the foyer and gave up.

Buzz and Rip were standing near me. "Who but God could touch that ceiling?" I asked them.

"Cheers, Jer."

"You know it, Jer."

And I went outside because I felt a bit cramped. I had drunk enough not to notice the cold, so I sat on the top step of the porch. I've noticed that whenever people step outside from a party for a break, they always look a bit wise—they wear a look that says they must be more interesting than the party inside. Smokers especially. I was probably wearing one of those looks.

I didn't really intend to think of anything but my mind seemed to want to go back to the hours before the party.

Kathleen had been wearing this pink spongy jumpsuit which she always wore when she was being efficient. (Jerry told me the other day that he used to try to avoid her whenever she wore it.) She had gotten up early and was banging cupboards, making the kitchen sound like a firing range. The theme of the day was "Why don't you help me? *Don't* help me!"

When I got down to the kitchen the first thing she said was, "I want every one of your tools put away before you do anything today, before you say anything to me. It's like two kids and not just the one."

It was fair warning to treat her gingerly, so I tiptoed behind her and went to make some toast.

"What are you doing?"

"Getting a bit of breakfast."

"Didn't you hear me?"

"What?"

"Pick up your goddamn toys from around the house. I'm not doing any cleaning until you pick up your tools. You were lying in bed, playing with yer penis no doubt, while I've been down here busy. You would think this party was for me."

Jerry walked by the door of the kitchen so I called good morning to him and offered him some toast.

"Don't you bring him on to your side now. He was in here when I came down this morning…eating…sitting up there eating his own peanut-butter toast like he was King Flippin Shit of the Manor. I've already told him off, so don't go bringing him on to your side. Just put the bread down and pick up yer toys."

So I got out of her way for a while, picking up my tools from around the place. You shouldn't believe her when she implied they were all over the place. But it took a surprisingly long time to

237

pick them up. I noticed one of my hammers had a hairline crack, which was something the manufacturer was going to hear about.

"Where the shit have you been?!" was the next thing I heard from her. "We have six hours before that doorbell rings! Have we got enough booze?"

"I don't know."

"Check!"

We had far less than I thought we did. "Where's all our vodka?" I said.

"How should I know? If we're out you'd better get some. Well?"

"We're out."

"Well? Christ, Jerry, a bit of planning, eh? You want to impress your bigwigs, eh? Your Big Mr. Larges? You go out and buy more booze than you have ever bought, and if you're not back in an hour, I'll hurt you."

So I did just that. I can still remember the bill for the booze but I still don't believe it enough to say it aloud. I was back in forty-five minutes but it took me another forty-five to unload it all. Jerry helped me—that's when I had the idea of making him bartender at the party.

"While you two have been out farting, I've mopped every fuckin floor in here. Every one." She poked my shoulder for every floor in the house. "And the bathtubs, I've cleaned the bathtubs, the sinks, your disgusting toilet. And you," she tried to backhand Jerry's face but he ducked so she grabbed him and shook him. "How many times have I told you to make your bed, and on the one day I need you to really make your feckin bed, you still leave it a mess. Get out of my sight. You get out of my sight, too," she said to me. "Go look around at your *self-cleaning* house and see how goddamn clever it is when I'm in it."

I did as I was told and set up a few things wherever Kathleen wasn't. I quickly whacked some legs into some chipboard, and behold, my friend, a bar. I set that up in the family room and covered it with a tablecloth.

"What are you doing now?" she said.

"Staying out of your way."

"Well, how about helping me? How many times do I have to ask?"

"For God's sake, Kathleen, you've been shouting at me all day. Take it easy."

"I'll take it easy when I know I have people in this house, men I can rely on. This is your party, Gerald."

"My name is Jerry. It has never been anything other than Jerry. What do you mean, it's my party? This whole fuckin thing was your idea."

"Oh, if that's the sort of grammar you're going to use in front of your bigwigs, you might as well call it off. And don't you start FUCKin well SHOUTing at me, Gerald McGuinty, because I'll tell all your friends tonight, Edgar and the rest of them, how bad you really treat me. I'll tell your bigwigs what you are *really* like, about all your poking and begging in bed. I'll tell them about your vasectomy, Jerry, and then we'll see how well your business does. They don't have to live with you like I do."

It didn't stop. All day she kept shouting like that. She told Jerry that he would embarrass the family if he was the bartender because he would cock it up like he cocked up all his chores. It was only ten minutes before the first guests arrived that I was able to bring him around to helping me.

And when Kathleen got out of her jumpsuit, when she showered, fixed her hair, put perfume on...when the doorbell rang and every hair on our three necks stood up...when she emerged from the bathroom looking like the woman every healthy man dreams of...when she smiled and said, "Oh, I wonder who that is?"...when I answered the door and she came down my intelligent stairs in the body I built them for...when she said "Hello!" and smiled at the guests...everything was all right.

It was a party.

I WENT BACK in and joined the party because my ass was cold. There were still a lot of people there. I had a few whiskies to warm up, and I was lost in thought for a long time. I found myself laughing and saying "exactly" to every guest I encountered. There was a strange, steady bang in the background somewhere but I didn't pay much attention to it—sort of a "whirr, BANG, whirr, BANG."

Guests left.

"Hey, Jer, you're going to enjoy living in this house, aren't you?"

"Exactly. Ha ha ha."

"See ya, Jer. Catch you Monday morning, as always."

"Exactly. Ha ha ha."

Whirr, BANG, whirr, BANG, whirr, BANG.

I went to get myself another drink and I realized I hadn't noticed Jerry behind the bar for a while. Whirr, BANG. And that's when I became fully aware of the noise.

I followed it around, through the kitchen, and came to the dining room. There was Jerry opening the sliding door and banging it closed, opening the sliding door and banging it closed.

"Testing your father's craftsmanship, are you, buddy?"

"No."

"How come you're not behind the bar any more?"

He didn't say anything and went upstairs to bed. He had a handsome little curl on the crown of his head, a sort of an elegant swirl, like a king should have. I realized he had got that from me, but when I felt my own head I noticed that most of my hair was gone.

A NORMALLY reliable principle of development is that once it starts, it won't stop. There are breaths, little pauses, of course. But they are only breaths. Put a house on a piece of land one year, and a hundred years later you can be guaranteed a suburb. It's partly based on the principle that people don't know that they want something until they see it, and once they see it they want and want and want. But there is also the obvious practical explanation that once water, sewerage, and electricity are set, the rest is inevitable, and as long as those webs of pipes and cables can be joined to new webs, we spider developers will be happy and fat and you flies can rest in peace.

Continuous development, my friend, is a beautiful thing.

But if something gets in the way, if something prevents those webs from linking, you have an abomination. My phase five and other future phases were encroaching on what the Government was calling the "Greenbelt."

I don't know whether I need to say anything about the Greenbelt other than its name: green belt. A *green belt.* Green, like leprechauns and fairies, weird, imaginary, squeaky little freaks that make everyone sort of uncomfortable. Just because green is the color of leaves and grass doesn't mean it's not a fuckin weird color. There's nothing natural about it. A green belt. I think we understand each other.

Somehow it was growing into a buffer zone. There were our developments on one side of it and the airport on the other. What was being saved? The airport? It made no sense. And if we had to stop our developments on one side of it, and we couldn't develop again for miles beyond the airport, there would be one of those breaks in the web. An abomination.

I'll put it this way. You've got a city with needs, you've got a developer with ideas. The developer stakes his claim, the city commits some money, investors come in, roads are laid, the buildings go up, the city spreads, the needs increase, and it hums along like music. It can be such a beautiful thumping piece of music, even from one house to the next. In blocks of ten, I would put foundations here, frames up here, walls up here, mechanics here, painting here. Progress blowing from one block to the next like seeds in a springtime field. That is nature. That is music. You can't put an end to that.

AND LET ME tell you about green, in Ottawa.

It doesn't exist.

That land in the green belt was flat, white, and bitter. They talk about nature. Life. Drive near that area in the middle of winter and the only thing alive is the snow kicked up by your wheels, the snow that curls in the wind like evil empty questions. There's nothing green, nothing to cherish. See, I'm there in my truck on this flat unused land, and I'm in an Espolito mood; those snowy questions blowing in through the cracks and down the neck of my coat.

I see Kathleen, you see, I see her parked near the future phase five, and I pull over feeling fluey, and I watch her, that yellow standing out all the more because the snow is blowing today, my friend, blowing sideways so the world is flat and is only the color of cold. I should have felt relieved to see that truck, but I am realizing, pulling over, that she is such a stranger that I'm afraid to get too near.

What is she doing here in the middle of nowhere? *Such* a *nowhere*. Our sites are a mile away. Her work is a mile away.

I just can't get near her any more. I sit about a hundred yards behind her in my truck and I think about inching toward her, taking my foot off the brake a bit. I don't think about racing up to her and hopping in for a warm embrace. I wonder why I don't, and I tell myself it's because she's here, in the middle of nowhere. What's she doing here?

Before I can admit that really I know perfectly well what she is doing, her truck takes off. She kicks up a cloud of snow, and I follow. I don't know whether she sees me or not, but I realize that she is in a rush. She is racing away from our sites, away from work, and definitely racing. I'm speeding to keep her in sight and chasing her along this shitty gravel road that's never plowed. It's straight but any turn of the wheel would put us in a spin.

"Why are you running away from me, Kath?"

The snow was so cold it was like grease. She must have put a bit of weight on the brake and turned the wheel. The road was still straight so why she braked and turned I don't know. I found out later she was drunk.

I watched her tip and start rolling, and the only thing I could do was worry about stopping in time, and not sliding right into the upside-down truck.

Kathleen was upside down, buckled into her seat and bleeding from her mouth.

Somehow Edgar went through the windshield feet first. Halfway through. He was stuck at his waist, moaning fuuuuuuck, like he had made a mistake.

A GOLF COURSE. That's one thing I thought of. Keep it *green*, but useful.

"WHY EDGAR?"

"Who are you?"

"Why Edgar?"

"He's a man."

"Are you saying I'm not a man?"

"Nurse! Fuckin, Nurse! Tell Jerry I've spilled my chips!"

"I'm right here, Kathleen."

"Tell him to clean the oil in the truck, and fry it. Please? Pleeease?"

"MR. HERLIHY?"

"McGuinty."

"Was that your wife?"

"Was?"

"Whom I just treated? Is that your wife?"

"Yes."

"Did you bring her in?"

"Yes."

"She's a bit confused. Did you see her crash?"

"Yes."

"What happened?"

"She crashed...snow. Snow."

"Had she been drinking?"

"I don't know."

"She has a high level of alcohol in her blood."

"I didn't see that. I didn't see her drinking."

"The painkillers I've given her shouldn't react with the alcohol. She is still intoxicated. She broke two ribs, Mr. Herlihy."

"Her mouth was bleeding."

"She lost a tooth. There's no point in seeing her for a while. She is delusional. She seems to be concerned about her fries."

"She told me."

"I haven't finished examining her, but the ribs didn't puncture anything. You should let her rest."

I DON'T LIKE GOLF. I don't like sports generally. I hate golfers.

"WHAT ABOUT EDGAR?"

"Who?"

"Edgar Davies. He was in the truck. I brought him in with my wife."

"Someone else is looking after him."

"He was bleeding a lot."

"I see."

I SLUNG THEM both on the seat of my pickup, bleeding bags of cement, the pair of them, my friends. That's how they tell me— broken pieces of meat, bleeding the truth on my smelly tartan seats—We fuck each other, Jerry. I had to lay Kathleen, passed out, on top of Edgar, across the seat. There was no room for me to drive. I had to rest Edgar's head on my lap, both of their faces looking up at me.

"My legs, Jerry, fuuuuuuuuuuuuck, Jer, I'm sorry sorry sorry sorry sorry sorry. I'm sorry."

I should have got out, let them take care of themselves. Or tossed them in the back. Or let them drive. How about you bleeding bags of shit drive my pickup? I'll get out of the way.

"Get her off me, Jerry. My legs!"

"She's passed out."

"Get her off me. My legs, Jerry."

"She's passed out."

"SHE IS STILL delusional, Mr. Herlihy."

"Is she healing?"

"She should be. I can't get a sense of how she is feeling. She has to stay still."

"How long?"

"There's something else, Mr. Herlihy."

WHETHER IT'S golf or houses... Listen to me... Whether it's golf or houses or a gray goddamn parking lot, it's essentials.

I'm talking about essentials. What people need. How about ambulances? How about ambulances for my lying friends?

Check out my bleeding tartan. It's this fuckin cold outside and that blood won't freeze. It's all soaked warm and forever into that seat.

I'm talking about services. Essentials.

Sit on my bleeding tartan seat, and tell me how green, how natural it all is.

"I'M SORRY, JERRY."

"How many stitches, Edgar?"

"They don't know if the muscles will heal. I'm fuckin jelly, Jerry."

"How many stitches?"

"It's not the skin, man. It's the muscles."

"How *many* stitches? Just give me a number. Tell me how many times they stuck a needle into your legs. I want to hear it."

"I don't know."

"You look like an idiot, Edgar. Your feathered little hairdo. You can't fuck my wife, Edgar."

"I know, Jerry."

_____

"Mummy's fine. She hurt herself badly, but she'll be fine."

"I don't call her mummy."

"What do you call her?"

"Little boys say mummy."

"That's true. And Uncle Edgar, he basically shredded his legs, you know, back here, those calf muscles. But he's fine."

"How come they were driving together?"

"Do you want to see them?"

"No."

"How come?"

"Kathleen."

"I'm down here."

"I know. Can you see me? Open your eyes. It's me: Jerry."

"Where's Edgar?"

"Fuck Edgar."

"Am I all right?"

"I don't know. How do you feel?"

"Trapped."

"It's your ribs. You broke two ribs."

"How many have I got?"

"What?"

"How many ribs?"

"I don't know."

"I feel like a feckin bruise."

"You lost a tooth."

"I can feel that."

"Doctor thinks you swallowed it."

"How long have I been here?"

"A few days."

"It hurts when I cry."

"So don't cry."

"Can you see my tooth, my…where my tooth was?"

"Is that what you're crying about?"

"Fuck off, Jerry."

"You fuck off, Kathleen."

"I wasn't…I'm flippin sorry, Jerry. I was only wondering if Edgar is all right. I crashed the truck."

"I know you crashed the cock-sucking truck. I was right behind you."

"I'm sorry, Jerry."

"The doctor says there's something else."

2

SIMON KNEW a man who could help. Technically this sort of thing was a matter of aeronautics. This man knew aeronautics.

But it would be so much more.

3

I BANGED MY NOSE against a wall, that's all I did. I was dazed, pretty sore, nose out of joint, yeah yeah.

Having worked in construction I reacted to pain as all workers should. There is the split second when you feel the pain, and you curse, but after that, reason, calm sets in. You have to think reasonably about what to do about your pain because usually it's serious—nail through the foot, sawn-off finger tip. I spent a lifetime training myself to be calm after pain so I'd know what to do to make it better.

I was smarting from their affair and I was sort of swinging around, cursing. I had to decide what to do.

I am a reasonable man. Praise me. I am reasonable.

There were moments, maybe one or two, when I lost control, but not seriously. Edgar was in a wheelchair, for example, while he was in the hospital, and one day, the only day, when I persuaded Jerry to visit his mother and Edgar, I asked if he wanted a ride in a wheelchair. He was a big boy of twelve, so he probably didn't want a ride, but I didn't really give him a chance to answer. I just picked him up and put him in the chair while Edgar was still in it.

"Owwwwwchaffak!"

But, generally, you know, I was calm, reasonable, a strong and patient mountain of a man, God love me.

I can't explain it. I'm sure you understand. I have no doubt that you have been cheated on.

Kathleen had spent twelve years draining my blood into little bags. Now she was standing in front of me, juggling the bags around, tossing them over my head to Edgar. I had to be reasonable.

KATHLEEN GOT OUT of hospital before Edgar did. When she came home I said to Jerry, I said, "Watch out for Mummy," and he said, "I don't friggin call her that," and I said, "K."

She had to lie on her back a lot, stay still. She was helpless.

"I'm feckin starving, Jerry," she said.

And I said, "Jerry, fetch Mummy some toast or something, K, big guy?"

That started a pattern. I didn't have time to look after her, because the rest of the world was humming, you know, white hot, so Jerry did a lot of the looking after, a lot of the fetching and what have you. I didn't really have time to see Kathleen, to talk to her, listen to her.

Edgar was out of the hospital after a while. Do you know, as far as I know, they never saw each other alone again?

I didn't visit Edgar in the hospital once Kathleen came home and I hoped not to see him for a long time, but he visited me on-site one day when he was able to use crutches.

"Jer."

"Edgar."

"Can I buy you a coffee?"

"Coffee shop's not built yet."

"True enough. Can I pour you a coffee?"

"If you want." I didn't really know how to react and my ass was clenching its fist. I said, "You've probably got something to say but there's probably no need to say it, Edgar."

And he said, "No, man, I've got to say it, I've got to say it all."

And I said, "No, you don't."

"I do. Shit, I do, I'm sorry, Jerry, I'm totally…you know, *Full of sorry.*"

"Right."

"I am, Jerry. I can't explain it. Kathleen…you know. I don't know what she told you, but, shit, you know, I don't know about her, but that accident threw me. Maybe she's told you everything, but…I liked her, sure, but I know she loves you. You know, she's difficult, Jerry, and I know it's not my place and you probably hate me, you *should* hate me, but I don't know how to explain. I know she loves you, buddy, and me and her was just, you know, I don't know what it was."

"You don't…"

"Yeah, I do buddy. Shit, yeah I do. You know, it's eating me up, man, and I've got to talk to you. That accident. My legs are like balsa wood, man, and you know, I can't eat, because I'm *so sorry.* I feel kind of scared all the time. I can't eat, seriously. I couldn't eat before the accident even, because, seriously, I was betraying you, you know, I felt bad. And now since the accident for some reason I can only eat Jell-O, and…I can't even shave, you know, I feel too weak to shave. Did you see my beard?"

"I see that, buddy."

"And it doesn't even suit me. I'm this bearded, skinny pussy now, aren't I, and I know you don't care, man, you *shouldn't* care, but I've got to tell you how sorry I am, and sort of tell you what happened."

"I don't want to know what happened."

"We just, you know, it was just in her truck sometimes, not even that much, and it was…I know it's not right to say…it was kind of awful sometimes."

"I don't want to hear it…"

"I've got to, man. It wasn't her, it was me. It was only sometimes, honestly, for maybe a couple of years, but…"

"Don't…"

"I fuckin have to. I'm sorry. Seriously. It was mostly drinking, you know, having a laugh, like the three of us do, and I missed you, honestly, it's what made me feel awful. She missed you. She's a sad woman, Jer. It's not my place, but…you weren't there in the truck and we just, you know, it was like friends. Mostly drinking, warming up at lunch, that sort of thing. Sometimes, you know, even most of the time, we seriously didn't even want to, but, you know, this fuckin job. And I'm going all sort of, man, I just went all sort of, and I'm this, you know, this pussy, since the accident, I'm terrified. I looked at death…"

"Look, I'll tell you what, pussy boy, you hurt your legs. That's all."

"I know, Jerry, I know, I don't want you to understand. I know you *do*, I know you *can* understand, but I'm not asking you to. I looked at death, you know, and I realized I'm not a man. I am a man because it's easy for me to die, I can die any minute because I'm a man, but I'm not a *man*. I looked at it, you know, death, but I can't *face* it. I don't know what Kathleen says, but that accident changed my life. That day…you know, on that day, Kathleen, she's looking in her rearview mirror, you know, we weren't doing anything, and she's looking in her mirror and she says, 'Shit! It's Jerry!', you know, and she starts driving. Both of us were panicking, it's Jerry, it's Jerry, and she was bombed. We were drinking because it was so cold that day, but she was really looped. We thought, I guess she thought, you were chasing us. I'm so *sorry*. And it starts tipping. This terrifying tipping."

"Do you know what? I *really* don't want to hear it."

"I'm sorry."

"Enough."

"I need you…I know it's stupid, fuckin corny. I know you hate me, but please forgive me. Please forgive me, my friend Jerry, I am *that* fuckin sorry."

I didn't hear any of it. I know I just repeated every word for you but I have special powers. I can build houses, I can repeat conversations for you. I didn't hear a word of it at the time. Forgive?

"Forgive?" I said. Real forgiveness comes from really hearing. I didn't really hear him. "Look at your fuckin beard," I said.

"I'm hungry, jer!"
"Jerry, can you fix Mummy some soup or something?"

I couldn't get rid of that golf-course idea. I have no idea why I wanted to build a golf course, why I hung on to that idea. But it seemed like a good one.

A whole community, you see, a whole community brought together by a game—it's a sweet idea, even if you hate the game. And there's all that *green*. If green is to your taste, there it is.

I have never had reason to doubt my ideas. I don't think I told you, for example, that a particularly admired feature of my self-cleaning houses was a central vacuum system. It was an idea I had—I didn't invent it, but I used it *way* before it caught on, *way* before you and your friends might have got one.

The people buying my houses were rich. Rich people, and people who hope that they really are rich, like to play golf. Plus, even though I prefer to look at buildings, I understand that people like to look at grass and trees so it makes sense to give them an orderly view of those things.

I could build the same sort of house, Big, Self-cleaning, add the fun of a game, and give them some orderly green.

What was slowly becoming clear was that Edgar's development and my development were maybe a bit too close to each other, and the mall might not be enough of a division when it was finished after all.

Different types of people, you see. Edgar's cheap houses were bought by poor people, rowdy people, nice simple people of the sort I belong to but stupider. And the people buying my houses were people like you. Already, before everything was finished, people in my houses hated having to look at the people in Edgar's houses: they found their mailboxes on fire sometimes, beer bottles in their yards that could only have come from the people over there. It wasn't such a serious problem yet (it never became one actually), but I thought it might turn into one.

The golf-course idea, if I could secure the land, would avoid that sort of problem. The land I wanted came off the back of my phase five. I had already indicated to the Government, to Schutz, that I wanted it, and some of the angel demons were willing to put some money into it.

Imagine: a vast area of pure McGuinty forming a broad crescent around this golf course. The airport was nearby: planes could fly over and make the golfers feel even wealthier, at the center of an International Destination. (Not that my houses would be under the flight path.)

Fantastic.

THERE WAS THIS other problem that the doctor mentioned, "something else, possibly a concern." While he was checking out Kathleen, making sure she was OK, he found that there was something wrong with her liver. Some test or something.

I tried to tell Jerry about it when she was still in the hospital. I said, "I think it's bullshit, my friend, but Mummy might have something wrong with her liver." I don't know where the liver is but I gave Jerry a little chop with my fingers in his side. "In her liver," I said, chop, and made him giggle despite himself.

I figured it *was* bullshit. This doctor, you know. Doctors. I'm happy for them to buy my houses but I have no respect for people who look up people's asses all day and then behave like the view up their own is delicious.

He was up there on the high ground: "Your wife drinks too much, Mr. Herlihy," as if he would know.

I put it out of my mind. She was sick, yes, I knew that, but of course you're going to feel sick if you've betrayed your husband, almost killed a friend, broken two ribs, and lost a tooth. You can expect to look a little yellow.

She needed a lot of attention. Once her ribs healed and she

could move around a bit, she still felt a lot better when she was lying down. She was helpless for a long time, even when she could probably help herself. And since I was so busy, Jerry looked after her.

"Jerry!"
"Jerry!"
"Jerry!"
"Jerry!"
"Jerry!"

Less and less was it meant for me.

I guess he fed her often, because I don't really remember eating with them together and I doubt that either she or I cooked. I kept the house stocked up with food and juice and booze but I didn't have much of any of it, as far as I can recall.

We didn't sleep in the same bed because it would hurt her ribs to have me rolling around.

"Where's my feckin painkillers, Jer!"

"Jerry, get your mummy her painkillers, please."

She was on those for ages, and when that doctor said he wouldn't prescribe them any more I found another who would. She was clearly in pain, and they helped her sleep.

"I'm going to be late again tonight, buddy, so if you're making dinner for Mummy, don't forget to give her her painkillers."

"I know, Dad."

"I know, buddy."

I was home one afternoon, picking up some paint samples that I wanted to show the real-estate agent, and I just poked my head upstairs to see how things were going. Kathleen was asleep in her room, looking no different from when I saw her in the morning. Jerry was in his room.

"Hey! How are ya?"

"OK."

"Did ya...how's things?"

"OK."

"You look tired, buddy."

"I am tired."

"How was school?"

"She makes me come home early."

"Cool. Get out of class early?"

"Yeah. Cool."

He was pretty grumpy so I thought I should leave him alone. As I was leaving he said, "Dad?"

"Yeah?"

"You know Kwyet? My old babysitter?"

"Yeah."

"I don't see her much now, do I?"

"No. We aren't going out much, are we?"

"I saw her the other day, you know?"

"Oh yeah?"

"She came by here. She's nice, Dad."

"Sure."

"And she asked me…she wants me…she said I could fly in an airplane. She said she's got, like, a friend with, I don't know, who flies an airplane. Can I fly in…she said they could take me flying."

"Fuckin A, buddy. When?"

"Maybe on the weekend?"

"Can I wave at you?"

"I can go?"

"Fuckin A, you can."

"What about her?"

"Who?"

"Mum."

"Right. What about her?"

"Who will look after her?"

"Right. She'll be fine. I'll look after her."

KATHLEEN'S TRUCK was totaled, front axle snapped, steering rod all stupid, frame bent.

I scrapped it.

I kept some of the parts that were working. You know that one shitty pickup I've got on my driveway out there? That's got the engine from Kathleen's truck in it. That's nice, isn't it, like its heart is still beating.

What can I say about that truck? I didn't want to chase it any more. I wanted to scrap it. I might have scrapped it even if it wasn't totaled. Edgar in there fucking her.

I felt like there was a load of concrete on my chest when I looked at the truck all bent in the junkyard.

She could get another one, if she wanted. Maybe when she got better we could have a talk and she might get another. I personally didn't think it was a good idea, but maybe.

I told her about it one night. "I had to scrap your truck, Kath," I said.

She said, "Augh, Jesus, Jerry," very quietly, and cried cried cried with her hand on her ribs.

"Where's he going?"

"He's going flying."

"What?"

"Yeah. That Kwyet, the babysitter, she's got a boyfriend or something who can fly a plane."

"He's not going flying."

"Yeah, he is. He's all dressed for it."

"You're not going flying."

"Go on and wait for your friends, Jerry. Have fun if we don't see you."

"You'll feckin die up there is what's going to happen. They'll, they'll be necking and lose control. I won't be sorry."

"Go on, Jerry."

"Yeah. Off he goes flying and I'm here in this flippin bed again. Who's going to look after me? You, I suppose."

"That's right."

"I don't need looking after. See how quickly he ran out of here? That's because he thinks he looks after me too much. I can tell. I spent twelve years looking after him, doing everything for him, and now he complains about looking after me for, what, a few months. I could get up, Jerry. I'm not that sick, but I think it's time I was looked after for a while. Not that I like lying in this… fffeck… freckin bed all the time."

"I thought I might do some tinkering in the basement."

"Yeah, well, you go on then."

I saw Jerry getting into a car with his friends when I went downstairs. Kwyet had called to get permission, by the way. Nice girl.

THE CHIEF PURSUITS, you might say, at that particular point in my life were selling a lot of houses and putting together the golf-course proposal.

As far as the house-selling went, I had taken the decision to get a real-estate agent, and that led to the less business-oriented decision to slide inside her for thirty seconds. She was a pretty girl, lipstick, just the type to sell a lot of houses, and we seemed to flirt with each other every time we met.

So I met her one day in a house that was going to be a model home. I brought a few color samples and got her opinion for the paintwork. She held my hand when I was holding a color and we laughed at the name, "*California Dreamin,* ha ha ha," and next thing you know I'm between her legs and my entire body is shouting. I was heavily aware of my own weight after those thirty seconds. I had a cramp in my leg so I couldn't get off her as quickly as I should have, and about all either of us could say once I did get off was "golly golly golly" whether we actually said it or not.

She was a really nice girl. I felt so guilty, and ashamed for feeling guilty, and embarrassed that it took me thirty seconds, and when I gathered together all those color samples with all the silly names it was like they knew what I was feeling. I wanted to run away and hide, but she had the Christianity to say, "That was nice."

Oh, my friend, it was not nice.

But enough. I am not going to explain myself for the sake of your weird curiosity. I was unfaithful to Kathleen, that's all you need to know. I bought her some roses and a nice bottle of vodka—to apologize without telling her anything—and spent the evening at home.

As for the golf-course proposal, my other chief pursuit: I told Schutz about it, gave him a bit of money, and he said he would do what he could, but as much as that guy puffed himself up he didn't have much power over his department. What I proposed was this:

200 houses, strong, self-cleaning;
1 golf course, 9 holes, green.

Like you, I had never built a golf course. My instinct told me it involved more than a lawnmower, so I made some inquiries and discovered that there is a type of human called a "golf-course architect" who seems to think it is a respectable career to build sand castles. If the game of golf seems a little silly to you, imagine a man who treats a blade of grass like a house, a lawn like a city, an acre like an empire, an empire whose only purpose is to support a small white ball and a clown.

Well, the fact is, I can admire that man's career more than most, and there were a few moments when I actually loved the silliness of it—when I learned how complicated it all is, the importance of soil, the drainage problems, the shaping of hills as walls or encouragements, the name of this grass: *fescue*. Fuck me, the world can be a wild shaken-up jumble of soul-tickling mysteries, so many little games for so many little people, and I want to play, yes, I want to play sometimes and make more mysteries.

Golf-course architects were not a common sight in Ottawa. I had to bring a guy up from Toronto who charged me for every breath he took once we got off the phone. And he said, "Well, see what the Government says first because there's a lot to consider these days, you know, environmentally."

And this is what the Government had to say:

Mr. Jerry McGuinty
McGuinty Construction
4 Kathleen Crescent
Ottawa K18 2N4

13 May 1982

File: 80814
Re: Blah blah, *Planning Approval Application: "The Green" Residential and Recreational Development* blah blah

Dear Mr. McGuinty,

Thank you for your application, yadda yadda yadda.

As you may know, the approximately 800 hectares of land in Ottawa South, now commonly known as the Greenbelt, is an area of uncommon potential and precious resources, which has come to be monitored closely by this Government and this Division particularly.

Why is it monitored at all? That is a question often asked, the guy says, yadda yadda yadda.

A Capital plan must consider attributes such as the symbolic role of the Capital itself, and it must reflect the trust that you and your countrymen place in the Federal Government to plan the Capital properly.

What is the symbolic role blah blah *reflect the values that are central to Canadian society, including freedom, democracy, peace, order, good government, our vast geography, tolerance, respect for both official languages and offering general access to people with disabilities.*

The Capital is a window on our country, and it is important to keep that window clean.

As you know, Sustainable Urban Development involves maintaining and enhancing the quality of the biophysical, chthonic, macrosocial, and petty economic components of the rural-urban cosmos for existing and future generations. Sustainable Urban Development is implemented through the protection of environmental components while understanding their inherent interrelationships and the both natural and artificially imposed balance between them. The quality of the biophysical environment can be enhanced through the protection of the air, water, land, flora, and fauna, and the evolution of an economy that respects the inherent limits of that environment.

We are all interested in creating a model of urban ecology, in developing a Capital Concept that fosters the emergence of a Healthy Community and that provides for continuous activities, throughout the day and evening.

So the little bloodless pencil goes on to say

4

that I look forward to considering your application more closely in conjunction with my colleagues.

As you may appreciate, this Division is overwhelmed with applications. You may be asked to submit supporting material, but we ask that you do not contact us with inquiries regarding the progress of your application.

Yours sincerely,

Simon Struthers
Melancholy Guardian of the Rural Urban Cosmos

IT IS A MASTERFUL little irritant, is it not, Mr. McGuinty? Please accept my apologies. A nice mixture, nonetheless, of modestly preposterous rhetoric and bewildering vapidity. I hope that you keep it; it is printed on acid-free paper and should last for generations.

I am sore, Mr. McGuinty. What is Eros spelled backward? That is right sir, sore from tip to tip from Love's return journey.

Saint Matty chanting her gospel of betrayal. What does a betrayer know of betrayal? Betraying me to cease betraying her husband.

He UNDERSTOOD that Mr. McGuinty was one of the builders who had had some dealings, a little quid pro quo with his boon companion Schutz.

Simon had his own designs on that land.

KICKED IN THE FACE by Time's busy boot. That's how he looked with those bags under his eyes.

He was getting uglier, there was no question about that. He caught glimpses of himself everywhere—at home, in the mirrors of his car, store windows—he looked constantly, and was patently disappointed with what he saw. Narcissus grown to hate himself.

Sometimes he would catch himself in a mirror smiling, and a look of self-awareness, shame, would cover his yellowing teeth. In restaurants, for example, a beautiful, incompetent waitress might knock his wine over and he might smile what he thought was a dashing boy's smile, "That's all right, that's all right, don't worry, it's funny," and he would see his smile in the mirror across the room. The change to his face!

The change was everywhere. The restaurants. They never existed before. That restaurant near Matty's which he now dined at as often as he could, that was never there before. Neither was the store next door where Matty often shopped. The restaurant was called an "eatery," a new word to him, more change. It was also a forlornery, a bringherbackery, an isKwyetintownery. From a window table at lunch he could see Matty shopping next door. If, on a Friday, she had an extra bag or two, it usually meant that Kwyet was in town for the weekend. If corn chips were visible in one of the bags—Kwyet had a weakness for corn chips—she was definitely in town.

He sat in the eatery every week and wondered if Kwyet would be near. He ate a lot of deep-fried zucchini and chicken wings, and the face in the mirror grew larger.

But what if Matty walked into the eatery and saw Simon there? Would she join him, have a happy chat? She had given him an ultimatum. "I don't want to see you any more. I can't even see you socially—it wouldn't work."

Simon considered that flattering: seeing him would be too much, he is irresistible, she would be overcome. Whenever he saw her from the window he was torn between calling to her, and wanting to hide. He would have no reason to give her for being so near her house.

He ate more chicken wings, more deep-fried vegetables, chili, veal schnitzel, the occasional Polish sausage.

It was what you men of morals call a State of Want.

Swedish meatballs, spaghetti bolognese, a half carafe of the house red, might as well make it a whole. Desire can be stupefying.

But if she was carrying the extra bag, if he saw corn chips through the shopping bag (like a leg through a sun-soaked skirt), he would spring to attention, crane his neck. Maybe Kwyet was still in the store? Maybe she was waiting in the car? Maybe he could run out before Matty noticed and slip Kwyet a note?

Week after week after week. The face in the mirror grew unrecognizable.

Chicken fingers with fries and the house plum sauce. Three-cheese melt. A bacon burger with salad and/or fries. Was he trying to look like Leonard?

The face grew shiny, sad, cruel. To be honest, it began to look like mine.

Dr. Paul Overington
National Research Council
1028 Montreal Road
Ottawa K14 6Z8

Dear Paul,

A voice from the past can be a pleasant surprise under controlled circumstances, no? So here I am, writing rather than calling.

This is a strictly professional communication. I was at a Cam-

bridge Society dinner recently and someone mentioned that you were now in charge of aeronautical research at the NRC. I have something that I would like to discuss with you—a proposal of sorts.

Could we meet? I would like to show you something, and I know a perfectly dreadful restaurant nearby. I could take you to lunch.

Feel free to call, or write.

Congratulations, of course, on your appointment.

Kind regards,
Simon

P.S. Do say hello to Evelyn, if you think it appropriate.

HE SAW HER AGAIN one Friday, sitting in the car waiting for her mother who had just run into the store. Now was his chance to talk to her. He planned to slip freely from the eatery, but he was stiff, awfully sluggish as he stood up, and slightly dizzy. He stumbled toward the door and the waitress said she'd see him later. It was very bright outside. When he got through the door he stopped defensively, shielding his eyes as if he had stumbled into some sort of inquisition. Out of the corner of his eye he saw someone emerging from the store next door. He realized it was Matty, already, so he quickly retreated into the eatery and watched her through the tinted glass door.

His car was near, so he decided to follow them when they drove away. Matty got into her car and Simon slipped more carefully out of the eatery this time and got into his own car.

Matty and Kwyet pulled away and drove the usual route to their house. But as they got near they took an unexpected turn left. Simon followed them at a safe distance. At one point Matty reached across and stroked Kwyet's cheek.

Imagine being inside the intimacy of that car.

Where were they going now? Another unexpected left, now slower, slower, careful. What were they doing? They were stopping.

Kwyet got out of the car. She stretched. Oh, she stretched! (When she stretches we can all stay still and hope.)

Then Matty got out of the car. She went around the front, Kwyet went around the back and got in behind the wheel.

Kwyet drove much more quickly than Matty. He could see Matty shrinking a bit, probably offering gentle suggestions about speed. He fell back from them, sped to catch up, fell back. They knew all the roads around there better than he did. They were all new roads (built by Leonard's friends, no doubt).

He knew where their house was though, and it was clear they were going somewhere else. It was a sunny day; perhaps they were just having a drive. Kwyet had sped up so much that he could see only the shine of the car's paint, and when she turned a corner he saw nothing.

He drove on, turned the same corner, but he couldn't see them any more.

He followed them like that for months. There were several occasions when he was sure he could see Kwyet's eyes in the rearview mirror looking at him.

And once there was Kwyet's face looking up from a book in their living room. She saw him, and her look was inscrutable—remote, warm, surprised, apathetic—every contradiction harmonized into an ineffably perfect calm that made Simon frantic.

And Matty. He realized middle-aged Eros would soon have run his course anyway, but, let's speak in unadorned language now: you tasted like fresh bread.

He knew he had developed an inevitable obsession with your daughter, but that would not necessarily have meant the end. He had the funds for an army of loves. Loving you and your daughter made perfect sense. The three of them could have met in the park for ever, never getting to know each other, laughing in green delight.

Now someone wanted to make that into a golf course.

HE WORKED busily behind the scenes. He avoided his office.

Eyebrows—Leonard's, Eleanor's, Renée's—rising two by two.

"Dammit, Struthers, why the delay?"

"Dammit, Schutz, the damned don't delay, they eat too much and thrive on venality. How are your developer friends?"

HE COULD NEVER hear their voices. Whenever Kwyet visited and they ate dinner together like this, Kwyet was the most animated. Matty smiled, made witty contributions. He knew they were witty because Kwyet smiled and Leonard continued eating. Kwyet tells stories. She moves her hands. She describes a world he doesn't know in words he can't hear. Windows shouldn't be triple glazed.

IN THE BATHROOM at work one day, Leonard was in one of the cubicles, shaking the toilet seat and quietly weeping. I was sitting in the cubicle next to him, trying to be quiet so he wouldn't know I was there. One is used to hearing one's colleagues at their most vulnerable when they are in the cubicle next door. It is a time when we all tacitly agree to be human, to put up with each other. But this was upsetting.

Everyone in there was listening intently. Was a man really weeping? There was a sense of shuddering nearby.

I suppose he felt his career was threatened. I suppose he was afraid that his income might be questioned. I suppose he knew that his wife had betrayed him.

It was chilling and dreary, I have to admit—a moment when I couldn't think of anything but emptiness and struggle and how remote the fictions were that baffle the struggle and emptiness.

WHY PUT KWYET amid such predictable geometry?

No line is an accident, every street a foregone conclusion. Mrs. Smith, who wears blue plaid pyjamas, lives at this end of the street, ergo the same Mrs. Smith, *ceteris paribus* (pyjamas), lives at the other end of the street. Every up has a matching down. Loops, curves, roundels, turrets, mere variations on a theme of straight. Why not squeeze it all together on every side, see what gives? Bend that house into this, let's wriggle cheek to cheek. Draw a cincture tight around each outside wall until cracks and comical bulges appear, until the space between us is just an idea. There is no need for streets; he can *traboule* through your living room when expedience dictates. Or if it is all too close, Kwyet, then run beyond the walls.

He can't keep walking down these streets. Every house has two dormers, on every slanted roof, staring forward, relentless, catatonic. He is walking down the aisle of a mental ward.

Neighbors, neighbors. He was not what he seemed, some common voyeur. He was never what he seemed. But he couldn't do this much longer. All these walls going up between him and Kwyet. Why won't you just come out of your house?

He was a giant, Kwyet. Didn't your mother tell you? When he was your age, he could accomplish anything, have anyone he chose.

"Struthers."

"Schutz."

"What's happening with this golf-course proposal?"

"I am considering it."

"What's the problem?"

"I beg your pardon."

"Look, Simon…I am not alone among our colleagues…I don't need to remind you that these are political appointments. They end, Simon. Approve the golf course."

"Are you telling me what to do?"

"Let me put it another way. Our Division needs funding, and if it doesn't get new sources of income, as well as higher public approval, we will all end up in Transport."

"I have been concentrating on something else."

"So I gather. And I am beginning to wonder whether it is all that efficient for you to be involved in these decisions."

"They are *my* decisions, Leonard. Remember who I am. I am well aware that these are political appointments, and if you think that I cannot get another one, you are forgetting who I *am*. It is the whole idea, the whole vision."

"Of what? Vision of what?"

"Imagination, Leonard. I am talking about imagination."

"What *are* you talking about?"

"How many golf courses are there in the world?"

"I don't care."

"Well, these phases, these proposals, these developments, the golf course...more houses, more houses, more houses, and a golf course, Leonard. What are we left with then? What has it all become?"

"A neighborhood."

"The end, Leonard. Death pretending to be life. Predictability, disappointment, and in the middle of it all a manicured fantasy for men in plaid knickers. A golf course, Leonard? I am talking about creating something wonderful, using the Greenbelt as a *proper* playground, where *imagination grows*, not where it ends, not where it has to fit into all the familiar vessels. We can put things there that renew possibility."

"Right. Like a worm farm?"

"Would that be worse than a golf course? I know what your interests are in this, Leonard."

"Enough with your threats. I need to know what you are talking about. There is pressure on me. *Why will you not approve this golf course?* What *exactly* are you talking about?"

"I'll show you."

"Yes?"

"I will show you."

"When?"

"Soon."

Dr. Paul Overington
National Research Council
1028 Montreal Road
Ottawa K14 6Z8

Dear Paul,

Just wondering if you received my letter of six months ago.
I can assure you I have something to propose that will interest you.
Should I call you?

Sincerely,
Simon

Distrust was rising to a point that was no longer fruitful.

It was indeed conceivable that all of their appointments could end soon—Simon's, Leonard's, all of theirs. Even if no one did anything wrong. He realized the truth. He was capable of realizing the truth.

I have been looking for a point where it all went wrong.

It was good that he moved quickly.

Someone fell from a window.

Mr. Jerry McGuinty
McGuinty Construction
4 Kathleen Crescent
Ottawa K18 2N4

Dear Mr. McGuinty,

Further to your application (file 80814), a number of supporting documents will be required before preliminary consideration by this office can take place.

We will require the usual written assurance that hydro-electricity can be adequately supplied and that you have obtained approval from the water board.

However, given the extraordinary nature of your proposed development, some initial environmental impact studies must be undertaken by a neutral third party before our most basic deliberations can take place. Noise and traffic studies, according to the guidelines set out by the City of Ottawa, should be completed over the next four seasons.

An inventory of vegetation and wildlife, compiled, again, on a multi-seasonal basis will also have to be submitted. Please ensure that this first gains the approval of the Provincial Ministries of Natural Resources and Energy and Environment.

Also, in relation to the environment, you may appreciate knowing that the Provincial Department of Land and Environment, in conjunction with the Regional Conservation Authority and the University of Ottawa, is currently engaged in a study of wetlands in the Manotick-Nepean-Ottawa-Carleton region with the intention of formulating a policy on conservation and appropriate development. You will note that near the proposed fifth hole of your golf course there is a large pond. Any decision from this Division on that segment of your proposal will be withheld pending the outcome of the wetlands project.

5

You may be asked to provide additional supporting material from time to time.

Once again, we ask that you do not contact us with inquiries regarding the progress of your application.

Yours sincerely,
Simon Struthers blah blah blah

"WHAT ARE YA reading, Jer?"

"A letter."

"Yer up late. Yiz are always up late."

"Are you feeling all right?"

"I was only wondering if ya wanted to come and sleep with me, like, not sleep with me but, like, maybe you'd like to join me in the room for the night."

"Are you feeling all right?"

"It doesn't mean there's something wrong if I want ya to join me, is it? Does there?"

"No. I was only asking. Yeah. I want to join you."

"Come on then."

"Fuckin Government."

"What's that?"

"Nothing."

"Don't be taking yer work to bed, cause there's no room for the three of us—not near these ribs."

"It doesn't smell very good in here, Kath."

"No one's cleaning, is it? Is anyone?"

"It's been a long time since I was in here."

"It's a good room. Ya built a nice room, Jer."

"It does smell though."

"And I'm...I'm sick to death of this room, Jer, to be honest witchyez. I'm sick of it and you say it stinks but it's a good room, Jer. Let me just lie my head on yer chest there now."

"It's been a long time."

"Yes, Jer, yes it has."

"Long time."

"Now, don't start getting into that, Jer. Just leave it. It's been a long time. Right. Yes. And if it's been a long time, there's all the more reason to forget. I haven't thought...the idea of having... with anyone...no. It's ages now. How long is it? Ages. Years. More than a year. More than a year."

"More than a year."

"That's right."

"I'm sorry."

"I'm sorry. Enough, now. Put yer hand back on my head there."

"Are you tired?"

"Fagged. I can't stop the tired, Jer."

"Well, you sleep then. I'll turn off the light."

"Don't turn off the light."

"OK."

"I'm sick of the dark."

"It stinks. I should open a window."

"It's cold. Don't. It just needs a clean. I'll be better soon and I'll give it a proper bang-up clean. I'm just tired. I can't stop it."

"Do you want a painkiller?"

"Yeah. Pass us a painkiller. Has it really been a year?"

"More than a year, Kath. Maybe you should see a doctor again."

"It's your son that should be cleaning. He should tidy up more, but he's bloody hopeless."

"He's been looking after you."

"Not much, I tell you. Not much, Jer. Have ya noticed that his voice is breaking?"

"Is it?"

"That's right. And you know what that means. He's off masturbatin on his sheets all the time and not doing what he's supposed to."

"Does it?"

"A breaking flippin voice. I've got a son with a breaking cracking voice, like with age, cracking with the passage of time. I'm not that old, am I, Jer?"

"You're not old."

"I notice yiz have lost some of yer hair there."

"Sorry."

"I like it. But it all means I'm old, Jer. He'll have hair under his arms, too."

"He will."

"He does. I've seen sweat marks, and he smells like a man, Jerry. And hopeless. Christ I feel old, Jerry."

"Relax your head there."

"I feel old."

"You're not old."

"Too old to change anything. Change is just happening, isn't it. It just walks in and out of the room with a breaking flippin voice. I want to change so much, Jerry."

"Just relax."

"I'll just get over the tiredness. Then I myself will change, Jerry. I promise I'll get better."

"You need some fresh air. That's all."

"Yeah."

"How would you like to live by a golf course?"

"Lovely."

"Yeah?"

"Yeah. I'll change."

"You just rest."

"Yeah."

"I'll turn off the light."

"No."

"Have a sleep on my chest."

"Yeah. Goodnight, my Jer."

"Night."

By the time my own voice broke I was on my way to my apprenticeship. When the world was iron and cold, that's what a young man did.

I don't believe in that sort of suffering. I believe in the fat of the land, milk and honey, yes. You might not expect that of me. I don't believe in work for its own sake. It's like believing in faith and ignoring God. There has to be a point to all that work. I was accumulating some sweet little vats of milk and honey for my son, my friend, and a whole lot of fat. I didn't want him to do a bit of work if he didn't want to, because I knew, somehow (faith), that he was a handsome piece of perfection who needed none of the necessary whittling that work can sometimes do. He didn't have to lift a finger. I had all those secret vats, all that tasty fat.

But up he comes with his cracking voice, saying, "Dad, I think I need a job."

Boy, he made me proud.

"A job, eh?" I wanted to hear him speak more because that voice was giving me little shivers of surprise.

"Yeah."

"What kind of job?"

"I don't know. Work. Have you got any work?"

"Have I got any work? Did your father marry a beautiful woman?"

"..."

"Yeah, I've got work, buddy. You're just in time. It's all happening. More work just got approved, so after we pop a cork in honor of your father and the wall-maker's trade, we have a lot to do."

I gave him a taste of everything. For about nine months there, he was working in the mornings before school, in the evenings. He worked in the site office, helped some of the girls with whatnot. He worked with the road builders for a bit, shoveling the tar. He worked on Cooper's team. He still loved Cooper. "He knows things, Dad. You don't understand," he said.

He built a wall or two, my friend, so praise his precious hands.

I paid him generously. He was the richest fourteen-year-old in Ottawa South, probably. I'm afraid that I didn't watch him very closely, though. I just heard what he was up to from other people, in passing. Turns out he was saving.

I was at the peak of my career. People knew me. "McGuinty's good. Builds a fine home."

"I see you live in a McGuinty home. That's fine."

"Oh, yeah. McGuinty. He built a lot of the best stuff around here."

That's the sort of thing you might have heard if people talked like wood. (It was from my radio ads, actually. Very effective.) People came to *me* with proposals.

"I've got a subdivision out in Nepean there. You want a piece of that?"

"We've got a nice little piece of land out Gloucester way— care to come in on that?"

I became a bit of a brand, a badge of quality. People wanted my involvement in their projects so they could put my name on their signs. You know you're a success when the least tangible thing about you becomes valuable. Not your speed, not your ability, not your fists or your possessions—your name. McGuinty.

I *am* Jerry McGuinty. I was scheming, planning, closing, laughing, struggling, having, wanting, growing seriously big in the gut. I was aware of nothing but what I had to *do*. And more than anything I was convinced that what I had to *do* was build a golf course.

I was too busy to wonder why. I caught myself imagining I would one day see Kathleen driving around the kingdom outside my window, my kingdom, in her own little golf cart. I imagined I could own the limits of her world: everywhere she drove was *Jerry*. I didn't think about why. That's the nature of business and dreams. I suspect that you have spent most of your working life dreaming of owning an art gallery or moving to an island to open a scuba shop or something laughable like that. When you get close to it you'll realize that you can't paint or you don't actually like art, that you'll be bored, that you'll be broke, lonely, frightened, that to succeed you would need twenty years but all you've got, at the most, is ten.

With me it was different. I was busy, sure, I was dreaming, yes, but the one was not unrelated to the other, and I am, after all, Jerry McGuinty. I could do anything.

An exclusive group of my finest homes. A golf course with an abundance of this grass: *fescue*. Elegant lines, straight, views of trees, glimpses of sport, a sense of belonging, a great deal of money for the man with my name.

I know, I know, I agree with you. The suspicion that we can't have what we dream of is what keeps us dreaming. We know that because we are wise. We didn't know it then.

I suspected this golf-course development would be hard to hold in my hand, and the more I suspected that the more I longed to hold it. It was more than a suspicion, too. You saw the letters. I was up against some secret department of powerful nerds.

Now, maybe the Government wasn't conspiring to destroy me personally. I'll admit that. I'm not armed for a revolution at the moment; no camouflage on me, see. But they were up to something with this land. They are always up to something and it's never something good for the simple folk—like they think I am.

Nine months Jerry worked. Close your eyes and count to nine. It doesn't seem like much could change.

I had forgotten that Kathleen might need some attention. Jerry working in the mornings and then again after school meant no one was around the house. She told me she was feeling better, she didn't need help, that us two Jerries could feck off with our mollycoddling and our moping moony faces.

She seemed better, a bit more of her old spirit back. I do remember that she made dinner once, the first time in ages. She burned a couple of things, Jerry tried to help, she pushed him away. She definitely had some strength left. It was still a good dinner.

She cut herself once, just a little cut on her finger but it bled and bled and bled. I thought that was odd but she just said feck, feck, feck, like it was just a little nuisance. Generally I thought she was getting better.

But Jerry knew. He was going home a lot, I later learned. He wasn't looking after her any less than before. Running off from work all the time, every day. She had him scared, I learned, so scared that she could make him do anything. He would run home, then run back to work, run home again, make all his own meals, do everything she wanted.

He came to work with me in my truck once or twice. Usually he was up even earlier than I was because he wanted to get some good hours in before school.

"You're a little nut," I told him when I was driving him one day. "Why are you working so hard?"

He has this silence that frustrates me.

"Seriously, buddy, you'll wear yourself out. Your career will be over by the time you're eighteen. You'll have to retire when your friends are just getting going. They'll be visiting you in the retirement home before you start shaving, eh?"

"..."

"Seriously. What are your friends doing? Are they working? What do they think?"

"..."

"Maybe we should have your friends over. Who *are* your friends?"

"Fuck off, Dad."

"OK, buddy."

THE GIRLS IN the site office, they say my Jerry's sweet, makes paper airplanes all the time but does his work. Spells OK, too, they say.

And Cooper—the only compliment I ever heard from him—he says Jerry's a good guy.

Dear Mr. Struthers,

Re file blah blah

Please find enclosed the preliminary approval of the water board and Ontario Hydro, as well as a list of concerned investors
The required studies will be forthcoming as the seasons permit, blah blah blah

You know, as the seasons permit!

I had to pay for these catalogs of leaves and goddamn groundhogs. I had to pay someone to tell the Government that, generally, the winter witnesses an abundance of sleeping groundhogs.

It turns out that there are birds and trees which might be affected by development.

Rock my world!

It also turns out that over the seasons, "There is change, such as erosion, delicately balanced. This is significant," is what one report said. That was the last sentence of that section of the report, which I spent money on: "This is significant."

As opposed to the small number of golf-course architects in the world, these little guys who do environmental studies were Legion.

"The world is changing." That's what the golf-course architect said to me, chewing philosophically. "You can't just lay things down any more," he said.

He was right. But he was also on retainer, so I didn't want him telling me what I knew. When he talked about his trade he interested me.

"You don't golf, Mr. McGuinty, so you might not know this. Golfers don't want to feel like they're playing on a suburban street. They don't want to see houses looking at them all the time. Now, you build houses so you probably do know this: homeowners want to see the golf course. They want to see the grass, the trees, maybe a golfer or two. What's the solution?"

Now he's earning his money.

"The solution is to put the houses on high banks, have the course lower, put berms and woodlots between the course and the subdivision.

"And we want it as natural as possible. I think we should have the course looking kind of rugged here and there. So a links-style course with a fair amount of fescue grass."

That was the first time I heard that word: fescue.

"Maybe even some stone fences here and there, and hedgerows. I'll need to do soil samples to consider drainage. Let's meet out at the land and I'll tell you some more. Ever been hit in the head by a golf ball, Mr. McGuinty?"

"Nope."

"Well, that's a very basic thing to keep in mind as well. I'll come up from Toronto and we'll have a good look at the land. You can find me somewhere decent to stay, I suppose?"

So I put him up in a shitty hotel that he complains about, but he comes out to the land with me and he earns his money a bit more.

"Irrigation and drainage, Mr. McGuinty, are probably the most important considerations in any golf-course development. If we've got impermeable clay here or porous soil, we're obviously going to have stability problems. Some of it might be easy to shift around, as I'm sure you know, and it might help the golf course drain, but you're going to have to decide whether your development can be supported, especially if we want to raise it above the golf course.

"Generally speaking, I build a course that I know can withstand the worst storm in any five-year period. I'll need to know weather patterns, certainly. We've got to consider how the houses are going to drain. Having them up high will be an advantage that way too, but you're going to need pipes, capital P, Pipes, to get the water we don't want away from the course.

"Now, there are some natural ponds, which will be good little challenges on the course. We might want even more of them so you can save on pipes. I happen to know some varieties of aquatic plant that can help make healthy ponds out of the drainage— keep the shape of things, settle suspended solids, even control coliform bacteria, Mr. McGuinty."

I know this guy bores you but I thought he was as exciting as New York. He was a regular freak, this guy, his feet solidly on the ground but his head in a place I never knew.

I threw my soul into that development right then.

And on he jabbered like a Jesus to me. I was so taken that I didn't notice for a while that there were two strangers about fifty feet away from us, dressed in suits and looking out at the land.

"Who are they?" I says to my Jesus and he says, "Beats me."

And we talk in a guarded way and then decide to leave.

I tried to get close to them to overhear what they were saying but when I got near, one of them said:

"Isn't it a glorious day?"

And I felt like it was a warning to stay away.

WHAT A GODDAMN IDIOT, with an I as tall as me.

1

2

3

4

5

6

7

8

9

A reverse birth, my friend, counting up to disappearance.

No Espolito feeling this time, just a vat of plastic wood that I forgot in my garage. That's all that brought me home.

Kathleen's getting feisty these days, maybe a little frisky, I thought, so maybe when I'm getting the plastic wood I might pop my head inside the house and see if we can't be a man and a woman for a minute.

I go in through the garage, through the laundry-room door, planning on hanging a right to go up to her room.

But there she is, face down on the family-room floor, a normally spinning chair tipped over on its side lying stiller than it was born for.

No Edgar this time, just Kathleen on her own looking small and bent, blood in her mouth again.

Panic? Tears? Ambulance?! Call an ambulance?! Check her pulse?

Nope.

I did what your standard lunatic does. I got a bit shaky and went to the kitchen for a tall glass of milk. Nice and cold, coating that taste in my mouth.

6

"Hello, simon, it's Paul Overington calling."

"Paul! Good of you to call. You got my letters then."

"Yes. What is it you wanted to propose to me?"

"I think you will like it. Quite a boon for your research, I should think. Are you well?"

"I am well."

"Shall I take you to lunch?"

"If that's necessary."

"You engineers, eh? Keen sense of what is necessary. Do you call yourself an engineer or a scientist?"

"Either."

"Do you know what a chicken finger is?"

"I think so."

"Meet me for lunch at this place I know and we will have chicken fingers with the house plum sauce and a side of fries. What could be nicer? Strictly business. And then we can go on a little field trip. I would like to show you some land."

"Simon struthers."

"Simon?"

"Speaking."

"It's Kwyet."

"Kwyet!"

"Hi."

"Hi! How…everything…really? A voice from the past. How are you?"

"Good."

"Great. Is everything all right? I don't suppose I have done something wrong."

"…"

"Kwyet?"

"Guilty conscience?"

"Naturally."

"No, I was just calling to say hi."

"Are you in town?"

"No, I'm in Montreal."

"How is the studying?"

"Good. I could still use some help. Final year coming up."

"I would be happy to…if, if that's what you mean… absolutely."

"…"

"Kwyet?"

"I'm here."

"Yes, well, everything here is going well, certainly. Something important in the works. Quite important."

"Good."

"Yes. And how is your mother?"

"Do you remember that I invited you to Montreal a long time ago?"

"Yes, I do."

"Would you still like to come?"

"Of course!"

"How about four weekends from now? The twentieth. Are you free?"

"Yes!"

"Good."

"Good! Will you...Can I get your address?"

"..."

"Kwyet?"

PAUL OVERINGTON, an Englishman with English teeth, was over-whelmed by Simon's idea.

"A wind tunnel."

An awestruck, grateful tone—not one of bland incredulity. Simon's investigations had told him that the National Research Council had been yearning for a wind tunnel, a huge testing site for aeronautical, military, civic purposes.

"Not just a run-of-the-mill wind tunnel, Paul."

"Really?"

"It is up to you."

They had always pursued the wrong channels. Meanwhile Simon found "wind tunnel" in the Dreambook, buried, with one small "!" penciled next to it.

"Are you interested?"

Overwhelmed. It took him a moment to trust Simon, but he was eventually overwhelmed.

A scientist's enthusiasm, once underway, can be messy.

"We have wanted a wind tunnel for years! Years!"

They had the funding, he said. They had sophisticated plans, but everything had stalled. An adequate site.

"Something huge, frankly, is what we need, Simon."

"Perfect."

"I don't think you understand. Huge."

"Fine."

"Do you know much about wind tunnels, Simon?"

"A little."

"Let me tell you more."

7

It was almost like a familiar chore, picking her up and taking her to the hospital.

"She is a very sick lady, Mr. McGuinty."

She bit a piece of her tongue off this time, broke one of the same ribs.

"She is out of her concussion. Was she drinking?"

"I didn't see that."

"She is a very sick lady, Mr. McGuinty."

"I didn't see that."

One interesting thing about a diseased liver, I learned, is that you bleed a lot. Your blood doesn't clot so well. I thought about the golf-course architect. Maybe he knew some sort of aquatic plant.

Doctors may not be decent people, but they do interesting things, sure, sometimes. The body. There's a game. There's a project. I couldn't do it, though. Too close to home.

"She will have to be admitted for a long time, Mr. McGuinty. She won't be any better tonight. You should go home."

———

HOME, YES. It had been hours. I hadn't done any work either. And there was Jerry to consider. I had found Kathleen at around ten in the morning. There had seemed to be no point then in getting Jerry from school. He would probably go to work after school, come home late. I could tell him then, at night, what had happened.

What would I say? I don't even know what happened. Did she just fall out of the chair? Who made her liver sick?

On my way home I thought of looking for Jerry, picking him up from the office or one of the sites, but then I figured he would just get worried—I'd make it seem more serious than it was. He wouldn't want to hear about that happening to his mummy. What did happen to her?

I got home and sat in one of the other spinning chairs. The tipped-over chair was near the bookshelf—not where it normally was. I went over and picked it up, straightened it out.

Mummy's sick again, big guy. That's all I needed to say. He was growing up, voice changing, but he didn't need to know everything.

What was she doing with that chair?

I saw an ashtray on the floor that I hadn't noticed. It usually lived on the bookshelf. I picked it up and put it back on the shelf, high up. That's when I realized she must have been standing on the chair to get something—maybe the ashtray. But she didn't smoke that much, only on bonfire nights and special occasions.

I pulled the chair over to the shelf out of curiosity and stood up on it. It nearly had me on my face but I hung on to the shelf. Up there behind our books—*Irish Castles, Castles of Ireland*—I saw a bottle of vodka. I guess she was after that and she slipped.

Pretty fuckin goofy, isn't it? A stash of vodka up there like she was a drunk. Your mummy's a drunk, big guy.

"SHE COULD DIE, Mr. McGuinty. I have to mention possibilities."

"Yeah, well, she hit her head and she's out of her concussion. I don't think it's that serious."

"Sit down, Mr. McGuinty."

"That's all right, Mr. Doctor."

"Cirrhosis of the liver is life-threatening, sir. If she lives she will have a very different life, a very different quality of life."

"Speak for yourself there, buddy."

I DRINK ALCOHOL these days with pleasure, but there's usually a sorrow that bites my later sips. I don't know what else to say. Sometimes there's nothing sweeter.

I drank a good dose of whisky that night, I tell you with little significance. Had a spin on the chairs. I woke up at dawn, still in a chair. I called Jerry's name.

He must have slipped in while I was asleep. I went up to his room, calling. His door was open, bed was made. He had probably gone out already, the nut.

I went to the hospital.

"It's quite serious, Mr. McGuinty."

"Yeah, yeah."

"Her esophagus is bleeding and the blood is coagulating abnormally. We have to watch her carefully. There are toxins in her brain."

"Can I see her?"

"Not yet. Now, you have to listen to me. She is not going to be as you know her. Not for quite some time. Do you know what encephalopathy is?"

Encephalopathy, cirrhosis, coliform bacteria, chthonic, petty economic, berms, woodlots, fescue. All the spiky words and bumps of blood and shifting mud.

"I haven't got a clue what it means."

"DID LITTLE JERRY turn up for work this morning?"

"I didn't see him. Ask Cooper."

"Hey, Cooper, you seen Jerry this morning?"

"He wasn't working with me."

"Was he in the office?"

———

"HI, LADIES. Was Jerry in the office this morning?"

"I didn't see him."

"No, I was here first. I turned the lights on. He never comes in before me. But he's adorable."

"Yeah."

"And he spells OK."

"HI, I'M LOOKING for my son, Jerry McGuinty. Can you call him from class?"

"Our intercom's not working these days, but I can get him. Why don't you come with me? Let's see what class he's in here. 9G. Come on with me. Oh, actually. No. All the grade nines are on a field trip today. Science Museum. Do you know where that is?"

"Yeah, that's all right. Will he come back here later?"

"No. They go home after all-day trips. They like that."

"CAN YOU DO me a favor, ladies? If Jerry shows up here after school, can you tell him I'm looking for him?"

"HEY, MARIO, do me a favor. If you see Jerry this aft can you tell him to come home?"

"Yes."

"And can you tell Cooper the same?"

"BASICALLY HER BRAIN will be poisoned. Her liver isn't filtering toxins from her blood and some are reaching her brain. I don't know about permanent damage, but she's going to be delusional for a while. And the withdrawal is going to get to her. How much was she drinking?"

"Not much."

"This doesn't happen from a binge. How many a day? Thirty?"

"No way."

"It would have been near that."

"Bullshit."

"She will be feeling serious withdrawal and that itself will make her delusional."

"OH. HELLO. This is Jerry McGuinty calling. Is that Kwyet?"

"This is her mother."

"I'm looking for my son, actually. Kwyet used to baby-sit him."

"Of course, yes. No, Kwyet is in Montreal now. She lives there."

"Right. I don't suppose you have seen him. Jerry? Little guy?"

"No. Sorry."

BY MIDNIGHT on the second night there was still no sign of him. I checked all my sites, called everyone. I still didn't know what to tell him about Kathleen, but, you know, I wanted to see him.

I didn't feel like a drink that night.

Next morning I did a round of the sites again. At the hospital I decided to call the police.

"My son has gone missing."

"Where are you calling from, sir?"

"The hospital."

"Is he hurt?"

"No. He's missing."

"In the hospital?"

"*I* am in the hospital. My son is missing."

"I'm not understanding, sir. Did your son hurt you?"

I went to the police station myself. I wasn't seeing Kathleen at the hospital anyway—I always chose the wrong time to see her and got stuck with that doctor.

"I want to find my son," I said when I got to the police station. "He hasn't come home for a couple of days."

I had forgotten that policemen are as stupid as professional movers.

"Can I have your name please, sir?"

"Jerry McGuinty."

"How long has your son been missing?"

"I just told you."

"Don't get scrappy please, sir. What is your son's name?"

"Jerry McGuinty."

"Your *son's* name, sir."

I WOULD FIND HIM. Nothing serious. I half suspected we were just missing each other—you know, ships in the night. He was coming home when I was at the hospital, and he was going to the hospital when I was coming home. I left him notes, see: "I'm at the hospital, buddy"; and I left a map, cab fare, whatnot.

"EDGAR."

"Hey, Jer."

"You seen Jerry?"

"You all right?"

"Yeah. No."

"What's wrong?"

"Kath's in hospital."

"What's wrong?"

"Ah, you know. You seen Jerry?"

"Not since yesterday."

"You saw him yesterday?"

"What's wrong with Kathleen?"

"Where did you see him?"

"I don't know. Yeah, I saw him near your place. Maybe it wasn't yesterday. No, it was. What's wrong with Kathleen?"

"She fell. Are you sure it was yesterday? I haven't seen him for a couple of days."

"Is everything all right?"

"Well, no, man, that's...I'm trying to sort things out. One or two things are out of place. My *son.*"

"I'm pretty sure it was yesterday I saw him. I saw him with Johnny Cooper."

"I've asked Cooper. He hasn't seen him, not for a couple of days."

"Sorry, Jer."

"Keep your eye out, will you?"

"You look pale, buddy."

"I'm tired."

"Sit down."

"I should keep looking."

HE STOPPED showing up at school.

A long period began when every noise in the house had me excited and terrified, like Fear could get a Hard On: *It's him! His body's found! Him! Death!* Imagine what the doorbell did to me.

After about five days of him gone the doorbell rang and I opened the door to Tony Antonioni.

"Jerry! I seen your Jerry!"

"Where?"

"Downtown! This morning. I seen him! I was in my car and I seen him. But, excuse me, Jerry, I cannot get out to see him. I'm stuck in traffic, I see him across the street, and I honk to him PAP! but I cannot get out because traffic! I call, 'Jerry Jerry Jerry!' but I forget to open window, and then he is gone and I cannot get out because fucking traffic, Jerry."

"What do you mean he's gone?"

"Down, you know, turn a corner. I cannot see him."

"Why didn't you tell me?"

"I try here all day. And at site."

"I told you I would be at the hospital."

"No. Why?"

"I did."

"No. You sick, Jerry?"

"No. Did he look all right?"

"Fine! Handsome boy."

"What the fuck is he doing downtown?"

"Who knows? Not me."

"HER BLOOD is clotting more regularly. We have taken the ligatures off her esophagus. She can speak now, Mr. McGuinty, but it is best at the moment to give her no reason to. She is in a phase of withdrawal."

"Yeah. She probably needs those painkillers. Those painkillers did her good."

"I suspect not, Mr. McGuinty."

"Yeah, well."

I DROVE DOWNTOWN, all around Bank Street there, you know, lower town, uptown, whatever you want to call it, because calling anything anything makes no difference, no, you can call for Jerry with your window up or down, you're not going to find him, and whether she's my wife or not it doesn't matter because she's my Kathleen and isn't, no matter where she is, hospital, bed, it's all the one place in your mind, Jerry McGuinty, the Jerry place, where everything is what it might be, so you can call, shout a city into being, name it, and it's yours and never will be, see.

Is that him there?

He's smaller than that. Considerably shorter, such as a baby might be.

IT'S BEEN THREE weeks now, so that's a bit too long. You know, come on, Kathleen, smarten up. Wake up, you know, we can have a bacon sandwich together and I'll go off to work. I can get you a new van and you can make us a couple of them, you know, you can make those goofy little things that you made at the party, because they probably made your heart a bit happy, eh, even though it was bitter and had its eye on Edgar, eh, for the time, for that little time? Let's have a chat, anyway, talk about what's up, you know, three weeks and Jerry's missing and you've had a drop or two out of sadness, was it?

"I SEEN HIM again, Jerry!"

"Where?!"

"Same! Downtown! Again, Jerry, same place, for sure your Jerry, and seriously? Fucking traffic!"

JERRY, I TELL YOU, he was not one of those kids who paint pictures for their daddy, you know, Here is my daddy with a hard hat, which I could stick up on the fridge. He was never one of those kids, that I ever saw, never even handed me a piece of paper, that I ever remembered, yet here comes this letter, in the mail of all things, stamp, my name in writing like mine a bit but shakier, with the address. Writing to his own home like he was a stranger, you know, Dear Sir.

Dear Dad,

I am writing to let you know that I am OK.
    I am OK. Is she OK?

Jerry

8

WHY SHE NEVER gave him her address was beyond him, although it might just be negligence, youth, carelessness, on the phone, carefree, in her bedroom. He would find her.

But it is not as though Montreal is a hamlet. He can't ask the baker where Kwyet lives. And he can hardly call her mother to get her address. Really, it was unforgivable and delicious of her.

For this journey he would need brown brogues for strolls across campus, black Oxfords for dinner, a dark blue suit, white shirt, blue shirt, brown hound's-tooth jacket, his larger khaki trousers, damn his waxing belly. He would need a map of Montreal, the usual toiletries, perhaps a packet or two of the terrific sheep gut, one lives in hope and fear.

Perhaps if he brought a squash racket she might consider him vigorous, you know, he used to play often, but no, no, and damn the house plum sauce.

She won't see him with his luggage, anyway. He will check into his hotel first, perhaps reacquaint himself with the city, and then he will stroll over to campus and make his Kwyet inquiries.

What a name. He wondered if she was well known. "Hello, I am looking for Kwyet."

"Peace as well, I suppose?"

It will be marvelous. He longed for sophomoric raillery. He wondered if he would meet her friends.

If mystery must have form and name, let it be hers and Kwyet's.

Three pairs of underwear, three pairs of socks, some aspirin.

He wished he at least had a phone number, though. He will have to leave her a note somewhere. If he were taking the train he could draft a note or two, but it is best to take the car, for this first visit anyway, since she may live far from a Metro stop.

And a gift, a gift, a gift, a gift. He would bring the following possibilities in the car: a small *Ficus benjamina,* Leonidas chocolates, one demi-bouteille of Chateau D'Yquem, a book. What book? Graves's translation of Apuleius—silly, inscrutably moralistic, a meaningful myth in the middle.

Does she have roommates? Housemates? Greek sisters? They may want presents.

How would he get it all to the car?

IT IS COLD TONIGHT, so cold that the faster he drives the more the engine cools. No danger of eagerness overheating.

He feels so alone when he drives. He should have taken the train.

And it is late. He won't find her tonight. Damn traffic leaving Ottawa. If that city would stop spreading there would be less of that miserable commuting. He might have been there by now.

She is probably out with her friends. Center of attention. Friday night. The city drawing toward her like plasm to taste her nuclear honey.

Has he thought of her possibly having a boyfriend?

Well, yes, certainly he was aware that she was once seeing a young pilot or some classmate who flew planes, but he long ago realized that anyone she was with would simply be a curious pause along her journey toward him. He mumbled in the car

with a worn-out smile: "If ever any beauty she desired and got
'twas but a dream of me."

And why the delays? Why, "visit me in a year," "visit me in
four weeks"?

Mystery. Simple, unfathomably complex mystery.

Aha. There is Montréal propre. St. Joseph's illuminated. Find
your way to the hotel, check in, contemplate your hunt.

"HELLO. SIMON Struthers. I reserved a room."
　　"Yes, Monsieur Strudders. Room one-one-seven-two."
　　"Is there a phone book in the room?"
　　"Yes, monsieur."

S
S
S
Saint-Jacques
Saint-Jean
Sansculotte (hilarious!)
Savoyard
Schmidt
Schuster
Schutz
Schutz!
Schutz B
Schutz Ernst
Schutz K
Schutz K!
992-1716
992-1/16
"Hallo."
"Hello. Is that Kwyet?"
"'Scuse?"
"I'm looking for Kwyet."

"Quiet?"

"Yes, may I speak to Kwyet?"

"What's dat quiet? C'est une blague. I'll 'ang up. Dere's de fuck*ing* quiet."

THE THING TO DO is to have a late, simple, solitary dinner in the hotel, get up early, go to McGill, find which...

Is she in a residence? Are there colleges at McGill?

There will be a main administration building, of course, and they will...

But it will be Saturday.

Why did she not call him last week? It would have been awfully simple.

"EXCUSE ME. What is that central building there?"

"That's the Arts Building."

"Ah, the Arts Building. Thank you."

The Arts Building, such as where an Arts student might spend her time, reading Classics, chatting to corduroy men. He will have a look.

It is dark in here. The Dark Arts. And empty. There must be a common room, or an office somewhere. Yes, here we are. Office. Closed. Hours Mon–Fri 9:00–3:30. Those are civil servants' hours.

There must be a common room. What's upstairs?

Not a *soul* about. What is happening to the Arts?

These all seem to be classrooms. Yes. Imagine Kwyet at one of those desks. She's not too young for him, is she?

Ah, here's an office. Professor Godfrey. And that must *be* Professor Godfrey.

"Professor Godfrey?"

"Yes."

"How do you do? Simon Struthers."

"Hello."

"I am looking for someone. A student. Kwyet Schutz. Do you know her?"

"I have too many students to know any of them. What does she look like?"

"Look? She is fair, and, fairer than the word, / Of Wondrous virtues: sometimes from her eyes / I did receive fair speechless messages."

"Sounds familiar. But the name doesn't."

"Where do students go, generally, to study?"

"They don't. This is a big city. On Saturdays Learning will be cast into the mire, and trodden down under the hoofs of a swinish multitude. Try Peel Pub or Bar St. Laurent."

"Excuse me. Is there a main administration building on campus?"

"Yeah. Totally. But it won't be open today."

"Oh. Perhaps you could help. Are you a student?"

"Yep."

"Do you know Kwyet by any chance?"

"Quiet? Are you a Christian?"

"No."

"No, man. I don't 'know quiet.'"

"Is Peel Pub on Peel Street?"

"Now you're talking."

"This way?"

"Off campus, right on Sherbrooke, left on Peel."

"Thank you."

"Wait a minute. Do you mean Kwyet? Like the girl?"

"Yes."

"Ohhh. No, I don't know her. Are you her father?"

"No."

"Uncle or something?"

"No."

"She's gorgeous. But I don't know her. Are you looking for her?"

"Yes."

"She's probably swimming. She's on the swim team. But I don't know her. Just in class, you know?"

"Do you know where she lives?"

"No."

"Where would she swim?"

"In the pool, man. Up the hill. Over there. Corner of Pine and Parc."

HE WONDERED if he should get his car. All these hills. But then he might have trouble parking. He shouldn't have brought his car at all. We invent cars to diminish space and now there is not enough space to park them. Sing his urban dirge.

But, really, Kwyet, a phone call last week would have saved a bit of exercise. He will be trim for you, of course, lithe, strong of thigh, but he might have been saved this hill.

Does this mean he will see you in a bathing suit? He wouldn't dare. There must be a lounge room or somewhere you will inevitably pass from the pool.

"McGill ID."

"Pardon?"

"ID please."

"What ID?"

"Are you a student?"

"No."

"Faculty?"

"No."

"Are you a member?"

"Of what?"

"The pool, sir."

"No. I'm…I'm looking for Kwyet."

"Do you want to use the pool, sir?"

"Do you know Kwyet?"

"If you mean adult swimming, it's at two o'clock. No children or games allowed. Membership is forty dollars for six months, that will entitle you to ten free weekday swims, but if you want free admission on Saturdays you will need to tick that box there,

'Gold,' and could you please step aside while I serve my next customer?"

"But I don't…Forty dollars?"

"Excuse me."

"Sorry. Forty dollars."

"Thank you, sir."

"Can I go in?"

"For one dollar, yes."

"I just gave you forty."

"You didn't tick that box there, 'Gold.' Dollar admission for regular members on Saturdays. Membership has its privileges, eh, sir, ha ha, stand aside."

He hardly needs this towel, does he? Good heavens, no lounge. He doesn't…He doesn't have trunks. "Excuse me."

"Yes."

"Is there a place to watch the swimming?"

"Bleachers. Follow that sign: Bleachers."

HE WON'T PRETEND that this is not a pleasure. In More's Utopia we would see each other naked before marriage. This is a more sensible balance, me in the bleachers, them in their swimmers.

He doesn't dare, he wouldn't dare to look. Is that Kwyet there? No. My God, the young…the young body is designed to keep the agèd young of mind.

Is she here at all? It is hard to concentrate on just one. Let's see, roughly fourteen women. Fifteen men. That old man in there should be ashamed of himself. The group over there must be some sort of team. The longer he stays here the more suspect he will seem. He should take off his overcoat, yes, and walk directly over to them. Look them in the eye, keep your eyes up and steady.

"Hello! Hello! Hello, down there!"

"Yeah?!"

"Sorry to trouble you! Sorry to interrupt! I was told that

someone I know…! I am looking for someone, you see?! Kwyet! Do you know someone named Kwyet?!"

"Yes! I know Kwyet! She's not here today!"

"Could you tell me where she might be, her address perhaps?!"

"Are you her father?!"

"No!"

"Uncle or something?!"

"I am a friend from Ottawa!"

"She lives at RVC! University and Sherbrooke! But you'd have better luck finding her back in Ottawa!"

"Why?!"

"She's gone home for the weekend!"

"To Ottawa?!"

"Yeah!"

"Are you sure?!"

"*Yeah!* That's why she's not at practice!"

"I was…! She invited me! I was supposed to meet her here this weekend!"

"Wait! Are you Simon?!"

"Yes!"

"*OK!* I thought you were her father, you know, or something! *OK!* I thought you were coming next weekend!"

"No! No, I am here now, you see!"

"Kwyet's expecting you next weekend!"

"No!"

"Yes! Next weekend!"

9

I NEVER RECOGNIZED Kathleen again. Once, maybe twice. I recognized her twice but the second time was after she did something completely nutty.

She wasn't talking for a long time because they did something to her throat. And she never looked normal. In that first ward she was always in the same position, always looking like she was about to cry or like she was looking for the place in her mind that let her cry. I was told that she was restless, but I never saw her like that. She just seemed still and strange.

Then they moved her. She was yellow. They put her in an in-patient ward, watched her, made sure she didn't break.

"Had a bad fall, eh, Kath?"

"Unn?"

"Had a bad fall, eh?"

"Unn?"

She looked thin and then she looked fat. I said to the nurse, I said, "What're ya feedin her, ha ha. Wow, ha!"

The doctor told me Kathleen didn't seem to remember how she arrived in the hospital.

"Memory's not important," I said. "What's important is you've got your health."

What?

I said some shiny stupid things quite regularly those days. I don't know why. The doctor made me nervous, like he had all the answers, and I always wanted to show him that I had some wisdom of my own. I could take care of her.

Dear Jerry,

Where the fuck are you? Why are you gone, writing me a letter, you fuckin little nut?

That's a letter I never sent, having no address or sense of where I was.

THE FIRST TIME I recognized her, she had found that place in her mind and a human Kathleen was sitting up in her bed having a wail of a torn-bodied cry. I held her. She didn't push me away. But she let me know that she didn't want me there, like her tears were a language she didn't want me to speak. I recognized her but she was telling me to forget her.

Every time I visited her I expected her to be better, to be up telling jokes and frying toast in her room. I thought she was over the worst. Her room was nice—big floor-to-ceiling window looking out over a parking lot—and everything but her was in place to make her better.

The second time I recognized her I was walking toward her room and I heard a noise, like BOUNGHK!, like a bird hitting a window but fatter. I went into the room and saw her lying in a heap. Good and solid, those big windows. Except for the bump on her head that was definitely Kathleen on the floor. Maybe the window knocked her back into herself for a while. I asked her if she wanted the doctor and she shook her head as in normal conversation.

She lay on her bed, staring at the window, not saying any-thing. It was a long time of silence, long enough for me to get over any shock I allowed myself to feel, long enough to think about golf courses.

"I'll build us a...we'll have a nice view, Kath. Grass. Beautiful."

She stayed quiet.

"I jon't," she said after a long time.

"Don't what?" I said.

"Want a nithe view." Her tongue was hurting. "I've got choo leave you, Jerry."

"Well, no. No. The doctor says you've had a little drinking problem. You know, lay off the booze for a bit."

"It'th you, Jerry. It'th not the boosh. I can't joo it."

"Do what?"

"I can't, I can't shshsh, thththink."

"Doctor says you've had thirty or forty drinks a day."

"Fuck the joctor."

"Is it true?"

"I have choo leave you. Jon't make it hard. Thith taketh, like, shtrength, Jerry, thoo shay thith from the feckin hothpital bed. Can you?"

"What?"

"Leave me alone. Will ya leave me alone?"

"Jerry's missing. He's run away. He sent me a letter."

"I thtill won't come back."

"Is that what you think I'm saying?"

"Eh?"

"What?"

"I'm confuthed!"

"Are you saying that I think that you...Did you just try to kill yourself, Kath?"

"Jid you shay Jerry'th mithing?"

"And you don't care? I don't know what is going on, Kath. What is going on? Why are you here?"

"Leave me alone."

"No."

"I can't feckin! I want to jie, Jerry. Let me be. Pleathe, pleathe, pleathe, you ugly ffook. Can ya? What joo I need to joo Jerry What joo I need to joo Jerry What joo I need to joo Jerry What joo I need to joo Jerry?"

"Fuckin smarten up is what you...I don't know you, drinking a bottle a day."

"Ecthactly! Ecthactly, Jerry. And may I shay that living with you hath been one...You're a ffff...Jerry, and yith have trapped me with yer fuckin ssshon. I'm in pain."

"Nurse!"

"Not a nursh! Jutht leave me. If I could run. I'll run out that god feckin winjow!"

"You'll settle down. You'll just settle down."

"I *will* NOT! I'm thick of it! You've made me thick!"

"How?"

"Ecthactly! Now leave. Leave leave leave leave leave leave! Yiv been sthdanding, yiv bin shittin there all my feckin life, thinkin yer big, thinkin yith can, yith could shtop me, thinkin yer a rock, feckin sholid, like yith can shtop me. Yer not. Yith have never NEVER been man enough. Never big. No one, ya fuckin old man...look at ya...FUCKIN no one, will shtop me. Again. Wheresh it all gone, eh? Kathleen, eh? Thish Kathleen? Am I?!"

"What?"

"You know me? You ever know me? Ya...ya crush me on a feckin bed, but ya shtill never got shtrength to know me. Shtrong fuckin man, but yish can never hold me. Let me go. Thatsh how I could have lovejyou."

"What?"

"Fuck off outta here now! Now! I'll run out the winjow!"

"Fuckin eh, Kathleen. Run out the window! Try again!"

"Leave! I want to leave! Jerriald Mac, yer a feckin iron WEIGHT!"

"Nurse!"

"Leave!"

I told the nurse when she came in, I snapped, I shouted, "She's a nut!"

"Calm down, sir."

"She's a fuckin nut!"

"It's normal."

"It's not normal. Look at her! No, it *is* normal. She's always on the floor! You're right. Look at her...yeah!...Go ahead and smile, Kathleen. She just tried to kill herself, but it *is* normal, because... look at her! Fuck *off*, Kathleen..."

"Sir..."

"Because she's blaming me! She's blaming my son! I don't even know how she got here. I don't know where our son is and she doesn't care!"

"*I care.*"

"She *doesn't* care! Listen to her. She changes her tone like that...pretends...all fuckin sweet. 'I *care*,' like she's breathing... like she's made of fuckin flowers..."

"Sir..."

"It's not new. That's what I'm telling you. She pretends. She's a good mother, a good wife, around you, yeah, other people, but she's a *bitch*. Ask her what she said, ask her how she got that bump. Ask her!"

"Perhaps you should leave."

"Get him out of the room. Let my shon in, but not him."

"Oh, *listen* to her!"

"You should rest..."

"Did you fuckin hear her?"

"Please leave, sir."

"I *will*. I'll leave, Kathleen. See?"

"Leave!"

"There. See her? I *will*. I'm leaving. *I* am leaving *you*. It's official. You're a witness."

"Yeah, she'th a feckin witneth."

"I'm gone."

10

"It's kwyet calling."

"Kwyet! You are very naughty."

"I didn't know you were coming. I said four weekends. I am very sorry."

"It *was* four weekends."

"Was it? I am sorry, Simon. How...Can you come again?"

"When?"

"Well, when would it...I'm *really* sorry, Simon. Could you come in another four weekends?"

"Really?"

"I'm sorry."

"So this Saturday is the third, yes?"

"Third what? Third of February, yes, yes, sorry."

"So the third of March. I should come on the second of March?"

"Could you?"

"Could I?"

Could he do anything at all?

Yes. He did everything.

He was frantic.

"Please, Paul, get your application together. Time is of the essence. I cannot delay other decisions forever."

His appointment might be running out. There were rumors, stronger rumors, that some would have to end. He still believed he was well liked, but one could never be sure with politics, as his father ponderously said. What if Leonard was replaced? Poor old Leonard, eh? These threats of revealing his arrangements. The land was Simon's as long as he and Leonard were around.

"Paul. Please."

They had more discussions. Simon got more excited.

"All you have to do, Paul, is send me an application. I can alter it as I see fit. All you need is my approval."

Paul told him about the wind tunnel he wanted. A continuous flow, closed circuit, atmospheric testing section.

That was not exciting.

"We can test everything in there. For everyone. Huge commercial possibilities, Simon. Not just aeronautics."

This is what Simon liked.

"Buildings. Can they withstand winds? Can cars be more fuel efficient? Can trains go faster? Will this spacecraft take us to the moon?"

"Space?"

"Of course."

"Go on."

"Millions of things. Any commercial material, any building material subject to natural force. This restaurant, for example. Could it withstand a heavy storm? Is it overbuilt? How will it age?"

"How will it age?"

"Exactly. We can look into the future. Applying the right pressure, the right environment, to any substance lets you see how it will age. If we get the proper facility built—environmental chambers, drop tower, maybe even a Clean Room—we can see what this city will look like in a hundred years."

"Paul, there is plum sauce on your lip. Wipe it off, get a new napkin, and when you receive that napkin, write your application on it. That is all I need. I will get you your approval."

11

THE THING IS, I told you earlier, remember, my friend, I told you earlier that I would smarten up, become myself again when I heard a woman hit a window. But that was boasting. I will admit that now.

As events turned out, effectively, I did smarten up. But I never really left her, you see.

She left me.

I went home in a smoking huff, and shouted fuck at all the walls, and I went into her room and put some *light*, some much needed light, in the room, and on the bed, right, under the bed. Everything I needed to learn was there on that regret of a bed. *Stains.* She was actually pissing herself. That's why the smell. She had been pissing in our own bed. And the smell. Of course, underneath. I flip up the mattress, and underneath is this graveyard of vodka bottles, this stinking frozen storm of labels and goddamn glass. You know, an affair is one thing, it's, there are muscles, and we're animals, so we have a fuck and maybe it continues for a while, because, certainly, there are beautiful honey-shaped muscles in the world, man or woman, but, fine, we are animals and we hide things, bury things, but what silly animals, with muscles, hide bottles, you know, Smirnoff, under the shitty bed?

I couldn't have learned a more depressing little secret. Ridiculous. The smell, like an armpit's ass, and that's my Kathleen making it because she really likes vodka and doesn't like me.

And, my good friend, that should have been enough. I should have had an easy time walking away from that. I was afraid of the truth for a long time and now here was the truth, so Run! But it tasted, in fact, better than the fear of it did. It was disgusting, but it wasn't enough to smarten me up. There was still me in me, the little freak saying aw, no, Kath will be fine.

I wanted to smash a bottle against the wall, but it was, see, a good wall, I'm afraid, so I cleaned up, disinfected, spick and spooky span, for all those unknown visitors who pass between me and my walls.

I didn't see her for a couple of weeks. I didn't visit her for a couple of weeks, and when I did, do you know, she wasn't there to be visited. She checked out on her own.

I have an account, a bank account, which I call "Kathleen." I deposit money every month.

SOMETIMES I just sat there, could sit there till I died.

> Now I taught the weeping willow how to cry cry cry.
> And I showed the clouds how to cover up a clear blue sky.
> And the tears I cried for that woman are gonna flood you,
>   Big River.
> And I'm gonna sit right here until I die.

I circled that block downtown, that block where Tony kept seeing him. Every night, I drove around, waiting for him to appear, waiting to club him over the head. When the mouse appears, club the little bastard over the head.

Can you believe him? Fourteen years old, or so? Quits school, writes home to his dad, dear dad?

I HAD a theory.

Jerry saw her fall off the chair. She was up early, being a thirsty boozed-up, underboozed thirsty freakin weirdo.

Kathleen was up on that chair and Jerry saw her fall. I had a feeling. That was my theory.

And he got scared, because: who wouldn't? She falls down and knocks herself out, he gets scared and runs away. But it's more than fear now, isn't it? You don't stay away so long because you're afraid.

"Is she OK?" he asks in that letter. He must have known something was wrong with her. He obviously saw her fall. Maybe he pushed her. Maybe he was feeling guilty.

(Look over here now, though, in my mind's eye, I'll get back in a minute, I'm on a bit of a binge, see, there, Look, look, I'm back there, Kath's left, Jerry's gone, early days yet, and I'm missing him, actually, but I'm mad, pissed, pissed, angry drunk mad, at everyone, and there I am, see, at Edgar's site office and, watch this, I stumble in there grumbling something dizzy, and I head straight for Edgar, "Whereshmyshun!" or something and I swing at poor skinny Edgar and miss and trip over my swing and pass out, yep, yes, drooling there, dribbling. Heh heh.)

I drove around that block a lot and I never saw him.

"I'M KEEPING my eyes peeled, Jer, seriously. Why would I...You OK?"

"Yeah."

"Why would I know where Jerry is? You know, look, shit, buddy, I was interested in Kath, you know, sorry, but not, you know, not your son. I don't know where he is. I've been looking. What about the cops?"

"They know. They're looking."

"I've been looking out. I've asked my guys to keep a lookout too. What about Cooper?"

"What about him?"

"They were chummy, weren't they?"

"Yeah."

"Yeah. Chums. Maybe he knows."

"Have you seen Kath?"

AS I SAID, it must have been more than fear at this point. If he was afraid of what he saw, Kathleen falling, he wouldn't have been gone for six months.

Dead?

No chance.

So what was wrong?

It was the Government. They had him scared. He noticed how much the Government was pissing me off, making me un-happy, so he was afraid. You know, he was entering the building trade: maybe he was afraid of them doing the same to him. The Government sent someone around to scare him—to scare me, but I wasn't home so they scared him. That's what I thought. The Government was up to something, certainly. First, there were those men I saw on the land, then there were months of no re-sponse at all, not a peep. And then Schutz—Jesus, Schutz. I tried to talk to him about what was going on, and he looked worse than Kathleen did. Miserable!

I said to him, "Schutz!" I said, "Jesus, Schutz, what is going on?"

He just grumbled.

"Are you guys going to sell me that land or not?"

He grumbled, stared into space, mumbled something about a colleague, couldn't look at me. He looked like he was drugged. Someone had him scared.

"My wife," he said (miserable! mopey!). "It is not a good time, Mr. McGuinty."

"You're right. You're goddamn right."

"Could we meet some other time? I'm a bit…I am a bit preoccupied."

"Preoccupied! Jesus, Schutz, 'preoccupied' makes the world go round. Who isn't preoccupied? You people, you want to stop the world going round. That's your problem."

He was shuffling forward. I was at his house, standing at the front door and he was shuffling forward, trying to keep me out.

"Can we please meet some other time?"

"Who got to you, Schutz?"

"What?"

"Someone's got to you."

He just wasn't talking. I thought for a minute that he was hiding Jerry. "Who's in there, Schutz?"

"My wife."

"Who's she?"

"What?"

"Stupid question, sure, but things are not as they seem, Schutz, you know, Jesus, if someone's got to you, if you're hiding Jerry, if you guys are trying to scare Jerry to get to me, you know, pick on someone your own size. Where's my son, Schutz?"

IT WAS TIME to force their hand, get an answer, because I couldn't concentrate on things, I couldn't focus, I could not, quite honestly, muster the right clear-headedness you need to build a plaster city, to build your necessary dreams, and the angel demons were asking questions about the man they invested in, me, and questions are no replacement for scaffolding.

Dear Mr. Struthers,

Re File: fuck

While fully aware that your office requests that applicants not make inquiries regarding the progress of their files, I am writing to ask your office kindly to consider the fact that there are many parties in-

terested in this application, that the various impact studies have cost money, and that the longer a decision takes, the more money private citizens are putting into a gamble arranged by the Government.

I write with all due respect to your office's limited resources, the sensitive nature of such decisions, etc. Spending money and delaying for land we do not own is unacceptable to my business partners and me, and we would like a decision on whether we can, at least, purchase the land.

I am sure your office is aware that our purchase of the land would benefit the public purse more than the prolonged engagement of your office in further deliberation.

Never threaten a bureaucrat, my friend; their skin is as thin as yours.

"YOU SEEN Kathleen, Edgar? You can be honest."

"In the hospital?"

"She's in the hospital?"

"That's what you told me."

"She's not in the hospital. You can be honest with me."

"I haven't seen her, Jer. Seriously. I wouldn't do that. I thought she was in the hospital."

"We had a little fight."

"Do you want to talk about anything, Jer?"

"I'm not a fag, Edgar. Don't talk to me like I'm a fag."

"No, man, it's just, you come in swinging at me, and you're asking where your son is, where your wife is, and you know, I hear things, you know."

"What?"

"I hear things, you know, some of your projects, some of your men. You know, if you need help, if you need time off, I'm your friend, Jerry, shit. You've got a lot on."

"That's real sweet, Edgar."

"Augh, you know...up yours, Jerry. I'm trying to help."

———

"You seen Jerry, Cooper?"

"You see this blow torch, McGuinty?"

"Yes."

"Suck it."

"Do you want your job, Cooper?"

"No."

"You're fired."

I threatened a bureaucrat. I got what I deserved: no response. I gathered my strength. I gathered a group of angel demons. We bought golf clubs, we rented a bus, we drove downtown to Parliament, I stood in front of the angel demons in their matching suits and we took our clubs and we smashed all the ground-floor windows of Parliament House.

Also in that dream I bench-pressed a cow and Kathleen worshipped me on her knees. I felt good waking up, strong, and then the day progressed with no news from anyone and night came again like an emptying glass.

The people need a king. They need a leader. The ladies in the office, the boys on the sites, Mario, Tony, more than a hundred people, they need their figurehead, Jerry.

"I have 114 messages for you here, Jerry," said a Lady of the Office to the King. "What do you want me to do with them?"

"Any from the Government, Schutz, Struthers?"

"No."

"File them, leave them, toss them."

And when they think their leader is not himself, is not there for them, is not his best, they will betray him. Mario Calzone, the filthy fighting pig, went to work with Edgar.

"It looks like he's got more work," he said.

I had to lay off a couple of crews and I forgot to do it civilly. One of the laid-off guys was married to one of the office ladies. She says to me in tears one day, "I have to go, Jerry, it's just not the same here any more," as though her leaving was going to help it stay the same. "You should see someone," she said.

"You're goddamn right," I said.

"You can't just let it all fall to pieces," she said. She straightened her skirt like it was all that easy, like all I had to do was straighten my skirt. "Everyone needs you, Jerry. They need some, like, guidance around here."

"You just straighten your skirt there."

They say they need you and they leave you. Most of them don't even say they need you. I'm their bread and filling butter, trousers on their legs, payer of their rent, braces and dentures, booze on a Friday, but they never say thanks and all of them leave.

I forget to order materials. A whole block of phase five has stood still for four months because I've forgotten to order things. Procurement. Procurement.

"You've forgotten basic procurement," says a hard hat to me.

"That's a big word for a man in a hard hat," I says.

"I'm an engineer," says he.

But it's still a big word, with cure in the middle like it will help me somehow: gathering things, ordering tiles, getting enough nails is going to cure me. Even words are betraying me.

"You've got to sign off on this," the hard hat says. "Basic infrastructure, Jerry, we're falling seriously behind. We need you to sign off on this."

They need me. They need a king.

I am not a king.

12

THERE ARE CERTAIN beauties about it, quite aside from proving him powerful: a fiery wind in the heart of calm, the sky on land, flight without movement, an epitome of chaos in a clean white tube. Certain beauties don't appear to people immediately, but the city will cherish his work.

And it could be gloriously large. Paul has the funds. Paul, Simon's helpful saint, had the zeal of the converted. He was in Damascus when Simon's earthly form appeared; he met him on a street called Straight.

"It could be bigger than anything the Americans have," Paul said.

SITUATIONS OCCUR to him. He is walking down a street called Nowhere and he sees Kwyet peering out of a colorless house, burning with ennui. He is her only hope. "Simon!" she cries.

He will save you. He will save you from this world of middling choices. When he finds her in her room she is glad as the spring. He lies down with her and they both grow hungrier the more they eat.

Right now she is in class tapping a pen on her lips. A lecturer speaks of the gigantic past, her pen taps more quickly and she resolves to make her world grow big with Simon. Tomorrow, in her favorite café she sits with her best friend, the one who met him by the pool, and shares some intimate thoughts. They talk about him together. They talk about many things but return to him as their theme, *he, him, Simon, me, he's.* Think of all the café confidences he has overheard from all the pretty women.

He wanted to be the *he* in someone's sentence. Then he would be big enough. He wanted Kwyet to speak of him.

NATURALLY, NOW that the four weeks had passed he found himself incapacitated with bronchitis. He had her phone number now but he could barely lift his lungs out of bed to travel to the phone.

He realizes all these things he coughs up are the impurities of his soul, but that is a morbid way of thinking which will not improve his health. What he has to do is rest, swallow the impurities so that perhaps he will be well enough to see her tomorrow. He will have a nap, call her in an hour, tell her he cannot come tonight, but can he please take her to a lovely restaurant in Montreal tomorrow?

He slept for twelve hours.

"KWYET, I am so sorry."

"What happened?"

"I am hoorwaghff…hwarff!"

"Simon?"

"Hem."

"Did you not want to visit me?"

"No! Good God! Hwoof, hwoof, hwoof, hwoof, hwoof, hwee! I…"

"You sound terrible."

"Yes, I cuh, cuh, k!"

"That sounds horrible. I thought you were mad at me or something."

"No!"

"I thought you were trying to get back at me. It didn't...you know...Are you all right?"

AND NATURALLY that was his last chance before her midterm break. Home with Matty and Leonard now, leaving him excluded in his Tomis for several black months.

"As soon as next term ends you should come. You should. When my exams are...**after** my exams."

PERHAPS IT WAS the fever. When he moved from one room to another in his house he felt like the room he left was chasing him, like there was nothing to turn back to. When he entered a new room it was not like he was filling a new space, but like the space he just left was following and trapping him. Loneliness was catching up.

Perhaps it wasn't the fever.

All these years later, I feel like every room in this house has breathed out, and won't breathe in again.

Someone fell from a window.

HIS LUNGS CONJURED nightmares every night. Every dol of his pain echoed a pore of Kwyet's skin. Such an exquisite body of anguish.

She was only twenty-five minutes away. Eleven stop lights. But it would not be right to appear at Leonard's door at dawn with a cough, and a tear in his eye. For Matty's sake.

He should have devised some means of communicating with her while she was staying with her parents. He was sure she would like a break. Matty was charming but he doubted that Kwyet wanted to spend her whole holiday with her.

Patience, though, patience. She is pining as much as I am.

He got better. He got more work done.

———

"HERE IS THE PLAN," says Paul. "A nine-point-one-meter-wide, nine-point-one-meter-high, twenty-two-point-nine-meter-long test section," he sings, "would make it the largest in the world. The complete structure would be enormous."

"Go on."

"Well, it will be huge."

"Largest in the world, you say."

"That's right."

"And that's just the beginning. We'll have other wind tunnels. A vertical one, a Trisonic one. And within these tubular structures, and surrounding them—look at these plans—we'll have all the other facilities. Have you got things under way, Simon?"

"End of the week, Paul. I will submit my memo with the approval of my chairman."

"Fantastic. I am so pleased you took an interest in this. I have no idea why. It wasn't...you know...I don't know why you have."

"What else would go in here?"

"Have I told you about the model of the city?"

"Yes. Tell me again."

13

My problem was I had no patience.

People leave their jobs all the time. I should have accepted it. My business had grown, now it was shrinking a bit. I should have been patient and kind.

Instead, I tried firing a lot of the people who didn't leave. Anyone who said something in the wrong way: "You're fired." I never showed up regularly, but when I did show up and someone was late: "You're fired." I fired a guy for getting a splinter. "Ow," he said.

"You're fired."

It made me feel good for a while. I recommend it. I didn't always mean it. The people who knew me knew I didn't mean it. But I fired some of the people who thought they knew me.

Cooper kept turning up for work after I fired him because he knew I didn't mean it. I tested him with a look, which, I think, said, "You know you pissed me off."

"Get out of my face," he said. "I've got responsibilities." He looked ashamed for using a long word. I assumed the responsibilities were to his parole officer.

"You're a big man, Cooper."
I didn't know.

I CLEANED THE house a lot. You could have eaten off my bathroom floors if that was to your taste. I figured Jerry would like to come home to a nice clean house. He might have associated the house with chores, so I didn't want him to see it all dirty when he walked through the door. (He was going to walk through the door any minute. I would have rubber gloves on, and a sponge in my hand, and he would walk in, I wouldn't be able to shake his hand, he'd say, "Dad, you look like a fruitcake," and we would laugh all the way to the fridge.)

When I was cleaning I kept finding hidden bottles, empty bottles. That was good for a laugh. I had thought it was a story, a bit of a wives' tale, that drunks hid their booze in the bathroom, like "all drunks have red noses." Kathleen had a pretty nose. But there were bottles in the bathrooms, in closets, behind the couch. I didn't know how she had bought them all.

I called people sometimes, her doctor, people I thought were her friends. ("You seen Kath?") I didn't do it seriously, just occasionally, just as a sort of hobby. I started to realize that she had no friends. I myself have no friends, my friend, but it is somehow more sad to learn that someone you know has no friends than to realize it about yourself.

The obvious way to catch her was through the bank, maybe even at the bank. She was still withdrawing money, you see. At first I told my bank manager to keep that woman out of my accounts. She had money of her own, in accounts I had set up in her name to beat the tax man (better the wife than the Government). But those would run out, and as my mood changed I told the bank manager to let her have access.

I planned to go to the bank, hang out there all day to see if I could catch her. I was ready to do it, but the closer I got to doing it I got such a tired feeling. So tired. Aren't you tired?

She wouldn't want to see me anyway.

Still, I waited near the bank all day, just as a hobby. She didn't show up. I opened the "Kathleen" account and told the manager to help her find her way to it.

She was alive. I knew that at least. But Jerry?

Dead?

No way.

The Government was still drugging him. Someone was. I knew that much. Someone was keeping him.

But the Government—I *fought* them. I called Schutz every day. I knew people who knew people, union boys who knew politicos who knew how to put pressure on the right people. I told the angel demons, don't worry, we'll get it, and when a couple of them pulled out, I took up their shares. "The National Capital Division answers to no one," one of them said, but for once I ignored their advice.

I moved the golf-course architect up here full-time and we worked furiously. I hired two new engineers and fired my long-standing trusted one because firing put the blood in my arms. We were going to go all the way, I decided: not nine holes, but eighteen. And I doubled the number of houses. Oh ho ho, yeah. If the Government wanted environmental conservation, the best solution was to double the size of the golf course. All the trees and grass in the world would survive beautifully if we made it all a golf course.

Thanks to the "vegetation inventories" I had been forced to do, we knew exactly what could grow. We knew the precise depth of ponds, how to keep them level across the seasons. We planned to stock them with fish, and I had a letter prepared for the Department of Fisheries and Oceans, explaining the benefits to each species.

We had been warned of a Wetlands Policy, so we planned the houses and ponds so far away from each other that no matter what the policy was there could be no complaints about disturbing whatever was so precious about a wetland.

I had fifteen different subcontractors arranged for the building work, all their men next to mine, the best in their respective trades. We planned ten separate house designs, more choice than I had ever offered. Six hundred houses all together.

A lot of my other projects were winding up, we had all finished the mall. Money was marching in, so I scaled back, took advantage of everyone leaving, fired more of the old people, forgot about other possible projects, ducked out of commitments, and put all my energy into the golf course. And I still didn't own the land.

Every morning from nine o'clock I had Schutz on the phone. Not Schutz himself, I mean—just his number. Schutz never answered, you see. The Government had become really French, so all the messages were in French and every time I called Schutz I got this message, in French, which I can still repeat the sounds of even though I have yet to learn what it said. It was all part of their ploy to shut me out. I figured there was some secret code in the French that would give me some way in, maybe tell me something about Jerry—but I wasn't going to stoop to playing their games.

I kept writing to that Struthers chump. No response from him, either. But I knew that as soon as I caught one of them I would be able to force them into selling me that land, force them because they would be so overwhelmed by the fact that I had every blade of grass accounted for and protected, that I was saving fish and improving the world. We planned to offer executives of the National Capital Division discounted memberships for the course.

I WAS ALL FIRED up again. I was in the office, jumping around in front of two new office ladies. They liked seeing me fired up. "It's all happening, ladies."

They loved it.

I was waiting for Cooper. I wanted to fill him in, tell him about the state of my project because ever since I started my company Cooper was the one to tell first. It was like a ritual.

And I was putting up new Jerry posters. The only picture I had of him was when he was eight or nine. I had these posters made, HAVE YOU SEEN THIS BOY?, and I got the printer to make him look older. There was this new batch of him looking even older, but he was starting to look a bit funny.

"It's all happening, ladies."

"We heard about your son, Jerry."

"It's terrible, Jerry."

"Well, these posters should work. He doesn't look like a freak like that, but I didn't have, you know, a...a nice picture."

"He's gorgeous. He'll turn up."

"You bet."

Cooper had walked in.

"Hey, Cooper. It's all happening, buddy, you've got to see these plans, all the plans are finished, and it's all in, and everything's go, so sit down here, there, stand if you want and listen, and I'll tell you, seriously, listen it's all bigger than ever, we'll force their hand, I'll make you a king..."

I was standing near one of the posters I had just put up and Cooper kind of put me off balance by punching the poster through the wall. Plasterboard. The ladies let out a little "owoohwoo."

"Telling you about his son, has he?"

"It's all right, ladies. This is Johnny Cooper. He's been out of prison for many years."

"These posters. What you got here, five posters in the office, eh, boss man? That's gonna find him."

"I want to talk to you about the project, Cooper."

He went over and punched another Jerry through the wall.

"Could you stop punching my son, please?"

"That's not your son, cunt boy."

"Should we call the police, Jerry?"

"No. Whose son is he, prison boy?"

"I don't know, tough guy."

"What are you saying? Are you insulting my wife?"

"Your son has a mohawk."

"What?"

"That's right, boss man. He's not a fuckin, not a fuckin five-year-old with a beard. He's a fifteen-year-old with a shaved head. And I got him a nice little tattoo, on his forearm."

"What?"

"Pair of wings."

"You've seen him?"

"He was living with me."

"Call the police."

"You cunts call the police and I'll eat you."

"You kidnapped my son."

"Fuck yourself, McGuinty. You don't have a clue."

"Where...*what* is going on, Cooper?"

"I looked after him. That's what the thing is, tough guy. I looked after him for a bit. And now he's gone."

"Call the police."

"What did I say?"

"Don't call the police. Get your hand off my neck, Cooper. Get..."

When I caught my breath again I was able to think more clearly. I was calm. Cooper explained. I listened.

"He left me this note last week," he said.

"'*Johnny, I'm off. Thanks, J.*'

"He slept on my floor. Since he ran away he slept on my floor sometimes. That's all I'm saying to you, golf boy. He's got friends. But I don't know where he's gone."

I DO KNOW THIS, I do know this: there's a flower, I've seen it in numbers, shoots up through snow like a sword. Dirty snow, hopeless snow. In reds, oranges, yellows.

Part Five

1

COOPER LIVED OVER with the crooks in Vanier, near downtown. He had some of Jerry's stuff but he wouldn't let me come over and get it. If I wanted to wait outside to see if Jerry came back for it, I could, he said, but don't expect him to send out coffee or blow me fuckin kisses. If Jerry was going to come by, he said, he'd be doing it at night.

I wanted to know how Jerry spent his days.

"He begs, I think. Mentioned a job. I don't know."

So I waited in my truck outside Cooper's place every night, for months. I grabbed some McDonald's on my way over, parked and waited from around five thirty, watching Cooper's door until two a.m., when the radio stations got all weird and Christian. I was at the ready, hand on the handle, a soldier every night, I tell you, a sharp old cop, ready to pounce, on the lookout, FBI.

Every night Cooper slouched home from the Brasserie, never looking toward me. He was getting old. Still a piece of iron, but smaller. I never thanked him for looking after Jerry because I continue to doubt whether that man could look after anyone. I saw him trip on his top step one night—a wooden step—and he fell over. He got up slowly, approached the step again like he was hunting it, and he kicked the top board off, stomped on what was left, broke through the next step, got his leg caught, fell over again, got up screaming, went over to a wooden pillar near the step, shook it, his head thrashed around, the pillar came loose at the bottom, he kicked it, and went inside. I don't like to think what Jerry learned from him.

Have you ever had two Big Macs every night with an apple pie and eight hours of diesel fumes? Ever shat by the side of your truck?

There was one person and one person alone who ever walked into Cooper's house, for months: the master himself. But one night I saw him stumbling along and a little fella ran up to his side and they laughed loudly and put their arms around each other. I tightened my hand on the handle, waited till they got nice and close. It was Jerry all right.

Just before they turned up Johnny's path I flashed on my headlights and jumped out. I ran toward them shouting "Jerry! Jerry!" and confronted them. They just stood still.

Cooper's lady friend had a shaved head and a laugh like smoke. She found me funny. When I got back into my truck Cooper fired a rock at my windshield and chipped it. Fair enough. I disturbed them. I looked like an idiot.

I docked his wage for the windshield. He laughed about it when he got his pay check, saying, "Huh, huh, I meant to tell you that night, huh, your Jerry got his stuff a couple of months ago. He broke in one day."

It's going to be easy. One little city. One little Jerry. One big Jerry. I'll find him. Can't trick me forever, big guy. I know what you look like. Put a mohawk on your head, whatever—I still know what you look like. Mother's eyes, smart guy. I know how to chase them.

———

I COVERED my floor in maps, made myself coffee. That was my morning business. Every map of the city I owned was spread across my living room. I trained my eyes to avoid that green belt. I got to know the flow of every street from above, learned short-cuts in case I had to chase him in my truck. FBI. Freeze.

So what are we dealing with here? We're dealing with paper maps, concrete roads, concrete buildings, marble malls, fruit mar-kets, flesh and blood, leafy trees to hide in, maybe. All these things, these materials, *will* come together. They don't know each other (what's more different than paper and concrete?) but they can't do without each other. From the map in my living room I will choose a road, go to a building, find my son.

Each morning I chose an area, sometimes depending on what I found the day before. I started downtown because it seemed the most likely. It was coming up on fall, late September or so, still warm enough for him to be anywhere.

Top of Rideau, work straight down, have a look around here, Sandy Hill, probably not, maybe around King Edward, right.

CORNER STORES are likely places.

"You seen my son? This is an old picture. He's fifteen or so. Mohawk."

"What color?"

"What?"

"What color is his mohawk?"

"I don't know."

"Fan?"

"What?"

"Fan mohawk?"

"What?"

"Is it a blue mohawk, orange fan mohawk, purple half mo-hawk, we get a lot of mohawks in here, sir, streetkids, punks, stealing things, sir, do you understand?"

"His name's Jerry."

"If I knew the names of the kids...if the kids stealing from me only left their names."

"Yeah, well. How much are these wine gums?"

"A dollar."

"Here's a dollar. There. You've made your fortune. My son's not a thief."

"No, I'm sure he's just another sweet kid with a mohawk."

"Tell you what, buddy, having a mohawk and stealing sounds a lot cooler than selling wine gums."

"You going to buy anything else?"

"No."

"Get the fuck out of my store."

THERE'S ANOTHER corner store over there, but I might save that for another day.

Gas station?

No.

Flower sho...no.

Frui...no.

Pi...? Maybe. Kids like pizza. I fuckin love pizza. Try the pizza shop.

"Hi there, can I have one of them, one of those pepperonis, a slice, two slices, yeah, and, I was wondering, and a Coke, and I was wondering if you might have happened to see my son, name's Jerry, his name's Jerry, about fifteen. Here's a picture."

"I can't touch, greasy fingers. Show me."

"There—that's about five years out of date. And he's got, someone said he's got some kind of mohawk thing on his head."

"I'm not here at night. Most of those kids come here at night, you know, later. Ask Vinnie. He's here at night."

"OK. Where's Vinnie?"

"He's not here. That's what I'm telling you. He's here at night. Come back and ask Vinnie."

"Thanks."

"Five seventy-five."

"Eh? Oh, right."

I COULD LOOK down some of these alleys, but, come on, he's, what's he going to do in an alley? I'll look. I'll have a look. What do you do down alleys? Fuck people, do drugs, get fucked, shoot people, get shot. That's television. You park your car in an alley. You put out your garbage. Is he eating garbage? Bet you Cooper taught him to eat garbage.

Is he still a virgin?

THE SHELTERS! What an idiot! Try the shelters! Where's he going to sleep? He's not sleeping on the streets. Try a shelter!

Shepherds of Good Hope, Salvation Army, Keepers of Sweet God-Lovin Faith and My Jerry. He's probably eating their soup and becoming a priest, the crazy little goof.

Here now. Shepherds of Good Hope. Jesus, look at the line. I don't need to line up. I'm not looking for soup.

"Hey, buddy."

"Whasssssssa?"

"Never mind. Hey, buddy."

"Fuck off."

"Have you seen my son?"

"Get the fuck away from me, man, or I'll shiv ya."

"How do you get in here?"

"Quit butting! Quit butting!"

"Who's in charge?"

"Quit butting!"

"I just wanted to speak to…where's the shelter? Where do you guys sleep?"

"Tell that guy to quit butting!"

"Get to the back of the line!"

"I don't want soup. I'm looking for my son."

"Get to the back of the line!"

I FOUND A GUY, someone in charge. I thought he was a priest. I said, "Father, I'm looking for my son."

"I'm not a priest," he said. "I'm an ex-cop. Drunk. How old is your son?"

"Fifteen."

"He's probably not here. We don't get many kids. I send them over to the Y sometimes, if they turn up here. Would you like some soup?"

"No thanks."

There was a tiredness about him that reminded me of Kathleen. "Do you get many women here?" I asked him.

"Sometimes. Your son a woman?"

"No. He's got a mohawk."

"Yeah? There was a kid with a mohawk turned up here about a month ago. I told him the Y would be better for him."

"Did he look like this?"

"Who's that?"

"My son."

"No, this guy had a mohawk."

"The Y, eh?"

IT WAS GOING to be easy now. I drove over to the Y right away. It was a much nicer place. It felt right, for a boy of Jerry's taste: no drunks, front desk, etc.

"Do you have the names of people staying here?"

"What would you like to know?"

"Whether my son is here."

"Why don't you know?"

"Why do you care?"

"Because sometimes people are staying here because they don't want to be at home."

"Well, that's not the case."

"But you understand that for that reason I can't tell you whether your son is here or not?"

336

"His name is Jerry McGuinty."

"That's nice."

"Yeah, it is nice. Is he here?"

"Sir…"

"I'm not picking a fight. You know, I understand. But in this case… You see, it was his mother. I don't have to tell you this."

"No. And I can't tell you who is staying here."

"How does it work here? You have rooms?"

"Shared rooms and private rooms."

"Private rooms are more expensive?"

"Yes."

"I want to stay in a shared room."

"I can't let you do that. We're full."

"You're full or you can't let me do that?"

"I can't let you do that because we are full."

"Not because I'm Jerry's father?"

"That's right, sir, not because you're Jerry's father."

"So he is here?"

"I didn't say that."

"You just said his name like you knew him."

"I was only repeating what you said."

"So he's not here?"

"Maybe."

"How long will you be full?"

"I can't say."

"Guess."

"We're always full."

"I could force you by law to let me see my son."

"How old is your son?"

"Fifteen."

"No, you couldn't."

"I could squeeze his name out of you."

"Then it is my turn to remind you of the law."

"*Then it is my turn to remind you…* Are you proud of yourself, little fella? Do you realize you are keeping my son from me?"

"I am doing my job, sir."

"Well I'm going to wait outside."

"That's nice."

"For as long as it takes."

"That's nice."

"He'll come out, we'll hug, it'll be none of your business."

"I look forward to that."

So I waited. I went outside, got in my truck, and waited.

Five weeks. I never wanted to lose sight of that door to the Y. I got thirty-eight tickets for stopping there in my truck during rush hour. I couldn't shit by the truck because this wasn't Cooper's neighborhood, so eating and your basic belly functions were the only things that kept me from that door.

I did visit Vinnie the pizza man one night, though, and that was my first breakthrough. Yeah, he'd seen him, he knew the kid I was talking about. But not for a long time—he hadn't seen him for months, he said. He didn't know where he was staying, he just served him pizza—pepperoni was his favorite, same as me.

A lot of young guys went in and out of that Y, all looking like the world's rough paw was tossing them for a tumble too often. It was getting near winter and none of them had anything more than a jean jacket. That's all right if you're a construction worker because you're busy, and tough as bad beef. I, for example, know how to relax my shoulders in the cold. That's the way to stay warm. But all these little guys, they would come out of the Y and hunch up their shoulders as soon as the wind hit, shrugging like they were saying *I don't know why* and couldn't say it hard enough.

So I had an idea. I got out of my truck and went up to this little guy, and I said, "Relax your shoulders."

"What?"

"Relax your shoulders."

"Up yours."

But my idea went beyond that. I just had to stop one of them long enough to ask him if he knew Jerry. The relax-your-

338

shoulders thing was stupid, sure, but I had to find a way to make them a bit grateful so they would tell me something in return.

Cigarettes were the obvious answer. (Everything is obvious now. Why did it take me five weeks to think of asking one of these guys if he knew Jerry? Nothing was obvious then.) I bought some cigarettes and waited for another little guy.

"You got a light?" I said.

"Yeah."

He lit my cigarette, kind of cool.

"Thanks. Here, you want one?"

"Thanks."

"Getting cold, eh?"

"Yeah."

"I'm looking for a fella named Jerry McGuinty. You know him?"

"Yeah, I know Jerry."

"Mohawk?"

"No, he grew that out."

"Right."

"Too expensive shaving that all the time."

"Right."

"More of a nothing now, you know."

"Sure. Sure. Do you want the rest of this pack?"

"No thanks."

"Sure?"

"You don't want it? I'll take it if you don't want it."

"Go for it."

"OK."

"Jerry live up there in the Y, shared room or anything?"

"He did, man. He did. He's not there now."

"Where is he?"

"Not sure. You his father?"

"Yes."

"I *knew* it, man. Same voice."

"Same, is it?"

"Yeah. Deep."

"He's got a deep voice now, does he?"

"Pretty deep."

"I probably gave him that."

"Guess so, man."

"But do you know where he is, where he might be?"

"Honestly, man, I don't know. That Jerry moves around a lot, doesn't stay in one place long. That fuckin Y is getting expensive, man. I can't stay there long. But it's safe, see."

"So where else does he sleep?"

"Everywhere."

"On the street?"

"Sure."

"Where?"

"You know."

"Yeah?"

"Warmer places. It's getting cold."

"Come into my truck. It's over there."

"No, I don't…I don't do that, man."

"Give me a break, buddy."

"No, man. I've got to go."

"Which warmer places? Where's warmer?"

"I don't know. Malls. Billings Bridge is good."

"Billings Bridge mall?"

"Yeah. Good places to hide in there."

"Wait. Wait. Look, here's some money."

"I told you I don't do that."

"Would you give me a fucking break? It's not *for* anything. I just need…Here. Look."

"That's a fifty."

"Take it."

"You don't want it? I'll take it if you don't want it."

"I want my son, my friend."

"Yeah."

"Does he talk about me?"

"Sure."

"Is he all right?"

"I don't know. Sure. He doesn't talk much."

"Right."

"Flying. Fuck it's cold."

"Relax your shoulders."

"He talks about flying, being a pilot. And he talks about some girlfriend in Montreal he's gonna visit sometime."

"Oh yeah?"

"And he talks about you."

"What does he say?"

"Says you build houses."

"That's right."

"Development, all rich and shit."

"That's right."

"And you were never around when his mum poured beer on him."

2

SMALL OBSERVATIONS HE had noted following discussions with various members of the National Research Council:

- we could witness winds of up to 90 m/s;
- men of science are generally not handsome;
- models can be made of anything to be tested, if the actual body or structure is too large to fit in the testing section;
- a testing section of the size proposed, aside from being the largest in the world, would accommodate many small craft, automobiles, and crucial scale segments of all known vehicles;
- models have long been the focus of this sort of testing, so please don't feel disappointed if everything gigantic cannot fit *in toto.*

The general civic purposes were infinite: all forms of transport could be tested and improved. Every imaginable form of weather could be conjured and thrown at every conceivable substance. But what caught his eye first, you see, what leapt from the pages of the Dreambook long before these discussions with Paul, was a note next to the entry "Wind Tunnel': *model of city to be built*.

A scale model of this entire city would be built and placed inside. That's what the initial dreamer hoped, and now Simon was making it possible. High-rises, bridges, perhaps the testing center itself. Every new shape on land would be made proof against the unexpected, would stand or fall before it actually stood. Would age, show its faults, tell us where we went wrong before we actually do it.

Do you see, you builders, mothers, dreamers? It is a place where mind, hope, and fact cohabit. Where the city becomes imaginary and our imaginings are real.

I will send a wind of whips and fire across this city, or a breeze that licks your walls. And you will never know me.

3

I got a birthday card from Jerry.

Dear Dad,

Happy Birthday!

Love, Jerry

It depressed me more than anything I had known. To re-member me but tell me nothing, like I wasn't worth telling. It was the cruellest thing you did, my Jerry, and then you did it again at Christmas.

I was out there looking for him like he was the future, but the most he could do was remember me.

And look at how empty that house was. Listen to it chattering away with itself like I wasn't even there, creaking, adjusting itself. We weren't getting along, that house and I; it was proving a point by adjusting itself, like a woman stretching out in bed to kick her husband out. I stayed in the living room, worked there, ate there, slept there.

The living room was where it all happened: mission control, the war room, the Penta-Jerry's-Gone, my friend. That's where I planned my missions.

I checked Billings Bridge mall, as Jerry's friend had suggested. I went during the day at first to have a look around and then I went back to the living room for a bit of strategy. I decided I should locate all the malls in the city on my maps in case I didn't find him at Billings Bridge. I would focus on different malls each week.

Billings Bridge was my warm-up, my practice mall. When I returned there, near closing time, I looked for teenagers and places they could hide when the shops closed. I saw roughly eighty-three thousand teenagers—armies of them, families of them, great swatting, kissing, giggling, gangly herds of zitty little monkeys. Boys giving each other a bit of the rough-house, girls smiling and kicking, holding their hands over their braces when they laughed. They made me want to cry, so ugly, sweet, and little.

Get it right, my spiky little friends, are you going to get it right? They're all in these tight little groups. Does Jerry have a group, a buddy for the rough-house? Have you got a pretty friend to hold a bit of your sadness? All these kids are on their way home, stopping at the mall on their way from school. Why not you? Come home and I'll listen to your sadness, buddy, you bet I will.

The groups disappeared, some of the shops rolled down their shutters, security guards waddled back and forth. Older, tougher kids hung around, smoking, spitting, checking me out. Maybe Jerry's like them. They wouldn't tell me if they knew him.

I found some hiding places. I kept clear of the security guards. It occurred to me that hiding in the department stores might be better than in the mall itself, but I was too late for that.

All the shops had closed now. I heard a "Hey!" from one of the security guards and a laugh from one of the tough kids. Billings Bridge was one long hallway, more or less, so staying unseen was a matter of being at the opposite end from the guards and hiding, somewhere, when they walked by. A janitor came out of a utilities room, did some mopping, talked to himself. I decided that that room might be the best place to stay once he left, if he didn't lock it.

When it got really late and the guards left I had that nervous *what next* feeling you get when you play hide-and-seek and your friends don't find you. I wandered down the hall as quietly as I could, and I was pretty sure that I was not the only one hiding. I heard footsteps at one point and I think I heard a sniffle. I went to that utilities room and it was unlocked. I felt for a light switch but decided not to flick it. If it was a good hiding place, maybe Jerry would know about it and come in later.

I felt around for a spot to wait. It turned out that Jerry wouldn't come in.

He was already there.

As I went farther into the room I tripped over my sleeping son.

ON THAT PARTICULAR occasion my sleeping son was a gray-bearded sixty-year-old who smelled like a pissed-on sock. He welcomed me to my shopping-mall life.

I returned to Billings Bridge every night that week, finding new places to sleep, new people sleeping. I brought a flashlight, a flask of coffee. I shone my light on people, scared some, pissed off others. None of them knew Jerry, few of them were actually sane enough to understand me. Those men in closets converse with no one but their past.

I shone my flashlight down the hall once and I scared someone, a young guy, Jerry, and he ran, ran, ran. I know it was him.

In my living room I chose some other malls on the maps. From four p.m. every day I hung out in some mall or other, with my flask and my flashlight. I started to recognize a lot of the teenagers at the end of their schooldays. They all made fun of me. In one of the malls, out near Woodroffe there, I was known as the Retard. I wore plaid shirts, wore my flask on my belt. Here comes the Retard.

WORK?

No thanks. Couldn't give a shit.

THE GIRLFRIEND in Montreal?

I was willing to bet it was that baby-sitter of his, Kwyet. Her mother said she was living in Montreal now. She was a beauty who deserved my son, but I expected fifteen was a bit young for her.

I called up her mother again to make sure she was still in Montreal, and she was. I got her number and address.

4

Here it is. Royal Victoria College. An all-women residence.

There is a front desk. Security.

"Hello. I am looking for Kwyet Schutz."

"Is she expecting you?"

"Yes."

"Sign in here, please. I will call her. Your name?"

"Simon Struthers."

"Are you her uncle?"

"Do I have to be?"

"No, sir. Hello, Ms. Schutz, there is a Mr. Struthers here for you...All right...She will be right down."

"Thank you."

What a dreadful place. Perhaps if he comes to Montreal often he should get an apartment. He could sleep on a fold-out couch whenever he misbehaved. He could wear silk pajamas. He would never get erections except at the appropriate moment.

"Hi, Simon."

"Kwyet! Yes...yes, two kisses is the Montreal custom. How are you?"

"Good."

"They keep you under tight security here."

"They do. But the clever ones find their way in."

"Do I look like your uncle?"

"I don't have an uncle. You look well."

"Well fed, yes. I welcome your dishonesty. You look…"

"Simon?"

"Yes?"

"Can I ask you something?"

"Yes."

"You know how you invited me to dinner?"

"Yes."

"And that's where we are going now?"

"Yes."

"Can my friend come?"

"Your friend?"

"You've met her. You met her by the pool. I know it's rude of me…"

"Not at all…"

"She seemed jealous of me going out."

"I understand."

"It's hard to explain."

"I understand."

"She's on her way down actually."

"Good! I am honored."

"And also…Here she comes…Hi…You remember Simon, from the pool?"

"Yeah. Hi."

"Hello."

"Thank you for inviting me."

"It's a pleasure."

"I had a party to go to, but I thought I might eat with you two, since you invited."

"It's an honor. I thought we might walk to the restaurant. It's only…"

"I'm starved, totally starved, aren't you, Kwyet? Famished. Is that the word? Famished?"

"The restaurant is only…"

"From practice, you know, Kwyet and I had practice today, Saturday, you know, so I, anyway, am like so totally starved it's not funny, and every Saturday it's the same."

"I see."

"Saturday's the big training day."

"I see. We aren't far from the restaurant at all…"

"Oh, I bet I know where we're going. I bet, I bet. Sorry. But I bet."

"It's just a block away…"

"Yes, yes, yes, oh, Kwyet, it's so nice, you are so lucky!"

"I'm sure."

"No…"

"Yes!"

"It's only…"

"Yes! Anyway, Kwyet, sorry Simon, I was telling Kwyet this story just before, earlier, sorry, so Bruce was told, Coach told Bruce that he had to, what was it, he had to, yeah, he had to knock off ten seconds, you know *ten seconds!* off his time or he wouldn't make the cut—sorry, Simon, swim talk—but, like, OK, ten seconds is a lot, but over fifteen hundred meters, maybe not so much, but, still, totally, can you believe that? And just to be told like that, you know, say I'm Coach and you're, say Simon's Bruce, and I get totally in Bruce's face, right, like I'm Coach, and I'm like, 'Si… Bruce, you cut your time or you're out,' like that, right, it is *so* rude. If nothing else, it is *so* rude. Right? Right, Simon?"

"I'm Bruce."

"He is so funny, Kwyet. But seriously, it's not only rude… it's…Bruce was so upset, I had to hug him, like he was a boy, you know, like this, let's say Simon's Bruce, like this…"

"I see."

"Sorry, Simon, I get like this, sorry, it's Saturday, I get like this on Saturdays, Kwyet and I do, maybe not her so much, but me, on a Saturday? I'm all wound up."

"Well, here's…"

"I am *starved*."

"Here it is. Le Caveau."

"This is the place! This is the place! You are so lucky, Kwyet. My uncle took me here. It's like…oh…I don't even know. You have *got* to eat here."

"Yes, well…"

"Thank you."

"Thanks!"

"Hello. Struthers. Table for t…I mistakenly booked for two people, but I meant for three."

"No problème, monsieur. This way."

"That is…oh, look, I'll tell you later. There's something I want to tell you about the…wait till the waiter…"

"Thank you."

"Thank you."

"Thank you."

"May I offer you an apéritif? Madame?"

"…"

"Kwyet?"

"Oh, I…"

"I'll have a Bloody Mary. While you're deciding, Kwyet, I'll have a Bloody Mary. I can chew on the celery."

"Madame?"

"I…"

"You better order, Simon. She never decides."

"Would you like champagne, Kwyet? Why don't we have champagne?"

"I'm having a Bloody Mary. Champagne's not good for me."

"Champagne would be lovely."

"We have Billecart-Salmon, monsieur."

"Good."

"That's…Wait till he goes…Yeah, that's what I wanted to say…When my uncle took me here, he was just like Simon. He didn't speak French, and I was so…I don't know, I'm sick of French, and, you know, I don't even know what I mean, but it's just so nice…"

"Yes, I…"

"It's just so nice here. So…"

"Simon is a civil servant."

"Yeah? I am *so* tired."

"Quite right."

"I haven't got a clue…you know, I'm in, Kwyet and I are in fourth year, and, I don't know about you, Kwyet, but I do not have a *clue* what I will do with my life, like, civil servancy, what?, that's, I bet that's good, but I feel like there's probably more for me."

"Probably."

"I don't know. Ah, celery!"

"Monsieur?"

"That's fine."

Pop.

"I'm jealous. I wish I could have champagne."

"Please do."

"No, I so totally can't. I'll be sick."

"To your health."

"Cheers."

"Cheers."

"I am afraid I never got your name."

"I'm sorry, Simon."

"You never told him my name? That's hilarious! It's like Bruce on the team, actually. I didn't know his name until we went out last year, and we're like in the middle of a date. I can't believe I went out with him. Thank God that didn't last. But I do feel sorry for him. Coach has got a serious attitude these days. He's a sweetie, to me, and, I don't know, to you, sure, but he has an attitude lately. I don't like it. I'm not sure it's good for the team. I mean, Bruce sucks, but I don't know what Coach is doing these days."

"How long have you been swimming, Kwyet?"

"Quite a while."

"We shouldn't talk about swimming in a place like this. Sorry. I started it. It's like with my uncle, you know, he likes books and things, like you, Simon, and I talked his *ear* off about swimming. We should talk about books. How do you two know each other, anyway?"

"Simon's a friend of my father's."

"That's so nice. I hope I still have friends at that age. Kwyet will be. For sure. You're my friend for life. God, seriously, if we want to get serious…"

"We should look at the menu."

"Yeah, definitely, but if we want to get serious, Kwyet, seriously, *what* are we going to do with our lives? I mean, I know you don't know because you can't decide anything, but *me*? Have you told Simon about some of the frat parties? Theta boys?"

"Me? No. Why would…"

"That would be *so* funny. If he came? Seriously."

"I don't think…"

"He's got to. He has *got to*. Let's order. He has to come. Can I tell him?"

"No…"

"Simon, don't worry about Kwyet. She has this…"

"We should order."

"I know what I'm having. Fish. Anything with fish. All fish. Any fish."

"They have a dégustation, a six-course menu. Perhaps you would like…"

"Does it have fish?"

"Yes."

"Then I'm there. Totally. Six courses?"

"Kwyet?"

"That sounds nice."

"I was talking about something…"

"Let's just order…Can…Hi…We…Could we have…We will all have the dégustation."

"Very good, monsieur."

"Easy."

"Thank you."

"Thanks."

"Fish. Can't wait. I should go to the bathroom. Excuse me."

"Of course."

"I am sorry, Simon."

"About what?"

"My friend."

"Not at all. I only…I hope we will have a chance to talk."

"No chance."

"As I feared."

"Are you staying overnight?"

"Where?"

"Montreal."

"Yes. Yes. At the Radisson."

"I would…If I had room I would…"

"Would you? No men allowed, isn't it?"

"No, no. Men are allowed, anyone's allowed. That's just general security."

"Perhaps we could have coffee."

"Yes, well, absolutely. You should…"

"I'm back!"

"Hi."

"Hello."

"What do you guys think of my shoes? I suddenly got worried that they weren't right, not nice enough, you know, but we've got this party. Did Kwyet tell you about this party? We've got to go to this party, and I always ruin my shoes, you know, frat boys, always these frat boys around spilling beer on my shoes. I have yet to meet one nice frat boy, except Kwyet's…"

"This champagne is fantastic."

"Her ex."

"Yes?"

"But still, you can't judge people for what they do when they're drunk. Is that the fish coming? That is such good timing."

WHEN THEY DEPARTED, they to a party, Simon to himself, he kissed Kwyet on either cheek and the corners of their lips touched. It was a confidence, a tactile contract, a formal recognition that when their lips met fully their animal skin would thrum.

With smiles, grimaces, melancholy, and the aid of his tongue he spread her corner kisses over most of his face and neck. That was his primary occupation since arriving at his room. And when he kissed his fingers, her kisses could go anywhere.

He had had too much cognac. Her friend had given him another hug, tight, and Kwyet had kissed his lips.

Hotels are such honeycombs of frustration. Memories of happy couples, eyelashes palpating this pillow, a thousand elusive sounds, no one here for Simon. Kiss me wherever you like, Kwyet.

If he presses his ear against this wall, he hears the elevator shaft, twang twang, but beyond it he hears whispers, a woman's cough, a tap on, off. A hundred pseudo-private holidays in boxes. You are dull at home but when you pack yourselves into this public space you abandon your restraint. Why not let me see? I can hear you. I can hear your television moans. Why not let me see? Here, on the other side of this wall someone is having a bath. Hear that? Plish, plish, plish, plish, plish, plish, plish. I know that rhythm. Are you alone in there? I never got the name of Kwyet's friend. Are you thinking of the same sporty swimmer, sir? Plish, plish, plish, plish, plish, plish, plish.

Kiss me here, Kwyet.

PROMISES OF private parties, see you in a month, my friend will be away, my friend really likes you, come and meet my friends, come whenever you like, I have lots of friends, we always have parties (they might not be your scene), sorry we couldn't spend much time together, I can't actually do coffee tomorrow, but please come again, again, again.

He was having trouble with his shoes. Again. Try a shoe horn. Again.

No need to despair. Plenty to do at home.

SIMON FORMALLY approved the application. The memo was submitted, one of Simon's greatest: cogent, irresistible, successful. Leonard had to affix his approval.

"There is money to be had from this, Leonard. There are military uses. The aerospace industry—just think how much money they can bring to you, to your neighborhood."

"One more veiled little threat from you, Struthers…"

"Yes?"

"Do you have any idea what people think of you?"

"Yes."

And the future was under way. He did it.

Have you had a safe flight? Does your car run smoothly? Train on time? Windows intact? Are you comfortable in that office? It looks like the roof on your tiny little house withstands every storm.

And can you see the man responsible?

Look up up up.

A FEW THINGS plagued him when he returned from Montreal, possibly thanks to the excess cognac. The old feelings about policy. Would he appear responsible when it was all built? Did Simon make *that*? Years away, when scientists, engineers were at work, would they be grateful to him? He was growing envious of some of the scientists. They would be working on the models, they would go into space, they would see how the city would age. Simon would be outside, as usual. He lost his breath when he let that thought cross his mind. Perhaps he could get some sort of a pass from Paul, carte blanche to watch the research once everything was under way.

The idea, however, withstood his doubts, remained glorious. He imagined the wind roaring through the city. If age and its cure were only functions of wind, how silent, how pure, how balanced life would be.

SHE KISSED HIM there, and there, the corners of his lips. "Come again," she said.

At home he waited for his glory to build.

He waited for Kwyet to call.

He waited six months. The old routines were starting again. Perhaps he was not as popular as he thought.

My God, he thought of those kisses.

He wandered, waited.

5

I DROVE TO Montreal to visit Kwyet. I asked if I could see her about
my son. She was sweet. Said she hadn't seen him. She had heard
from him. Dirty postcards. Not dirty like you think—just funny
postcards he had found and sent, smudged with dirty fingers like
he had been living on the street. She let me read them.

> *Dear Kwyet,*
>
> *I'm writing this near the airport. There's a corner of the ~~field~~ feild here*
> *you can lay on your back and the bellies of the planes blow your cheeks.*
> *I don't understand the picture on this card.*
>
> *Love,*
> *Jerry McGuinty*

> *Dear Kwyet,*
>
> *Staying with a buddy. See the guy on the front? I got a tattoo, too.*
> *You don't like tattoos, do you?*
> *Here's an address if you want to write.*
>
> *Love,*
> *Jerry*

(The address was Cooper's.)

She said she wrote, told him he could visit her, asked him if he was all right, told him I'd be worried, his father would be worried.

But he never visited. She was going to call me, she would have if he visited, but she didn't want to interfere if he didn't. How is your wife, she said, and I'm sorry, I will do anything I can.

I wouldn't want to lose my heart to beauty that complete, my friend.

"I know you are his friend, but will you send my son to me?"

"Yes, I told him you would be worried."

CHECK THIS OUT.

I'm driving around my developments, and I veer off, absent-minded, heading to the edge of the green belt. I'm driving along near the land I wanted, I see an airplane taking off and I think Jerry, Jerry, Jerry, Jerry, Jerry, Jerry, Jerry, Jerry. I coast by, shaking my head, and there to the left, I know I saw them, are dump trucks and men at work on what was supposed to be the fairway of a seventh hole. I see them but I coast on by, looking at the belly of the airplane, blowing out my cheeks.

I believe with the deepest conviction that my son turned me into a moron.

GOING TO WORK was about stakeouts, hunting, figuring things out, having a coffee, talking to street kids, policemen, eating at McDonald's. My other work was nothing. I got served with a law-suit or two over incomplete jobs. I got some subcontractors to finish things, and I lost a fortune. I dropped some plums, yes sir. But I had a fortune, my friend: rich. If you look closely at me now, here, under my eyes, my skin is lined with velvet, see. I could, and can, buy anything.

So Jerry was my career for more than a year.

I was closing in. I had my contacts, my agents, my ears on the ground. There was a new guy working at the Y who liked me. He said he knew Jerry and he would call me if he came in. He said

Jerry was going around with a few different names these days: Tim, Johnny, Kevin. (I laughed at that last one: Kevin. Ha ha ha. I don't know why.) If any of those Jerries came in, he would call me right away.

The name-changing was a good sign, I learned. When kids, young guys, do that it usually means they've got some fake IDs lined up, that they're growing into the smarter sort of *cheat*. I admire the smarter sort of *cheat*. Legitimate purposes, you see— that's what he was *cheat*ing for. He was trying to get work. I found this young guy who did fake IDs for a lot of kids. Most of them are just trying to get into bars, but there are some, he said, who get IDs to get jobs, who don't want their families to track them down through work or social insurance.

I wasn't exactly certain about all this. The ID kid was a little crook and he wasn't telling me whether he knew Jerry or not. "I might know a Kevin, I might not." But Edgar made me certain.

Edgar was coming around every now and then, checking up on me, telling me who wanted me, who wanted to sue me, who had resigned and was now working for him. He was being kind: "Just giving you a heads-up, Jer." I don't know whether inside he thought he was a bit smart or superior, having escaped Kathleen and not having a son, but poor old Edgar was certainly not growing smarter.

He comes around with a case of beer and news of some new lawsuit against me and we're talking away, and he says:

"Oh yeah, shit, Jer, I meant to tell you. I was down at Mickey D's on Baseline the other day, you know, grabbing a Big Mac, and I get served by this young fella looks exactly like your Jerry. I'm like, you know, take...double take...I'm doing a double take. What's the fuckin expression?"

"Was it him or not, Edgar? Christ."

"Well, no, he didn't...I looked at him, but he...This kid was a Kevin. You know, across here: Kevin. Some of these young guys look alike."

"Yeah, well, that was my son, you fuckin heel."

"Your son's named Jerry, Jerry, don't start with your grumpy fuckin craziness again."

I got the exact address of the McDonald's and went straight away. I knew I had him. When I was in the restaurant I looked carefully at everyone in uniform. I still didn't know how he looked. He wasn't emptying the trash, he wasn't mopping. I looked at the people serving, one by one. I tried to see the guys making burgers in the back but I couldn't see them properly.

This one kid was mopping the floors. I went up to him and said, "Kevin working today?"

"Kev? No."

"When does Kev come in?"

"I don't know. The manager does the schedules."

"Who's the manager?"

"Guy in the blue shirt."

I told the guy in the blue shirt, I said, "I'm looking for Kev. Is he in today?"

"Kevin McClinty?"

"That's the one."

"He's in tomorrow morning."

"That's good news, my friend. I'm his buddy Johnny Cooper. Don't tell him I'm looking for him. I want to surprise him."

I WAS HUMMING that night, I tell you with a tingle. Couldn't sleep a wink. I was proud of him for having a job and I walked around my bedroom thinking Kevin, Kevin, Kevin, what a funny little kook. I was setting him up for a real surprise—he'd be expecting Cooper, if the manager spilled the beans, and then I, his father, would swing into view. That is a clever and sweet little surprise, my friend.

So I go back to the McDonald's at six thirty the next morning, but I'm too nervous to go in right away. I drive to another McDonald's and sit on the can there for a bit. Then back I go to the other one, courage, bravery, through the door, and I see a young guy behind the counter who looks pretty familiar.

Courage, my friend.

Up I go to the counter slowly. He's serving some people in front of me. There's another little server guy saying, "Can I help you? Can I help you, sir?" but I pretend to be deaf or stupid and I stay in Kevin's line.

And then there's nothing between me and my son but a low counter and a little beeping register.

"Hi, Kev," I said.

I realized quick enough that the surprise wasn't all that sweet for him.

"I've been looking for you," I said.

JERRY WAS my height now, taller in his McDonald's hat, taller because I was leaning toward him. I was scaring him. I just wanted to touch him, hold him still.

He didn't say anything. He backed up, spun around, and ran.

I jumped up on the counter and shouted after him. I tried to run but first I slipped on someone's fuckin hash brown on the counter, and then when I landed the manager in the blue shirt shouted, "Hold it, Johnny!" and tried to get in my way. He was a stocky little guy, but, you know, look at these arms.

I ran through the back where Jerry went, past all the buns.

"Jerry! Jerry! How dare you run! How dare you run!"

I ran through the garbage room, which he left all dark, and then BANG! through the door and I was out in the parking lot. There he was, running away.

I found a *shout* from the earth beneath that parking lot, I tell you, a shout from the hole in the middle of everything.

"JERRY McGUINTY! JERRY McGUINTY!"

And he stopped.

"Don't you fuckin run from me!"

"Don't you fuckin come closer!"

"Just fuckin wait!"

"What the fuck are you doing here?!"

"Fuck you, what am I doing here! Why are you running?"

"I don't fuckin need you!"

"Yes you fuckin do!"

"No, I fuckin don't!"

We were about twenty feet apart. His hat fell near my feet.

"Just wait!"

"I'm waiting!"

"I've been looking for you, Jerry. Fuck me, I've been looking for you!"

"I didn't ask you to."

"I don't need you to ask me to."

"I don't need you for anything."

"Yes, you do."

"I don't, fuck. I don't need you. I've got a job."

"But your name's Kevin!"

"So?"

"It's depressing. I named you Jerry."

"I'm not you."

"But you're not Kevin. Every Kevin I know has...has hair parted on the side!"

"What the fuck are you talking about?"

"Just take it easy for a minute, Jerry. Jesus, I've been running. I just want to talk to you."

"Stay there!"

"If you stay *there*, I'll stay *here*, Jerry. Just take it easy."

"It was that Edgar loser, wasn't it? I knew he recognized me."

"Edgar's an idiot."

"You're an idiot."

"I am an idiot. But that doesn't mean, I mean, Jesus, Jerry, why do you run from me? I haven't seen you in...I've been fuckin looking for you for more than a year!"

"You're an idiot."

"Shut your hole, little man. I've given up my life for you."

"Bullshit."

"You were a kid. You had a little chest like this, for fuck's sake. How was I supposed to know you could survive like this, get a job, look after yourself? Every fuckin day I was just guessing you were alive, you little shit."

"Don't call me a little shit, you FUCKIN ASSHOLE!"

"Just take it easy."

"No! You don't have a fuckin clue!"

"I know."

"You don't."

"I know."

"You don't."

"I know I have no clue. No clue why you ran. I know you had a reason, but why are you still running? What's your reason now?"

"You want me to explain?"

"Yes!"

"No! It's too late. It's all too late. I don't want to see you."

"Why?"

"I don't."

"But why? I just want to talk."

"Why?"

"Because everything's...because your room's empty."

"What?"

"And I want to try to make toast for you, Jerry. I want to talk to you. You know. You can come over and I'll make some toast for you. I can...Just take it easy. I could wake you up sometimes, or you could wake me up—I don't know, kick my bed in the morning."

"What are you talking about?"

"I want you to tell me things. Can't we just grab a coffee?"

"No."

"What did I do?"

"Nothing!"

"It's...you know, it's sad for me if you don't like me. Because, look at you. How did you do it? You're all tall. You look, you know, you look like one of the good guys, one of the popular guys. It's sad for me if you don't like me."

"Take it easy, Dad."

"I'm your dad."

"I know."

"She's gone, Jerry."

"So?"

"I thought you should know. I haven't heard from her. You saw her fall or something, didn't you? She was sick. She was a drunk, Jerry."

"You think I don't know that?"

"But she's gone, buddy. And I...I haven't been looking for her. I promise I haven't been looking for her."

"So?"

"Do you hate me?"

"Who cares? No."

"If you come home, if you visit or whatever, it will just be me there."

"I'm not coming home."

"I'm not letting you go."

"I'm faster than you."

"I'm stronger than you and I know your name's Kevin. I know you crash at the Y sometimes. I know your name's Johnny and Tim, and I'll catch you, Jerry, and I'll sew you into my side. You're not getting away from me."

"What do you want?"

"Can I see your tattoo?"

"No."

"Do you want to get a coffee?"

"I've lost my job now, because of you."

"You haven't lost your job."

"How can I work there now that you know I work there?

You're not catching me. You think you can catch me, but I've escaped from you and that fuckin house for a long time. I'm grown up. You think I can't escape again? You have no right over me. You can't sew me anywhere. You're a fuckin weirdo. You're a total stranger. I don't live in your world. I won't live in your house. I don't want to see you. I have my own life. I was a kid, you fuckin idiot. I was scared all the time. Now I'm not. I don't need to be scared like that any more. I don't need to live in that fuckin house."

"But she's gone."

"Well, so am I."

"Oh, don't run, Jerry, goddamn it! You don't have to be so dramatic. Don't run! Don't! 'So am I'! Listen to yourself! Come back and listen to yourself! Fuck, Jerry! Stop! I've got your hat! I've got your hat! You can't get anywhere without your hat!"

WELL, HERE'S HIS HAT.

It wasn't quite an anchor or a magnet. That clever trick of mine ("you can't get anywhere without your hat")—he didn't quite fall for that. So here's his hat as a funny memory of his days as Kevin.

I'll just grab a beer.

I can't tell you what a relief it was to see what he looked like. Everything was possible again. His voice was deep, yes, shoulders big, but he still had a bit of the puppy in him. When he said he wasn't scared, his voice broke.

Do you think I let him out of my sight? For the record, for the history of the battle between Jerry and Jerry: Jerry never escaped from Jerry.

So he wasn't as happily surprised to see me as I thought he might be. Have you ever been happily surprised to see your parents? In the future I would give him some warning that I was coming, prepare him for the pleasure.

When he ran away from me across the parking lot I ran to my

truck and sped after him. He ran over a grass bank and into the next parking lot, which was attached to a mall. I guessed he would run for the mall so I drove around, out on to the street, into that parking lot, and I just saw the back of him swing into the mall. The stores weren't open yet, so he wouldn't have many places to hide. But I figured it would be better if I just watched him for a while instead of confronting him again.

I stayed in my truck and drove from one end of the mall to the other, watching the exits. After a couple of hours I thought he'd slipped away, fuck, but I saw the little chimp sneaking out eventually.

I followed him again. He didn't see my truck. He got on a bus, and I tailed that for about half an hour. I think he noticed me then. I saw people in the bus looking at me all the time because every car on the road was honking at me for driving at forty k and pulling over at bus stops, and the bus driver himself kept honking at me and waving me ahead.

When Jerry got out on Bank, he ran, flash, faster than any McDonald's suit had ever been taken. He deked down a street which was one-way against me, but that didn't stop me, then he ran into a park but it was only a block wide and I saw him run out the other side.

"Where can I lead the old man in the truck?" I could hear him thinking. I'm on to you.

I was a bit embarrassed for him at one stage. He ran through a car wash thinking that I would try to drive through and be compelled to get a wash. Maybe it was a glimpse of his low opinion of me. I drove around and saw him at the other side of the car wash getting on another bus. I started feeling sorry for him at that point. He was spending money he probably wouldn't otherwise have spent. I decided to turn away.

HE DIDN'T GET AWAY, no no. It was just a trick. I let the bus out of my sight and then caught up to it again. Genius.

367

He got off the bus looking different—just a white T-shirt (his trousers were all that was left of McDonald's Boy). The disguise didn't fool me.

He had no clue that I was watching him. We were down near the market now—daytime crowds, one or two hoors still kicking around from the night before—easy to stay hidden from him, but hard not to get the attention of the hoors by driving slowly.

Jerry ducked down an alleyway at one point. When I looked more closely I realized it wasn't an alley, but a passage to the basement of a building. He went in and didn't come out for a couple of hours. When he was inside I took the risk of getting out of the truck and looking at the building more closely.

It was where he lived. My big Jerry. His own place, or maybe his and someone else's. I don't know. It smelled like piss and I wanted to sing with pride. It reminded me of Mrs. Brookner's basement. Remember? Ah, buddy, you're a brick.

I had an idea—just to let him know that I was proud. I went back to my truck and wrote a note:

Jer,

If you don't care about me, how come you sent me cards for my birthday?

Love,
Jerry

When he came out of the basement and walked down the street a bit, I hopped out of the truck again and left that note for him for when he came home.

And I hopped back into my truck and kept following him.

I GOT NO SIGN that he wanted to see me. I never saw him swing by my place. He never acknowledged my truck.

I left more notes for him.

Jer,

How come you sent me a Christmas card?
    You wanted to make me sad?

Love,
Jer

I just wanted to give him little reminders that I was around. Every Friday night he went to the same field out by the airport to lie down and watch the planes (Friday was the busiest night in the sky). I started leaving him a six-pack out there with little notes.

Jer,

Cheers.

Jer

But he never touched them.

WHERE DOES he end up one day?

Closer to the house, closer to the house, his bus is getting closer to the house, and it sets him down at the mall that McGuinty, Davies, and others hammered out of their dreams. Westview Mall, it has become, despite being in the south and having no view. And there it is, embracing my son.

Something told me to get out of my truck for a change. I didn't know what he was doing there—I never knew what he was doing—and I guess curiosity made me follow on foot.

I couldn't believe all the people in that mall. It was lunch hour, and there were men in suits walking around, women in suits, old ladies shopping, people jabbing fries into their mouths. It was still new, but it was *full.* I felt like I had planted a few seeds, forgotten about them, and now here was a forest with wildlife, flowers and nuts.

Can I admit to something, just between us? I forgot about Jerry. I completely forgot about why I was in that mall. You will understand that I felt pride for having had a hand in the making of the building, but there was some other feeling that made me forget about Jerry for a minute.

Look at the man looking for an electric knife, the granny looking for a bluer rinse, the woman here looking for the right speckled frame for her glasses. They depress me, my friend. They're all looking for something, and their sad little faces are telling me there's a reason for their looking and it's not roast beef or a weak shade of blue. There's something outside, I tell you, and it's making them all come in here, something scary, something waiting for all of them.

I'm sitting there chinning my thoughts, having a cup of coffee, and I recall my Jerry and the reason I'm in the mall. My Jerry. I realize that to him I am probably that thing outside, that reason for getting lost in knickknacks and the faces of strangers.

My quiet friend, let us take this moment to weigh the heaviness of that thought.

I WENT BACK outside to my truck. I resolved to leave the boy alone. If he needs me like I need him, he will come to me.

It is time to return to work. Maybe it's time to build another mall. I believe my Jerry could use one.

I started my engine and got ready to reverse when on my back window I heard a THWAP, a dirt-bomb whacking the glass.

I turned around and there's my Jerry, smiling.

6

EVENING.

A weekend coming. A dinner. A party. Amen.

Thickening.

Uncle Simon's invited to a gathering, with friends, frat boys, freshmen.

Reckoning.

A dinner, à deux, with Kwyet. All thoughts to be spoken, veins scissored open, minds considered and weighed.

Ripening.

After months she called him again.

He is in love. Simple. Always. He loves love, Kwyet is Love, and all other loves have been steps to her altar.

Back to Montreal for a seat at the Feast of Venus. The introductory event, on Friday night, will be a bit of a bacchanal, a dorm party, of all things, where Simon will meet Kwyet's young friends and a handful of faculty.

On Saturday night is the main event, when Simon and Love will have dinner by themselves.

Until then he worked on a few scenarios, which you might be

interested in. Some of these are noble, some downright salty, all of them end with Love's splendid triumph.

When Kwyet first appeared naked to my mind's eye, I had to turn away. But gradually I have shed my pudeur and I am now, then, capable of indulging some robust and vivid imaginings. It is all in this spirit of testing that I had lately come to enjoy. Will a house survive? How will Kwyet and Simon most successfully unite? One very simple scenario has the two of them enjoying their meal on Saturday, growing warm, frank, close, and returning either to Simon's room or Kwyet's to grow warmer, franker, closer.

KWYET HAS *a bottom like a pillow, where I rest my head to consider what I look like from above. I send my soul up there to have a look. Kwyet on the bottom, me on hers, my graceful raffish soul tilting his head in Botticellian pose above my grateful rakish body (recently sated on Kwyet's adaptable bottom). I smile and my soul winks back at me. I look good, I should say.*

And she never had a lover as curious and adept, I tell her to tell me. We are sitting on my windowsill (naked: downstairs), and we are both immensely pleased with me. She is at a loss for words.

"SIMON!"

"Yes!"

"You never got my name, did you?!"

"No!"

"That is *so* funny! Where's Kwyet?!"

"I thought you would know!"

"No, sir!"

"She said she would meet me here!"

"She'll be here! For sure! She's probably here already, but these parties are *so* big, so totally out of *hand*! It's not just this room! This is just one, like, room! Let me introduce you!"

"Yes!"

"These are some of my buddies!"

"Hello!"

"That's Gretchen! Tony! Tom! Ashley! Jodie! Bruce! Robert! Sean! Jodie Two! Dee! Peter! Alan! Michaela! Jay! France, Francoise and Francine! (They're always together and French!)"

"Hello!"

"Here, talk to Bruce! I told you about Bruce before! His name's Bruce!"

"Hello!"

"How's it going?!"

"This is Simon! He's! Like! He knows Kwyet!"

"Right on!"

"Yes!"

"Where is she?!"

"I don't know! She said she would meet me here!"

"She'll be here! Totally! I've got to go! I'll be back!"

"So!"

"Yes!"

"Kwyet, eh?!"

"That's right!"

"Right on!"

"Yes!"

"You one of her profs?!"

"I know her from Ottawa!"

"What do you teach?!"

"I don't teach anything!"

"Cool!"

"I might see if I can find Kwyet!"

"What?!"

"See you!"

"OK!"

"Excuse me!"

"Yeah!"

"Excuse me!"

"Sure!"

"Where are the other rooms?!"

"We were talking!"

"Pardon?!"

"You interrupted us!"

"Forgive me! Excuse me!"

"You bet!"

"Are the…! Excuse me! Are the other rooms through here?"

"You bet!"

"Have you seen Kwyet?!"

"Right on! Are you the Dean?!"

"Have you seen Kwyet?!"

"Right again, Mr. Dean!"

"See you!"

"Hi!"

"Excuse me!"

"Simon!"

"Hi! I am still looking for Kwyet!"

"Have you met anyone?!"

"Yes!"

"Cool!"

"Where are the other rooms?!"

"Cool!"

"What?! Where are the other rooms?"

"All of them! The whole floor! This is the biggest! Go into any room!"

"Really?!"

"Totally! That's the fun part! Surprise! Ha ha ha! Let's look in this one! Come on! I heard they've got a bong going! Whoo, Tony! Lookin buff! Excuse us! Hey! Whoo! Excuse us! In here! Whoo!"

"It smells like Morocco!"

"Totally!"

"I don't think she would be in here!"

"You don't know her! Look! Whoo! I know that guy! I know you! You're one of my profs! Hey, Simon! Talk to him! He's a prof! This is Simon!"

"Hi!"

"Chatty! Don't be shy, boys! Hey! You gave me a D!"

"Sorry!"

"Totally!"

"I might go look for Kwyet! Excuse me!"

"Sure! I'm going to see if I can't get my mark changed!"

"Bye!"

"Bye!"

"Where can I get a drink?!"

"There's a keg down the hall!"

"Thank you! Excuse me!"

"Make way for the Dean, everybody!"

"That's not the Dean!"

"Yes it is!"

"He's going for the keg!"

"Go for it, Mr. Dean!"

"The Dean's a woman!"

"No he's not, he's going for the keg!"

"Excuse me! How do I...?!"

"Grab a cup! Help yourself!"

"Thank you! Like this?! Thank you! Do you know Kwyet, the girl, Kwyet?"

"Sure!"

"Have you seen her this evening?!"

"Yeah!"

"Where?!"

"Dancing! She was dancing with the boys!"

"Which boys?!"

"That's right!

"Where is the dancing?!"

"Down there! Fourth room along!"

"Thank you! Cheers!"

"Cheers!"

"See you! Excuse me!"

"Make way for the Dean!"

"Excuse me!"

"Where you going, Mr. Dean?!"

"Dancing!"

"Whoo! The Dean *is* a woman!"

"Ha ha!"

"Whoo!"

"Cheers!"

boom, Bom. boom, Bom. boom, Bom. boom, Bom. b-boww, b-boww, b-boww, b-boww, b-boww, b-boww, b-boww, b-boww, b-boww, b-boww, b-b-b-b-b-b-b-b, b-boww, b-boww, b-b-b-b-b-b-b-b, b-boww, b-boww, b-boww, b-boww, b-boww. Pssht pssht pssht pssht. Pssht pssht pssht pssht. How does it feel, to treat me like you do?

"DO YOU KNOW KWYET?!"

"WHOO-OO! IS…IP…CHA…WAY! YOU-OO"

Pssht pssht pssht pssht. Pssht pssht pssht pssht.

"DANCE, BUDDY! DANCE! YOU CA…IF…ZI…ONTOE… ZI…YEAH HA HA!"

Tell me how, do I, feel. Tell me now, how do I feel. Pssht pssht pssht pssht. Pssht pssht pssht pssht.

"SIMON!"

"KWYET!"

"I'VE BE…LOOK…FU!"

"I'VE LOOKED EVERYWHERE!"

"WHA…TI…SIT!"

"PARDON!"

"TIME!"

"HEY, TEACH, YOU STOLE MY GIRL!"

"EXCUSE ME!"

booh booh

"HANG ON! WAI…! KWYET!"

"SOR…SIM…HE ISN'T…I'LL…WHEN WE GO!"

"WHAT?"

"WHOO-HOO!"

THE NEXT NIGHT would be better. Quieter.

The desperate flesh of Simon had ripened to the verge of rotten.

"DO YOU trust me, Kwyet?"

"Trust?"

"I suppose it's not trust I am getting at exactly. Do you know me?"

"I…"

"It's an odd question to ask you over your pork. Is it nice?"

"I finished it."

"Yes, mine is good. 'Do you know me'—that's not what I meant at all. Let's just chat."

"Yes."

"Pork is difficult to do properly. The balance between over-cooked and trichinosis."

"My mother would kill me if I got trichinosis."

"Ha ha."

"HAVE ANOTHER cognac with me?"

"No thanks."

"Sure?"

"No."

"You will have another?"

"Will I?"

"Yes. Do."

"Thanks."

"I could suggest anything to you, couldn't I?"

"Could you?"

"Yes."

"I don't know about that."

"There are quite a few of them, though. Aren't there?"

"What?"

"Suggestions."

"Where?"

"Here. Between us. Generally. I believe there are."

"I think your cognac's coming."

"Kwyet, I...I may have another. Will you?...I...No?...I thought...I was hoping...I'm sorry—I feel as though I have been talking too much...Chatting, yes, but too much, and not enough, never what I want...I don't know what you were hoping about tonight, but I should say, I thought I might say that I would...Thank you, and perhaps the bill please...I wanted to tell you that perhaps I could help you in some way, and what I mean by that is not...Do you consider me paternalistic?...Uncle, yes, ha ha...I could perhaps come and visit you more often, and get to know you, in a, I remember, I, so fondly remember those days in the park with you and your mother, with you primarily, and really, there is no reason...Did you?...Yes, you still call it home-work do you, how sweet, yes, I would be happy to...And that is what I mean, to visit more often, have those meaningful, delicious...My cognac? Delicious, thanks. Would you?...No?...I'm... You don't look tired, really, you are so, so...But let's go, yes...I would like to give you something, see you more, perhaps, I love running after, you see, but, I wonder, in my experience, the balance...Like pork?...Yes, ha ha. So you understand?...No, well, I'm not making myself clear, but I am not sure that I want to... This is your coat, yes?...Let me...I thought I might walk you back to your room...I'm not tired, no...It's only ten minutes and we can chat...It's probably just the cognac—you don't look tired. I, certainly, drank the last too quickly...Anyway, I must tell you...I know I am sounding a bit serious, and...ha ha, yes, lovely...It is dark, isn't it...Run, yes, I thought you said you were tired...Yes. Hey! Run! Ha ha! Wait! Ha!...Oof!...No, no, I'm all right—crack in the sidewalk...Run...Run...Be careful...Run... Run...Please come back...Pardon?...No, I said...! No, it's fun...I was only...I will catch up, no, do, I will catch you before your room, and, and, chat...Run! Ha!...And tell you, Kwyet, and have you, Kwyet, I can grit these teeth, kiss your teeth, bite the rust from my lips, Kwyet, if you, will you...Hello!...No!...You're coming back, how nice!...Ha ha...No, no, I will walk you, it's still another, still far, and it's dark, I'll just see you to your door or what have you...'What have you,' yes, silly expression...Let's just, let me just say, Kwyet, that, oh, you are all out of breath... It's nice, lovely, that's, that's what I was going to say, Kwyet, you are, when you are out of breath and when you are not, you are... No, really, I am not tired at all, I enjoy the walk—honestly—and it is really such a pleasure to be walking with you, to be alone with you finally, please, let's keep walking. I might, I might walk you to your room, if that's...No...Sorry...Walk ahead if you like, yes, do...God, you look...What?...Did I?...I didn't say anything, mumbled, maybe, I think walking, the fresh air is certainly a good idea for me, after a meal like that, sign of age...Age...I wasn't the oldest person at that party last night, did you notice? Not by any means was I the oldest, there was a, a Professor of Some Description who could only be described as old, and I assure you that it wasn't age that drove me from the party, finally, it was really just a sense, do you know, in certain situations one realizes one has little to contribute, little to offer to enhance the situation and one clams up, rather, and also, of course, you were dancing, so, you were dancing with all the younger, perhaps that was age after all, do you, I won't ask that, well, do you think of me as old, older than you?...Ha ha...That's, that is, you are very, on top of every-thing, you are a very funny...Are we? Oh, yes, there it is...No, no, certainly I will walk you all the way, no, no, it is good for me, and, it is a shame there is no common room or something of the sort, a place to have a nightcap, up there, near your, near all the rooms, but, I suppose at least it is good, you must be grateful, that you yourself have no roommate, it really must feel private... Mmm...There's something, there is something I wanted to talk to you about this evening, I don't know whether you, whether I should have mentioned it earlier, nothing serious, more interesting, really, more, I don't know whether you are keen to chat a bit longer, I know I have chatted too much, but...Yes, here we are, I'll just, oh, no, there is no security, no one at the front desk, good thing, ha ha, good thing you have had an escort, yes, I wonder, is that unusual, no one there?...Yes, I'm sure it is perfectly safe, but I will just make sure, I will see you to your room then, no one around at all, how strange, I will just, I have never seen your room...I've wondered, I have thought you must be keen on getting your own place, apartment, but perhaps it is perfectly nice, your room...I don't mind a climb, no, no, but there is an elevator, why not take...One floor?...No, honestly, all in the spirit of walking off spirits, I am keen, I am grateful, really, lead on, I have nothing, I certainly have nothing to return to, I...No, I will go home later, if you don't mind, I would really like to see your room, and talk to you about something...Steep climb, isn't it? Let me...Is this the floor...Broom cupboard...No...Yes, soldier on...Yes...Yes...Let me, is this the floor? Let me hold the door for you, here, here, lead on, this way, is it?...You really don't look, you do not look tired...Well, yes, but I assure you, you at least don't look tired...This is your room here, is it, yes, well, Kwyet, well, Kwyet, if I could just, oh, Kwyet, yes, what?...Perhaps if I could just say...Let me help you with your coat...Yes...God, Kwyet, you are so beautiful...Kwyet, if I could just, please, Kwyet, God, Kwyet...I, we could, just a, please, Kwyet, hold, please hold still, I just...Why...I thought you said come here, I thought all of this...You just aren't sure, that's all, because, if you try to run, I, I want to run, you see, Kwyet, none of this, that's the window, you're not...Why?! Why do you keep inviting me?! What am I supposed to think?!...I'm not coming closer, just, please, you are so…Stay!…Calm down…Please…I'm not pushing…Come away from the window, please…I'm not pushing…I only want

"I ONLY WANTED to keep you away from my mother. You keep following us, Simon. Please, just, stay, away."

SO I SAID TO HER, I said, listen, I said, Kwyet, I said, Kwyet, I said (the eager chasseur), I want, I said, to run. My little humming Quiet, my little thread of Kwyet, a birdbreeze lower than a breath said Come, she said, or so I had imagined, Come she said, Here I am.

She said nothing, but I took her to mean much, as she ran more than walked, cowered more than curved up the stairs through the door by the window.

I want to run, I said, but None, I said, of this Come here. My goose was bumped all over from the breeze of disquieting breath; to run was my need, not my wish. I was prepared to get song-of-songsy, all hinds and harts and panting, to sing with her as we ran. But when I was there, when I was right there with her, there was nothing but quiet: an open window and an invitation. Come, she says, here I am.

SHE FELL ALL that way to the ground.

Part Six

1

THE LITTLE MONKEY smiling through my window. He ran away and I didn't chase him. Flower in the snow. More than a flower in the snow, my friend, it was a smile from the God of Yes, the God of White, the Man in Black, the shy, shy welcome of deep and dark and sweet, my friend, I don't know, I tell you, I do not know what I mean, but look at that smile and hope.

I did not chase him, no, I went home, changed, had a beer for several months, I even, you know, dieted, exercised, got back to work, birth of a new world, patience, hope, light beer, moistening my bones, and then:

The doorbell rang and I thought Paperboy? and I opened the door to Jer. I told you this already.

"Jer!" I said.

"Hi, Dad," he said, and came in.

I knew it was my job to be cool. "How are ya, Jer," I said, cool.

And he said, "How are ya."

And I said, "Beer?"

And he said, "Yeah."

And I went to the fridge and came back with a couple.

He was still standing there in front of the door, and we clinked them together, me and Jer, and no two beers in the history of man were sucked back faster, I tell you with no shame. We finished at the same time.

"Another?" I said.

And he said, "Yeah." So I came back with two more.

"Come in. Sit down. Come in."

He had a knapsack on his shoulder full of his father's hope. I couldn't ask if he was going to stay. He sat down over there, across from me.

"How are ya, Jer?" I said.

"OK," sip of beer, "OK…You?"

"OK. Beer?" I said, and he said, "Yeah," and I got another case from the basement and put it in the fridge.

"So, you've been OK, eh, Jer?"

"Yeah. OK enough."

"You look thin."

"Yeah."

"Healthy?"

"Yeah."

"You hungry?" Too early, too early.

"No."

"Me neither."

"*You* look thin," he said, after a while.

"I've been on a diet," I said.

"Yeah?"

"Yep. Twenty pounds."

"Yeah?"

"Yep…I know the guy who makes this beer."

And he said, "Yeah?"

"Yeah." And there I was talking about yeast, a grandmother's recipe, a guy named Buck who made one or two himself, and there was Jer, a familiar stranger, older, smaller, a growing man, and as he politely nodded himself to sleep I might have walked over and put my hand on his head.

NEXT MORNING, he's in his bedroom, back in his bedroom, just down the hall there. Peek in the door you'll see his big feet poking out from all those crazy *Star Wars* critters, the woolly one and whatnot.

"HEY, DAD, can I borrow the pickup?"
    "You can drive now?"
    "Yeah."
    "Catch."

"HEY, JERRY, you know how I make you toast in the morning?"
    "Yeah."
    "You like that?"
    "Sure."
    "I've got...I've become pretty good at it."
    "Sure."
    "I like my toast."
    "OK."

"HEY, DAD, can I borrow the pickup?"
    "Sure. Catch."

"JERRY, I'VE GOT a few jobs coming in. You know, rebuilding the McGuinty name and so on. You have any interest in helping me here and there?"
    "With what?"
    "This and that."
    "Sure."
    "I'll pay you."
    "I'm not working for free."
    "Fuckin A, my friend."

"HEY, DAD, can I borrow the pickup?"
    "No."

"Why not?"

"Because it's mine."

LIVING WITH a teenager was hard. I've heard all you ladies say the same thing to your friends: "Living with a teenager is hard." Fuckin A, ladies.

There was something about his feet. His goofy big feet were everywhere. He put them on every table, no matter how high the table was. He left his gigantic running shoes in my path, no matter where my path was. He owned more running shoes than he could ever possibly wear, but he wore them all and the smell was a unique and terrible thing. Mud on his boots... Yes, I could go on, oh yes.

But we love them anyway, don't we, ladies? And he was stretching into those years when we can do anything, when he could do everything. He slouched and loafed, but when I watched him at work he was a beautiful sight—strong, an athlete, smooth, patient. He could have been a great builder if he had wanted. He learned new skills like *that*. He was like one of those lizards, you know, all slow-looking and sleepy except when a fly comes along and then FLEEM that secret tongue comes out and that fly is *his*.

I think I was even jealous of him sometimes. I knew that if he put his mind to it he could do anything better than I could, except plastering.

"No, NO, JERRY, you're moving the trowel like it's a trowel. Move it like it's a feather or a thought or like it's absolutely nothing."

"Plastering is dead, old man. Plastering is dead."

I WISHED Kathleen could see him.

I told him once, I said, "I tried on a number of occasions to communicate with her, buddy, and introduce her to the spirit of Johnny Cash and everything solid and deep."

"Well, you don't have a clue, old man."

And the fact is, I don't. I have no idea at all what went on in my life, in Jerry's life, in your life, in any life, no clue about anything but what happens in the space between me and my big white walls. I asked Jerry occasionally why it was that he hated his mother so much, but, between us, I never believed his answers and eventually we never talked about it. He never understood how pretty she was.

I started thinking about her more. I sometimes found myself driving around aimlessly and realizing that my aim was actually her.

"Don't you miss her sometimes?" I asked him.

Maybe she would surprise us one day, "How are yiz," at the door with a blink of an apology, or even an explanation, and a case of soda water. Maybe it would be nice. I suggested that to Jerry and that's when he showed me a scar—said he got it while she was cutting his hair once.

I don't know. I suppose he wouldn't make up stories like that, but I don't know. Kids don't know any better than I do what is really happening around them. I don't know.

TIME FOR ANOTHER move, my friend, a smaller place, this one here I'm sitting in. I believe, with a strong sense of justice, that it sits bright among my whitest creations. If you invite me over to your place to tell me a story I will fully expect an inferior building.

My son helped me with this one, my son and some of the old crew. It is true that McGuinty Construction was not what it used to be, but there were quite a few houses left in these arms when Jerry moved in with me and this house was by no means my last.

We moved in as soon as we finished it. Jerry was desperate to get out of the old place. He even wanted new furniture. I decided that a good way to let Kathleen know secretly that we were keen to see her back was to give her the old furniture as a sort of message: "Remember your home?"

My bank manager said he had her address. I never asked him for it. He let the movers know where to leave the furniture, and as far as I know now Kathleen is sitting on our couch.

Don't tell Jerry.

Come down the hall here and I'll show you a feature I like. See, here: two studies. One there. One there. Father. Son. Jerry wanted a place where he could catch up with the years of school he missed. He said he had to be a sharper human being if he was going to be a pilot, so we made this room for him to hammer on his brain. His study is twelve square feet smaller than mine because I am his father.

What with work, school, dreaming about planes, he was even busier than I was at his age. He didn't have all that much time to talk to me. But we worked in these rooms next to each other sometimes and those silent hours made us closer than any conversation could. We had coffee breaks and shared some solemn despair over how little I could help him with schoolwork.

I was very busy, of course, catching up with years of paperwork, figuring out what I was going to do, deciding which debts to pay first. On the advice of one of the angel demons I had invested in a few things that actually made me a fortune—no building, no skin off the hands. The paper in my office, the plaster in my houses, nothing's real any more, I tell you: the world is made of numbers in the air. I paid my debts with a smile on my face and I tried to think what on earth I should build next.

Remember the golf-course idea?

2

I'VE SEARCHED FOR an event, a point in my life when it all went wrong. Can you see it here somewhere?

A lifetime getting to know myself has led to a fatal suppling of the truth. It languishes invalid somewhere in this buttered body of mine. With effort I can find it, but the older I get the more I hate effort.

I can walk to my wine downstairs, climb the stairs to my bedroom, but any quick movement, even a flash of my old desires, makes me ill. I have to take short breaths in my house, not just because there is so little air in my little life, but because I'm afraid of awakening myself. If I breathe deeply, move vigorously, I might start pretending again that I am young and remotely desirable.

I never admitted anything. I never went down to the lawn to see if she was all right. I simply went back to my hotel and wondered whether yearning for someone who never wanted me was actually the same as pushing. I'm sure I never pushed her.

This silly little city. If only I wasn't…I can try telling you everything again—everything I really thought, everything I really said—but it would all seem even emptier. I would like to tell you a story about a man named Simon Struthers: servant of the public; giant; fiction; me. I would like to tell you where I am, but I have never really known. I believe it is somewhere between me and you. I know for certain that I was rarely in this body unless it was against someone else.

Lonely people pretend in public that they like their own company, but solitude is never comforting. It is just a heavy blanket that smothers, blocks out vision, feels safe but encourages fantasy. I am telling you, though—I assure you, that I was once perfectly likable.

Everything is new. How can I show you what it was once like for me if everything around me changes?

I have had a lot of time, far too much time. I was removed from the Division. We all were. Nothing to do with Kwyet. A simple change of taste, a new regime—even greener, thank God. For a while, anyway. The Greenbelt has become a feature of this city, no more contests around its edges; and there at one edge—believe me, I was responsible for that. But Leonard ruined me nonetheless. Never another high-ranking job because he put it about—I suspect it was Leonard—that I was hopeless, lazy, shifty, everything he thought I was. It was widely known that in all my years at the Division I accomplished only one minor project.

But he would never understand. None of you would understand unless you went inside.

One day, perhaps, I will go inside.

And I am not really ruined. No, no. Still plenty of my father's money left, and three days a week I shuffle over to the National Archives, pretending to be old and stuffy, and I organize records, keep things in order, occasionally glance at long-dead plans, monuments of what this city might have been.

And I wander. If I have the energy I wander.

No one attractive ever visits the Archives. If I allow myself a breath of vitality, I wander around malls, generally. One in particular. I saw Kwyet there once.

You see, I tried to make amends.

I went to my hotel at first that night, but I returned to her residence later, to the lawn outside, and there was no one there. I was going to climb the stairs again, just to explain, but how could I possibly explain why I loved her so much? That is what I have been trying to do.

I tried to track her down at home, but I was afraid to get too close, afraid to give myself away, because no one would believe that I didn't push her.

She must have known that I was following her again, because I received a note one day at my house. *Stay away.* Kwyet saying *stay away* or she would press charges.

Then I saw her, once, in this mall. I know it was her. I only saw her from behind.

So I come here, I keep watch.

Look at that, you see, that woman in the short white dress, face of Diana and hemline of Venus. There is a paradox I could wrestle with for weeks, if I should allow myself.

Mind you...

Look at that!

Mind you, I have no idea what she told people. She mustn't have told Leonard. She mustn't have been seriously hurt.

But I am in this mall to make amends.

I don't understand why someone in a skirt that short would scruple to pull it down whenever it creeps up. Let it creep.

I have to sit down.

I did see you, Kwyet, I am sure of it. I need to explain, get *back*. After all, it wasn't me. Do you understand? What I have to do, when I find her, is explain, even apologize, at least explain to her that it wasn't me.

Perhaps if you see her...if you are taller than I am, I would ask you to look around for a moment and tell me where she is. We can come back tomorrow, or the next day, and if, one day, you notice Kwyet and you see me near, warn her, or wish me luck.

Kathleen on Saturday

IT'S A FINE, it's a furry warm slush, in that glass, is it, and all, keeps me warmer in, no way in winter, sploosh! and your feets are in a puddle cause ya think it's ice, clink clink.

To the Dewar's tank! On ya go! Up! To the Dewar's, tap it. Gallons left in there, is it, and there's no need for your services this evening, Robert, dial-another, dial-a-boy, smokes are low, but there's gallons till tomorrow. Smokes are low. I could call, early delivery, first thing, smokes are low, and another of the usual. Dial-a-boy.

Come on, on the couch, Nancy Whiskey, we'll share the last, have a smoke or two. We could read, or write, or that, put the feet up, catch up with friends, and how are yiz all these years. I've been away, write to them, have a think, I'll get round to writing tomorrow. I'll catch up with all of yiz tomorrow.

Kathleen on Sunday

"Robert!"
"No, ma'am."

"Where's Robert?!"

"He's making a delivery, ma'am. Where are you calling from?"

"What?"

"Are you calling from home, ma'am? Home delivery? Two-three-six one-one-eight-seven?"

"What are ya feckin…mathematicking? Tell Robert I want my Dewar's."

"Mrs. Herlihy?"

"McGuinty to you, ya feckin. Where's Robert?"

"Two Dewar's, is it?"

"Something else, something else, something else…"

"Anything else?"

"Smokes!"

"The usual? And the two Dewar's."

"Who is this?"

"Comes to…"

"I know!"

"Sixty seventy-nine."

"I know! I pay. I keep you flippin flips in business. Robert's seen my couch. He knows. It's McGuinty."

"Goodbye, Mrs. Herlihy."

Up yours is where it is, ya fuckin. I worked harder than you could ever, with the cleaning up after a pair of filthy, and the cooking, driving my truck, more miles than. Did I order smokes? Call up.

"Did I order smokes?"

"Who am I speaking to?"

"Who's that?"

"Mrs. Herlihy?"

"Did I order smokes?"

"Yes, ma'am."

"Is Robert bringing them?"

"Robert's on another delivery."

"Who's bringing my smokes? You know. I can't. I pay for yiz. A service."

"If Robert's not back, I'll deliver them."

"I don't care. Who are you?"

"You know me, Mrs. Herlihy."

"Who?"

"Jerry."

"You're Jerry?"

"Jerry."

"Oh? That could be nice. Jerry the bigger, is it?"

"Could be."

"Jerry with the filthy arse, never does what I tell him. Who is it?"

"Your delivery will arrive shortly."

So Jerry's being delivered, is it, that's how life works out. Jerry. Two of them of course. They're not staying. Drink and a smoke, how are yiz, and then go, because I'm not doing any more of that I can tell yiz, the losing of this, here, this Kathleen, looking after the likes who never, feckin. His voice is, how old am I? Look at that skin. I used to be, in the bars, all of them, Espolito and them, hard men, fuckin, fan, fuckin hard, fantastic men all with the shit yiz are beautiful Kathleen, real men, and round the back, and Edgar. Ha ha! What sort of an idiot. Hard men, is it. I'll give yiz hard. Freedom's the hard one, is it, the one ya never find. So Jerry. Now he's found me, delivering smokes, was it, did I order the flippin

"Did I order the Dewar's?"

"Mrs. Herlihy?"

"Who's that?"

"It's Robert."

"Where's Jerry?"

"Gone, ma'am. Delivery."

"Gone, is it? Fuck em."

"You want your Dewar's, ma'am?"

"Where is it?"

"I'm bringing it to you. And your Players."

"Bring both of them. Bring Jerries."

"Cherries?"

"I'm not feeling well."

"I'll be over soon. Twenty minutes. You called early today."

"I don't feel so good."

"Twenty minutes. Nice glass of something. That's all you need."

"Eh?"

"That's right. Two fingers of Dewar's and you'll be fine."

"I'm so tired, Jerry."

"It's Robert, ma'am. Give me twenty minutes."

"Are you really coming?"

"Every day, ma'am."

"I love you, Jerry."

4

Before you leave, there are some facts you should know:

I am fifty-seven round years old.

My son is now a man.

I am stronger than I look.

I no longer build houses, I restore old plaster.

I am probably no better than you, but I am wealthier and stronger.

I have been on one or two dates recently and when the women get a shine in their eyes I know it's because of a memory and not the man across from them. I know my eyes do the same.

I tell stories to my walls and to whoever will listen.

And i have one little story I want to tell you, for now, which begins with a goofy truth: sitting on that land that I wanted for a golf course—broad, flat, useless land, between the airport and the city—is a wind tunnel. It looks like a bendy big drinking straw, and for years it made me sad.

Thanks to a lack of concentration, a few personal difficulties, a...I don't know, I should have gone higher, dealt with MPs, the powerful people, concentrated…I lost my dream development, and on it sits this tube…and…yes, there it is.

And a few weeks ago my son visited me. He visits often, I love it, and I talk his ear off. On this one visit it occurred to me to ask him a question, a real *question*, not just one of those conversation starters. I know him well enough, as well as one man can be pleased to know another, but there were some things, some big things. Find me an old man who is interested in the little things, in the empty conversation of others, and I will show you a fool with no opinions and no sense of time. I said to Jerry, I asked:

"Jerry," I said, "what's it like to fly?"

He's a pilot, you see. Wears a cap, sees the world, makes me proud as a blood-full heart, you bet. I believe he flies the big planes. I recently became concerned, however, you see, that he would turn out like other pilots I've met who go on about stewardesses, long holidays, the uniqueness of their ability and so on. You know the kind: square jaw and whatnot. Cap. I was concerned that he would no longer be the sensitive, sad, prickly little mystery that I had raised him to be.

Plus, he threw away a lot of talent—he could have made McGuinty Construction more glorious than ever.

He comes over all the time, wears his cap (as a joke, I think, although it's like he wants to tell me that he doesn't work in construction), and this time, on this occasion, I wanted to get at the kernel of the thing.

"Jerry, what's it like to fly?"

"What's it like?"

"Yeah."

"What are you doing next Sunday?"

"I'll be here."

"I'll come and get you."

So Sunday morning comes around, you know, down, you know, the song, the way the Man in Black sings it *there's nothing short of dying that's half as lonesome as the sound*...I'm wondering what she does these days on a Sunday...you know.

Jerry comes by on this Sunday, knocks on the door, lets himself in looking sort of mischievous, and I know perfectly well what he's up to. He'll take me up in some small plane and he'll tell me about stewardesses and show me some tricks. Could be fun, but I'd be no closer to him, and, frankly, I'm not all that comfortable in an airplane flown by my little boy.

I felt one of those days of fatherly patience coming on, especially when we get in his car and he says, "Can I play some music?"

"Johnny Cash?" I say, and he says, "No."

He says: "Listen to this song, old man. I'll tell you what it reminds me of."

He pulls out of my driveway and the song begins, a nice little old-time guitar or banjo thingy going quiet on its own at first, kind of teasing in the corner of the song.

"It reminds me," he says, "of the tractor, old man, riding high in the shovel when you drove."

And then it starts.

Shooky-shooky shooky-shooky shooky-shooky shooky-shooky, tambourines, and Bom...Bom...Bom...Bom...Bom... Bom...drums going strong at the pace of travel and life, my friend, guitar strumming steady and forward.

I would have bounced right away in my seat, I tell you, were it not for an old man's sense of dignity. And this nice little voice— no Man in Black, but a nice young man's voice—comes in:

> *Tender is the night*
> *Lying by your side*
> *Tender is the touch*
> *Of someone that you love too much*
> *Tender is the day*
> *The demons go away*
> *Lord I need to find*
> *Someone who can heal my mind*

And on he goes singing some nice corny truths about life, Jerry, Jerry, and Kathleen. My son is in the shovel, high in the air.

"You really remember that?"

"You bet I do, old man."

> *C'mon, c'mon, c'mon get through it*
> *C'mon, c'mon, c'mon*
> *Love's the greatest thing*
> *That we have*
> *I'm waiting for that feeling*
> *Waiting for that feeling, waiting for that*
> *Feeling to come*

If you don't know it, I've got a tape of it here I'll lend you before you go.

That wasn't flying, however, no, there was more to it than that. But I asked him to play it again once or twice while we drove.

> *Oh my baby, Oh my baby, Oh why, Oh my*
> *Oh my baby, Oh my baby, Oh why, Oh my*

Next thing you know, I'm in some familiar territory. We were heading for the airport all right, but Jerry turns off, and there, getting bigger before me, is that ridiculous big wind tunnel.

"Where we going?" I ask him.

"There," he says.

Well, when we parked the car I let him have it. I told him the whole story. What this land meant to me, how I fought for it, how it symbolized the end of the glory days, all the letters I wrote, humiliation, emptiness, failure. I didn't tell him how stupid I really was at the time and that in my heart I still hated golfers—that in fact I think I was building my neighborhoods just to get a hold on Kathleen, keep her from driving away. But I talked his ear off. It's every old man's right.

Poor, patient Jerry, he says: "Just get out of the car." He gets a big duffel bag out of the trunk and he leads me toward this wind tunnel.

"Fact is, my bitter old pop: I love this place. The world is in here."

He gets me back by telling me a long story of the research done in there. He says they test submarines, dragsters, ships, trucks, models of skyscrapers, airplanes, wings, even models of houses, he says. Everything is tested so it floats, flies, or stands, he says.

Yadda yadda yadda.

I know how the world stands.

"Anyway," he says, "you want to fly or not?"

Now, my friend: Listen.

I am fifty-seven years old, and I have to say that the moment of my life of which I am currently most proud was that moment there, in front of my son, when I agreed to wear a helmet, goggles, and a wacky orange jumpsuit and I leapt in a column of wind.

I won't tell you the whole story. You see…No, I won't. Some time. There's a skydiving club, they train sometimes in the wind tunnel, Jerry's a member. Never mind.

I flew.

I stared down at this noisy gale of nothing and it kept me up, kept me alive, supported me, punched me, made me think of everything, nothing, what I am, walls, women with regret in their eyes, chasing, chasing, running and never getting, but here I am, *getting*, my mouth open and the world blowing through me, flying but staying still.

Whoooooooooooooooooooooooooooooooohoooooooooooooooo!

Whoo!

The feeling is still in me, my friend. My Jerry gave it to me.

I'm resting, the world is blowing, I'm alone and nowhere, like I've always been.

And I figure, if I hang on to that, there's enough going on, you know, here, in the middle of a room I built. If I just sit here, heavy on this chair, and remember, let some of that impossible sweetness drive across my mind. If I watch that bone-white door, I will hear a knock or a key. Someone come in with the gust.

Acknowledgments

I WOULD LIKE to thank Anne Carson, my editors Robin Robertson and Drenka Willen, and, especially, my agent Bill Clegg. My greatest thanks are to Jaclyn Moriarty, for suggestions at every level and support more solid than one of Jerry's walls.